Fiona Farrell is one of New Zealand's leading writers. Born in Oamaru and educated at the universities of Otago and Toronto, she has published volumes of poetry, collections of short stories, non-fiction works, and many novels.

In 2007 she received the Prime Minister's Award for Fiction, and in 2012 was appointed an Officer of the New Zealand Order of Merit for services to literature.

The Broken Book, a book of essays relating to the Christchurch earthquakes, was shortlisted for the non-fiction award in the 2012 Book Awards and critically greeted as the 'first major artwork' to emerge from the event. *The Villa at the Edge of the Empire* was also shortlisted for this award in 2016.

Her work, which *The New Zealand Herald* has praised for its 'richness — of both theme and languages', has been published around the world, including in the US, France and the UK.

*For Susie – with warmest wishes
Fiona Farrell 2017*

DECLINE & FALL ON SAVAGE STREET

Fiona Farrell

VINTAGE

VINTAGE

UK | USA | Canada | Ireland | Australia
India | New Zealand | South Africa | China

Vintage is an imprint of the Penguin Random House group of companies, whose addresses can be found at global.penguinrandomhouse.com.

First published by Penguin Random House New Zealand, 2017

1 3 5 7 9 10 8 6 4 2

Text © Fiona Farrell, 2017

The moral right of the author has been asserted.

All rights reserved. Without limiting the rights under copyright reserved above, no part of this publication may be reproduced, stored in or introduced into a retrieval system, or transmitted, in any form or by any means (electronic, mechanical, photocopying, recording or otherwise), without the prior written permission of both the copyright owner and the above publisher of this book.

Cover design by Sarah Healey © Penguin Random House New Zealand
Text design by Rachel Clark © Penguin Random House New Zealand
Illustrations by Rachel Clark
Author photograph by Inez Grim
Printed and bound in Australia by Griffin Press, an Accredited ISO AS/NZS 14001 Environmental Management Systems Printer

A catalogue record for this book is available from the National Library of New Zealand.

ISBN 978-0-14-377062-6
eISBN 978-0-14-377063-3

The author gratefully acknowledges the assistance of the Creative New Zealand Michael King Fellowship in the writing of this book and its companion volume, *The Villa at the Edge of the Empire* (Vintage, 2015).

The assistance of Creative New Zealand towards the production of this book is gratefully acknowledged by the publisher.

penguin.co.nz

FOR NGAIO, HUIA,
ELENI AND ALSEIA

...unaccommodated man is no more but such
a poor, bare, forked animal as thou art...

Part One

one

THE SITE

SPRING 1906

...**sand dune,** left behind as the sea receded to the east. It wavers, a stretch of high, dry ground, across swampland. At its foot runs a river. Not one of the great rivers of the region, surging in a tangled bed from mountain to sea. Nor one of those rivers' dark cousins, the aquifers that find their way to the coast through hidden channels below ground.

This river is small and shallow, running swiftly from its source a few miles inland where it bubbles up, clear water from cones of fine white silt, among tutu and flax, toetoe and fern. It forms an estuary behind a coastal bar, before pouring through a narrow opening into the wide blue waters of a bay. At one end of the bay, to the north, there's a fretwork of mountains, white-tipped, even in summer. At the other end there are the truncated remains of two ancient volcanoes, leaning companionably back to back, their calderas long since flooded as indented harbours, their hills meeting the sea as a peninsula wheel of tiny bays cupped between jagged cliffs of ancient lava.

The sand dune curves along the river's northern bank. It slopes gently down to its swift waters. The dune is made up of schist and granite, ground to dust, and shells and the fragments of monstrous creatures who once swam in warm oceans, all teeth and predatory purpose. It contains the bones of seabirds and seals and fish, the ash of fires, the remains of centuries of human feasting.

They lie beneath fern and tutu, shimmering from time to time when the earth jumps as it is wont to do. These are restless islands, forced to the surface by the collision of vast continental plates set in opposition, grinding endlessly against one another.

The surface shimmers at their meeting, and people on the surface have imagined restless things: a waka, rocking on a primeval sea. A giant fish dragging at the hook. They have imagined also a woman lying as the curve of hills and valleys and the sky leaning tenderly over her, filling her with life. They have imagined, when the earth shimmers, a baby god stirring, rolling within her great belly, kicking beneath her skin, making mountains fall, boulders rain down, wide chasms open. The little foetal earthquake god, forever in a state of gestation, forever about to be born.

All that, within the sand dune.

And now its surface is dotted with white pegs. A mile or so to the west, a city has been laid down on fern and tutu, devised by military men with a military precision at this outpost of empire. A city of right angles built about a central cruciform square. The swamp has been divided as neatly as pounds of butter into uniform blocks, for ease of sale and purchase. The original inhabitants have been consigned to their inevitable decline on a few reserves about the perimeter, while at the centre have risen a cathedral in the Gothic style for the Anglicans, another with a Roman cupola for the Catholics, banks and theatres, churches, places of commerce, offices, shops, factories, foundries, schools and parks for healthful recreation. And houses, of course, for the accommodation of those who will labour here. Whose hands and eyes and minds can be harnessed to that great cause which is the advancement of civilisation. The citizens.

Year by year, their houses have sprung up as the suburbs have stepped steadily from the centre across swamp and plain.

And here. To the sand dune by the ...

two

THE FLOORPLAN

SPRING 1908

... and rules a line. It's a wall. A side wall. Four windows. One, perhaps, a bay.

A villa. Not too large. Not one of the twenty-seven-roomed fantasies that introduce his magnum opus: his catalogue of *One Hundred Designs for New Zealand Residences*. Not the two-storeyed extravagance of Smoking Room, Billiard Room, Fernery and the rest, but something more modest: ten rooms, perhaps. A substantial villa for the man who is on his way, and for his dependants. A villa combining tradition with modernity, the best of the past with contemporary comfort, for that is the style for this country, where public buildings favour imperial gravitas with columns and Roman porticoes, along with ample windows and modern plumbing.

And when they leave the public realm, the citizens whom luck and industry have favoured like to stroll home to one or two storeys of vaguely Gothic timber and gabling, or perhaps Georgian brick, with bathroom and kitchen in the contemporary American manner, ideally linked to the modern marvels of metropolitan sewerage systems, gas and electricity, all set behind the fences of a pleasantly private quarter-acre. A house like this, for example: the ten-roomed villa, taking shape beneath the architect's busy pen.

Other men among his colleagues in the Institute of Architects might occupy themselves with theory, debating the relationship between art and architecture, fretting at the absence of a distinctive New Zealand style, lamenting that the nation's cities are simply a palimpsest of architectural quotation, arguing over how to satisfy the airy ambitions of the government's new Workers' Dwellings Act to design the ideal hygienic home for the labourer. But he does not concern himself with theory and debate. He is a practical man. A New Zealander, born and bred. He simply wants to get on and *do*.

Once, he had other aspirations. There was a time when he hoped to be an artist. His sketch of his sister as the Lady of Shalott at her loom drew the admiration of his mother and her friends. They insisted he must travel, just as soon as he was old enough. He must view the great masters. He must be properly educated if he is to realise his talent. They offered money, tickets, a whole directory of relations and useful connections Back Home, and he accepted, though, in the event, travel had the opposite effect from the one his sponsors anticipated. Lonely in a strange city, standing before Rembrandt and the full-throated swagger of *The Night Watch*, he had been overwhelmed by the certainty of his total mediocrity. He was not an artist. He would never become an artist. He could never hope to create that glorious incandescence. He returned home, attended some classes at the School of Art where, surrounded by others infinitely more talented than himself, he was confirmed in his self-assessment. He was completely ordinary.

But an ordinary man has his place. He attached himself to the architectural practice of a family friend, completed his articles and now he sits at his desk in an office just off Cathedral Square, drawing a house.

Its rooms will be spacious. They will open from a central hallway. A broad breezeway permitting the circulation of fresh air, for the modern home must be properly ventilated if its inhabitants are to escape the diseases of enclosure and foetid air. Coughing, lethargy, pallor, death. Opening from the breezy hallway will be the proper sequence of rooms: a drawing room at the front, impressively proportioned and 14 feet from floor to ceiling, where a ceiling rose — he imagines white plaster, an ornamental wreath of lilies and acanthus — supports a gasolier or, better yet, for this is plan, this is dream — an electrical light. The city's gas company has mounted a stout defence against their encroachment, but already wires are loping along the streets, strung from pole to pole, working their way out from the centre. Already electricity illuminates offices and shops and the city's premier department store, casting its cool unwavering glow over dinner sets and bed linen, shirts and ladies' millinery. Its supremacy was asserted in the summer of 1906 when it made a fantasy of the vast dome of the International Exhibition that rose overnight in the cool green acres of Hagley Park.

'HAERE MAI' beamed a thousand lightbulbs to the multitude come to view the triumph of empire. Forest, plain and swamp had been subdued, as the prime minister declared, and industry and thrift prevailed. 'WELCOME' to the halls crammed with machinery and the evidence of progress in science, art, industry and the general march of civilisation. 'WELCOME' from atop snowy towers of plaster and stuccoline.

The architect had joined the crowd, walking across the park toward the beckoning glow, along with his wife, who, upholstered in fox fur and feathered hat, had assisted the ladies arranging the display of Home Industries.

'HAERE MAI!' to the Prairie Province in the country that is showing the way to the Workers' Paradise with minimum wage and old age pension, first in the world to grant women the vote, though the architect thought privately that might have been overdoing things, a thought he would never have voiced to his wife, who had grown somehow from the flower-like creature he had married to a redoubtable proponent of Domestic Engineering. She was forever quoting some Yankee female ranting in *The Ladies' Home Journal* or a similar publication of high scientific purpose, and really something of a bore on the science of kitchen bench heights and the arrangement of kitchen appliances for maximum labour efficiency. An enthusiasm derived, the architect suspects, from her deep loathing of the whole business: managing a home, organising dinners, children and, in particular, the distasteful business of their conception. The sex act she regards as something to be got over with as quickly as possible before a quick rebuttoning. She is bored by it all: babies and family and the domestic round, however scientifically arranged. She wants something other: to do and make and earn her own money, to marshal whole battalions of workers, to govern a medium-sized country. She'd be good at that. In the meantime, she fusses over the placement of a kitchen sink.

The architect finds sinks a terrible bore. For him, the excitement lies here: in the drawing room, with its handsome side bay window and the cunning ceiling rose that doubles as frame to the marvels of illumination and also as concealed vent to draw warm air and contagion from the room beneath. Beside the drawing room, another as ample, as well lit, for dining, where glass-panelled doors open to a side verandah with — why not? — a conservatory. Vines and ferns, camellias and the scent of jasmine on a summer evening.

He sharpens his pencil, adjusts the set square, turns his attention from public rooms to private: the bedrooms across the hallway. The owners', with its fireplace and wide bay and window seat, and next to it a room that might be office or library, calm retreat for the master, and beyond that the children's rooms, one for boys, one for girls, and, to the rear, a bathroom with bath on clawed feet and handbasin, plumbed to a supply delivered by progress and ingenuity via pipes fed by tanks high on the peninsula hills. He allows himself also the fantasy of a water closet within the bathroom in the American manner, a closet that will quickly and hygienically deliver the owners' waste to the municipal sewers that are in construction, the first waterborne sewerage system in the country. All that mess and stink will be carried off to the east unseen beneath the city's streets to trickle into the sandhills of the estuary.

In the villa of ten rooms there will be no need for the scurry through the rain to the dunny by the back fence with its hovering flies, its little box of squares torn from the daily paper, its cloak of passionfruit vine framing the view of the distant back door beyond the damp ranks of silverbeet. No need for the nightsoil man in his noisome cart, creaking by at 2 a.m.

And finally the architect turns to the kitchen, doing his best to accommodate his redoubtable Efficiency Engineer with an arrangement of coal range and chimney, larder and scullery, meat safe on the southern wall as advised. And the two small adjoining rooms that will house the cook/housekeeper, one a bedroom, the other her sitting room, or perhaps a bedroom for her child. So many cook/housekeepers seem to have suffered an identical fate: widowed in a distant place, husband fallen victim to some unspecified accident, leaving a child who must be supported by her own endeavour. For her use, the architect adds a second water closet next to the washhouse and adjoining coal house by the back step: a desirable addition, according to the Engineer, if staff are not to intrude on the privacy of their employers.

And then it is as though all this efficiency, this modernity, has become too much for his pencil to bear any longer. It takes off on its own little fantasy, as it does occasionally when he finds himself designing houses of interlocking octagons or great turreted chateaux that will never conceivably find a place in this pragmatic country. He finds himself adding an inglenook to the drawing room, a massive thing, the kind of fireplace where whole Yule logs might be burned, whole pigs might be roasted, watched over by merry peasants clad in worsted who sit in high-backed settles, tankards of homebrewed ale in their merry hands. He momentarily regrets the absence of flagstones and blackened oak, but compromises with a pointed Gothic arch to each of the windows in the bay. And above it all — his pencil flying, the clock on the landing outside his door chiming midday, the prospect of lunch: pea soup, a cutlet, in the club across the river in the company of men as comfortable as himself — he adds a turret. In a moment he will walk out onto streets that were, within his own lifetime, only lines on a white page when all around was swamp and primeval wilderness, inhabited by savages. This city then was fantasy, and behold: here it stands, in timber and solid stone. The lines on a page have risen up. They have taken shape. Who knows what a line on a page might become?

He adds his turret. A little hexagonal fantasy with carved wooden walls open to the elements and a sharply pointed roof ending in a finial. A gazebo, accessed by an external staircase from the side verandah, where a young woman, the owner's wife, might recline upon a cane chair on a warm spring afternoon. She is pale and fair, her long hair worn loose, her book drooping from her hand. Her mouth is sweet, her eyes dreamy, her breasts rise, uncorseted, beneath the fine fabric of her gown. A woman unconcerned with the science of kitchen sinks. She has kicked off one shoe and her slender ankle. Her slender ankle . . .

The architect rules a line. Tirra lirra, he thinks for no particular reason, as the knight rides, young and happy, toward the turret rising on the river's flowery bank. How did the poem go again? Tirra lirra. Tirra ...

three

THE NAIL

SPRING 1910

...rises on an acre of hummocky paddock sloping down to the river where, until recently, cows grazed: sleek Jerseys with lustrous brown eyes, demure lashes and swollen udders slopping milk and cream for the billycans of the city. The cows have given ground. They have fallen back toward the east, dawdled off downriver to tough little farms grubbed from the wetlands of flax and raupo. They have made their unhurried retreat, tails flicking, green shit dribbling into circular pies in the dust, while their former pasture has sprouted an overnight mushroom growth of surveyors' pegs. Their paddocks now feature among the advertisements in the daily paper as Barchester Estate, where might be found 'Charming sites overlooking the river. A delightful situation close to the city.' Plans and particulars concerning the estate's development might be obtained from the auctioneers and estate agents, Craddock McCrostie Co., whose sales at 12 noon every Saturday in their rooms on Cashel Street have been, they report with quiet pride, 'conspicuously successful'. Those in search of bargains in Farm, City and Suburban Properties cannot do better than attend.

    The bargain has been struck, a charming site secured, a design selected from a massive catalogue supplied by the builder, and now the residence is taking shape. It is a skeletal thing as yet, poised on a small regiment of totara piles dug into a sandy ridge in defiance of any biblical caution. Bearer and joist, stud and brace. The frame is of totara dragged from the peninsula hills, for it is impervious to rot. More totara clads the structure, laid in horizontal rows of weatherboard like the overlapping feathers of waterfowl. Water will be shed from board to board as it is shed feather to feather.

The interior, too, is finely dressed in timber from a single pine that took seed a thousand years before the sawyers sought it out and set to its destruction, boots scraping for a purchase on muddy ground, sweat soaking woollen vests, as the blade cuts deeper then deeper yet until the tree groans and falls, taking with it that dense habitation of bird and insect and multitudes of living things. Trimmed, dragged to the mill by straining oxen, cut and sliced and here it is: rough-cut rimu nailed to totara stud, both timbers still green so that they will hold straight and true as they dry, slowly, slowly.

This sarking is nailed in place by a young man from Alsace, a miner, son of miners, come to see for himself exactly how life might be lived in the workers' paradise. This idyll in the South Seas described to him with accompanying lantern slides by a lecturer from the SPD to a roomful of men like himself, scrubbed up for night class, though the coal dust can never quite be expunged from the crevices of the body: a gritty rim at groin and hairline, black crescents beneath the fingernails. The lecturer, in stiff collar and woollen suit, was from Strasbourg, and his eyes were alight with enthusiasm behind wire-rimmed spectacles as he quoted the observations of a fellow socialist, Albert Métin, a man who had visited this distant place and discovered the Workers' Paradise of minimum wage and maximum hours, pensions in old age, compensation for injury, compulsory arbitration in dispute. The great estates of the wealthy had been seized and broken into many smaller holdings, 176 properties redrawn as 3500 farms where plainer men might make their living. And all, said the lecturer, tapping the lectern for emphasis so that a lantern slide of a worker's cottage, sturdy and snug within its own garden, jiggled on the screen. All, he said, without bloodshed! Without revolution! Without, according to Métin, any debate whatever concerning social doctrine! Yet here it was, made manifest beneath a benevolent sun. The peaceful and inevitable triumph of good sense. Socialism! The faith and hope of the working man, 'for when the masses,' said the lecturer, glancing at the wall clock and reaching for Liebknecht by way of rousing conclusion, 'have become socialists, the time of militarism will have come to an end!' The slide of cottage and garden dwindled to a dot, the lecturer stuffed his papers into his case and left at a run to catch his train. And the young man with his dirty nails emerged onto the street, chill rain falling through smoke-grimed air, filled with new resolve.

Denniston, when he finally reached it, was not quite the paradise he had imagined. He arrived in spring. Drizzle and fog cloaked the dank hills, and mining was as it had always been: the descent into darkness and the uneasy knowledge he had never been able, quite, to set aside, of the great weight of earth above his head.

But in this country, released from tradition and custom and the weight of the past, it was possible to change. He could walk away from the dark. He could lay aside his shovel and take up a hammer. He could become a carpenter.

He is Friedrich. His mother called him Frédéric, with her native uvular 'r', but that was just at home, where they might be as French as they pleased. At school, he was Friedrich, because it was simpler that way in a place that switched identity as regularly as a clock ticking: now French, now German. The border swinging a few miles to the east, a few miles to the west.

Frédéric. Friedrich. And now Fred, though his workmates insist on calling him Fritz. It's a joke, a strange Anglo-Saxon joke, like asking him on the first day on this job if he could go and ask Bingham the foreman for the glass hammer. 'Glass hammer?' he had repeated, forcing his mouth to the shapes of this flat New Zealand speech.

'Yeah,' they had said. Taffy and Curly and the others whose names he had not yet mastered, heads down, grinning as they rolled their cigarettes and drank the bitter brown stuff they insisted on gulping mid-morning with every appearance of satisfaction. This thin smoko, when back in Forbach their German brothers paused for their zweites Frühstück of beer and sausage. The glass hammer was clearly a joke, but he went along with it, for were not all working men united in this, their good humour, as in all things? They gave their bodies, their hands and backs, to toil. With their sweat they created the wealth of the world, wealth seized by 10 per cent of the population, by those fat capitalists, Krupps and Siemen and the rest of them — while the working man and his weary wife and sickly children lived like pigs. Working men were united in this, too: their suffering, and the struggle to ameliorate that suffering. Germans and Americans, Englishmen and Frenchmen, and here, too: these New Zealanders, sniggering as he sets off on his fool's errand, to find the glass hammer. United in their common cause. United by laughter. As he laughs also and answers to any name his brothers care to bestow on him.

The main thing is that he is above ground, not buried deep. He's perched upon a ladder, his hammer striking each nail dead centre. He likes the sound of it, ringing in the open air. He likes the way he has become accurate and fast. He likes the flex of his boots on the ladder rung. He likes the feeling of doing something that is clear and has a purpose. He is making a house and what could be more purposeful than that?

He is fixing in place lengths of sarking, roughly cut, the stuff with knots and imperfections, the signs of the saw still visible. It doesn't matter, for it will never be seen. Its function is to brace, lending its invisible strength to the whole framework, holding everything steady.

Over the sarking they will nail a web of scrim, coarse woven jute that had its beginning in a Bengal bog, as a tall green reed with its roots down deep where the sacred river abandons herself to the sea. Men have waded through mud to cut its stems, small girls and women have clawed out the soft core with nimble fingers, and the fibres have hung and dried and been carried off in the dusty holds of ships to Dundee. And there they have been sprayed with whale oil, boiled from the bodies of the great creatures that swim in all magnificence along the sweep of coast a few kilometres from where Frédéric/Friedrich/Fritz perches on his ladder in the morning sunlight. Someone has discovered somehow that whale oil renders jute fibres malleable enough for machine weaving. More girls and women have stood at their looms, lungs filling with dust in the deafening clatter. And other men, other workers, have heaved the woven stuff into other ships and here it is, carried back across the world to this place, where it is being unrolled and nailed into place over the carcasses of dead trees. Over it will be pasted paper patterned with pink roses and acanthus, purple grapevines on an acid-green lattice, irises and tulips reduced to their stylised essence. Mouldings will frame the imagery of the flowery mead, scotia and skirting board and ceilings of rimu and floors of matai and windows framed with more totara and a roof overhead of corrugated iron, and the whole will sit, bare as an egg and newly painted, on an acre of cleared earth on a ridge overlooking a river.

Frédéric lifts his hammer, hits a nail square, one of a chorus of hammers at work, a saw grinding back and forth, back and forth, a young man singing on the roof: *Oh! Oh! Antonio* — that would be the one they call Taffy who fancies himself as a bit of a singer — *Oh! Oh! Antonio, he's gone away* from overhead where his brothers, the workers of the world, are mortaring bricks on chimneys, tall chimneys varicoloured and cantilevered around the pot, another of the architect's little flights of fancy. *Left me alon-io, all on my own-io* . . .

The nail slides through the sarking and into the stud, straight and true.

Birdsong, the sound of . . .

›
four

THE ROCKERY

SPRING 1912

'... shouldn't have come,' said Crosbie. And really she shouldn't. There was no place for babies on this expedition. Not when it would require every ounce of strength they possessed to face the challenges that lay ahead. The Great Man had told him so when they were taken to see the huskies. What was required for such ventures, he had said in his abrupt naval fashion, was a team of stout-hearted fellows capable of immense endurance. Nature was a stern taskmistress and nowhere was she more intransigent than in the polar regions.

Sybil's face has taken on that mulish look everyone knew so well. The one that could erupt into tears and a scream so piercing it guaranteed immediate adult intervention. She stood in the middle of the road, thick little legs in dusty boots, pinafore stained and crumpled, though it was hardly an hour since she had been buttoned into a clean one after dinner. In her arms she held a sack that dripped ominously.

'She has to come,' said Margaret. 'I have to look after her, and if she doesn't come, I can't either.' Margaret was a necessity. Not a stout-hearted fellow exactly, but a very tall and strong one. Taller already than Crosbie, though she was a year younger. He was taking ages to grow. His mother said he would be tall eventually: all the men on her side, the Mulcahys, were six foot, so 'Don't fret. You'll be towering over the lot of us soon enough and endangering the furniture.' He'd just have to wait. Sometimes it felt as if his entire life was spent waiting. Permanently stuck at the starting line, knees flexed, ready to spring, ears alert for the snap of the starter's pistol. Margaret could already reach the biscuit tin on the top shelf in the larder without the aid of a chair. She could also run faster on her long legs, and easily flipped his arm sideways when they wrestled.

But soon, all that would change. Soon he'd be tall. Taller than his father and his father's brothers, who were Sinclairs and stocky. Taller even than his grandfather, who had been a military man in India and could be picked out in any crowd, upright above a field of swaying hats. He would be strong. He was working on that in the privacy of his bedroom, standing in his underclothes before the wardrobe mirror, lifting rocks he had removed surreptitiously from the pile that was going to turn into a rockery. Special rocks, his father said. Granite and kyanite, brought as ballast from Antarctica in the hold of the *Discovery*, which had been another of the Great Man's ships, and gifted to those who had rendered special service. His father, for instance, who had overseen some electrical installation. The rocks were blue-black, smoothed by the scraping of ice, and very very heavy. Crosbie sweated and strained. Soon he would be tall, he would have muscles. While Margaret would be stuck in long skirts and a stupid hat.

Meanwhile, however, she bears the oars and the pole for the Union Jack over one shoulder and the flag itself, part of the bunting they hung from the verandah on Dominion Day, stuffed in her school satchel.

'She's too small,' said Crosbie. 'It's dangerous.'

'Why?' said Sybil. 'Because of the polar bears?'

'There aren't any polar bears,' said Crosbie. 'That's the North Pole, silly. You don't get polar bears in the south.'

'Anyway, I've got meat for them,' said Sybil. 'I brought enough for the dogs and the bears.'

'Is that what's dripping?' said Margaret. 'I thought you were just bringing biscuits.'

'It was on the shelf,' said Sybil. 'It's huge. There'll be heaps.' She opened the sack. A blood-soaked joint lay among a litter of biscuit crumbs and some withered carrots.

'Oh, Syb!' said Margaret. 'Mrs McTurk will be furious! You'll have to take it back.'

'But what about the dogs?' said Sybil. She remembered the dogs. The funny Russian man had told her all the animals' names. Each of the ponies who were going to pull the sleds like Jingle Bells, jingling all the way to the South Pole, had two names, one for everyday and one for the schools that had donated it to the expedition. The stumpy little bay was Floreat Etonia but everyone called him Snippet. The grey was Westminster but generally known as Blossom. There were Nobby and Snatcher and Chinaman and Jones and Jimmy Pig. There were two rabbits and a stripey cat and a squirrel who had taken a nut from her fingers with its tiny hands reaching through the bars of its cage. She had never seen a squirrel before.

The dogs had pale eyes and were not to be patted. They had two names too, one Russian, one English, because school children had donated the dogs also, along with the sleeping bags and the tents that would keep the men warm. There was Bristol after a school in Bristol, but the Russian man called him Lappa Uki, which meant lop ears, and Hampstead for a girls' college whom the Russian called Ishak, which meant jackass, because he was so stupid. Beaumont and Bluecoat and Bristol and Mac... She had been making up a little song from the names as she marched down the dusty road to the river. The joint had been terribly heavy, but she had borne it because of the dogs.

'You'll have to take it back,' said Margaret. 'There aren't any dogs. This is just pretend.'

Crosbie hated that. For long stretches he was still capable of forgetting that what he was engaged in — some battle to defend a beleaguered British redoubt against Zulus, this expedition over towering seas — was pretend. The redoubt was a pile of builders' spoil in the part of the garden that was going to be an orchard, the spears were sticks of flax, the towering seas a river between sapling elms and willows, their icy destination a muddy islet a few hundred yards downstream. And their stout ship, rigged for Antarctic waters, was a raft constructed from weatherboard offcuts the builders had left stacked behind the stable and gighouse, now lashed to half a dozen firmly sealed kerosene tins. He and Leonard had spent the first week of the school holidays on its construction.

Leonard was a stout-hearted fellow. Exactly the kind of chap one wanted on an expedition. Son of the cook and a year older than Crosbie, heavy-set but even-tempered, happy to play Zulu to Crosbie's gallant British officer, crew member to Crosbie's expeditionary leader, prepared to shoulder more than his fair share of any burden. And, best of all, always convinced of the reality of what they were about. For the duration of any enterprise, Leonard understood that this was not pretend.

'You gowk,' said Crosbie. 'When we're almost there. You gowk.'

Sybil's lip trembled. Tears threatened.

'Here, Syb,' said Leonard. 'Give me the bag. I'll carry it. You can take the scientific instruments.' He took the reeking sack as if there were indeed huskies waiting to devour its contents and added it to his load: a sugarbag of provisions, a bottle of fresh water from the tap in the yard that went straight down to another invisible river that flowed far beneath their feet. ('Ahh,' said Pat the gardener, smacking his lips whenever he drank from the faucet, 'Adam's ale!') A jar of preserved peaches, the pocket knife he had received for his last birthday, which was his most valued possession, a hammer for collecting rocks, a jam jar for specimens, a ruler and pencil and a selection of woollen hats and mittens because, although the day was warm, Crosbie's vision of snow and ice was compelling. Just as Leonard saw the Zulu warriors advancing, heard the cries of wounded men beneath the wide blue arc of the African sky, so today he saw the icy plateau, the snow billowing around them in dense clouds. He had seen real snow in flurries over the city, but a whole land of ice and snow? Now, that would be something ...

Sybil smiled up at him as he took the bloody sack and as soon as she was relieved of it she was off, skipping ahead, holding the jam jar. A crisis had been averted. It had rained all morning, but the clouds had cleared and now the sun shone on a world that seemed to have risen newly formed from beneath the sea. On the road ahead, puddles gleamed in ruts, while all around the ground steamed so that trees and cows stood on white cloud. Leonard shouldered the load, Sybil danced along singing her pony song, Margaret swung into line, and Crosbie took the lead.

They should return the joint. Crosbie knew that would be the wiser course. Along with the flag. His father was very particular about that flag, referring to it always as 'the good old Union Jack' and folding it respectfully after use, before stowing it on a shelf in the hall cupboard. He would take a dim view of its current destination, pinned to a manuka stake on a muddy islet standing in for the South Magnetic Pole. For that is where they were headed. And there lay the greatest transgression of all: in Crosbie's jacket pocket is the heavy weight of the compass.

He had taken it from his father's desk, tiptoeing into the office with its scent of varnish and Havana cigars. The compass knocked against his heart, the red tip on its jittery needle trembling always toward the north while the silver tip pointed south. His father had laughed when Crosbie first tried to make the needle point east–west. It was a mystery, the entire point of another Great Man's expedition when more stout-hearted fellows advanced the reach of the empire to the farthest corners of the globe. They had been willing to endure cold and injury, possibly death, hauling heavy sleds themselves when the motor car had failed them and their ponies had died of cold or accident. The men had nobly suffered hardship, and why? In the cause of science. They planned to discover the exact location of the South Magnetic Pole.

That was a place where a whole lot of energy was released by the molten rock that sloshed about mysteriously somewhere beneath the Amritsar rug in Crosbie's father's office: rock dense with particles of iron — that same iron that made steam engines and bridges and the very roof beneath which they stood — well, all that energy gathered to a point at the northern and southern extremities of the earth, not the North Pole or the South Pole exactly, but somewhere in their vicinity. He had imagined a gleaming shaft of dancing light reaching up from the ice as he concentrated on trying to look intelligent while his father sketched a few diagrams on scrap paper, talking of azimuths and degrees. Here. You see? The south is zero degrees, east 90 degrees, west 270 degrees, and the little pinman is the observer and this horizontal line is the sea or maybe it's ice, and this is a star and this — a quick row of dots — is the projection of a perpendicular line from the star to the horizon . . .

It was another of those forces that were at work, mysterious, unfathomable. Like the comet that had arced over the city when he was ten. He had squinted through his father's telescope at its strange blunt head nosing its way through the reaches of space. The same comet, his father said, had hung like a sword above Jerusalem, arousing fear in Roman and Jew alike. The same comet had terrified King Harold and his Saxons as the Norman knights sailed toward them, bringing all that history. And here it was again, hanging over Christchurch, though there was no need for superstitious dread. It was to be understood simply in scientific terms as a natural and entirely predictable phenomenon. Yet Crosbie had stood, his feet cold, the night air penetrating the gaps in his pyjamas, looking up into the night sky and, despite science, he had felt a tremor of fear. Here they were, tiny pinmen, on a suburban verandah, caught up in the tail of a comet 14 million miles away. Tiny particles were raining down upon them, filling the air they breathed. They were rolling through space, entangled, and he had felt dizzy, weightless with the knowledge of it.

Crosbie would have liked to bring the telescope on this expedition, but he had time only to scoop the compass into his pocket. It knocked at his heart, cool and scientific, its weight worth the risk. A whipping, and not just six of the best either, but a thorough pasting, his father's razor strop whistling through the air, stinging into bare flesh.

But there was the track leading down through flax to the river bank where *Perseverance* lay concealed. Not sunk overnight, which was a relief.

Margaret set down the oars. 'Is that it?' she said. She poked at it with her foot. 'Is this your boat?' And once again Crosbie felt that sinking of the heart as *Perseverance* shrank from rigging and spars and hull reinforced to punch a passage through pack ice to a kids' thing, a dubious assembly of weatherboard and tin cans. He could hardly bear it, this loss of the grand idea, the way everything always dwindled.

'She's sound,' said Leonard. And in that one word 'she', he restored the vision. 'She' was a ship, a sturdy ocean-going craft. 'She floats and that's what matters.' *Perseverance* dipped beneath his weight as he stepped aboard. 'Come on, Syb. Take my hand.'

One by one they came aboard and *Perseverance* settled low in the water, but remained buoyant, as Crosbie untied the rope and, using the manuka flagpole, pushed off. Sybil was told to sit amidships and not move because she couldn't swim yet and was forbidden to go anywhere near the river. She sat cross-legged, looking at the sky and the river as the dogs crowded round and the ponies, too, Nobby and Jehu and plump little Jimmy Pig. The river gleamed and dimpled. In the paddock, Rajah the gig pony lifted his head to watch them pass. Drops hung heavy on every flax leaf and the Dobsons' cows paused in their drinking, big pink rubbery tongues cleaning their nostrils the way cows' tongues can, and even though she knew there were no polar bears and she had got it wrong again, really when you didn't look straight on but from the corner of one eye, they could almost be mistaken for bears. In white shaggy coats, standing on their big bear feet and wondering perhaps whether to leap in and paddle over and eat them up. She wasn't sure if a polar bear could eat a person, and she wouldn't dare ask and risk further ridicule, but she was glad just the same that she had brought the meat. She clutched the damp sack, blood seeping into her pinafore, looked straight ahead and sang her pony song.

Margaret stood to one side, steadying the craft with one of the oars her father had used when he was young and rowed for the Canterbury Club, and Leonard stood opposite with the other oar and Crosbie sat between them on a butter box calling, 'Row on! Hands to port!', the way the coxes did when they were racing, though now the river had taken them and no effort was really required to propel them forward. The raft swept with the current out into the open sea where great icebergs could pierce even the strongest hull and bring all on board to ruin and a watery grave. Crosbie kept lookout in that part of himself that was present, though he could feel it fade. The cries of warriors, the screams of the wounded, the press of ice. All that would fade and that is the exchange he must make if he were to become a man like the Mulcahy men, tall and muscled and a risk to the furniture. But for now, on this bright day, he takes out the compass and sets their voyage south. And Sybil amidships looks out at the shining river. There is something glittering, something moving toward them, just beneath the surface of the water. She bends over to look more closely. A great shimmering mass of tiny fish is swimming upstream. Hundreds of tiny glassy creatures.

'Oh, look,' she says, jumping up. 'Look!' And the water, amber brown ...

five

THE RIVER

SPRING 1914

Nothing happens.

The river flows. Leaves fall. They spin and drift. Rot.

A little thing flicks from the open ocean into the estuary, borne by dark currents from its birthplace thousands of miles to the north. It has burst from the egg, a minute glassy leaf, gut and nervous system visible as fine wiring beneath the skin. And, in the genetic either/or, female.

She has been swept up. She has been carried south until she came to this estuary where she has swum upriver. Just one tiny sentient creature among thousands.

She has made her way against the current to a safe place, beneath a muddy bank.

She settles into her life.

six

THE SWITCH

SPRING 1916

...**finds his** bicycle where he left it that morning, parked in the alley behind the solid rump of the new Government Building. There has been a directive that bicycles must be parked out of sight lest they spoil the dignity of Classical portico, Renaissance ornament and rusticated stone, brand-new from the box. Around the back it's a tangle of racing machines with down-turned handles, ladies' cycles with skirt guards and baskets, power-assisted models capable of 30 miles an hour up even the steepest slopes of the Port Hills, along with a fair number of touring machines like his own. It takes a while to pick out the Spinaway's green frame, its sturdy Dunlop tyres, its little leather repair kit strapped to the saddle.

He could have taken the tram this morning, rattled into the city down North Parade, Stanmore Road and so to the Square, drawn not by labouring horses, their feathery hooves slipping on mud and gravel, but by a single wire. It amazes him still, this effortless journey powered by the fall of water. Water surging through tunnel and penstock. Water generating this force that can be transmitted from the high country's blue dazzle, step by giant pylon step, across the plain (the highest voltage, the longest wires) to the city. And by a process that is all scientific rationality but is as close as humanity can come to magic, it is delivered to this vehicle, with its consignment of men like himself, destined for the offices and business premises of the city, smart young shop girls, lady typistes, students of school or college, factory workers, men in khaki, a little self-conscious, neatly shaven beneath a newly issued hat, boots highly polished, eyes down, ignoring the glances of the girls in their sweet spring hats. Modestly accepting the congratulations of commuters.

George had sat opposite one such new recruit yesterday. The man next to him had clapped him on the shoulder as they stood to alight at the corner of Hereford Street. 'Well done, my boy,' he'd said. 'We need more chaps like you.' George had watched as the young man blushed. Muttered something about 'Just doing my bit', then stepped down into the crowd, marched off toward the barracks by the river. Youthful back ramrod straight. Youthful shoulders square. Youthful spring to the step.

George has a family. George does vital work in the Ministry of Public Works. George spends his days at a desk overlooking the Square designing reticulation systems for the distribution of electrical power across the city. George is unlikely to be conscripted, though he is forty-two and of military age. He has registered, as all men in the dominion between seventeen and sixty must. Not to do so risked a fine of £100, but George would have registered, fine or no fine. It was, after all, a matter of duty. For months, the government denied that registration was a prelude to conscription, while the country erupted in uproar. Meetings and conventions have ranted against conscription. Those Red Feds who have made a career fomenting riot, elected by men and women as unpatriotic as themselves, have used their seats in Parliament to argue against conscription. Thousands of men — socialists, Red Feds, so-called Christians, Maoris with no proper appreciation of the benefits civilisation has bestowed upon them, fit men pleading ill-health — have stated that they are unwilling to serve overseas. Over two-thirds of the entire adult male population, cowards and shirkers the lot of them.

And now the government has introduced conscription, as everyone had known it would. The ballot box has been set in motion. The little marbles are rolling. Fate is taking a hand. And should his number come up, George will go. He will leave wife and children, though it would pain him to do so. He will don his country's uniform and be proud to do so. He will complete what has been begun by those brave men whose names form dense black columns in the daily paper.

And yesterday there was that soldier on the tram and the commuter congratulating him while George stood by, unregarded in his civilian suit. He was trim and clean-shaven and he knew he looked young for his age. He felt the scrutiny of others and their question without it being asked. It was not a comfortable sensation.

So today he has avoided the tram and ridden his bicycle to work instead. He drags it from the mass and wheels it out onto Worcester Street where a brisk easterly is blowing straight from the sea, bearing a salty whiff of kelp and fathomless depths. It mingles with the familiar scents of the city: horse dung and benzine, coal smoke and wood smoke, the rich blend of hops and malt from the breweries and the stink from the towering stack of the city destructor. Its plume hangs overhead, reeking of fish and offal and factory waste and horses killed while their owners wait, and stray dogs drowned in the cage, all consigned to the furnace. The city's detritus purified by fire, transformed to that benevolent energy that warms the municipal baths. And to think that only fifty years ago the settlement had depended upon scavenging pigs especially imported to consume its mess.

Beneath the plume, trams circle the cathedral, before setting off toward the villas and bungalows, mansions and one-roomed apartments of the suburbs, and there is that feeling of release. Across the road, the lights shine in the offices of *The Press* where the events of the day are being arranged back to front on the linotype bar for the morning edition while a boy stands at the corner yelling 'Pa-ya-per! Pa-ya-per', selling what is over and gone. From Warner's Hotel comes the roar of men having a quick pint before home. For an instant, George considers joining them. But they will be waiting: his children, his wife. And tonight he wants very much to be with them. He wants to be with her. He polishes his glasses, clips his trouser cuffs, mounts the Spinaway and kicks off into the evening traffic.

The street lights are being lit, and in the west the sky blooms. At his back, swags of crimson close off the end of Worcester

Street and the entire city is taking on a luminous quality. Shop and hotel, the newspaper office and the Government Building with its pragmatic tenancy of Customs and Stamps and Fire Insurance and State Coal and Public Works — all are colouring up. They are transforming into theatrical palaces alongside the gleam of asphalt canals. Even his skin, when he looks down at his hands gripping the handlebars, has turned pink. He glows. On such an evening he might, once, have been tempted to turn, right there, right then, into the light. He would have cycled west into that fiery furnace of luminous possibility. He would follow the straight roads from the city towards the mountains where he would take up some other destiny entirely: mountaineer, musterer, fisherman, farmer, the whole tinker/tailor litany of occupations for a man.

No. He tugs his hat low and sets his star for home. His body draws him, the longing for her that had settled upon him that afternoon as he surveyed a twelve-panel switchboard designed to receive the influx of power flowing towards the city from the high country. There have been problems with the project. Dissatisfaction among the men who laboured through icy winters, home a bare tent among tussock, engaged on building a tunnel they mistrusted as inadequately braced, but what was one to do? Timber was expensive, the railhead 32 miles away, and the contractor was working to a tight budget. The entire structure had its difficulties: the only power station in the world to be constructed on bottomless moraine, its foundation a pile of shingle drawn down the mountains. The landscape looked solid and sleek beneath its cloak of golden tussock, but it was shifting stuff, difficult to work, an awkward base for surge chamber and powerhouse.

But they had done it. Concrete gleamed in the wilderness, penstock slope, tailrace and tunnel. What had been imagined on a government desk had been constructed. The very shape of modernity, the lake glistening among mountains, the pylons marching away, and at its end the power of sixteen candles delivered to a frail bulb above his own kitchen table, at the flick of a switch. Magic.

He cycles among the evening crowds along city streets that will soon, within a matter of months, be lit as bright as day. Ahead of him lies his home. His wife.

He still feels the jolt of the word. That she is there. In his house. There have been other women. Of course there have. He was good-looking, broad-shouldered. Women noticed him. They liked his manner, beginning with the redhead who had called to him one night on St Asaph Street, as he walked home from cricket in college cap and jacket. There had been a cousin, Edith, who was not at all the young lady her parents presumed; Isobel the typiste at his first job, married but up for a good time. Dorothy and Catherine and others whose names he cannot remember.

And then there was Violet, measuring out sixpence worth of peppermints into a paper cone, pink lips pursed in concentration in a small shop on Tuam Street. Blue eyes studiously avoiding his own. Raven hair pinned up, but loosened already so that some curled about her neck. A stunner. Porteous, who was with him, whistled under his breath. 'Mine,' he said.

He'd spotted her first and he knew his way about the lolly shops. The ones with front shelves selling licorice allsorts and cigarettes while out the back they housed another trade entirely. 'Bet she'd be sweet to suck,' he'd said. But George had shoved him hard against a wall, arm against his throat and said, 'Don't ever speak like that about that girl.' Porteous shrugged him off. 'Calm down,' he said. 'Just saying . . . lolly shop.'

Porteous was mild, however, in comparison with George's parents. They knew, within seconds of meeting, who Violet was and where she came from. His mother had surveyed her from behind the silver teapot. The pink dress. Cheap fabric. (George had thought it beautiful, some stuff that made Violet's eyes shine.) Shabby boots, though she'd done her best with the polish. You cannot, though, disguise heels worn down from walking to her job from the tiny house on Hurley Street with its scrum of kids squabbling in the kitchen, her mother cooking stew, sweat pouring from her, and her father benevolent after a drink with the lads at the brewery, tickling the latest baby while he waited for his tea.

And George besotted. Head over heels. They would have to be very firm if he were not to make a complete fool of himself. Girls like this were for casual recreation, not for marrying. God forbid. She rang the little bell for Amrit, who had come with them from Simla years ago, so devoted. So endlessly faithful. No future for her in India after the death of her husband, an equally loyal and trustworthy infantryman.

But George was stubborn. He thought himself in love with the most beautiful girl in the city. He found himself walking up Colombo Street, Violet on his arm. Her little straw hat with the striped ribbon. A bunch of flowers — violets, of course — pinned at the neck of her shirt. He caught the glances of the other fellows passing by: their envy.

He had felt it later when they were strolling in the Botanic Gardens on a Sunday afternoon, he pushing Sybil in her perambulator, Crosbie dragging at Violet's hand while Margaret took an independent six-year-old's route on her tricycle. He had put his arm about Violet's waist then and said, 'I am the most fortunate man in the world.'

He feels it still. Her slim waist. Her belly flat after three pregnancies. Her slender legs, and the bush that lies between them, the damp declivity that opens to him, his face buried in her hair, the cries she utters, quickly muffled lest she waken the children. He loves driving her to indiscretion, the way she rises to cock or tongue or fingers, arches in the moonlight through the bedroom curtains that he leaves slightly parted, the better to see her writhe at his touch, the way she flings back her head, bites her lip so hard sometimes with the effort to hold back the cries that in the morning he can make out the tiny bruise left by her teeth.

And she has learned, too, to be shameless with him. Porteous had been completely wrong. She was no whore. Just a girl working in a sweet shop. She had no experience of other men. When they were first together she shied away, not wanting to put her hand on him, but he had shown her, placed her hand on his body, and then her lips, her mouth, and they had come hard together, hip bone grinding against hip bone, him anchored in her as they rocked and moaned and came in an explosive burst that left tremors afterward. Tiny aftershocks that gripped and fell away, gripped and fell away.

It happened less often now. She was tired, of course, exhausted by children and the running of a house and he was busy at work, preoccupied. But tonight, perhaps tonight...

Away from the luminous city, across the bridge into the suburban streets, the sky darkens to blue-black. In a few houses, lights are coming on, for the wires are weaving their way from the centre, suburb by suburb, month by month. His own home already stands like a lantern on its ridge, a block back from the river, amid flowerbeds and rockery and young trees. He opens the gate and wheels his bicycle through, feeling a sudden need to be quiet, to sneak up on the house, enjoying the suspended feeling that is arrival and the longing that draws him here: the longing for his wife's cool sweet skin.

Margaret is in the drawing room, thumping the life from some unfortunate sonata. She is persistent, but she will never make a pianiste. Round the side of the house light falls from the dining room where Crosbie, lanky Crosbie, sprawls, chair tipped back as is strictly prohibited, frowning over a book. His careless, clumsy son, forever losing things, breaking things and too big now to be sent off to collect the razor strop, to bear it from the bathroom to the study carpet where he had learned to stand, as he himself has learned to stand, head up, back straight, hand out, no blubbing, taking his punishment like a man. Now Crosbie towers over his father, skinny, lightly bearded. He sprawls on another fragile chair and idly picks his nose, while Sybil crawls about the carpet, dancing a bit of paper on a thread for the latest kitten and George looks in on them from the darkness, ambushed, despite the chair, by such a wash of love for them, for his family, that he can hardly breathe. His children. His wife. His home.

He pushes his bicycle past the conservatory and around the corner to the back door. There is no light on in the kitchen, but there is a sudden shout of laughter he takes a moment to recognise as Violet's, laughing as she has not laughed with him, he realises, as he bends to remove his cycle clips, in a very long time. It was something he had liked to begin with, this laughter of hers, loud and uninhibited, though it had begun after a time to grate. He found it slightly embarrassing, a little coarse, too close to the laughter of the women who lounged about the rowdier hotels at the southern end of Manchester Street. There is another voice, too. Lower pitched. A man's voice, talking on and on with a kind of eager insistence. Pat. It's Pat Shean, the gardener. He is talking. He is addressing Violet as if she were an audience of hundreds in a hall, not a woman at home, in her own warm kitchen.

'Why should we fight for a nation that left our ancestors to die in their millions? And why take up arms against men with whom we have no argument? Why—?'

'Stop lecturing,' said Violet. 'You always lecture me. You always have. It's not me you have to convince. I'm on your side, remember?' But there's no rancour to it. There's laughter and banter between people who know each another well. He opens the door. He switches on the electric light.

The glare is shocking and a gust of warm air fogs his glasses. Through the blur he can make out his wife seated at the kitchen table with her feet up on a chair. Pat is seated opposite, scrawny little Pat, jittery with the ferret-like energy George has always associated with such red-haired men. Between them a bottle stands on the table: Lagavulin. His Lagavulin. White Horse. Ten years in the cask. His wife and the gardener are drinking his whisky. And there is a distinct fug of cigarette smoke, though his wife is hastily removing her feet from the chair and rushing to the sink to extinguish something at the tap. And all this is mixed up with the smell of mutton stew, because today is Wednesday, Mrs McTurk's day off, when she goes into town for her shopping and they must eat Violet's cooking: a stew of greasy chops and potatoes he cannot abide, having been raised as a child on Amrit's delicately spiced curries and pulaos with spices ordered especially from Fortnum and Mason. Cumin and fenugreek, coriander and turmeric, at which Violet always crinkles her delicate nose. She called them 'stinks'. When it is her turn she cooks the food of her childhood: stew and perhaps a doughy pudding swimming in golden syrup.

Back when they walked arm in arm down Colombo Street she'd said, 'I'm warning you, I'm a hopeless cook', and he had laughed and said, 'I'm certainly not wanting to marry you for your cooking.' The other chaps glancing at her, at him, with envy.

But now the room stinks of fatty mutton, and it is surely the saddest, most doleful stink on earth, and she is laughing as she never laughs with him. She is sitting in the dark drinking whisky with …

seven

THE TILE

SPRING 1918

...snatches of sound from the north where the crowds are gathered for the procession. Little brass-bound musical phrases pop and fade. Pop and fade. Margaret is not among the crowd. Nor is Sister Adams, who no doubt has her own reasons for avoiding celebration. They stand instead at the corner of a street. Narrow, muddy, lined by mean little cottages that stare, dull-eyed, from windows curtained with rags. Smoke trickles from chimneys and the whole place stutters along in its grim mean fashion until it runs full tilt into the tall brick wall of some kind of factory, a foundry perhaps, for the air has a gritty metallic edge that catches in the throat. There's a skewbald tethered in a rubbish-strewn yard, head drooping in the rain.

Sister Adams hooks her basket onto her arm.

'You take that side,' she says. 'I'll take this. Any problems, call cooee. All right, Sinclair?'

'Yes,' says Sinclair, hoping she looks more confident than she feels. Sister Adams does not look the type to countenance a ninny.

'Over the top!' says Sister Adams, and off she marches to rap at a shabby front door.

Margaret stands with her kind little basket filled with nourishment — shortbread, a dozen eggs, some lemons, a jar of beef broth, a little brown packet containing cream of tartar, chief component of Imperial Drink, sovereign remedy against infection as demonstrated back at the depot by Sister Adams: one teaspoonful in a pint of water, a slice of lemon. She surveys the street, sensing the twitch of those rags, unseen eyes looking out at her: intruder, foreigner. A dog barks over and over. She had no idea such places existed a few miles from piano and inglenook. She may just as well have strayed into some savage encampment in Afghanistan.

But Sister Adams has disappeared, swallowed up by the hovel, and there is nothing for it but to be brave and follow suit.

She steps through a puddle, careful not to slip in the mud, and knocks at a door. She can hear a kind of furtive scrabbling. 'Hello?' she calls. 'I'm from the Relief Depot. I've brought some food.'

The door opens a crack. A small girl is looking up at her. Maybe three, maybe four, hair in dirty tangles, face smeared, bare arms, bare feet, stained dress, fingers in mouth.

Margaret bends down. 'Hello,' she says. 'Is your mother home?' From the crack oozes a dense suffusion, sour and cloyingly sweet like nothing she has ever smelled before. The child scratches one scabby arm and regards her solemnly. 'May I speak to your mother?' says Margaret. She has to be brave.

It is important to be brave. Everyone has had to be brave. Ever since the night when their father sawed a slice from a leg of hogget and said, 'Well, we shall have to start without him.' At the other end of the dining table their mother lifted a lid on the serving dish and drove a spoon into the mashed potatoes as if they might fight back. No one spoke. Sybil had her hand under the table where Floss waited out of sight, her nose on Sybil's knee.

Bother Sybil. Their father's moustache was already bristling with annoyance at Crosbie's empty chair. If he noticed Floss it would be all over: the full barrage, their father slamming down the carving knife, their mother trying to defend the wrongdoers as usual, being feeble, doors slamming and then a whole evening of silence wound tight over the house. Everyone walking on eggshells.

Bother Sybil. And bother Crosbie for being late, on his own birthday, making everything difficult when it needn't be. Why did some people never understand that it was much better to just follow the rules? They were there for a reason: to make things simple, so everyone knew exactly how to behave and where they should be and when.

Don't bring animals to the dinner table.

Sybil constantly broke that rule, smuggling in a stray kitten, a baby hedgehog wrapped in a handkerchief, her horrible white rat Snowy, who never stayed quietly under her jersey but wriggled up to peer with his nasty pink eyes over her collar. Or Floss, who was quite audibly snacking on titbits and practically ensuring a scene.

Everyone to be seated, pet free, at the table by six o'clock, hair brushed, hands washed, don't speak unless you are spoken to, don't stretch for the butter or the gravy boat, don't slouch, eat everything on your plate without objection, don't swing back on your chair.

Crosbie had always known the rules as well as anyone, along with the rules applicable elsewhere: don't play ball games in the garden, don't slam doors, pull up your socks, straighten your tie. 'Why do you always insist on being a nuisance?' she had asked. 'It's not just you who gets into trouble, you know. It's all of us.' Tiptoeing about, unable to practise when it was only a matter of days before Miss Beaufort's pupils' recital and the tricky passage in the 'Rondo alla Turca' not yet up to speed. Everyone whispering, their father erupting at intervals from his room in wreaths of tobacco smoke like God on his way to smite someone or something.

Crosbie was late. Mrs McTurk was annoyed. 'Don't blame me, but it's all dried out,' she said as she slammed down the hogget. 'And Leonard's not home for his tea either. He's beyond me, that lad.'

Margaret surveyed her plate. Two slices of wizened meat. Creviced mound of mashed potato. Damp rags of boiled cabbage. Disgusting. And to be fair, it was not all Crosbie's fault. Mrs McTurk was an appalling cook, though no one but Margaret seemed to be aware of it. When Margaret married, she would be much more particular in her selection. Her mother was so disorganised. Margaret intended to be better prepared. She had a list of things she wished to achieve in her life: 1. Mastering all the *Songs Without Words*. 2. Developing a stronger backhand. 3. Visiting London to walk the length of the Mall. 4. Falling in love with someone at least 2 inches taller than herself. She was so very tired of having to dance with boys who reached only to her chin. Then marriage, she supposed, four children at regular intervals, a calm and properly run home.

She made a start on the meat. It was indeed dry. Their father ate with fierce concentration, their mother fluttered, nudging cabbage about her plate. Sybil had passed her share to Floss. And then there was a thump from the hall, the slam of the front door, the thud of rapid footsteps and the dining room door crashed open.

For a moment they stood swaying in the doorway, then in they came, marching round the table, a furled umbrella from the stand in the hall over the shoulder, one behind the other, eyes front, arms swinging, while Floss erupted from cover, yapping and jumping. They came to a halt, stamp stamp, One, *two* — in front of the fireplace.

'Private Sinclair, Second Canterbury Battalion, reporting for duty, *sir*,' said one, saluting smartly. 'Get down, Floss.'

'Private McTurk, Second Canterbury Battalion, reporting for duty, *sir*,' echoed the other, before stumbling backward over the fire irons.

Crosbie and Leonard, and both, if Margaret was not mistaken, drunk. Her mother put down her glass. Her father rose from his chair.

'We signed up, went in together a month ago,' said Crosbie to his father. He was alight. Excited. 'It's been the devil's own job keeping it secret. But here we are! We embark for Trentham tomorrow'.

'Tomorrow?' said their mother.

There was a pause, astonishment, then, 'Oh, well done!' cried their father and he was crossing to the sideboard, he was reaching for the whisky, he was saying, 'My word, this calls for a toast!' He was handing glasses to these strange young men, he was raising his own and saying, 'To youth and daring! To all young Britishers brave enough to take on the battle to preserve liberty and justice in the face of Prussian—'

The gravy boat flew through the air, landing with a crash in the inglenook behind their heads. A crack opened in one of the ornamental tiles, right across a crimson rose. Gravy bled to the hearth.

'Youth and daring!' said their mother, on her feet now, eyes blazing. 'They're boys! Off to kill some other mother's darling boys! And for what? Not liberty, that's certain. The British don't know the meaning of the word.'

'Don't you go quoting that Fenian chum of yours in my house,' said George, and he is blazing also. 'Too feeble to fight.'

'Feeble!' said their mother, two pink circles forming on her cheeks. 'He's imprisoned for his beliefs! For liberty!'

'Best place for him,' said their father. 'A firing squad. That's what he deserves.' And for tuppence, he'd place his hands about her neck, he'd squeeze as the villains did at the moving pictures, forcing the life from the doe-eyed maiden.

The look she was giving him was anything but doe-eyed.

'You utter fool,' she said. Icy with contempt. 'You stupid little man. I wish I'd never married you.' And she left, china snapping beneath her boots while the boys stood aside as if she were a stranger on a street, and Floss returned to her meat, and Margaret sat and wondered if she should add to her List of Ambitions. Maybe she could be like those Russian women she had read about in the paper who served in the Legion of Death, 'charging over shell-torn fields when men comrades deserted them in battle' and when their honour was threatened stepping forth like the Jewess who had stopped some men visiting their billets with evil intent. 'Begone!' she had said. 'Leave immediately or we will shoot!' Ah, yes. If she were in Russia, Margaret could join them, she could be brave, she could charge over shell-strewn fields, like her brother, wielding a gun.

She had gone to see him off. Another shambles. The barracks crammed with thousands intent on nothing but disruption, women and children mostly, hooting and jeering, surging into the roped-off area reserved for the men as they were called up to form ranks for the march to the railway station and the train to port. The names were completely inaudible above the row, rising to a howl when the mayor appeared on the balcony for the formal farewell. Margaret found herself pressed up hard against a woman in a shabby feathered hat, who yelled, 'You'll not be mayor much longer!' as the crowd roared and they were all carried toward the doors, fists flying as police tried to drag men forth into the line. Margaret caught no more than a brief glimpse of her brother and Leonard, standing quiet amid the tumult in one corner with the handful of the willing. Among the press of bodies she missed their departure, only a couple of dozen when there should have been a hundred and forty-three, a brave company, marching behind the brass band between flags and cheering crowds down Montreal Street.

And now the bands are back and the music plays, but far away, far away from this room where the child has dragged her, reaching out from behind the door and taking her hand in a fierce sticky grip, leading her into a room where there is a broken bed, a tangle of bedding, and something on the bed, a woman, but not a woman, for she is purple, like a ripe plum. She lies on filthy sheets, eyes closed, bare above the waist with some other little thing at her breast and the child is scrambling up to curl against her purple side, and all the time she is staring unblinking at Margaret, who stands there with her good little basket and her school coat and the smell in here is overpowering, and suddenly the purple woman convulses and red froth pours from mouth and nose and the thing at her breast rolls away into the sodden filthy tangle . . .

There's a draught of cold air from the front door.

'So,' says Sister Adams, 'what's going on here? Oh Lord—' And she's moving fast, she's pushing Margaret aside, she's saying, 'Come on, Sinclair! Stop moping. Breathe through your mouth and give me a hand here. We need to raise . . .

eight

THE WASH HOUSE

SPRING 1920

'... left my tools here,' he says, standing awkwardly, cap crushed in his hands, on the washhouse step. 'In the shed. Meant to pick them up but ... well, things went too fast. Didn't have a chance ...' She stands in the shadows, a dark silhouette he'd know anywhere. He is in bright sunlight, his eyes unadjusted to the gloom. Steam rises from the copper and the smell of wet linen and lye soap. 'That's if they're still there?'

His spade, whetted to a sharp edge, with the square tread that exactly fits his boot. Mattock and scythe for the rough ground in the orchard. Sharp also and properly peened and oiled. His rake, his hoe for clearing between the rows of young seedlings. He'd been meaning to come back the following morning to attend to the vegetable beds he'd mulched over winter and made ready. But they'd been waiting, hadn't they? Skulking behind the hedge when he got home that evening: the big officer, jacket straining over heavy muscle, his two fairy helpers, onto him before he'd had a chance even to unlatch the gate.

'Pat Shean?' said the fat one, planting a heavy hand on his shoulder. 'Patrick Francis Shean?'

'That'd be right,' said Pat. He'd been expecting them. They'd arrested Archie Bushe only the week before, in the middle of Colombo

Street in front of his wife and kids. He'd known it was just a matter of time before the heavy hand. He'd had a suitcase packed in his sleepout in readiness. The heavy hand slapped him around a bit on the way over the hill to the damp stone cell in Lyttelton, while one of the fairy helpers proved surprisingly handy with his fists and the other applied a boot to the balls. He'd expected that, too.

A few weeks later, snow sifting over huddled scrub on the Kaingaroa Plateau, he had missed his spade, its wooden handle worn smooth by his hand, its sharp blade. It would have made quick work of the rootbound volcanic soil. Better than the tools they had been issued by the guards, blunt and uncared for. The long row of men in grubby prison clothes stretched across the plateau, bent into the wind, hacking with mattocks, dibbing in the little seedling pines, moving steadily uphill through waves of scrub and tussock. Men given to persistent thievery or too ready with their fists, along with a sprinkling of men like himself: men fighting in their own way for the freedom of a country they had never set foot in, fired up by her rebellion songs and tales of heroes bearing pitchforks into battle. There were also a couple of Holy Joes, earnest bespectacled men, mild of manner but sternly determined to adhere to that inconvenient commandment that says, 'Thou shalt not kill.' Some Maori blokes from up north, unwilling to fight for a government that had stolen the land from under their feet. 'Nah,' said one of them, a soft-spoken bloke called Moko, as they stood side by side, peeling spuds. 'Bugger that.' And he had delivered a short history of the country that was in every respect at odds with the version Pat had learned from Mr Fraser back in Otira, which had begun with the noble navigator Cook, worked its way onward and upward via the enterprising visionary Wakefield to the noble pioneers who had tamed the wilderness, driven back the forces of cannibalistic darkness, established peace and plenty. Moko flicked a spud, deftly stripped of its length of curling skin, into the pot. 'We're not fighting for that fella,' he said. 'He's not our king. We got our own king.'

Then there were the men who would not fight with miners and factory workers like themselves. Not bloody likely, they said as they rolled their cigarettes, eking out the ration, on their narrow cot beds, the wind forcing the tent walls to belly in and out, the beast that had consumed them whole, breathing. Not bloody likely when the real enemies were the bosses and a system that condemned the many to near-slavery while delivering profit to the few. Men who remembered Waihi and Fred Evans going down under the boots of felons released from Mount Eden to do the government's dirty strike-breaking work. Men who remembered the cockies' cavalry clattering down Featherston Street with their government-issue batons, their government-issue guns, ready to kill, to do battle, and for what? To enforce the loading of a bunch of racehorses headed for Cup Day down in Christchurch. Working men and their wives and kiddies asking for nothing more than a fair deal, a working wage. Paddy Webb was among them, one of the wavering line inching across the plateau, convicted for speaking out in the House against conscription. In an eyeblink, translated from Member of Parliament, the Honourable this and that with suit and fob watch and an office on the third floor, to the tent, the icy blast, those regiments of tiny saplings forming ranks that stretched to the skyline.

She stands silent in the half light of the washhouse. Water bubbles in the copper. Her sleeves, now he can make her out a little more clearly, are rolled to the elbows, her hair drawn back in a dishevelled bun. Her stillness unnerves him. He's not quite sure what he'd expected. A smile? Yes. A smile, a 'It's you! You're home! Welcome back!' The old familiar Violet he's known since they were part of that noisy rabble playing bullrush on Hurley Street, shrieking and racing for the safety of the gas lamp that was home. The long-legged girl, heavy plait bouncing on her shoulders, skinny but fast. Hard to catch. Slippery to hold. 'I would have said goodbye,' he said. 'I wanted to but there was no ...' He trails off into silence. She takes a stick and lifts some heavy damp stuff from the copper, dumps it with a splash in the rinsing tub. 'I can come back later, if you're busy? To get my tools? If they're still here?'

She turns towards him at last. Steps forward into the light. He sees with a start that she's older. Lined. As he is, too, no doubt. He hadn't thought of that while he was away: that she might change. He had held her, constant and unchanged, warming his cold hands as he planted pine trees on the desert plateau.

But here she is saying, 'No, it's not a good time. Go ahead. Take whatever you want. But it will never be a good time.'

And now he sees, with astonishment, that she is angry. What he had taken for amazement at his unexpected arrival was in fact fury. Her voice shakes.

'One week,' she says. 'Did you know that? He was there one week. Then he was killed. Near somewhere called Grevillers, I've been told. Someone saw him hit, but they couldn't retrieve his body. So that's where he is: somewhere called Grevillers. While you've been fighting for Ireland, sitting in your safe little cell, three meals a day, nice warm bed . . .'

Ice spinning through canvas, raining down on a thin grey blanket . . .

'I'm so sorry,' he says. 'So sorry for your loss,' hearing the banality of the old phrase, but unable to think of anything else.

She'll have none of it.

'Sorry! One week! And thousands of others like him. I don't think sorry is adequate, do you? You and your mates with your causes, your ideals. And now you come around here, saying sorry.'

'But we did it for them,' he says, because she's not being fair. She's never been fair in argument and they deserve his defence, those men on the plateau. 'We were trying to stop it, fighting for peace to stop lads like him being killed.'

'Well, it didn't work, did it?' she says, dragging another tangled mess of white linen from the seething copper. 'He's gone and all the rest of them, and you're still here.'

The heavy load lies in the tub like something dead, something without muscle or breath, clad in a heavy shroud. Water splashes over the floor. She plunges her arms into the tub, swirls the mass about, then drags it forth.

'Why are you men such fools? The one I'm married to is bad enough, but you're just another. All gas and wind and big words. All fighting for this or that, peace or freedom. It's all poppycock.'

She is feeding one corner of a sheet into the wringer and her voice emerges in a kind of gasping desperation as she turns the handle. He wants to help her, to lift the sheet so that it will feed more readily between the rollers, but he's held back by the sheer force of her rage. He stays where he is, on the step.

'But then what could I possibly know about all this?' she says, gasps. 'Me. A mere woman. What I do know is: it took a week. First pains on a Sunday, and he didn't arrive until Friday morning and he was skinny. So small. We wrapped him in cottonwool, kept him warm. And he was always difficult. Colicky. Not like Margaret. Not like Sybil. They were calm and easy. But he was restless. Right from the start. Never slept. Always running off. Had to keep an eye on him all the time or he was gone in a flash. Broke his arm falling out of the plum tree. Caught everything: measles, mumps, chicken pox. But I nursed him. Made him better. Kept him safe. What a stupid, pointless mess ...'

The sheet has emerged from the wringer and folded down on itself in the basket. She bends to pick it up.

'So now you can leave. Get your tools, wherever they are, and go.'

She gathers up the basket. Brushes past him on the step.

'Take your big ideas, and get out.'

He watches her walk away from him towards the washing line, strung — because he had strung it — between trees in the orchard. He blunders into the toolshed next to the washhouse where his hoe is hanging where he left it on the hook, and his scythe. It is dark in the shed, filled with the shadows of implements and empty sacks and he can't see very well. His sight is blurred and he is frantic to get away. Of the spade, there is no sign.

It's gone. Gone completely. And for the rest of his life he will miss it: its smooth skin, its sharp true blade ...

nine
THE RIVER
SPRING 1922

Nothing happens.

Leaves fall. Dragonflies burst into existence, fly about, dazzling. Die.

She flickers in the dark place. Watches.

Eats whatever comes too close.

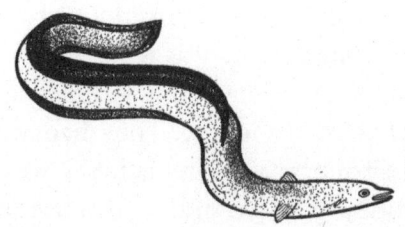

ten

THE WINDOW SEAT

SPRING 1924

… had been a pesky nor-wester stirring up the dust and making the girls hold onto their hats to stop them taking flight across the field. George had stood in the crowd on the terrace, making a thoughtful selection for the Cup. The Toff's tips in *Truth* were Sherwood ('full of ginger') or Albert Cling ('should do well').

Albert Cling, he decided after some deliberation. A quid for a win. But Finlayson was in no mood for caution.

'No point going for the favourite, old chum. Let's take a chance here.' And he'd placed ten quid on a little bay mare called Reta Peter, for no better reason than that he fancied a girl at the office, Johannson's new secretary, whose name was Rita.

'And the odds of having your wicked way with her are about as good as that horse winning,' said George. They had watched her in the birdcage being led about by a skinny lad. She was small and skittish and she was a trotter. A mare, and a trotter, the only one in the field. All the rest were pacers. Only one trotter had ever in history won the Cup against pacers. 'You'll be lucky.'

Finlayson had tapped his nose. 'Luck's the name of the game,' he said. 'In love or war.'

Reta Peter. Seventh favourite in a field of twelve. 'Don't waste your money,' advised The Toff.

She came in.

Nowhere to be seen as they went down the back stretch, Minston out in front, followed by Erin's Queen and Willie Lincoln. At the six furlong it was Willie Lincoln in the lead, where he stayed as the field rounded the bend for the last time. The crowd swayed as one to peer down the track, binoculars trained on the big beautiful beasts, all muscle and sinew and coats shining with sweat, giving it everything they possessed. General Link was in second place, then Erin's Queen and six lengths back were Trix Pointer, Sherwood.

And Finlayson's little bay mare.

She was holding her own as they raced for home into the roar of the crowd. The great collective roar as the pacers swayed in that strange unnatural rocking motion towards the finish line, hooves tossing up the dust, drivers on their frail bouncing sulkies laying on the whip, urging their charges on, and all the horses had their heads out, ears flattened, flakes of soapy foam blowing from heaving bodies, hearts and lungs bursting, bred for just this moment. Those early morning runs at the edge of the surf, a wide beach opening as they raced into the dazzle. Those winter sessions pounding tracks laid down on the plains, breath and sweat cloudy in the icy air that blows over the flat land straight from the mountains. All the cosseting and grooming, the brushing and the scrape scrape of the curry comb, the tending of hooves tucked against the blacksmith's leather apron. All the breaking to harness, the feeding and mucking out, the long patient hours of training: it comes down to this.

The finish line was racing towards them and Author Dillon was making a bid for the lead, challenging General Link, but here was the little bay mare, tiptoptiptoptiptop, coming up fast on the outside. Here she was, Reta Peter against all the odds, by half a length from General Link, a neck in front of Author Dillon and the crowd went mad. It was one roaring mass that lifted George, a solid man of middle age, clean off his feet. Then Finlayson was dancing him around in a puppyish headlock, punching his shoulder in jubilation. 'Did you see that?' he said, over and over. 'Did you see that? What did I tell you! Luck!'

And Albert Cling? George's choice? The favourite? Jibbed and broke at the start, left behind in the dust the whole distance.

The bay mare paid a dividend for a win of £20 11s – £20 11s for every pound wagered! Finlayson took George for a drink on the strength of it, still giddy. Still babbling with excitement.

'A lesson for you, old chum,' he said as he slammed down a jug. 'Don't play it so safe! We beat the odds at Menin Road! We beat the odds at Colincamps! Born under a lucky star, I reckon.'

George sat amid the uproar in the Star and Garter, fifteen minutes supping up before six o'clock.

Lucky? Was that it?

His son had been unlucky.

While he, who had also gone down to the barracks, who had attempted to enlist, had been turned down as too myopic to be of any use, had returned to the drafting desk, to his family and his home — he was lucky. Was that it?

He had never bothered to enlighten Finlayson concerning his war record. Let him suppose what he liked, this cocky fellow from Clinton, certain it was all going his way.

Two days later, George backed Reta Peter for the Dominion Handicap. Five quid for a win. More than he had ever placed on a horse before. The little bay mare started badly, then trailed the field the whole way. He watched her coming in amid a crowd who had, it seemed, placed as much faith in another miracle as himself. The cheering became muted and George stood, hearing hope fade, and with it, a strange sensation. He did not feel disappointment. Instead, what welled up was a weird satisfaction. It gripped him. It filled him with deep pleasure. This was failure. His old familiar. He settled into it, as if it were a comfortable overcoat.

Horse after horse had trailed since. Had jibbed. Fallen. Stumbled. Broken. Dumped its jockey. Been disqualified. Missed by a nose. A length, several lengths. And George watched them fall and break, taking his bet with them. And all he could feel was a kind of exhilaration. It was like falling into something dark, something bottomless.

Each week he had managed to hand Violet her allowance to

maintain the house, though sometimes it was a scramble to fill the envelope. He was a long-serving member of the department, a trusted figure with access to the strongrooms that stood by the lifts on each floor within the Government Building. He worked late. He fiddled and added and altered, careful never to take too much and keeping an accurate private accounting, because when he won, he would pay it all back.

He gave some to Violet, and some, more discreetly, to Daphne, an affable, easy girl with a little flat on Victoria Street. 'Ooh, ta!' she said, tucking the notes into a china biscuit jar shaped like a pink pig on the mantel. 'You are a sweetie, Georgie-pie!' At least she didn't think him a fool.

And he paid his regular visits to Charlie, who ran an illegal but nevertheless businesslike bookie's above a Chinese fruiterer's on Manchester Street. Full and prompt telephone and telegraphic connection to racecourses throughout the country. Charlie also had a poker game going out the back: a curtained room of dark and peaceful intent, lights lowered over the table, cards snapping to green baize, the muted voices of men saying no more than they had to, men he didn't need to know, wouldn't even recognise should he see them on the street. He bought tickets, too, in Tatts, or in the Art Unions. There were dozens of them suddenly, in this new era after everyone had been so serious for so long. And the prizes were no longer art, paintings nobody wanted to hang on their walls, but houses, cars, boats and, more and more often, a gold nugget. It was not legal to offer a simple cash prize, but a gold nugget! Ah! Who wouldn't want to win that! A nugget worth £4000, the proceeds from its lottery designed to fund the building of tennis courts and cricket grounds around the city. This was not gambling. This was a donation to a noble communal cause. And the gold nugget could, of course, be turned instantly to actual money.

George placed his bets, he picked up the hand, he pocketed his tickets. And week after week, year after year, he awaited the proof that luck was an operative force.

And the horses stumbled, the cards never added up, the gold nugget fell to someone else who had their photograph in the paper, smiling with delight as the recipient of good luck and civic benevolence.

And at night, when the house is quiet, his wife asleep in the room she moved into when the cook/housekeeper left along with her big, soft, lucky son: dismissed in an hour one howling afternoon ...

When his younger daughter, square and simple, sleeps in her room, content to share her bed with a dog or a cat ...

When all is quiet, when all is dark, George goes to his silent office, and underneath the lid of the windowseat, where no one will ever think to look, he pastes the lottery tickets. The Art Union tickets. The tickets in Tatts. Duds, the lot of them.

And when he looks at that mosaic, when he sees the horses stumble, when he sees his cards trumped upon the table, he feels nothing but the sweetness of failure. The deep sour certainty that he is meant to be unhappy. The satisfaction of ...

eleven

THE KOWHAI

SPRING 1926

...**straps on** her grandfather's old solar topee and loads Floss into her bicycle basket wrapped in a blanket. The dog is much too old to walk all the way. She can scarcely manage to totter from the house. At night Sybil sleeps with one hand on her side so that the minute Floss stirs she can waken and carry her out into the garden. Despite her best attention, however, there are accidents and her father is becoming impatient.

'That dog is past saving,' he has been saying for months now. 'Needs a bullet.' He had said it again this morning, irritable on the back step, scraping off a turd Floss had deposited in the hallway. 'This is ridiculous. It's disgusting.'

Sybil had cradled Floss, who whimpered slightly at her touch, her side smarting from the boot that had sent her staggering against the wall, and Sybil howling to her aid, 'Don't! Don't!' and her mother emerging from the bedroom shouting, 'Oh, for the love of God! Enough! Enough!'

'The dog has to be put down,' said her father. 'You know that, don't you, Sybil? No more nonsense.'

'You can't kill something just because it makes a mess,' said Sybil. 'People don't kill babies because they make a mess.'

'It's an animal,' said her father. 'Not a baby. And you are being silly. Worse than silly. You are being cruel.'

'He's right,' said her mother. 'You are not doing Floss a kindness, keeping her alive.'

'I'll attend to that dog when I get home tonight. But this is her last day. Understand?' And he stamped off to catch his tram.

'She's got to go,' said her mother, striking a careworn pose. 'I simply cannot be bothered cleaning up after her all the time. It's impossible.' Not that she could be called a fastidious housewife, forever dusting and polishing. Dustbugs rolled like puppies under the beds, dishes piled in the sink until mid-afternoon when she finally emerged from the turret where she spent all but the chilliest days. Reclining on the faded chaise longue that used to be in the drawing room. Reading novels from the penny library. Lighting cigarette after cigarette.

She's up there now. Sybil can hear the scratch of a match, smell the sweet dry burn of tobacco. She has been up there herself only once, years ago, one afternoon when she had the house to herself. Her sister was nursing somewhere on that distant planet called Up North. Her mother was in town at a matinee. Sybil climbed the staircase from the side verandah, opened the door and entered the turret. It really was the nicest room in the house, even if a little chilly, though her mother had had the window arches glazed, their tips ornamented with stained glass wreaths of crimson roses. You could look down onto the tops of trees. No wonder her mother had chosen it as her own. Sybil walked about, picking up the novels piled higgledy-piggledy by the chaise longue, fingering the faded shawl tossed over the arm, looking at the ashtray overflowing with butts, the smeared glass sticky with the veronal and honey-sweetened milk that her mother drank for her nerves. She sniffed and touched, then put everything back exactly as she had found it. She closed the door.

Floss's last day is warm, a day for the solar topee. Sybil wears a pair of men's trousers, cuffs folded and cinched at the waist with an old tie, and a comfortable shirt. Probably she looks a guy. She doesn't care. No one will notice. No one ever notices her, while she is busy noticing them: the planes and angles of their faces, the lines sketched around mouth and eyes. Notices without having the least idea what those lines might signify. The world beyond the garden gate is a curious and inexplicable place, filled with surging emotions she has neither hope of nor interest in understanding. The girls at her school are awash with feeling, chattering endlessly of love: that some boy is a dish, a dream, a corker. She has tried to see what they are seeing, but the dish looks simply odd to her. His head is a heavy cube, a thing of bone, from which his ears stick out like cup handles, while his eyebrows are a single charcoal line. If she were to draw him, he would resemble something you kept on a shelf.

She has never understood what made people love, or laugh, never anticipated anger, aware that she annoys people without having the slightest idea why, except that suddenly they are shouting, saying, 'Oh, Sybil! You are such a bore. Do go away. Vamoose, kiddo.' So she does. She has never understood, not since the water closed over, amber brown, dazzling ...

The art teacher alone seems to approve. Miss Delamere had stood at Sybil's shoulder watching as she painted the jug, the apples, the Japanese fan. The other girls were carefully blending complementary tints on the colour wheel, while all Sybil could see was the round black hole that was the mouth of the jug, an emptiness from which anything — armies of ants, flights of beetles — might emerge, and the apples were other circles, flushed with rot, decay bubbling beneath the skin. And the Japanese fan was ridiculous: a simpering, silly pink and white thing in the face of the dark well that was the jug, the hectic apples. Look, look, she wanted to say. Just look ...

Miss Delamere laid a slender hand on her shoulder. 'Interesting,' she said and she called the other girls over to see. They viewed the work coolly and returned without comment to the effort to get the shading just right.

Miss Delamere wanted Sybil to study further. She took her to lectures where earnest men promoted the cause of art: a nation without art, they said, was a nation unconscious of its soul! People had come to doubt the worth of civilisation. Old forms had been shattered and humanity found itself lost in a welter of new possibilities.

Art was truth. Art was the spiritual core of humanity. Science and intellectualism may have been promoted in the nineteenth century, but their role was narrow and could not compare with the power of art.

Sybil sat on hard chairs in darkened rooms watching lantern slides of the great works of this civilisation flick by: Venus riding in on her scallop shell, a woman standing by a window reading a letter, a boy in a velvet suit they said was blue, though everything of course was black and white and shades of grey. A Virgin in a damp grey field, holding out her pallid infant to pet a grey lamb. Art, said a lecturer, was the salvation of the nation. In times of financial collapse, 'when we are up against it materially, we should cultivate those things that better us culturally.' This young nation needed art, in order to properly perceive itself. An art rooted in the landscape, pronounced a man from the British Museum, visiting the dominion as inaugural guest of the Society for Imperial Culture. An art that blended new forms with tradition. 'New Zealand's artists cling with haughty exclusivity to the art of Britain and are the better for it. So far as they are concerned, China and Japan, those nations that exercise a voguish influence on the artists of Europe, have no other mission in the world than to launder shirts and produce green tea.' The audience tittered, the sound of cups and teapot audible behind the kitchen slide. 'The artists of this nation,' said the man from the British Museum, reaching for his conclusion, 'are creating work that is without a doubt the unstudied expression of the ideal of White New Zealand.'

Applause.

'Well said,' said Miss Delamere, clapping wildly. 'Oh, well said!'

Sybil clapped, too, without understanding why these things mattered: form, tradition. What mattered to her was the line on the page, the paint hanging full on the end of the brush, the black circle. Other girls went on to classes at the School of Art, where they cropped their hair and wore exotic black berets, drove their little cars out into the landscape to discover this culture, this civilisation, this soul that lurked beneath the brown hills in railway sidings and factory halls. While Sybil stayed at home, where it was less complicated and she didn't have to make the effort to understand all the time. There was more than enough here: the corner of the conservatory with the sunlight flashing halos through the grapevine. A camellia with leaves like scales. This garden, this house, contained multitudes, if only you were quiet and looked about. She left it rarely.

But today she has opened the gate. She has loaded Floss into the basket, tied a sugarbag containing the necessities — sketch pad, pencils, corned beef sandwiches wrapped in newsprint, a bottle of water from the garden tap, the best water, the clearest, Adam's ale — to the frame of her bicycle, and set off. Floss sits up in the basket, looking ahead, though of course she can't see, but her nose is up, her world a dizzy palette of smell, as clear and bright as it is to Sybil, pedalling carefully along the river and down Fitzgerald Avenue towards the hills. It's a long way and at the bottom of Dyers Pass she has to dismount and push. The bicycle with Floss on board is heavy and after only a few yards she is scarlet, puffing, but a lorry comes up behind her before she has gone very far and a man leans out the window.

'You going far, girlie?' he says. And she says, yes, to the top. And he says they'll give her a lift because that is where they are headed, too. 'You boys hop on the back. Give the young lady a hand with that bike.'

She sits in the front, the dog on her knee, while the men climb on the tray, off to build a road around the summit. 'You heard about that?' says the driver. Sybil says no, she hasn't heard about that. So all the way up the hill, grinding slowly, the driver tells her about the road and she listens and Floss sticks her nose out the window, tongue lolling, panting with the pleasure of being in a truck, zigzagging up hill above the city, past the tram terminus, past the pines of Victoria Park, up to the summit where they unload her bike, and say, 'There you go, girlie. Hooray,' turning right while she turns left onto the stretch of road that is already complete and leads along the crest towards Sumner.

A golden day. The road winds creamy white among tussock, and the light up here above the smoke is crisp and clear. The city lies beneath them, in its orderly grid, and beyond it stretches the countryside, broken into squares and rectangles by black rows of sheltering pines. And beyond that is the rim of mountains, white and angular under spring snow. She pulls over after only a few hundred yards and unloads Floss from her basket. The old dog totters about, sniffing at grass and sheep poo and the round black pellets left by rabbits. Her legs are stiff but her tail wags and you don't have to understand anything because it is as clear as can be that, for a dog, this is happiness.

Sybil leans back against a tussock and takes out her sketch pad. There are plants up here, tiny things that have missed grazing by sheep or rabbit: a plant with leaves that are silver on one side, grey on the other, a tiny kowhai with two leaves and a single yellow-tipped bud. She draws it where it grows, then uses her pencil to dig it up and folds it in the newsprint that wrapped her sandwich. Floss smells the corned beef and finds her way unerringly between the tussocks for her share. And the two of them sit eating their sandwiches, sharing a bottle of water, up in the sunshine overlooking the city.

Then Floss falls asleep, nose on paws, and Sybil sketches her: a beautiful drawing, one of her best. And when she has finished she lays the sketch pad aside. She unwraps her father's gun from the sugarbag, and the matchbox in which there are two bullets: one to hit, one to be sure. Floss doesn't flinch. She doesn't see it coming. She rears up at the first impact, then falls back at the second, her legs racing, racing, as they haven't done in years, over some wide sunlit hillside, populated by rabbits and whole flocks of silly tractable sheep. She races, ears flat, tongue lolling, then stops and is still. And Sybil can wrap her in her blanket and load her into the basket for the return journey. She's heavier now, heavier than before. No breath inside to lighten.

But Sybil manages it, then begins the descent, braking carefully, holding the bike steady as they come back down into the city, back along the avenue, the road beside the river, into the garden where she digs a hole at the end of the lawn where the ground is soft. She lays Floss down as if she were in her basket, and she unwraps the little tree and . . .

twelve

THE RIVER

SPRING 1928

Nothing happens.

Leaves fall. Rain dimples the surface. Ducklings wheel above her head, their tiny black feet paddling furiously, nervous by instinct of what might lie beneath. The dark void.

They try to keep in line. They try to keep moving forward. They try to keep as close as they can manage to safety, to the downy maternal breast.

She watches their efforts.

The water flows smooth against her skin. Her eyes look about ...

thirteen

SPRING 1930

...had come to the door. A Yank. Or maybe a Canadian. North American anyway. A talker and too cocky by half. Gold front tooth. Wide lapels. Smart fedora at a jaunty angle. There were a lot of such men around, men who struck a confident pose, talked too fast, looked you in the eye, but if you glanced down, their shoes were over at the heel, the shiny polish unable to disguise the scuffmarks of heavy use.

George was not normally in the habit of standing at his front door engaging in conversation with such men, all of them desperate to sell something: general knowledge or vanilla essence or eternal salvation. This one, however, was more persuasive than most. Or perhaps it was the accent. He sounded slick.

He wasn't about to waste George's time. He knew what a nuisance men like himself could be, interrupting the lives of men busier and more prominent than himself, men who had made a success out of life, but he thought it would be a crime if he neglected to inform George of a never-to-be-repeated opportunity. A once-in-a-lifetime chance to take the future into his own hands, secure guaranteed personal wealth and happiness for himself and his loved ones while also making a lasting contribution to the economic well-being of the nation. It was all described at greater length in this brochure, which he would like to take the liberty of presenting to George for his perusal. Should its contents prove of interest, he could be contacted care of the post office box listed on the final page, and now I'll be on my way and leave you to enjoy the remainder of the evening in your family's warm embrace, good night, sir. And he tipped his hat and headed to one of the new houses across the road.

George takes the brochure with him to work the next day. He sits at his desk when the others have gone, delaying the moment when he must leave. The bean-counters had been at work all day. Quiet grey men, who slipped into the office one morning a week ago and have been busy ever since, poring over the books, gathering for hushed meetings behind closed doors, checking, comparing notes, adding things up. He can feel the cloud coming down: eight hundred owed to Charlie, another hundred to the Chinaman who runs a pakapoo game alongside the apples and bananas. There's the new car, a sleek Buick Marquette, 10 to 60 in 31 seconds, to be paid for by the end of the month, and the grey men fossicking, checking, double-checking. He can feel it all falling around him, that sweet catastrophe.

What is a man to do? A drink in the roar at Warner's? Go home, to the unforgiving chill? Go around to Victoria Street, to one of Daphne's successors, some other dull, accommodating girl?

He looks out the high window to the Square, where the trams circle and people trudge, coat collars raised against an unseasonably cold blast.

And over it all, another image begins to take shape.

It's the image on the shiny brochure: of trees, tall pines, stretching over rolling hills beneath a sky of azure blue and a rising sun. Men with shirt sleeves rolled are employed in honest labour, muscled arms sawing at the base of mighty trees while piles of logs wait to be loaded into wagons. An image of industry and purpose.

'Wealth from the Pine!' reads the title page. 'For it is Better to be Without Gold, than Without Timber!'

By way of preface, a world is described 'where plains stretch bare to the horizon, mountains rise starkly to the skies, rivers flow between banks bare of timber to a sea girt by shores without shade. Truly a desolate picture, a parlous state of things for mankind.'

This was no fantasy, no nightmare, but an accurate depiction of the current condition of the planet. Its natural forests were being destroyed by the march of civilisation 'as man selfishly cuts down mighty forests to feed presses with newsprint, to build cities, to span continents with railroads'.

But a solution is at hand. In the place of those forests that have been cleared, new forests must be planted, laid out on scientific principles.

In New Zealand, thousands of acres of wasteland are at this moment being converted to productive forest. Millions of seedlings — a judicious blend of *Pinus radiata*, *Sequoia sempervirens* and *Pseudotsuga douglasii* — stand ready in the nurseries of Sequoia Forests NZ, for transplanting to soils uniquely suited to the rapid growth of softwood trees, as analysed by Mr Owen Jones (BA, Dip. Forestry, Oxford). The directors of this venture are men of equal authority: accountants, lawyers, Robert De Vere-Ffrench, P. Harold MacArthur. Their very names sound solid: a hyphen here, a hint of nobility there.

And what might the ordinary citizen contribute to the enterprise? Why, for £25 he might purchase an acre of this burgeoning forest! He might buy trees in their infancy that, by maturity, at twenty-five years, will realise £500, supplying comfort for himself in the evening of life and continued security for his loved ones.

It concludes with a poem:
Wind of the west, wind of the east,
Wandering to and fro,
Chant your songs in our topmost boughs
That the sons of men might know
The peerless pine was the first to come
And the pine will be last to go.

And an application form: I hereby apply for ... Bonds of £25 each. Full Name. Occupation. Residential Address.

George is filled with clear resolve. He completes the form and sends off a cheque representing every penny he can raise. He sells the Marquette to a gullible Pom, new to the game and flush with the proceeds of a suspiciously good hand. He pawns what he can gather up without detection — guns, watch, silver, jewellery. He borrows another five hundred from Charlie Conroy. Security: the house. For what could be more solid, more reliable, than *Pinus radiata*, *Sequoia sempervirens*? He can do nothing to make things well for his son. Too late for that. (Stiff back, chin up, hand out for the sting of the strop.) But he can bequeath security to his wife, to the daughter who has gone away, to the daughter who remains at home.

Not such a fool after all.

And when the cheque has been posted and the engraved certificate has been received by return of post, he places the envelope, heavy paper, reassuringly solid and addressed to Violet, upon the desk in his office. He pours a large whisky, the Laphroaig. He pours a deep warm bath. He lies back tasting peat and the sea, watching the steam circle toward the electrical light dangling from its central cord above his head. He looks up into the halo about the glowing bulb and finds himself thinking about cycling, out and away from the city, free as a bird, free of all responsibility, all failure, all hint of bad luck. He sets out across the plains into swags of glory, a crimson sunset colouring paddocks, barns and shelterbelts, catching the tips of the pylons that march across the landscape carrying down the perfection of pure energy from the lakes of the high country. They buzz and hum. They crackle.

And when he is quite ready, he stands in his bath up to the knees in water warmed in that miraculous transference of power. He stands up, naked. Not husband, nor engineer, nor son, nor any name. Just a man, who reaches up and squeezes the lightbulb until it shatters between his fingers, and the filaments make contact with bare flesh, 30 milliamps coursing in perfect synchrony with his unhappy beating heart . . .

fourteen

THE TURRET

SPRING 1932

... screws a cuphook into the wall and gathers up the curtain. It's cheap stuff, but pretty: white cotton with pink roses to conceal the corner cupboard.

It will do. Everything must do. Make do and mend, ever since the day the men arrived. She had seen them soon after the flash and sudden darkness, the thud and fall. Looked down from her place in the turret as they climbed the steps to the front door. She was vague, suspended in mid-air. She looked down in her half-dreaming state and thought they might be swaggers. There were lots of them that year, camped out on the riverbank netting for whitebait, then fanning out around the streets selling their catch door to door. But there was a car at the gate. Glossy black, like a hearse. So not swaggers.

Sybil was below in the garden, dabbing away at her easel in front of the walnut tree. From above, Violet could see the top of her head, bent closely, myopically, an inch from the canvas, a couple of cats writhing at her gaitered legs, one minus its back leg, the other wonky with a broken spine. The magpie perched on her shoulder. At times this house felt like a kind of desperate Noah's Ark, one in which all the creatures had been broken: accidentally shot, maimed, run over, a leg lost in a trap, amputees and strays dumped over the front fence or deposited by the gate in an apple box. Rescue did not make them grateful: the cats were grotesque and short-tempered, given to scraping at the door jambs and ripping the wallpaper, while the magpie staged ferocious attacks, screeching on broken wings half airborne while you tried to peg out the washing.

Sybil was intent. She did not look up, while Violet went down to open her door to cold, hard fact.

One man stood a little way back, heavy and looming, eyes averted. The other was shorter and older but he was the boss. He did the talking.

'Mrs Sinclair?' he said, and she said yes, assuming another former associate of her husband, come to offer his condolences. But not a bit of it. Mr Conroy was here on business, a delicate matter. So she asked them in, where they took a seat either side of the inglenook and no thank you to a cup of tea.

She sat looking at them as Mr Conroy set her straight, laid it all on the table. There was something familiar about the heavy one, something she couldn't quite put her finger...

'Mick?' she said. 'It is you, isn't it?' And the heavy one looked up and saw her properly. 'Mick Shean! How is Pat these days? How are your family?"

And he knew her, too. Violet Mulcahy, the girl his kid brother was always sweet on. The pretty one from next door on Hurley Street. Violet Mulcahy! Looking a bit rough, but then she'd had a shock and it was a long time since she was flying for home in the twilight on those long legs on hers, Pat in hot pursuit. So, what do you know!

Which made the simple purpose of this visit a little complicated. There was the debt, of course: that couldn't be waived simply because of a brother's affections, even if that brother was dead, took a knock to the head when hundreds of cops emerged from Colombo Street into the Square where the tram workers were singing 'The Red Flag' and chucking stones at the trams and the posh boys who were playing at being drivers. Then the cops poured in, and the specials, farmers and more posh boys with their new batons, and drove the singers into the corner by the post office, where Pat was hit. And then there was the headache that would not go away and the shaking, the twitching, the gathering confusion until he died, a year later, babbling, at their sister's place in Kaiapoi.

Violet teared up at that, big blue eyes filled with grief at the thought of Pat babbling.

You couldn't go forcing a woman like that from her home, could you? Clutching a bunch of fancy bonds worth less than the paper they were written on. You couldn't drive her out simply because she married a fool. Made the wrong choice years ago when they were all young and stupid.

Violet could keep her house and she could pay off the debt, £2 a week. Seven hundred weeks, and never mind the interest, said Charlie, tugging on his gloves. Defender of the weak. Protector of the widow and the orphan.

Violet climbed the stairs to the turret to watch them leave. The handsome car glided soundlessly off along the street, turned onto the road by the river and headed toward the city. It was warm up there, the sun pouring through the narrow windows from every angle. A bumble bee had become trapped against the glass. It buzzed mightily, its heavy body fighting to get through, and the sweet waxy smell of its panic hung on the air. Below in the garden, Sybil continued to dab at her painting. The trees over by the river swayed a little. Everything was quiet. Sound muted.

And suddenly the door swung open. Caught on the easterly, it crashed against the wall, leaving a dent in a rimu Gothic window frame. Cold air from the wide ocean penetrated every crevice. The latest novel flapped on the floor beside the chaise longue, like something wounded on a road: *His narrow, heavy-lidded eyes were green and strangely piercing. She sprang to her feet, flinging her broidery from her carelessly, and waved agitated little hands. 'You speak of love, but you mean to disgrace me!'* The little glass, with its sweet honeyed froth disguising the bitterness of veronal, tipped on its side. And suddenly she was awake.

She was wide awake again. The long spell of being here, half sleeping, feeling the phantom weight, the curve of her son's fragile skull filling the palm of her hand, the way he suckled then fell back, her milk dribbling on his chin and looked up in that sweet funny fashion, looked right at her, saw her as no one else had ever seen her. Her son. The weight of him against her breast. And then the way she had failed him, over and over. The snap of the strop. The way she had let him go. She reached for the honeyed drink, picked another silly fantasy of happy endings from the pile, dozed in the sun in her turret above it all.

But now she is suddenly awake. She can see the trees on the riverbank, the men sleeping rough beneath their branches. No knight is going to come riding, tirra lirra by the river. Knights fall from their horses. They are struck down in anger. They rot and burn and babble and there is no getting over this. The grief is a hard lump within her. Something she must simply . . .

fifteen

THE RIVER

SPRING 1934

Nothing happens.

Torn branches churn downstream to the coast in spring flood. The water is dense with silt.

She hugs the bank, her lean body a muscle intent on staying exactly where she is.

sixteen

THE RIVER

SPRING 1936

Nothing happens.

Dragonflies hover, wings glinting, dart and kill, choosing their prey from the multitude of tinier creatures that skitter about on the smooth curve of the meniscus.

She takes what she can reach.

seventeen

THE PICTURE RAIL

SPRING 1938

'... the afternoon sun,' says the woman, tugging aside the heavy curtains that make the room dark and shadowy. Anna stands in the doorway clutching her purse. A good purse. Egyptian crocodile skin.

It is so cold, this room. There is a massive fireplace on one wall with hideous tiles and an ornate carved mantel, so perhaps they will be able to have a fire. All the rooms they have seen so far have been cold. It seems that in this country they do not believe in heating. She has yet to see a single radiator.

The woman is tugging aside a cheap cotton curtain to reveal a cupboard with an enamel basin and an electric ring. She talks quickly and Anna can barely keep up. Something about being able to use the kitchen though many of our guests, says the woman, 'prefer to cook in the privacy of their own apartments.' She calls this room an 'apartment' when it is nothing like an apartment: just a single room with a bed, a small wooden table with two stools, two overstuffed armchairs pulled up having a stiff conversation either side of the fireplace, a great carved mausoleum of a wardrobe with an oval mirror. Anna can see herself in the glass: pale, with a very bad haircut. Her hair is curly and requires a skilled cutter and, so far, she has found no one who can cope with it. No one to match Toba in her white overall, her quick frowning concentration as she clipped, stood back, admired her handiwork, deft hands finding the natural fall of the hair and working with it so that the result framed her face. No. There has been no one since Toba. The mirrors in her salon shattered, the chairs overturned, the paint smeared like blood upon the door, the curious onlookers, standing by, indifferent...

Anna shakes all that away and tries to pay attention. The nervy woman is talking in the rapid gabble of this country. Her voice tips up constantly as if she is asking questions but there's no room for response.

'... a safe in the kitchen for milk and meat. Our guests supply their own crockery and utensils.' She bats a dead fly from the windowsill, makes some minute adjustment to a folding screen that attempts to divide bed from cupboard. It's covered in pictures cut from cheap magazines: pallid flowers, film stars with full red lips, cute dogs, fashion plates. Cheap. Ugly. Everything in this room is ugly. Anna grips her purse while Morris nods, giving every appearance of being impressed with this horrible room, its heavy plaster ceiling, its stained glass panels across the top of the windows that leave squares of red and yellow light over the cheap furniture, the bed with its slippery pink cover, its floral eiderdown that would never, she could tell from the doorway, be able to combat the cold. The terrible cold of this room, this house, this hallway stinking of mutton fat, the ghosts of cutlets, the wraiths of bacon.

Morris is taking a close interest in the way the key to the front door must be inserted just so, not too far, and turned clockwise twice. He is following the woman along the hallway that smells of ancient meat. Morris has glanced over at Anna, made that little gesture with his head that says, 'Come on. This is the best we can get. It's not too expensive. We'll be able to save a little and it's not forever.' So she follows the woman to view the bathroom (shared) with its lavatory (shared) and its fearsome bath poised on the claws of eagles (shared), to a dark and doleful kitchen (shared) with electric oven (shared) and cupboards with handprinted notes attached bearing the names of the individual owners of sad packets of cocoa and tins of sardines. The cupboards of lives lived like their own, in transit. It's not forever.

How she longs for 'forever'. She longs for her own apartment, her own home, and no dependence whatever on kindness. People have been so kind. The rabbi who met the boat in Auckland had been kind. The people who invited them to their homes had been kind. People who had already found forever and wished to share their good fortune with these newest arrivals, handing them from kind host to kind host, city to city, like parcels down the whole length of this strange empty country. Sheep sheep sheep from the train and damp green paddocks and forests separating funny little settlements where the buildings looked like tents, as if they could blow away in an instant. Houses built of wood, clinker-built like upturned boats, beached on a strange shore. Those wide empty streets where no one walks after nightfall.

She could not bear the kindness. Nor could Morris. It was one thing they shared completely, this detestation.

'Thank you, but no,' he had said, to another kind offer from kind hosts: a kind dentist whose parents had emigrated from Bavaria fifty years ago and his kind wife, all of them struggling to converse, for their German was rusty with disuse, while their hosts' Polish and Yiddish were non-existent. Which left a fractured English in which to offer a room in their own home: their daughter is married, a doctor in Auckland, a specialist in diseases of the lungs, so there is just so much room here in this big house, too big for only two, Morris and Anna could have a room, two rooms of their own, a sitting room and bedroom, they could stay just as long as . . . 'It is very kind of you,' said Morris, smiling. 'But no.'

'Another week of this and I shall go mad,' he whispered against Anna's neck as they clung together in another strange bed as if it were a boat, a liferaft, and they the only two survivors of wreck. 'Tomorrow we find somewhere to stay. Just us.'

Just us. Father. Mother. Brother. Sister. Cousin. Aunt and uncle. Toba with her deft little hairdresser's hands. Who knew where they might be at this very moment? Just us.

She examines the shared kitchen in the Villa Bella, Refined Accommodation for Permanent and Casual Guests. She accepts the piece of paper the woman presents for them to sign, once they have read it carefully, translated every word, understood exactly what the document contains. Documents must be scrutinised. People have simply disappeared after signing pieces of paper. They read carefully while the woman stands to one side, tapping one foot and keen to get back to whatever it was she was doing when they arrived at her door saying, 'Please? Excuse me. We read advertisement. Is possible?' She looked them over quickly, that up and down, but they have done their best this morning: Morris in best suit and tie, shoes polished; Anna in her good frock, the one she keeps for the most special occasions. Blue crêpe, silk stockings, black oxfords with a small heel, smart slouch hat with a pheasant's feather. She debated over wearing her coat, the musquash her aunt had pressed upon her as they stood on the landing, saying goodbye, but not forever. This was just a little holiday, after all. Two weeks in Venice. Gondolas. The Piazza San Marco. In July.

'Here,' said Aunt Rosa, after they had embraced, about to descend the stairs to the noise and bustle on Szeroka Street. 'You might need this.' And she had laid it about Anna's shoulders, gripped both her hands in her own, then turned away and closed the door firmly behind her before Anna could say no, no, it will be much too warm in Venice for fur! In London she had worn it, and on the journey across Canada, and now here, where it wrapped itself about her: silk lining like the softest skin carrying the faint scent of someone old and gentle and deeply known. Anna had worn it today though the sun was warm, and they had passed muster. The woman is nodding, smiling, handing them their keys, saying she hopes they will be comfortable, pocketing the first week's rent in advance. And they are able, at last, to enter their own room.

Their own ugly room with its heavy drapes and misshapen furniture. Its terrible emptiness. But Morris is shutting the door and putting his arms around her, saying, 'Never mind, bubala. Someday you'll live in a palace. Promise. At least it's our own, and it will do for now, won't it? It won't be forever.'

But she is saying, 'It's all right. It will be all right. Look.'

And she is fumbling about in the depths of the Egyptian crocodile purse and taking out the tiny scroll she has brought with her all the way from Szeroka Street. The words have been written with care on a scrap of parchment and furled within the wooden vial.

She is slipping off her shoes and standing in her stockinged feet on one of the ugly chairs so that she can reach. It should be on the door jamb itself, one third of the way exactly from the top, on the right-hand side as you enter the room, passing from the public world with its joys and terrors, to the private. It should be tucked into a crevice dug into the wood, but carving is out of the question here. And anyway, it's not forever.

Outside a bird is singing, a bird she's never heard before, the same rippling scale, up and down, over and over. Near the top of the door there's a narrow railing that goes all the way round the room, meeting the doorframe at more or less the correct height. The railing has a lip and a hollow behind where the mezuzah from Szeroka Street fits as snug as a baby in its cradle.

She jumps down from the stool and looks up to where she knows the words are. *Hear, O Israel. The Lord is our God.* The blessing. The cry for safety. She has carried them in the lining of her purse from home to new cities, across continents and oceans and who knew the world could be so wide? She has tucked them in, knowing that, for others, the words are falling on deaf ears. There is no safety on either side of the doorframe. But she does it anyway. And Morris takes her hand, though he has never shared her conviction, placing his faith rather in the last and greatest of the prophets, Karl Marx. But today, he takes her hand and they say the words together.

Baruch atah Adonai.

And they hope that, this time, the words will confer safety on this room, this ...

eighteen

THE PLUM TREE

SPRING 1940

... in the orchard when she becomes aware of him: a shadow, standing at the front gate, looking up at the house. He cannot see her because she is screened from view by a plum tree in full spring blossom. She had been intent on catching the dark diagonal of the ladder leaning against its trunk and the way light danced about it through the branches, white, pink, black, green, ochre, purple, running the spectrum on a single tree.

It's hot. She wears the solar topee her grandfather wore back when he was sorting out the Punjab, but sweat trickles down her forehead nonetheless. She stands to straighten her back, wipes her face with a handkerchief smelling strongly of turps. Performs her midday affirmation: feet apart, toes clenched, inhale. Left hand above head, look up. Exhale. I fill my body with Life, Love and Power. Inhale. Exhale. And as she straightens, there is one of those moments.

They fall upon her without warning. Moments of suspended stillness. There is a faint buzzing, a click in her head, and everything stops. She is small. She is nothing. She cannot move, cannot think or name anything, but she is aware, acutely aware, of everything around her. The sky arcs overhead, an unnamed expanse of intense colour.

Every sound resolves to a single chord, amplified. A warbler singing its scales, the rattle of a tram over on Stanmore Road, staccato of duck quack, rippling of river water, buzz of bumble bees, slip of worms in dark earth, it all rings in her ears. And with sound comes smell: river silt and dog shit and damp spring earth.

She stands transfixed before the plum tree.

It's a seedling tree, one she planted years ago and now fully grown. Its fruit, to be truthful, was bland, though borne in great quantity. It made good sauce and jars of jelly of a rich deep pink that always reminded her of the Queen of Sheba in the print in the hallway: that satin gown she wore to pay a visit to Solomon. The plum tree occupied a prime site, sheltered from the easterly and in full sunlight, and every year, her mother said they should cut it down and replace it with something more useful: a greengage perhaps, or a nice Victoria plum. But every year at this month, the plum tree played its trump card: a full head of blossom so delicate, so perfect, that its survival was guaranteed for another season.

Sybil stands before it, a tiny sentient thing, not thinking about her painting, nor planning lunch, though only a minute ago she had been ravenously hungry.

1 pint of potassium broth, 1 small salad of carrot, beetroot, parsley, dressed with olive oil from the chemist's and a squeeze of lemon juice. A single cubic inch of tasty cheese.

Her mother poked doubtfully at such food. 'Is this what we're having?' she said. 'Eat it. It's good for you,' said Sybil, who was attempting to live radiantly in accordance with the laws of nature. 'If I were a sheep . . .' said her mother and doused her plate in plum sauce. (Plum sauce was not alkaline. Nor was plum jam. They contained sugar and other substances that could have no role in impregnating the blood with vital energy.)

But now Sybil stands before the tree in its purest form. It is alive with bumble bees, writhing ecstatically in every blossom, and at this moment her skin is transparent. It has dissolved and her inner self is reaching out from beyond the confines of her body to rise weightless above the garden, above the streets of the city. She is weightless and yet she is firmly anchored in her big working boots, she is putting down roots into the soil, she is at one with the plum tree, putting down her long white roots, her fingers sprouting leaf, like the woman in the statue touched by the god.

That is when she sees him. A dark shadow, peering up at the house. What's he doing? He has something in his hands. A camera. He's taking a photograph of the house. He has a bag on his back. A prospective lodger perhaps? In which case he will be disappointed as their rooms are fully occupied. Less happily, perhaps, a thief? Conducting some kind of reconnaissance? He seems tall and solidly built. Nothing for it, thinks Sybil, shaking herself free of the moment, her ears still ringing slightly. She steps out from behind the tree.

'Hello,' she calls. 'Can I help you?'

'G'day, Syb,' says the man. And now she is able to look more closely she sees that he is in uniform: army khaki, army kitbag on his back. And then he smiles and she knows him.

'Leonard!' she says to this man who left the house years before, younger and wearing a bulkier, earlier version of this same uniform, driven out, the lucky one, along with his mother. Mrs McTurk had scurried down the front path swinging a bag at the mad woman who was running after them, screaming, 'Shoo! Shoo! Out of my house!'

But here he is after all this time: Leonard.

'We're all set to go,' he said. 'Got an afternoon's leave so thought I'd come over and see the old place. Didn't know if you'd be around.'

'We're still here,' says Sybil. 'Just Mother and me.'.

'Oh,' said Leonard. 'Might be best if I don't hang about.'

'Mother's at the pictures,' says Sybil. 'And I'm not fourteen. Haven't you noticed? Come on. I've made fruit cake. Do you still like fruit cake?"

'Too right,' says Leonard. So she opens the gate and he steps into the garden. Though he draws the line at entering the house. 'Don't think that'd be good idea, Syb,' he says. Instead he spreads his army coat on the overgrown grass while Sybil, her heart weirdly singing, runs up the path to the kitchen, fills the teapot, begins slicing cake, then gives up and puts the whole thing on a plate. She'll find a paper bag and wrap whatever is left over for him to take on the train. She sets the tray with two of the best cups and the teapot in its cosy that is a little wooden cottage with rows of scarlet hollyhocks and carries it out to the orchard carefully, carefully. One misstep and the whole afternoon could fracture, could break in pieces. Things could break so easily.

Leonard is standing by the easel.

'Did you do this?' he says as she sets down the tray. Carefully, carefully.

'Yes,' she says, concentrating on pouring. Ordinarily she would have whisked her work away, concealed it somewhere beyond scrutiny. Her paintings were not for people to look at, to stand back saying thoughtfully, 'Interesting.' They were stacked in the attic and belonged only to her. But Leonard is simply standing there quietly before her painting. He is seeing it. She remembers this quality he had, of being quiet. The way he stood aside while her family argued or fussed. He stands in front of her work and says, 'How do you do that, Syb? Make it look so beautiful? Like a real tree? Do you mind if I take a photo?' And he makes her stand by her painting with the plum tree in the background while he peers down into the viewfinder on a little Box Brownie, making sure he has it right before he presses the shutter.

And then they sit side by side on his coat with one of the dogs, eating a two-egg sultana cake while she tells him how she makes a tree look real and he tells her about working on the railway line up north and the freezing works, too, for a spell, in Hastings, and how he signed up. Had wanted to have a go at them ever since Spain. 'And what about you, Syb? What have you been up to?'

Sybil feels shy. 'Oh, you know . . .' she says. 'I paint. I do the garden. I look after Mother. She doesn't look after herself very well.'

'I thought you'd be married,' says Leonard. He's looking at her hands, wrinkled gardener's hands, paint-spattered. 'Thought you'd be out in the country. With six kids and dogs and horses and all that.'

'No,' says Sybil. 'Not me.'

'Thought some bloke would have snapped you up,' says Leonard.

A little breeze ripples through the orchard, releasing a shower of petals from the plum tree overhead. One catches in her hair. 'Snapped you up long ago,' says Leonard. And he reaches out his hand and takes the petal in his fingers.

Then there is another moment, her second in less than an hour.

Perfect stillness. Just his face, his brown eyes close to hers, his hand stroking her face as if she were the most beautiful creature in the world and not a dumpy little woman in rough woollen trousers and a gardening shirt.

And he's saying, 'I wanted to come and see you before I left. I wanted to see if you would . . .

nineteen

THE PHOTOGRAPH

SPRING 1942

... with watch and dogtags. A woman standing in an orchard, the corner of a house in the background, a black Labrador by her side, both of them looking straight at the camera.

The nurse slips it into the envelope on the locker, hangs a new bag and taps the line. Morphine drips into the vein. The other hand has gone entirely, a bandaged stump. The leg too, blasted to shreds of flesh and bone by a landmine the sweepers had missed in the dark. The nurse, fresh from training in Johannesburg, checks the cannula, though this one doesn't look recoverable. It goes against everything she has been taught. A harsh lesson. In military triage with limited resources, nurse, it's not the most seriously wounded that require your first attention, but those who might be got going again. You must concentrate on those who might be returned to active service.

So this one is palliative. Breath passes through his jaw, hesitant, with rattling pauses. One who survived Servia Pass and Maleme, Mersa Matruh, Sidi Rezegh. When the orderlies brought him in they had had a job holding him on the bed. A big man, still strong and perpetually trying to get out, get away, toppling from the stump of his leg until they upped his medication and he settled at last to his long deep sleep.

He is walking forward into the dark. Wilson is on his right, Quinn on his left. Lucky bastard. Kept beating them at poker. Eight quid down on yesterday's game when he'd produced a royal flush, ace, king, queen, jack, ten of diamonds. All of them seated round an upturned jerrycan, smoking, waiting, while the whole bloody show threatened to close down around them. That's what Wilson had told him. He had a mate in communications. He said the Germans and the Ities had them rounded up. They were just waiting for reinforcements and it'd all be over.

Wilson had a good pair of binoculars. They'd climbed up one of those little flat-topped hills you got around here that looked like some cowboy picture, Hi-yo Silver! rearing up on the skyline. They scrambled up on loose stones, keeping their heads well down. 'Here,' said Wilson. 'Have a shufti.' He handed Leonard the binoculars. He was keen on birds, Wilson. Even here in the desert he kept an eye out, noted them down in a little black book he kept in his shirt pocket. It was surprising what he noticed: the white spread of a vulture circling overhead, though come to ground they were transformed to those ugly waddling scavengers called Pharaoh's chickens that Wilson said ate anything, including shit. 'Cleaning up after us,' he said.

The hillock was just high enough to give an angle out across the desert. The late afternoon air shimmered, and away on the horizon was the glint of metal, a narrow black wash over the dusty earth like an incoming tide, a wave drawing in over the gleam of mudflats. Tanks, guns, trucks.

'Doesn't look too flash,' said Wilson. His mate said the official word was they were finished: the whole New Zealand Division. Freyberg was out of it already, hit by shrapnel. Gott had telegraphed high command that New Zealand had fallen out of the bedstead. Done for.

Well, bugger that.

Leonard waits in the dark. They were going to make a run for it, the New Zealanders. Like bullrush back at school, all of them lined up across the playground, charging through the mass in the middle who were intent on bringing you down hard onto the tarmac. They knew how to play this game. Here he is, with the others in the 19th at the front, the 28th and the 20th on either flank, transport and ambulances in night formation at the back behind the field guns. Bayonets at the high port.

He can feel the cool metal in his hand and the click as the bayonets are fitted home. He can hear Quinn muttering some of that Mick stuff he always mutters while he's waiting. Wilson is whistling tunelessly.

And Leonard? He fixes and refixes his bayonet. He touches the photo in his pocket. Fixes his bayonet. Touches the photo. Fixes his bayonet ...

They've laid down a line of shaded lights across the front of the column and that's all that's holding them: 400 yards of dim light. He's not that keen on the lights, not when you're up here at the front. And there is a moon tonight, which doesn't help: one of those big yellow moons that you get out here in the desert, bigger than any moon he's seen back home. It casts its steady glow over them all, lined up and visible surely from the crests of Bir Abu Batta and its flat-topped twin, Mahat Abu Matta. They loom ahead on either side, two lowering beasts that must surely, at any second, burst into action. The single shot, the alarm, the batteries trained down on them, hanging about, waiting for a signal that never seems to come.

Behind him, someone's snoring. Some blokes can sleep anywhere, anytime. He can hear the rhythmic inbreath, the whiffle of the outbreath. An odd calm hangs over them.

Ahead lies the col between the twin hills, dozing in moonlight. The word is they're waiting for some blokes who had gone off souveniring before the order was announced. There are some who like to do that, scavenging for guns, knives, whatever can be slipped into a rucksack. He himself has a knife. Someone has cut it down from a bayonet and it's a neat piece of work. A slender blade that will cut through any number of layers of clothing, straight to the bone. Someone knew what they were doing when they made that knife.

He didn't take it from a body. He draws the line at that. It was simply lying among some stones and he had picked it up. That was clean. Taking stuff from the dead as some did, tipping over a body swollen and fly-ridden: he couldn't do that. Leave them for Pharaoh's chickens, sailing up on their wide black-tipped wings on the thermals, rising in lazy circles before dropping to ground, graceful as circus acrobats, to hunch and tear. He'd come upon a flock after Mersa Matruh, gathered round some bloody gore, fired into them and they rose, beaks trailing some poor bugger's guts, up into the blue blue sky. But at least that was natural.

The moon sailed overhead. If they didn't get a move on soon, it'd be dawn and there they'd be, dogs' balls, out in the open without a show. But there is some muted movement behind him, men getting to their feet, a sudden intensity he knows from all the other times when the order is about to be given. They know it's coming before it has been issued, like dogs knowing when they're going to be let out and are at the door waiting. He's up on his feet, too, hands wrapped about the smooth reassurance of his rifle with its own scratches and tiny fissures he'd know anywhere after all this time together. Then, without any audible order, they are stepping over the shaded lights and beginning to move.

Out into the col, the slit trenches that had given them some temporary security falling away to the rear. The mine detectors sway over the land ahead, looking for a safe way through. He walks in their wake, steadily. Quinn has shat himself. Lots did, guts run to water, like weka when they're cornered nicking your gear in your hut back home and they're panicking, running around, trying to find a way out. Shit everywhere . . .

Fifty yards. The rattle of boots on stone. One hundred yards. He feels cool, the way he always does at such moments. Cold as water. Once he's on his way, he's clear. It's the waiting he can't stand.

One hundred and fifty yards and up ahead there's a shout. Someone has spotted them at last. There's a rattle of automatic fire, the pink and green flash of tracers, and Leonard can feel the whole column round him for a split second, hesitate. But there's a yell from the back where the Maoris are roaring into a haka and it grows in strength until they are all running, boots slipping on stones and they're amongst it. Smoke and fire and detonation and the howling of hundreds of men, bayonets sliding through meat, and there's a man running towards him, and in strange suspended state he is able to see that he is wearing pyjamas. He has bare feet. He is wearing pyjamas, tousled from sleep and his eyes are wide as the howl sweeps them up and there is nothing but steel on bone and he has taken leave of himself in a scarlet haze where men rise before him then fall away and he's running until somehow, he's through and the howl and roar is falling away and then there's a flash, a blinding blast that lifts him silently from his feet into the air and he is rising on the thermal like some bird with his wings spread. He is circling up and up into the sun and the sound of men has become the sound of sheep bleating, a great flock spread over distant hills and he is circling down slowly, coming to ground on a city street. There are houses, a hedge and a gate and he's standing outside, uncertain. There's a path on the other side that leads to the house and a woman walking towards him, a black dog at her side, lolloping along the way Labradors do, tail wagging. The woman appears to have shed her clothes and when he looks down he sees with some surprise that he too is naked, bar a pair of shiny black shoes. But it seems completely ordinary to be so. He can feel the soft cool lick of the wind on his skin, and the woman is looking at him. She is saying, 'Leonard? Leonard? Is that you?'

And indeed it . . .

twenty
THE RIVER
SPRING 1944

Nothing happens.

Leaves fall. The sun makes a warm pool where she is suspended, body rippling.

Meat is dangled before her, strung on a length of twine. She hangs in the water, watching while others take the bait.

She watches as they are lifted up, squirming.

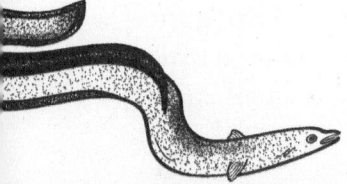

twenty-one
THE BOUNDARY FENCE
SPRING 1946

... in the slightly foetid warmth of the Regent stalls with some cigarettes and a bag of licorice allsorts. Violet has never quite got over a feeling of mild wickedness at going to a matinee on a sunny afternoon. She should be in the garden or cleaning the windows instead of being ensconced here beneath an Arabian sky, sprinkled with stars.

She shrugs down into crimson velour. Not too many this afternoon, drawn to the enticement of The Most Dazzling Colour Spectacle Ever Filmed! Esther Williams in *Bathing Beauty*! The girls, Girls, GIRLS! of the Aqua Ballet.

She should definitely be cleaning the rangette in Number 2 in readiness for the new tenant, but The Most Dazzling Colour Spectacle Ever? Fifty girls, in pink bathing suits, executing perfectly synchronised overarm in a bright blue pool?

The other solitaries are seated as far apart as they can manage. No one behind rattling their lolly packet or whispering during the picture. No one nudging her elbow from the next seat. No one with an enormous head seated right in front of her obscuring the screen. Bliss. So few here, in fact, that she doesn't bother getting up for the king and the national anthem, making a small stand against hundreds of years of Irish oppression. She stays firmly seated in number 42, dead centre, row L, midway down and lights up as the wee worried man waves from the balcony before giving way to *Looney Tunes*, the ball dancing maniacally along the words so she can join in, should she wish to sit there singing 'Mareseatoatsanddoeseatoats' in the middle of the Regent, all by herself.

The smoke from her cigarette wafts up into the beam, dreamy, secretive. It's one of the reasons she likes coming to the pictures. Sybil doesn't like her smoking, obsessed as she is with her lentils and pure living. But where's the harm, thinks Violet, watching a duck in a sports car driving over a cliff. And then *Metro News* and the courtroom.

All year the courtroom, the grey huts and piled bodies and the rows of men listening intently through headphones. The grey functionaries, Keitel, Jodl, Kaltenbrunner, names she has heard of only over the past few months. Functionaries, coolly doing their job. And the familiar faces: Von Ribbentrop, the big bullhead of Goering, denying, explaining, lying, forgetting, not knowing, only partially informed. *That is correct. That is not correct.* All their testaments have been delivered and the justices have withdrawn to discuss their verdicts . . .

And then there's New Zealand.

You don't often see New Zealand on the screen and when you do, it looks strange. Stranger than Piccadilly Circus or Broadway between the skyscrapers. They look real, unlike this strange place, a New Zealand city. She leans forward trying to identify it. Cramped wooden houses, smoke hanging heavy over corrugated-iron roofs. Probably Wellington, for there are hills and a view of a harbour. A young couple is walking the grey streets, looking for a home, and the upper-class English newsreel voice is announcing a battle. Not the one just won, with that vast cloud rising above devastation nor the long succession of shattered cities, homes reduced to mountains of rubble. But a battle to be conducted now, in the peace that follows devastation.

The young couple are looking for a home. They are clear-faced and respectable. He could have been a soldier until very recently. He has that upright bearing, Italy, Egypt not far behind, the memory of forming columns, eyes front still imprinted in the bone. He wears a suit, his hair is trimmed. She wears a coat that cannot conceal the fact that she is pregnant. Their first child is on the way, says the voice, and like many New Zealanders, they are suffering from 'house-hunger'. They are desperate for a house in a country where many are forced to live in crowded unsanitary flats. They walk from door to door down the dingy street and are turned away. The houses are already taken.

The houses: she knows them, the thin walls, inadequately shutting out the sounds of neighbours fighting, laughing, making love. She knows the buckled paper running with damp, and her brother fighting for breath, doubled over and wheezing as the asthma comes on with the advent of winter, smoke and fog mingled over the city. His chest swelling with the effort to breathe, their mother lighting the sulphur lamp in a futile attempt to clear the air in that street within range of the city's destructor with its filthy smoke, its stink of burning. She remembers that house. She will never forget it.

Up on the screen the young couple are seated in an architect's office. They have given up on finding a place to rent. They will try to build their own place, but the architect is telling them this will cost £1600 plus £200 for a deposit for a mortgage and the young couple cannot afford that. Their faces are furrowed with anxiety. Driven to desperation, they take a single room in a slum area, one crowded room which is 'no place for a baby,' says the woman. 'But you'll take anything when you're house hungry.'

And then the camera pans back. There is another city vista, this time a street of sturdy houses, properly designed by the state for the working man and his family, with separate bedrooms, a small but efficient kitchen set to catch the sun, and a section large enough to grow vegetables in the sweet suburban air. The woman mows the lawn while her child, now a toddler, plays. And the young man arrives home from work and swings the toddler on his shoulders and off they go, the little family, down a street lined with solid homes like their own, filled with happy, healthy citizens. Their house hunger has been satisfied.

The lights come up on the trellised balconies and minarets and Violet lights another cigarette while she awaits the main feature. She knows what she will do. She will divide the land around the house.

She and Sybil don't need so much. She will sell off part of the garden, clear debt, fix up the apartments, and the rest — the orchard, the strip of land she still calls the pony paddock, though it's a lifetime since Rajah grazed there, and the Dobsons' cows — she will gift to the state. She will move the boundary fence and there will be room for three, maybe four, of those houses. It is dry on the sandy ridge, sunny on the slope above the river.

She feels such lightness at the thought. She offers it up.

To the young man on the screen who had fought, to the young woman with the baby, to all those young men and women piled behind the wire who might have had such a home, a baby, a sunny lawn . . .

twenty-two
THE WINDOW
SPRING 1948

... site, carved from the garden but overhung by one beautiful walnut tree. Who would not wish to have such a tree leaning across the fence into their garden? Its big naked branches studded with fistfuls of crimson leaf preparing to open like generous hands. Each branch studded with the tiny green knobs that will swell and harden to be cracked at the proper season from the shell: nuts for cakes, for pickles, for the little Hamantaschen Anna persists in making each year with prunes and apple, though here she makes them in autumn. Leaf fall. Nut fall. Not spring. They make no other observation. Just this sweet lingering aftertaste of festival.

The walnut tree is still bare, its branches a gaunt sculpture framed by the horizontal lines of the kitchen window. In a few weeks it will be covered with leaf and the villa behind will be completely concealed. He has set the house square on the subdivided site, kitchen, dining and living areas one continuous flow, one big room fronted by a wall of glass reaching from floor to ceiling apex, with a view over street and houses to the river. Sunlight pours in, the clear light of this country so pure, so seemingly devoid of guile, though you can never quite forget those tiny cramped notes that had arrived for a time during the war on paper scented with violets. Nazi. They called him a Nazi. A spy. So stupid, some people. The pen had dug so furiously into the paper that it had caused the ink to splatter. He had taken each one between the tips of his fingers as if they carried contagion, torn them in pieces and buried them in the garden.

Now he stands in a new room, open for all to see. It is as if he has stepped on stage, made his entry at last. The guileless light pours onto pale timber, simple stuff, plywood. The walls are off-white, the doors palest grey. Dining table and chairs shorn of all pretension, curtains a simple print of seahorses and kelp, hand stencilled. Having been raised in a city 400 miles from the sea, Anna now seems obsessed with fish, stamping fish and crayfish, seahorses and trailing fronds of seaweed on curtains and cushions. Otherwise the room is bare. Just that pure light.

'Like a goldfish bowl,' says Bob, who is first to arrive, waving to the windows, the high ceiling. 'You realise that's what they're going to say. "It's like a goldfish bowl."' It is not, it seems, exactly a compliment. It means that everything inside will be visible. There can be no privacy.

But that, says Morris, is exactly how he had planned it. A house of glass and air, leaf and water.

Anna places some willow branches by the window in a pot someone has brought as a gift. Claire perhaps. It looks like her work. Rough textured, a beautiful raw thing, the mark of fingers clearly visible on the clay, the thumb print of muddy humanity, not the smooth veneer of some dull machine. The willow leaves are green spikes set to unfold in the warmth of the room. People are coming in. They climb the stairs of uncarpeted timber, drop coats and hats on the plain bed covered in grey linen stencilled with sea urchins. The people look about at the stairs, the plain bed. They enter the goldfish bowl, the big luminous room where rain spatters the windows. They stand about holding glasses: real champagne, rather than some sugary New Zealand approximation of gewürztraminer. Krug. 1938. A single bottle, obtained from the importer on Colombo Street with effort and at great expense. The wine glows in the glass, shoals of bubbles rising.

A wine worthy of this celebration. Not so long ago they had been in flight and they had come to land on this empty street. It was so very quiet. At night, nothing moved. They had felt deeply lost. But here they were at last, about to live their lives on this bright stage. No need to hide, to crouch in a corner, behind a cupboard, under the floorboards, buried beneath straw or under leaves. He has heard the stories: the cousin who had somehow survived Theresienstadt, who had sung alto in the requiem staged to impress the inspectors from the Red Cross. She had clung to the alto line through rehearsals in the underground room where they sang while overhead there was the shuffling as the chosen were herded toward the trains. He dreamed of it: the miserere swelling in anguish to the accompaniment of those hundreds, thousands of doomed feet. And he rose from the dream gasping, Anna's hand on his back saying shh shhh. But here they are, standing in this house, the one he has made from glass and air, a place where one can breathe.

Anna has made a cake. Walnut torte. They sit in the big clear room on chairs of leather and tubular steel, plain chairs, not some chesterfield suite drawn up like heavy beasts on a field of floral Axminster. These are chairs stripped to their essence. Nothing more than objects on which one can sit.

Bob leans back to survey the ceiling soaring up to double height above their heads. His hand cradles one of Claire's coffee cups. The cups are small and apple green, perfect for the drinking of coffee.

'Not bad,' he says, regarding the ceiling, the white walls, the high window. 'Not bad at all,' which Morris has learned constitutes high praise. 'I like its modesty, the absence of decoration. It's like a shed. A New Zealand shed.'

But Morris says, agitated, 'No, no, no. None of this regionalism! There is no place for this in architecture, in music, in art! This is a shelter, and our ideas of shelter, they know no borders. They move freely about the world, these ideas. Without limit, without restriction. This is a cube for living. That is all.'

'Exactly,' says Bob. 'Anonymous. Like a European terrace.'

'It has nothing to do with being European,' says Morris. He can feel himself become agitated, the little green cup shaking in his hand. 'Not European. Not New Zealand. Not a shed, not a terrace. It is four walls, of weatherboard stained black with creosote. Plain, simple, a box. White to outline doors and windows, the way a child might draw a house. I wanted to make a box for living, a beautiful box.

That is all. Plain wooden walls, plain wooden floors. I would have liked flagstones, but Anna said no. No stones.'

'I like to lie on the floor,' says Anna. 'It is good for my back. You cannot lie on stones.'

So: no stones. Wooden boards. A plain mat. A plain box that holds just the essentials for existence.

Like a suitcase really.

You need so very little. You can live with no more than can be contained in a single suitcase. And who knows when you might have to pack again, hurry with your suitcase to the railway station, carrying just a photograph or two, a change of clothing, some precious thing, a ring perhaps, that might be exchanged at some critical point for necessity. But here, in this room, the selection has been made already. On one wall, a painting, splashes of vivid red and green that if you look closely enough, resolve to hills and clouds. Everything broken in pieces and reassembled as in a dream, recognisable yet strange.

The bones of his house are laid bare. No ceiling conceals ducts and pipes and wiring. No weight of hidden things hang above their heads. Everything is light, everything exposed. He wants to explain this to his friend, his good, well-meaning colleague, but though he has a reasonable command now of this awkward English, some things defeat him. He cannot always find words to express what he is feeling.

But maybe there are no words, not in English, nor in Polish, nor in German, nor in any other tongue. Perhaps there are no words to describe the way he feels looking from this room through the simple rectangle of glass above the kitchen bench at the pitched roof of the old house to the rear, with its ornamental turret, its fussy frill of lace about the verandah. Looking through the high front window at Savage Street, newly formed to link Barchester Street with the road alongside the river. Berms and asphalt have been laid and houses line both sides: older villas and newer bungalows and a new row of sturdy cubes built by the state, all these places where people are going about their lives on the very edge of a chasm that could open at any moment. For anything can happen to anyone, anywhere, at any time. How can he express the poignancy of this insouciance: the way little humans constantly pitch their tents upon the lip of disaster. The way they live as if the act of building conferred security.

It is beyond architecture, or fashion, or regionalism or style, this business of making shelters.

We each inhabit an empty box. A suitcase abandoned on a road...

He gets up. He opens the plywood door that conceals the radiogram. The record is already on the turntable: Miles Davis letting loose. Charlie Parker chasin' the bird. He places the needle delicately within the groove. The party lifts into the light...

twenty-three
THE RIVER
SPRING 1950

Nothing happens.

Leaves fall.

The moon passes overhead, trailing a gleaming path on water.

The river is a thing of light and shadow.

She glistens by the bank where the darkness is deepest.

twenty-four
THE FLOORBOARDS
SPRING 1952

... regretting as he does so the absence of a moustache. Close clipped. Precise upon the upper lip, giving greater definition to the lower face, which he fears may be a little weak about the chin. But a moustache, he has decided long since, would be inadvisable. Too memorable, when his overreaching ambition is to be anonymous. He needs to be the face you cannot make out in the crowd, the man who slips unnoticed from the room. A man like the Saint, taking cool note of his surroundings while standing a little aside, the unseen watcher in the wings.

He smooths his hair with just a dab of Brylcreem, flattening it across the temples and regretting the thinning visible upon the crown. Baldness could be also be disadvantageous in this game, a distinguishing mark as memorable as a moustache. He adjusts his tie. An unremarkable tie without chevron, crest or stripe. Serviceable woollen trousers, bland shirt, bland V-neck. He checks the shirt pocket for notebook and pencil stub, the tools of his trade.

He puts on his cap. A flat woollen cap, a worker's cap, wishing just a little, as he always does, for a fedora: a fedora, like Bogart's, worn at a casual angle, the sharp suit, the bow tie. But that would definitely be remarkable. He might get away with that in LA, but here, he'd tend to stand out. Besides, he is too short for a fedora. He had tried one once and had the uneasy suspicion from the smirk on the shopgirl's face, that it made him look ridiculous, like a small standard lamp with a very large shade. He sets the cap straight, shrugs on a raincoat. It's wet outside. He checked just a minute ago as he ate baked beans heated on the electric ring in his room, straight from the saucepan. Rain seeps through the shrubs that cloak his window.

He likes the rain. The slow secretive trickle of it. The way it makes the streets of the city slick, the way people walk along the streets not noticing those they pass, heads down. Rain distracts people. It makes them careless. He pulls the belt on his coat tight. Tugs the curtains across the window, debates whether to leave the lamp on but decides against it in the interests of economy.

He has never failed them, always filed his reports accurately and regularly, often supplied more detail than was strictly necessary. He has gone that extra mile. But they are sometimes careless with payment. The money — always money, never a traceable cheque, always a crisp little fan of new notes — is often slow to arrive. He is careful as a consequence. Keeps a little in reserve in the tobacco tin, ensures that he is always able to pay his rent on time, leaves no trace of debt and unpaid bills. But sometimes it's a struggle. He deserves so much better. He should be treated with respect by his superiors, as the professional he is. It irks him.

This is one of those uncertain weeks when he must be thrifty. He switches off the light, though he leaves the wireless on, quietly enough not to annoy his neighbours but loudly enough to suggest his continued presence within, enjoying a quiet night by the heater. He takes one last quick look about the room as is his habit, then slips out, with just the faintest clicking of the latch. There are lights on in the other rooms along the hallway, the rattle of cutlery and plates. Miss Clitheroe in Room 3 is singing along to some of her usual nonsense *ay round the corner ooh-hooo* while rinsing out her nylons which she will peg, with her usual lack of consideration, over the bath. And from the front flat a radio audience brays inanely. The smell of other people's dinners lingers, a sticky blend of chop fat and fried onions. He slips past it all and out the big front door and no one will be able to say later, 'He left about . . . oh . . . half past six? Quarter to seven?'

He walks away from the house quickly, keeping to the side of the footpath where the shadows are deepest. Passing other houses with their carelessly uncurtained windows, their sashes unlatched, their doors left unlocked. He catches glimpses of others living their lives, casually seated round a dining table, standing by a mantelpiece talking to some unseen other, as if no one were watching, no one taking note. Confident in their untroubled security. Comfortable with the illusion of peace.

But he is passing by and he is taking note. And he is neither confident nor comfortable.

The rain has eased but the road gleams and there are halos round each street lamp. He likes to walk before working, taking his time to marshal his thoughts before he enters the room where they will all be assembled. The subject of his scrutiny. The members of the deceptively mild-mannered William Morris Society, gathered tonight for their spring concert.

He knows how it will go. He has been taking note for some time now. There will be branches of plum blossom arranged in tubs on either side of the stage. Ted Miller will sing, accompanying himself on the guitar, perhaps in duet with that sharp little woman who always looks at Eric warily as if she knows exactly what he is up to, but will give him the benefit of her considerable doubt. He gives her a wide berth. It's quite possible she has penetrated his disguise. In this country it is so difficult to avoid the person who knew you before, went to school with your brother in Onehunga, worked with you before the war over on the coast. He longs for a wider world where a man like himself might slip like Simon Templar into the anonymity of a crowded street, some tree-lined boulevard or Algerian souk or Shanghai slum. Lithe as a cat, his eyes two glinting chips of steel that miss nothing . . .

But this is where he lives, on these narrow constricting islands, where no matter how carefully he has constructed his camouflage, at any minute there could come that matey slap on the shoulder, that snap of recognition. Tonight he must walk again into the hall, hailed as 'comrade' by men he must pretend to like, some of them men with whom he works on the wharves in Lyttelton. Another place where he takes note. He will stop and have a yarn, crack a joke or two with the ladies busily setting out the teacups in the kitchen behind the closed slide. He'll buy a sixpenny raffle to help defray the expense of hiring the hall, take his seat before the stage with its dowdy red curtains. The curtains will jerk apart and there will be, inevitably, the folk songs, the people's songs, the songs collected by the Workers' Music Association, doleful ballads featuring coal miners and rural labourers or surprisingly chirrupy little numbers concerning cotton pickin' or ridin' freight cars and Good night Irene and So long it's been good to know ya and everybody join in!

There will be the cello solo and the humorous recitation: our Albert with the stick with the 'orse's 'ead 'andle, who got et by a lion, delivered in broad dialect by Harry from Newcastle, who seemed amiable enough when encountered on such an evening, but is just another of those Geordies who make it their business to cross the globe stirring up trouble among men previously interested only in doing a decent day's work for reasonable pay. The Harrys of this world are set on revolution, spreading agitation with their Communistic notions of class struggle and the oppression of the workers, opening the doors to chaos, encouraging men to walk out, to strike, and it is a strike, no matter how much Harry and the comrades insist it is the bosses and the government who have locked them out. Just as they called blowing up that railway bridge at Huntly an 'action' when it was terrorism, as Holland said. 'Infamous terrorism', no question.

Eric sees himself as a soldier in a war, a just war against this contagion of subversion and foreign ideas. He is a soldier, every bit as much as the men who have volunteered to go up to Korea to help stop the Commies there. Every battle must begin somewhere and here it is beginning with Eric himself, striding along Kilmore Street in his raincoat, fiery sword in hand, intent on driving out the forces of evil at the William Morris Society's spring concert. An evening of caterwauling followed by weak tea and gingernuts.

He will listen, without being unobtrusive. And when he returns home he will write up his observations in the quiet of his room, ready for posting in the morning. He will note every detail:

Mrs Adamson of Bangor Street is about 49 years of age, 5'2" in height, brown hair greying, sharp features and wears spectacles. Secretary of Housewives Union.

Mrs Wisniewski is about 35 years of age, thin, dark complexion, brown eyes, divorced with one son. Friendly with Mr Jones who was overheard inviting her to a party at their home during Christmas...

But first there will be the walk home, along the dark streets. And perhaps a quiet pause by the window of Miss Clitheroe, who is a silly girl, given to sleeping leaving the curtains wide open and the sash raised an inch or two for fresh air. He will peer in from the darkness, noting the body at its ease upon the bed, the eiderdown tossed aside, one bare leg exposed. He will stand unobserved, imagining the night when he lifts the sash quietly quietly and slides over the sill, the way she will stir as he bends over her, her blue eyes opening, not focused, then suddenly wide with fear as his hand clamps over the full red lips as he slides into her, holding her down, the silken cord he has concealed in his raincoat pocket unfurling at last and stretched about her neck, the thrash and fight of her but he has the power now, and she has none, she'll not ignore him again in the hallway, she'll know at last who he is, this unremarkable man, as the air leaves her lungs and her body goes limp beneath him and he comes in a great juddering...

But first the caterwauling. First the biscuits. Then the report, written up tonight while the details are fresh in the memory. Two copies, one for posting in the morning, the other for filing in his secret place, the small cavity he has cut in the floorboards in one corner of his room. It is covered ordinarily by the Feltex square and he has also placed his easy chair above it. It pleases him to sit there in the evening, knowing his secrets lie beneath him: his notebook, his reports, the silk cord. A single wrinkled stocking...

twenty-five

THE GLADIOLI

SPRING 1954

...takes down the photo. The one where she is seated with her family on a rug on the lawn, as if they are having a picnic, except Prince Philip is wearing a suit which seems a little formal for a picnic. Prince Charles is sitting beside them but they are both looking at Anne, who is crawling off the rug towards a border of flowers. The flowers are tall and pale: lilies perhaps, or gladioli.

The queen was fond of gladioli. They had been one of the flowers chosen to decorate the city in preparation for her visit over the summer. The entire floor of the army barracks in the centre of the city had been covered in gladioli and gypsophila, marguerites and roses as Christchurch strove to Say It With Flowers. To say Welcome to the Garden City, to the city that is more English than England, the city that, if you did not know was actually midway down an island in a Polynesian archipelago, might be confused with Salisbury or Cheltenham!

The call had gone out for flowers of patriotic red, white and blue, or in her Her Majesty's favourite colours, which were pink and pale aqua.

Sybil had picked armfuls of lilies and daisies and roses from the garden and every single gladiolus, gathering them in the earliest morning when they were fresh and packing them carefully into an applebox on the carrier of her bike. Gladioli are her favourite flower: tall stems of orange and pink and crimson, frilled and generous. Each year she divides the corms, peeling away the papery husk and poking them back into the soil, and each year they re-emerge in spring: green tips that in summer explode into flower. She cycled across the city to the barracks where a brisk, distracted woman said, 'Oh, how lovely. Just pop them over there,' waving a pair of secateurs towards a mountain of flowers growing by the minute against the wall with its gilded honour roll. 'I don't suppose you've got a moment,' she added, clipping the stems from marguerites, 'but Lois could do with a hand with the arch.' She was bossy, but someone had to be bossy. It mattered that it was done correctly. The floral arch would be the first thing their majesties would see as they alighted from the royal train and stepped forth from the railway station, which had been scrubbed up for the occasion, onto the streets of the city.

Sybil had watched her arrive, one in a throng of fluttering paper Union Jacks, a citizen among thousands, notable and otherwise, Girl Guides and Boy Scouts and school children lined up in white panama hats, gold commemorative medals pinned to their uniforms, the whole rising at her emergence to one communal roar of approbation, not a hurrah exactly but a vast exhalation of joy.

All over the city, gardens had said it with flowers. They were decked out with blue lobelia and red begonia and white alyssum.

'Lot of nonsense,' said her mother, who had no intention of putting on hat and gloves and joining the joyful throng. 'I don't know why you bother, Sybil.' She was angry because there had been letters to the paper protesting about the state of the old houses in Sydenham, her grandmother's girlhood home among them. They were too dingy to give a good impression of the city as the queen drove past on her way to view the manufacture of sports shirts and underwear at the Lane Walker Rudkin factory.

Personally, Sybil could think of nothing worse than a morning spent viewing machinery. The queen seemed to have spent a lot of time on her visit looking at car engines and assembly lines between brief spells at the races and the occasional garden party.

'The thing is she always manages to look interested, doesn't she?' she said. 'It's one of her great skills.'

Her mother had been unimpressed. There was her cousin, daft old Eugene Mulcahy, who had a house near the factory and had stayed up, according to an article in *The Press*, until 1 a.m. doing his best to cheer the place up with crepe paper and sixty-four balloons he could probably ill afford. But at least they had not demolished the houses the way they did up in Auckland where they set fire to Maori houses deemed unsightly along the royal route. There was a photo in the *Weekly News*: shadowy figures standing by watching as their homes went up in flames. At least they had avoided flame in the Garden City.

Sybil stood waving her paper flag, then followed the crowd up Colombo Street where the shops were hung with flowerboxes trailing carnations and gypsophila. In the Square the tram shelters had been cloaked in golden marigolds. She stood among the throng, chanting, 'We want the queen. We want the queen,' until she stepped forth onto the balcony of the Clarendon Hotel, waving that special thumb-in-palm wave that only royal personages can wave.

'Mrs Bloody Windsor,' said her mother, wheezing as she pushed her custard aside. 'And that chinless bloody wonder she married. You're a fool like your father, Sybil.' Her hands were thin and white, webbed with blue veins.

'Are you not going to eat that?' said Sybil.

'It's got lumps,' said her mother. 'I can't swallow lumps, you know that.'

'No, it doesn't,' said Sybil. 'I sieved it. There are no lumps.'

'Just a cup of tea,' said her mother.

'You've eaten nothing all day,' said Sybil. 'You can't live on tea.'

'Yes, I can,' said her mother and she turned up the wireless.

'I don't know how you stand it,' Margaret had said at Easter when she visited, smart in woollen coat and fine kid gloves. Her first visit in twenty years and she couldn't even bear to remove her coat, so eager to leave. 'Why don't you put her in a home?'

'I heard that,' wheezed Violet from the sunporch on the back verandah where she was wiping the worst of the grime from the windows with crumpled newspaper.

'We get along all right,' said Sybil. 'We manage.'

The place stank of cats and oil paints and old food and one of the dogs, a degenerate terrier, was clearly on heat. Margaret shuddered.

She couldn't wait to get back on the ferry, head back to Whangarei and the warm sweet order of brick and roughcast, built to a pattern selected from the Parade of Homes, the logical next step when Jock retired and their sons took over the running of the farm. She stood in this hideous kitchen where nothing much seemed to have changed in twenty years, other than mess and clutter and strangers occupying rooms that had once been their own. She longed desperately for her Formica bench, for the view of the sea, for the ladies gathered in her lounge for bridge and dainty club sandwiches.

Sybil was unbothered by mess. She and her mother got along. They managed.

In the summer when the queen visited New Zealand, newly crowned, Violet resolutely looked the other way while Sybil clipped photos from the *Weekly News* and pinned them to her bedroom wall. The photo of the queen and her sister as princesses with curled hair, seated at the microphone preparing to give hope to the victims of the Luftwaffe in the East End. The queen in her wedding gown, the queen carrying orb and sceptre, her head holding up that heavy crown. The queen waving from the royal train. The queen standing sombrely to commemorate the people who had been on that other train, the one that tumbled down into the churning river. The passengers had been seated in their carriages, their Christmas shopping stowed in the rack, and then the lurch, and fall, the mud and water, the choking and darkness. The queen had been present in the country to give her blessing to their terrible end. And then she had been driven to Waitomo where she had been taken in a little boat on the underground river to look up at the lights sprinkling the roof of the immense cavern. A great galaxy of stars, though each star was really a worm. A worm trailing a kind of mucus, lit up so that another worm with its mucus could find its way toward it in the dark.

Sybil pinned up the photo of the queen and her sister seated on a wall with corgis and the old queen and the old king, the shy one who had had to take over when his brother was a cad. She liked looking at them through the winter, pinned to the blue floral wallpaper in her room. She liked the calm reassurance of their distant lives.

By spring, however, they had become yellowed and wrinkled and today she is taking them down. There are other photos in the news now, but she does not think she will pin them in the queen's place. These are photos of the two girls, sixteen-year-olds in school uniforms. The pretty aloof one and the dark intense one, both of them condemned, unsmiling. Their hands are stained with the dark girl's mother's blood, the woman who ran the fish shop, a plain woman smelling of cod and flounder. They invited her to walk on the hills overlooking the city, to walk along the little gravel paths, to admire the view. And then they hit her with a brick. The thud of it on the mother's skull. How could they? How could they?

But then there was the orchard. Those green aisles of apple, pear and cherry, petal-strewn. The way her mother had simply handed it over, without warning or discussion, until only the plum tree remained, its trunk hard against their new boundary fence. Violet had given it away, and seemed delighted to have done so, pleased with her own generosity.

Sometimes, thinking of the orchard, watching those fretful skinny hands prod at soup or custard, there is a brick.

Sybil would never.

Of course.

She would never.

But just for a second.

The phantom weight, heavy in her hand . . .

twenty-six
THE RIVER
SPRING 1956

Nothing happens.

Leaves fall. Rowing skiffs pass overhead, the oars sliding cleanly, rhythmically, through the surface.

The water is cool against her sleek skin.

twenty-seven

THE RIVER

SPRING 1958

Nothing happens.

Leaves fall.

She is long and lean.

Her belly gleams silver by the dark bank. Her eyes like steel studs.

Watching.

twenty-eight
THE RIVER
SPRING 1960

Nothing happens.

Leaves fall.

The glittering shoals of glass arrive, swimming strongly upstream.

The big wire nets drop into the water. She watches as some swim into their fastness, beat against obstruction but are lifted up, wriggling.

Others swim by. On up the river.

Lucky.

twenty-nine

THE AERIAL

SPRING 1962

'... to the left,' says the old bat in the woolly hat and paint-spattered trousers tied roughly at the waist with a striped school tie. She stands below them in the garden, keeping one eye on the television which is parked, gleaming in polished oak veneer, in a corner of the tip she calls her living room.

When they first arrived, unloaded the console from the back of the truck and wheeled it past a row of rubbish bins up an overgrown path, cracked by tree roots and liberally carpeted in moss, Froggy had said, 'What a dump.' But it was nothing compared with the mess inside the house.

They'd found her seated at an easel, painting a picture that looked like it was supposed to be the back porch and the purple stuff that was growing all over it. She'd stood up as they came around the corner, wiping filthy hands on even filthier trousers. Her hair dangled over her shoulders in a greying mane.

'In here,' she'd said. 'Now, mind your step.' They didn't have to be reminded. She opened the door into a kitchen. A kind of kitchen. Benches supported pots and plates, boxes of walnuts, milk bottles, some green and unrinsed, every surface laden. Light filtered in through grimy net curtains. And cats. Bloody cats everywhere.

Vince couldn't stand cats. Dogs were all right. They knew who was boss, but cats always had something of the jungle about them. One glared at him balefully from the top of the fridge. Another occupied a sagging sofa in the sun. A third crouched among the plates on the table. 'Christ,' muttered Froggy. 'I thought I'd lived in some pretty rough places, but ... whoooo ...'

The old bat cleared a way through, tossing aside cartons and boxes to another door that opened into a room as cluttered as the first, though clearly intended to function as a sitting room. Chairs laden with books and ratty rugs, a fireplace with a dusty arrangement of wilted flowers all faded to sepia, canvases stacked against mildewed wallpaper. 'Here you go,' she said. 'Just pop it in the corner.' She had cleared a space to the left of the hearth with its avalanche of spent ash.

Vince held the console steady while Froggy slid it from the sackbarrow and then they set to work with cables, unpacking the antenna with its awkward spindly arms. She had a ladder ready, leaning against the back wall. It was ancient and wooden with one rung missing.

'Got one in the truck,' said Froggy hurriedly.

They climbed up onto the roof among the ornamental chimney pots, a bevy of them gathered on corrugated iron that hadn't seen any maintenance in years. A small forest of seedlings was taking root in the spouting and water dripped from an overflow pipe, leaving a long slippery green stain.

'Big place,' said Froggy. 'Must have been pretty impressive once upon a time.'

There had been a fire in the nearest chimney at some point and its decorative cantilevered pot was stained with soot, but it seemed sound enough. They attached the aerial, then Vince stood up top twisting the arms this way and that while Froggy climbed back down the ladder and attended to tuning in the room below.

'Yeah ... yeah,' he called. 'More to the left. Yeah. Back a bit ...' The old bat stood by the living room window, filling in whenever they could not hear one another's instructions clearly.

'He says "Back a bit,"' she yelled.

It was nice up there on the roof, looking out over overgrown trees. You could see the river and across the rooftops to the southern suburbs and the smooth brown bulk of the Port Hills. Vince had always liked getting up onto the top of things and looking about. So often you spent your time in this city between fences, down on the flat, but he had grown up in the foothills back of Oxford and liked a bit of elevation. That was what he liked when he was out hunting with his brother: the moment where you broke from the bush onto the tops. Up in the sunlight, among tussock and speargrass. You could breathe up there.

'Left down a bit,' called Froggy, relayed by the bat. 'Yep. Yep. Cracker. Got it. That'll do.'

'Now, how about a cup of tea?' said the bat when they had finished and were packing up. She had a tray set, the kettle boiling, a floral plate with custard squares. 'No thanks,' they said in unison. They didn't trust those squares. A cat was skidding off out the door, licking its lips, and a trail of crumbs led back to the table. Nah. They'd better get on. The bat smiled, unoffended, and 'Here,' she said, dragging a ten shilling note from her pocket.

'Thanks,' they said. She was a bit daft, but nice enough. Could have been quite good-looking in her time. They showed her how to adjust the vertical hold if the picture started to roll up the screen, how to turn the ring on the fine-tuner if the static meant it was unwatchable. 'If all else fails, get someone to go up on the roof and fiddle with the antenna, but first, just give it a bang on the side, like this . . .' And they showed her how to thump the set. 'That'll jolt the tube inside. Nine times out of ten, that'll fix it.' And then they drove away, leaving her behind in her overgrown garden, among the cats.

And later that day, as the sun sets and transmission begins, Sybil switches on her new television. She takes a cup of tea and all the custard squares on a dinner plate and settles herself on the sofa. Sooty jumps up for his share, and the two of them sit side by side watching as the screen lights up with the evening news: the whole wide world in black and white emerging from snow and static in a corner of their living room.

Grainy aerial shots of some blurred things they say are nuclear missiles and launchers and the Russians are sailing towards Cuba with even more and the Americans are standing by. If Violet were here she'd know what to make of it. She'd liked him, young and handsome, like a film star, and Irish. An Irishman in the White

House. She said she was glad she'd lived to see the day. And then he'd sent warships and planes to try and overturn the other one, the big one with the beard, Fidel. 'What's he doing?' she'd said, fretfully tugging at her bedspread. 'He should know better than that, being Irish. They'll fight.' And they did, the Cubans. Killed or captured the entire invading force. 'Coulda told him,' said Violet. Wheezing. Fighting for breath herself.

And now they were at it again, only this time there are those blurry things: the missiles that will take them all out together. Sybil sits with Sooty watching it in her cluttered room: the end of the world. Like on that film she'd taken Violet to see. Her usual matinee, seat 42, midway down at the Regent. She couldn't manage the steps in the bus, so Sybil called a taxi and they went in together.

Fred Astaire. Ava Gardner. Gregory Peck. *On the Beach*. She'd expected romance. She'd expected dancing, on account of Fred Astaire. But he didn't dance. Instead he roared around a racetrack in a Ferrari, while other cars hurtled off in flames, crashed recklessly, their drivers choosing sudden death over the slow decline of radiation poisoning. He won, but it was no victory. Not for Fred Astaire, the bespectacled scientist, drunkenly insisting to a room full of people gathered for a party, 'We're doomed, doomed by the air we are about to breathe!' For the cloud was rolling down from the northern hemisphere, flowing steadily south towards Melbourne, though everyone was pretending it wouldn't happen. The woman was planting flowers as if nothing would happen. The man was doing up his car as if nothing would happen. And the old gents at the club were drinking all the fine wines.

But of course it did happen. Soon the young mother was sick and her husband was injecting their baby daughter before they both swallowed their pills, for there was nowhere now where they might escape. The cloud had reached as far as Christchurch, New Zealand. Violet nudged Sybil's arm at that: the first time ever she has heard Christchurch mentioned by a movie star on the big screen! On documentaries, yes, those travel shorts that preceded the main feature, where the city generally appeared as a river lined by daffodils in bloom, the usual more English than England, the Garden City. But here it was, from the mouth of Fred Astaire! And its mention meant that the entire world was now incontrovertibly dead.

Fred Astaire put a blanket across the garage door and climbed into his Ferrari and waited for death. Gregory Peck set sail at the helm of the USS *Sawfish*, steadily steering his submarine and its doomed crew toward certain death and dead America, while Ava Gardner sat in her sports car on the headland and watched them leave. She, too, had her suicide pill. A newspaper blew down an empty Australian street between deserted buildings, and everyone had died. The world had died. And the banner unfurled across the dead city saying, 'There is still time, brother. The End.'

Then the lights came up and she gave her mother her arm and helped her out onto the busy Square. Tears were streaming down her cheeks for Fred and Ava and the whole doomed human race. The only comfort was that it was, after all, just a movie. It wasn't real. The people in the Square were real.

But now it was the cloud that could be real.

It could roll forth from the television set in the corner of the living room, seeping out from Cuba, from that tiny distant island.

It could overwhelm them all.

Tomorrow, perhaps.

Tonight . . .

thirty
THE WINDOW FRAME
SPRING 1964

...old chap who came in every day for a pie. The same lunch, every single day. She didn't even bother to take his order. Just said, 'I've kept your seat.' He liked to sit by the window and watch the lunchtime crowd on Colombo Street, eat his pie while reading *The Press*, big plate of thin-sliced bread and lots of butter, cup of tea and a lamington. And then he sat contentedly smoking — he preferred rollies, taking ages to tuck in the tobacco, lick the paper — and then a toothpick from his shirt pocket to delicately remove coconut threads from teeth too white and even to be his own.

She was his favourite. He always told her so. He didn't like Linda or Doreen. Only Beverley, he said. She was generous with the butter and topped up the teapot without him having to ask.

'Here's your boyfriend,' Doreen said, slamming a metal milkshake tumbler onto the machine. They teased her about him. Asked if he'd popped the question yet. When was the Big Day? Got her hope chest ready? Chosen her frock?

'He's just lonely,' Beverley said. He reminded her of her granddad back when they'd lived in Methven. He'd been a skinny old bald guy, yellowed from years of Albanys, quiet, not given to chatter. The bad times had come after, when he'd died and they had moved to the city so their mum could get a job. Shifting from one grim flat to another until they had ended up crammed into the big room in the house near the river. It had been divided with thin asbestos partitions into two bedrooms and a kitchenette, one bedroom for her and their mother, the other for Noel and Gordon, but you could tell it was really a single room because the partitions did not quite meet at the top, where a border of white fruit and leaves ran around the ceiling above her bed then continued into the boys' room on the other side. It carried through the next partition, too, into the kitchenette, though there the fruit and leaves were no longer snowy white but greasy yellow and not nearly so pretty.

Beverley liked her room. She liked its angular shape, set in a bay, with windows all around with panels of crimson roses at the top, though Gordon had broken one kicking a ball and Miss Sinclair, who owned the house and lived out the back with her cats, had had to clamber up on a rickety ladder to cover it with some plywood, their mother holding the bottom because she couldn't climb. She couldn't do heights. They set off her giddy spells. But the landlady had hitched up her trousers and taken the sheet of ply while their mother clutched the ladder saying, 'Don't fall, don't fall,' until Miss Sinclair said 'Oh, for goodness' sake, Mrs Jamieson. Just give us the hammer and be quiet.'

Beverley liked the roses, and the way her room was actually a tower. She lived below a turret, like in a book. She liked the border of fruit around the ceiling and the gap at the top of the partitions that meant that at night, when their mum was out late cleaning, she and her brothers could lie in bed and talk to one another or shine patterns on the plaster with the torch. Unless it was one of those times when their mum wasn't coping, between jobs and not enough from the Child Allowance if you were a woman left on her own with three kids to clothe and feed, not if you'd never got around to marrying the last one, father of Gordon and Noel, who'd done a runner to God knows where, no sense of responsibility. Those were the times when the kids had to pack their little suitcases, one toy each for company in the girls' dormitory and the boys' dormitory in the home over the hill where they stayed until their mum was better and they could come back to the roses and Miss Sinclair's cats. Where they stayed until their mum lost another job and it began again. Their mother didn't seem to have the knack of getting on with people.

Beverley had the knack. She had got a job the day after she turned fifteen and could finally leave school, though one of her teachers had pressed a book into her hands — *The Golden Treasury of Poetry* — and said it was a shame, she was a bright girl, could have gone on to university. But Miss Gething didn't understand about the hilarity when their mother burst into life, bouncing on the bed, taking them off to buy shoes on layby, making cakes all night, slamming about in the kitchenette until the other boarders bashed on the wall and yelled at her to shut up. And the slump that followed this feverish activity, the dull despair. Miss Gething didn't understand that and how someone had to make some money to pay the rent and sort out the bill at the dairy and buy the shoes.

Beverley had burned her panama hat on the riverbank on her way home, tossed the *Golden Treasury* under the bed with the other rubbish and next day she got a job. Easy as that.

And one afternoon, Wally came in for his usual and when he'd had his pie and she was clearing away, he'd grabbed her hand. 'Oh no,' she'd thought. 'Here we go. He's going to pop the question and everyone is going to laugh. They'll give me beans.' She could feel Doreen's satirical eye glance over. But Wally wasn't popping a question. He was pressing two bits of paper into her hand. Tickets. He was giving her tickets for a concert.

'Can't say they're my cup of tea. I'm more a Johnny Cash man myself. Hank Snow. That's my kind of music, but you teenagers seem keen, so here you go. Take your boyfriend and enjoy yourselves.' And he'd tucked £5 into her hand along with the tickets, for a programme, he said. And a nice box of chocolates to share with the boyfriend.

'I don't have a boyfriend,' she said. But Wally's hearing wasn't good and he was sitting there beaming with the pleasure of giving her this treat so she didn't press the matter.

Doreen was impressed. She squealed at the sight of the tickets. 'You lucky pig,' she said. 'Wish I'd been nicer to him. But if you don't have anyone else to ask, I wouldn't mind.' Linda already had a ticket. And a boyfriend.

So there was Beverley, crushed in the crowd outside the Majestic along with Doreen, who had had her hair done for the occasion, backcombed with an Alice band, flicked up at the bottom, her cardigan buttoned up at the back, her breasts two sharp peaks beneath pink cashmere for it was cold out. A snappy wind blew along High Street and they were waiting for the crowd to come out from the 6.30 concert. There were two, to accommodate everyone. They were queuing for the second, while the first emerged, dazed, dishevelled, as if they had just experienced some amazing transformation. Like Beverley's mum, that night when they'd gone to hear Billy Graham at Lancaster Park, thousands of them among the lights and the throbbing of choir and organ that had drawn their mother up out of her seat, propelled to the front where the tiny spotlit figure was calling her to believe. She had gone for a while, leaving her children in their seats alone, and the choir was singing and she was saved; she'd returned lit up with the glory of salvation. That was how the 6.30 crowd seemed as they pushed their way back out onto the streets, as if they had just witnessed some kind of glory.

'Come on,' said Doreen and grabbed her arm. 'Elbows out. Let's get through here.' And they had fought their way in where police were trying to hold things back, maintain order. Girls mostly, like themselves, though there were some young men, too, a few of them already wearing their hair long and fringed, their shoes pointy-toed, up with the play.

They found their seats: front row of the stalls. 'Best seats in the house!' said Doreen. 'Good old Wally!' The theatre filled and they sat close together and ate the whole top layer of a Dairy Milk selection while they read the programme. It was a proper magazine with advertisements for sophisticated things like coffee: 'Gregg's Instant Coffee. The modern Coffee for the smart younger Set!' And several kinds of acne cream. And there was a special introduction to these 'four British Bombs' whose visit to these shores illustrated the 'importance of this country in the world-wide show-business scene'. The best part were the bios for the musicians: for Johnny Chester, who was going to sing first and came from Melbourne and was a 5'10" bundle of dynamite. And a band called The Phantoms and Johnny Devlin. And The Beatles, of course. John who was 5'11". His eyes were 'sincere brown', his shoes were size 8½ and he didn't like 'thick headed girls.' Paul also preferred girls 'who could make intelligent conversation', whereas Ringo liked girls who were 'well built'. Doreen said she wouldn't stand a chance with Paul, though he was still her favourite and the rows of seats filled and the police walked up and down and eventually the lights dimmed and Johnny Chester sang and The Phantoms and Johnny Devlin in black leather and there was some half-hearted applause. No one was listening. Everyone was waiting, time was passing, over an hour and still The Beatles had not appeared and then the lights became brighter on stage and into the empty space they walked: four figures she recognised from the magazines, but actually, truly here. Only a few yards away, straightening their guitars, picking up drum sticks, taking their places at the microphones.

Actually here. Not in the pages of some magazine, nor on the little flickering screen of the television set. When their mum was out, Miss Sinclair sometimes invited them in to watch her television. They sat in a row on her grubby sofa among the cats watching *The Hit Parade*: Cliff, and Elvis. Or *I Love Lucy* and, once, a man being shot. The handsome president with the beautiful wife in the open-topped limousine. He looking like a movie star, she in her suit and becoming little pillbox hat, and then there was that tiny snap. Miss Sinclair turned up the volume to full so they could hear it. 'Hear that?' she said. 'That's history.' The snap. The sudden consternation as the man slumped and the woman in the beautiful suit was trying to climb over to him but too late, too late. They had watched it, this little scene from overseas. From the wide imagined universe that lay beyond the coast at Brighton, beyond the cloud-topped horizon. And here was another bit of overseas, something that belonged to the television and the magazines, but now it was here and adjusting its guitar.

The scream.

A single, deafening, high-pitched scream, a single wall of sound where individual voices were completely submerged, individual people were irrelevant. The music was irrelevant. The young men on the stage, tapping their toes, were almost irrelevant. What mattered was the scream. All those girls' voices in one ear-splitting sound that drowned out everything else, so that even from the front row the music was completely inaudible. They were playing. Their hands were busy strumming their guitars and Ringo was bashing at his drums and George was tapping his foot and Paul and John with his sincere brown eyes were singing into the mic, their mouths opening and closing, but they might as well not have sung at all for there was nothing. Just the vast wall of the scream. And a hail of jelly beans raining down on the stage and — splat! — an egg that landed just behind the mic. And another.

Someone was throwing eggs at The Beatles. But the girls were surging down the aisles, they were clambering over seats, making their way forward, forming a dense mass at the foot of the stage, arms reaching up toward the four young men who stood there, making the gestures of music. Doreen was among them, and Beverley, too, was swept up, her body caught in the press of bodies, Cliff and Elvis forgotten. For twenty-six minutes the scream was all. There was a moment: she looked up and John caught her eye. He was definitely looking back at her, and shrugging. A tiny amused shrug as if to say, 'Isn't this ridiculous?', and she smiled back, one of the girls he liked: intelligent, above such silliness, but eventually she surrendered to the scream, mouth open wide, her eyes streaming with tears but for what and for whom she could not quite tell.

And then it was over and she emerged onto High Street where she joined the crowd moving as one to stand in front of The Beatles' hotel, chanting, though truly she had no voice left. And after a while they appeared once more. They stood above them on the fire escape. And once again the barrage of eggs until the second-floor balcony railings dripped with mucus and The Beatles moved up a flight out of range while fights broke out down below between the egg-throwers and the young men with fringed haircuts.

So she left the crowd, ears ringing, and walked home alone, down the dark streets. Ordinarily she might have been frightened, being well schooled in never getting into cars with strangers, never walking too close to the hedge, staying away from dark corners, making her cautious way like a cat on hostile territory.

But tonight the moon was crisp and clear. The stars twinkled and nothing could reach her, lifted as she was by the power of that scream, by the sincere brown eyes, the tiny amused shrug.

Her mother was asleep when she got in, lying like a baby with her arms wide spread. Beverley undressed and slipped into bed without waking her. And then she took the knife her mother kept by the bed in case of burglars or rapists and on the window frame by her pillow she scratched a tiny JL and next to it a BJ, contained with a single heart and . . .

thirty-one
THE RIVER
SPRING 1966

Nothing happens.

Leaves fall, spinning in spring sunshine.

A dog floats by, its legs tied and long dead, trailing shreds.

She tugs away strips of sweet flesh.

Strips the bones clean.

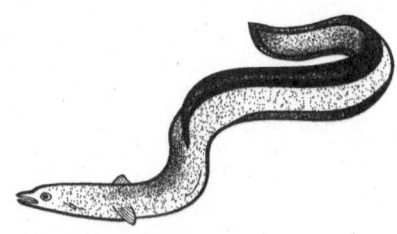

thirty-two
THE CAT FLAP
SPRING 1968

'... puss,' she says. 'Here, Boots.' She keeps her voice low and calm. She is almost within reach, but the cat lashes out at her extended hand and backs away, hissing, ears flat, and Sybil has no choice but to edge further, her legs straddling the branch with its rough bark and awkward twigs. 'Silly Boots. Come on, now. Don't be frightened.'

Around her, long tendrils of new willow leaf whip in the wind and, though the worst of the storm has passed and the sun has come out, the river surges, mucky brown in full flood, bearing its seething cargo of broken timber. Swirls of creamy froth billow by the bank. Boots sometimes forgets that she has only three legs and can no longer leap and climb as she once could. She has already fallen once, but managed to catch hold of some twigs and clamber back. Her fur is slicked close and she looks so very small and frightened out here on the willow. She can climb out, but not back, driven from the safety of the kitchen through the cat flap by the invasion of the Souchotts' miniature poodle, who looks like butter wouldn't melt in his mouth but is a killer with a long tally of cats, kittens, rabbits and small furry creatures to his name. Sybil has found the torn remains often enough, laid in a misplaced display of canine affection at her back door: broken-necked, spread-eagled. The poodle doesn't bother to eat them. It's the chase he enjoys, the dragging down, the snap of the small neck.

The branch bounces lightly in the wind and Boots is unsettled, scrambling for purchase on her three legs. Poor creature. Her fear catches at Sybil's heart. Sometimes she cannot bear the fear of animals. Those desperate sheep she has seen sometimes on the road, the truck spraying piss and terror, the frantic eye looking down from among the press of bodies, on the way to the works. The cows in paddocks whose sons are torn from them when they are no more than a few weeks old, still suckling with their soft pink mouths. And the way people eat their dead terrorised flesh, suck at the bones, cut and carve and swallow. How can they? And then there have always been the horses forced to take the metal rod between their big lips.

The farthest memory is of Rajah, glossy flanks gleaming, harnessed to the gig. His mouth frothing green about the bit. Tossing his enormous head against the restraint of leather and metal. 'Doesn't the bit hurt him?' she'd said, and her father had gathered up the reins saying he'd never hold him without the bit and didn't she want them all to go for a nice drive to the beach? She had tried the bit herself, surreptitiously slipping into the tack room one afternoon and putting it in her own mouth. It lay heavy, icy cold, tasting sourly of metal against her teeth. And Rajah had rolled his eye, white rimmed, as he stood waiting, harnessed and restrained in the yard. He'd looked down at her and cried, quite distinctly, 'Help me! Help me!'

Then there were the lions and elephants and sad chimpanzees captured for her entertainment as a child in some big draughty reeking circus tent. And only a few months ago, the dog that had passed overhead, strapped into that tiny glittering capsule, poor Luka. Probably already dead from sheer panic by the time she looked up from the garden to see the pinprick of light peep peep peeping as it flew among the stars. *Help me! Help me!* She could not bear it: that the beauty of stars and moon had been infected by that terrible fear.

So here she is trying to make up for all that. Here she is, reaching out to a little cat whose leg was caught in a possum trap and half torn away in her effort to escape before she'd been rescued, brought to the house near death by an earnest child, who had wrapped the little creature in a dirty cardigan. Boots, whom she had kept safe with her other animals, all of them living the way they were intended to live their lives, fed and cared for and free to roam about. Boots, who snuggled down each night, warm against her body in the bed.

'Boots,' she calls. 'Boots.'

And at that moment, the willow cracks in two and one part, the branch, begins to fall. It falls and Boots yowls and makes one final desperate leap for safety, clawing her way up Sybil's extended arm, across her shoulders and down her back to the bank, where she sets off as fast as she can on her tottering legs up Barchester Street, ears flat, around the corner onto Savage Street, through the garden, avoiding the poodle who yaps from behind the fence and clickety click through the cat flap to the sofa.

While Sybil falls, her trousers snagged on a twig. She falls with the branch into the churning river and there is nothing to hang onto, nowhere to get a foothold. Tangled in willow leaf, she tumbles in and is carried downstream, water closing over her head, as it has closed over other heads in river or lake or safe harbour: the waka capsizes on the reef and its crew are turned to stone. The ship drifts, sails full-bellied, onto some rocky promontory and all are lost. The ferry overturns within view of a suburban living room. And only a few hundred yards away the lifeboats dangle useless on the high exposed flank of the ferry, or they are launched and flip in the wind and all the people are flung into the water. It closes over their heads.

This is the way Sybil falls. The river takes her in its grasp, sweeping her downstream the way it did long ago. She looks up and, there are the same golden brown bubbles rising from her mouth. They rise about her like stars, while the raft sails onward above her head, leaving her to be swept along alone, caught up in the flood of water and time. She looks up and can see the rough wooden boards sailing away from her, and she waits, because any second now, his hand will smash through the dazzle. His big kind hand will reach down into the water and he will grab her by the hair and pull her up, up into . . .

thirty-three
THE WISTERIA
SPRING 1970

...was Min who found it. Midwinter, damp and grey, the river a ribbon of low-hanging fog. And there it was, half-buried beneath periwinkle, its walls dimpled with damp rot under a cloak of ivy. A leafless vine entangled the front porch, ornamented with the fluffy seed heads of old man's beard and fallen leaf lay knee-deep on the path between overhanging branches and the whole place reeked of damp and decay, cat pee and desolation.

Perfect.

Min stood in the overgrown garden, jeans soaked to the knees. She'd regret that later: flares took absolutely ages to dry. Beneath her sodden boots lay bricks and broken glass. Beer bottles littered the porch, and someone had set a fire at the foot of the steps where a half-burned wirewove rusted over charred wood and a shabby sofa and armchairs slumped either side in a parody of three-piece gentility. She stood, in uncertain territory. Maybe some old hermit still inhabited the house, an unpredictable type, savage with unexpected visitors?

In her hand she held the leaflets: Uncle Sam in his stars-and-stripes hat wanted YOU, except that Pete has redrawn his head as a skull and his pointing finger as skeletal bone. MOBILISE AGAINST

WAR! The plan was to gather in Victoria Square before marching through the central city. She had pinned one leaflet to a suburban library notice board, put three in church foyers, asked to place one in the window of a dairy whose owner had said yes, and one in the window of a butcher's who had said no without looking up from sawing a rack of lamb chops. And now she was tramping the suburban streets, posting the remainder in letterboxes. A man in a singlet and Stubbies, despite the cold, was in a driveway, peering into the upraised bonnet of a Holden.

'Hoy,' he called. 'Hoy! You!' She turned. He stood on the footpath, the leaflet in his upraised fist. 'Here's what I'm going to do with this!' And he made an elaborate mime of wiping his bum. 'Now fuck off! And take your rubbish with you!' The balled-up leaflet landed between them and rolled into the gutter.

Min walked on. Don't enter into argument. Look straight ahead. Keep moving. She posted more leaflets but a little more quickly than before, with that uneasy prickling at the back of the neck that signalled that she might be under scrutiny.

And that was when she found it. A letterbox, stuffed to bursting with sodden newsletters and unattended mail, a rickety gate drooping from a broken padlock, a copper nameplate green with verdigris: Villa Bella. And beside it, tacked to the gatepost, a faded For Sale sign. And beyond the gate, the damp dark path, the green tunnel...

She had always liked such places. It was something to do with childhood, with *The Secret Garden* which she had received as a prize for regular attendance at Sunday school. Her parents had no time for reading. There was only a Bible, in Dutch. And an atlas. And suddenly, miraculously, *The Secret Garden*, with its robin and crocuses and the peevish sickly children made well by growing things.

She glanced over her shoulder. The Holden was revving away. No one was paying attention. She pushed her way through the gate and up the overgrown path, and the house rose before her, wreathed in wisps of fog like one of those Mayan temples rising from the Yucatan jungle. A big villa with bay windows and a kind of pointed medieval turret at one corner. She stood before it in a sudden silence. Among the trees and shrubs, the Holden faded to a distant throb, the entire city to a faint persistent hum. She could have been standing miles away, out in the country.

The front door was ajar, so she knocked, twice, called tentatively, 'Hello?', on account of the hermit, and when there was no response, no shaggy madman with a shotgun, she stepped into the hall.

Panels of coloured glass around the door cast a pale pastel glow over walls festooned with swags of scrim and paper, which swayed like banners in a castle chamber. On either side, tall doors opened onto cramped arrangements of cubicles and kitchenettes, crudely partitioned, but if you looked up you could see that these had been carved from much larger, grander rooms with plaster ceiling borders of fruit and flowers. The big bay windows had been smashed and the carpet crunched underfoot with broken glass and dry leaves, while all around was the startled scurry of myriad small lives interrupted as she walked about. In one room, french doors stood half open to a side verandah, where an immense creeper had cast aside any pretence of garden ornament to become the jungle strangler it had always been at heart. Writhing limbs twisted around verandah posts and skinny tentacles waved for a grip. At one end of the verandah more plants jostled in the remains of a conservatory and there were those distant wraiths who always hover in such places: the lady in a white dress, plucking a gardenia; a gentleman in suit and high collar considering a rare plant. Formal people in formal clothes doing formal things.

At the other end of the verandah a staircase led up to the turret, which was also broken and abandoned and completely perfect. More rooms lined the dark hallway all the way back to a bathroom with a yellowed tub perched on clawed feet and a lavatory whose bowl was filthy but ornamented with pink roses. The kitchen was gloomy and through the broken floorboards there were glimpses of bare earth. The back garden was a tangle of plants and tumbledown sheds of indeterminate purpose: heaps of sheds, heaps of rooms, space for everyone, for Mack's band, and her loom and Pete's studio, for meetings and rehearsals and maybe a proper printing machine and a darkroom, a communal garden, a kitchen for shared meals, all of them abandoning the cramped flats and the looming spectre of the life lived behind suburban fences from which they had all, in their various ways, made their escape.

Her friends. Met at parties in crowded flats, beer bottles clanking in coat pockets and some dubious punch in the washing machine bowl for the girls. At meetings and demonstrations, or in classes at the university or across a sticky table at some cafeteria, or simply sitting on the riverbank in Hagley Park one spring afternoon. Like Liz, who sat among the daffodils arguing with an earnest anthropology student that 'man' was not a neutral term. It didn't mean the same as 'people' or 'humans'. 'I mean, it's not neutral, is it?' she said, ripping a daffodil in shreds. 'Nobody ever says, "Man breastfeeds his young." Or "Man gives birth vaginally."' Min had never heard the word 'vagina' said out loud before. Her mother always used the term 'down there'.

And Pete, who had designed a poster for a production of *Antigone* for which Min had been the costume mistress, sewing dozens of identical white shifts, splattered with cosmetic blood. *There is no more deadly peril than disobedience* ... Antigone confronting Creon and the power of the state. Lysistrata and her mates refusing to sleep with men until they stopped the war. The shifts got a lot of use that year.

And Steve, who had walked beside her in an anti-Vietnam demonstration and given her a hand to control an unwieldy banner. *Hey Hey LBJ! How many kids did you kill today?*

And Mack, whom she first noticed sitting cross-legged in a ratty flat above the takeaway on Riccarton Road playing some song about his mama not 'lowin' him to stay out all nigh' long. He had been going out with her flatmate, but one night as she was sitting on the verandah roof having a cigarette, he climbed out the window and sat beside her. 'You're gorgeous,' he said. 'You, too,' she said.

Simple, but effective.

Her friends. People who said things she'd never heard before. Who made her laugh unguardedly, happily. Who made her feel like herself at last, rather than that weird Dutch kid.

And here it was: a place where they could live together, all of them under a single roof. A single, slightly leaky roof, to judge from the stains on the ceiling, but that was a detail Min chose to ignore as she walked about. She said yes, instead. Yes to the house and the big beautiful rooms, yes to the tangled garden, yes to the hallway and the turret which she intended, though it must of course be a communal decision, to claim as her own. (Herself in flowing muslin at her loom in the tower above the treetops, like Tennyson: the Lady of Shalott, tirra lirra by the river.) Yes to the flowery lav and the tumbledown sheds, yes yes yes.

The owner lived in Whangarei, a difficult woman, said the agent, demanding a high price for what was in effect a demolition property.

'Oh no!' said Min. 'Not demolition!'

'You're going to live in that?' said the agent, who was about to move into a nice new architecturally designed townhouse with an angular roofline, central heating and porthole windows. Morpeth Mews. Within walking distance of an equally contemporary village of boutique clothing shops, delicatessen and European-style bakery. A hint of a sweet colonial past, but no more. One could have entirely too much of the past. One could have too much weatherboard and rot and an open fire struggling to heat a 14-foot stud.

But this young couple seemed keen. She supposed a couple, though you couldn't always tell. His hair was long, straggling over the collar of a coat that in the heat of her office was beginning to smell distinctly of goat. He sprawled with his long legs on one of her office chairs, with a kind of louche insolence she did not entirely like, his eyes barely visible behind lemon-tinted spectacles. The jeans were skinny and had big silver buttons at the fly and she couldn't help glancing at them and the curve they struggled to contain, and of course he had noticed. She had the uncomfortable feeling that he might be laughing at her, behind those lenses. The girl was a mouse by comparison, pretty and pale in kneeboots and fur coat. (Min had decided it didn't count if the animals had died before you were born.) They sat side by side on the other side of the agent's desk, looking eager. There were others involved, in some kind of communal arrangement the agent imagined would involve complicated sex and copious amounts of marijuana, but for the moment these two signatures would do.

The owner was driving a hard bargain: $12,000, she said over the telephone. She lived up north and had not visited in years, had absolutely no idea of the state the place was in, was completely unrealistic, asking twice what it was worth, but $12,000 or no sale. She would rather see the house rot into the ground than let it go for less. After two years on the market and no maintenance for decades before that.

Min listened as the vision faded. The big cleared rooms, the studios, the garden, her turret in the treetops. They had made an offer, all chipping in as much as they could: $500 from Steve who had a job that year at the Botanic Gardens, $1000 from Pete who had sold his car, the entire bequest left to Min by her Auntie Eve who had married a GI during the war and gone to live in Wisconsin, $2500 from Mack, and $1000 from Liz, who had a scholarship, was doing law and drafted a proper contract that used phrases they had never before encountered, such as 'tenants in common'. That's what they were now: tenants in common, who between them had managed to raise $7000, which the agent said was reasonable.

The owner up north said no. Not even close.

But what was this? Mack was saying $8000. The owner was saying $12,000. Mack was saying $10,000. The owner was saying $12,000. And then Mack was saying, 'Ah, to hell with it: $12,000,' and it was done. Mack was standing up as if this were an everyday occurrence. He was shaking hands with the agent and he was turning to Min, completely as his ease, saying to her silent question, 'It's cool. No hassle.' And there they were signing an agreement. She glanced down at Mack's signature as she added her own. Richard Fraser Treadwell McClintock. She'd never known his name before. He was just Mack. Slinky. Elusive.

And then they were leaving the office and the house was theirs. As they walked up Manchester Street she said, 'Where did that come from?' But Mack simply shrugged. Richard Fraser Treadwell McClintock. 'It's just money.' Was he planning on selling something? His bike? Did he have more — a lot more — of the black he had brought back from Kabul last summer? Was there some other source? She was aware suddenly that she knew nothing whatever about him. He was always evasive. 'Here and there,' he said, if anyone asked where he came from. And he said it with such indifference that it would have seemed uncool to press the matter further. He walked with a loose loping stride, owned a single pair of boots scuffed and intricately tooled, rode a temperamental Triumph that required constant tinkering, carried with him from flat to flat his guitar and a single soap carton containing a collection of blues albums of great rarity, which he played on a painstakingly assembled stereo system: Denon turntable, Bang and Olufsen amp, Wharfedale speakers. And that was it.

Just money.

Min thought of her parents' careful accumulation of wealth:

'Money doesn't grow on my back,' her father said. (He was a man of many sayings.) *Het geld groeit niet op mijn rug*. And her mother anxiously complied: plain meals, nothing bought on tick, nothing thrown out or wasted, rolls of wool carefully unravelled for reknitting, bundles of rubber bands stored in the kitchen drawer, paper bags folded and saved, rugs stitched from braided rags so that you could find the remains of your summer skirt, your brother's grey school shorts and the old kitchen curtains woven into the mat by the back door. All this restraint in the name of paying off a brick and tile in Nelson before retirement to a bach in the Sounds where her mother could put her feet up at last and her father could spend the remainder of his life fishing. Penny by penny. Dollar by dollar. *We moeten goed op die kleintjes letten.* Look after the little things, the pennies . . . Just money.

But here they are, her friends, all equal, all together in this purchase, gathered at the gate to the Villa Bella, which they have rechristened, after much argument, Lothlorien. Pete has painted the name on the gate. The sun is out after days of rain and they are filing up the overgrown path from the van laden with bags and cartons. And the house rises before them, no longer clad in drab winter leaf, but newborn. Sprays of yellow banksia wave above the chimney pots. The side verandah is disappearing under a curtain of purple wisteria. There's plum blossom and golden kowhai and tiny blue flowers among broken glass and smashed brick.

Back in the van there are more leaflets that must be delivered later. There is to be an action on Armistice Day.

Remember the Victims of Fascist Aggression in Vietnam! will be laid down among the RSA's wreaths at the cenotaph.

Yes. *Remember My Lai.* The bodies flung in a ditch, women and children for the most part, randomly killed but counted with that weird military exactness: 504.

Remember Agnew. Winging his way into the country with his cosmonaut at his side as evidence of American superiority, rulers of earth, sea and the universe. Remember the melee of security men and Holyoake, primped and oiled, prancing up the steps while the crowd rioted at his back. Remember the gleam of his little pointed shoes, so delighted to be dancing attendance.

Remember the marches. The thousands gathered on streets and squares. Remember the headlocks and scuffles and arrests, the thunk of the baton on bone, the knee to the balls, the fist to the jugular.

Remember the marches here and in America where the guardsmen had truly gone all the way and opened fire. Remember the girl at Kent State kneeling by the boy who lay face down by her side and the way her mouth stretched in that wide silent scream you could hear all the way over here.

Remember all that.

Remember the leaflets.

Remember, too, a curtain of purple flowers around an open . . .

thirty-four
THE MATTRESSES
SPRING 1972

…can hear them out in the old stable. They're rehearsing. Mack and Danny and Frankie the drummer and the new keyboard player, whose name Liz doesn't know — they change quickly, walk out snarling, 'You're a fascist, man!' The music stops and starts and stops. 'You're ahead again. Why can't you keep to the fucking beat?'

It's only a matter of time before Danny walks, too. He doesn't want to play covers. '"Mustang Sally?"' he says. 'Why the hell are we playing "Mustang Sally"?' He wants to play his own stuff but Mack won't budge.

'*She left him/halfway down Colombo Street,*' he says. 'What kind of crap is that?'

'My kind of crap,' said Danny. 'That's the point.'

He'll walk. They all walk, all except Frankie the drummer, who, while the others argue, sits fiddling with the hi-hat, smiling and sweetly beatifically stoned. Sunlight slants through gaps between the mattresses they have nailed around the stable walls. There were several in the house when they arrived: frayed, faded, striped, floral, all disgustingly stained. They made perfect if somewhat dusty insulation.

The music starts again and off goes Sally, ridin' around. The band has a gig tonight. A minuscule stage in a basement near the Square, a bar dispensing overpriced beer and orange vodka cocktails for the girls, a racket of music and voices rising toward midnight when it all closes down and the band will lug its gear back up the stairs — amp, speakers, mics and the rest — into the van and it's late and everyone's buzzing, they want a drink but only a couple of places have late licences and they'll be packed. So they'll head around to the club in the Loop where all the bands go after hours. All except Frankie. Irish Joe will have set up shop in the gents at the Grantham, dispensing little yellow matchboxes of weed, Thai sticks in silver foil, tiny deceptive dots of acid. Frankie will head off happily into the night.

And Liz will walk into the club, girlfriend of the bass, and there will be that rapid scrutiny, that quick up and down that began when she was eleven and became suddenly visible. Until then she had been the skinny gawky one, youngest of six in an argumentative family, 'a good Catholic family' as Father Daly said approvingly when he dropped by for a whisky with their dad. In that family she had learned to keep her head down, her nose in a book. Invisible.

And then her body changed. Without her consent, patches of wiry hair sprouted in odd places, while two thimble points on her skinny chest swelled until she had breasts and a bra, size 36B. Simultaneously, she grew upward until she towered above her classmates with extra allowance for her hair, which sprang without restraint into a curly tangle. Complete strangers began making muttered asides to her on the street. Workmen digging holes in the road looked up and whistled, and her aunt's husband, Uncle Bernie, made a grab for her as she was fetching a cardigan from the car at her cousin's wedding. He pressed her urgently against his dusty Jag, prodding at her with his fat stomach and rubbery lips. 'Get off!' she said, youngest of six and seasoned survivor of headlocks, armlocks and assorted wrestling holds. She kneed him expertly in the groin and left him crumpled in the carpark, but her nice pink bridesmaid dress had been spoiled, one of its Thai silk roses torn.

She has become accustomed to the scrutiny, but still when she enters a place like the musicians' club she can feel awkward. There are never many women there. She's the odd one out, just as she had been at university: one of four women in a class of thirty law students, all of them from private or Catholic boys' schools, who wore jackets and ties and that air of inalienable right. 'Whoops,' the worst of them would say, knocking her books from the desk. 'Sorry...'

Or at work where she is the only female clerk, head down drafting deeds and wills, trying to avoid the wrath of the boss, a man given to explosive rage at idiocy, you silly girl. Solitary female with her tracing paper and coloured pencils at the Land Transfer Office, outlining boundaries and easements, or lined up at the post office with all the other clerks in town, waiting her turn to use the fax machine.

Solitary female when the boss shouted his clerks lunch at his club, a grand Victorian edifice where she sipped something called Châteauneuf-du-Pape, which was obviously something to be appreciated with deep reverence, though to be honest she didn't like it half as much as Asti Spumante. At home, her family have a cup of tea with their dinner, and sliced white bread already buttered on a plate. The club took some adjustment.

And if she does make a mistake — gets a boundary line wrong, ordered steak tartare and recoils when it arrived, and it's not a nice steak with some spicy oriental condiment, but a saucer-shaped mound of raw mince tasting of blood and smelling like tampons — if she makes an idiot of herself, it's not her who's the idiot, but the whole of womankind.

She is representative of every woman on the planet.

Every silly blonde, simpering on screen with her big bouffant hair and pointed breasts, every blonde in all the jokes, the actress who said to the bishop, the silly woman driver, the absurd mother-in-law, the ridiculous little old lady, the chicks, the birds, every woman whose silly little mind can manage clothes but not serious matters like government, like law, like business, which are best left to men. Every stupid cow, every bitch, broad, dog. Every silly pretty woman whose beauty has unleashed evil, chaos, war, Helen coolly watching while men suffer on the plains of Troy, Eve saying to Adam, 'Go on! Try it! What's the worst that can happen?' Every silly woman lacking talent, so she can never hope to play a violin as well as a man, or run a marathon or write a book, or lead a country. Every woman who possesses talent, but not the nerve to handle it, who sticks her head in a gas oven or leaps into a river, overburdened with her unnatural gifts. Every silly creature since she first began to read about the silly chicken who didn't recognise an acorn when it fell upon her silly little head.

All of them are present when she misreads an easement line, or orders steak tartare, and sometimes it feels a bit crowded and she wonders if it was worth the effort, the exams, the debating team, the general attempt to make the most of this God-given Opportunity, the one denied all previous members of her family. 'You're a clever girl, Lizzie,' her mother said. 'You've inherited the O'Neil brains. None of us got to go to university, but you've got the Opportunity. You can become a lawyer. You could stand for Parliament. You can change the world!'

It's a heavy load to carry: the expectations of all her family, living and dead, all the way back to the bogs of Ireland, not to mention the entire weight of womankind.

Out in the shed Sally rides and rides, that's all she wants to do. Min is in the kitchen making one of her chickpea casseroles. And Liz is sitting under the kowhai tree, apparently reading but in fact reframing her entire existence.

One of the reasons Danny is sulking is because she doesn't want to marry him. He had taken her out last night: pasta at Tregatti's, a bottle of Mateus Rosé and a terrifying diamond solitaire in a little velvet box.

'So, why not?' he'd said, picking moodily at the wine cork. 'Is there someone else?'

'No,' she'd said, and it was the truth. There was no one. She simply couldn't bear the constriction of that ring, the way it bruised the knuckle as she tugged at it, frantic to remove it from her finger. Frantic at the thought of their washing tangled in a single basket, frantic at the prospect of the weekly trip to the supermarket, the shared holidays, shared car, shared bed. The cork lay in pieces between them. 'So, why?' said Danny.

'I don't know,' she said.

It was complicated.

Everyone was getting married that year. They wore muslin with flowers in their hair, they had bridesmaids and groomsmen, though sometimes they replaced the suits with shirts with big romantic collars, they replaced the church with a windswept beach or a patch of bush by a river, they replaced the *Book of Common Prayer* with Kahlil Gibran. But a wedding nevertheless, with promises of eternal devotion and a banquet to follow where the elderly relatives stood about poking at their lentil croquettes instead of a nice roast chicken.

And then, there was Irene.

Irene was the boss's secretary, a neat little woman, the perfect legal assistant. The kind who soothed the boss and maintained order in a busy office before returning home at night to confer similar calm on the suburbs. Mainstay of the PTA, secretary of the tennis club, kindly husband with his own business selling heating appliances who coached their son's soccer team, holiday once a year to a bach in Wanaka. Or so Liz assumed. Irene was much too discreet to conflate private and public life. But she was another woman around the office, and sometimes, when everyone else was out at lunch, they found themselves having a coffee together in the tiny kitchenette off the main office, a little female chitchat.

Irene stood by the bench waiting for the kettle to boil, a teaspoonful of instant in one hand, the *Woman's Weekly* open on the coffee table and her sandwich neatly wrapped in greaseproof. And crying. A neat kind of crying, a tiny discreet sniff, eyes welling, tears deftly wiped away with a folded handkerchief. The teaspoon trembled.

She was going to Australia. Just for a few days, back next week, and when Liz said, 'Lucky you! That sounds nice,' presuming a bikini and the Gold Coast, Irene shuddered and coffee granules spilt all over the bench and it turned out there was no kindly husband, no PTA, no soccer team. She was single like Liz, and her doctor had left for the UK and the new one would not prescribe the pill, not to single women, not unless you supplied the name of your fiancé and the date of the wedding and she couldn't do that because, well, it's complicated, very complicated ...

And Liz thought, as she made Irene a cup of coffee and Irene sniffed into her hanky, wasn't it always? Because tucked away in the deepest pocket in her brain was the man in the brown V-neck pullover, the back bedroom with flowery carpet and grubby eiderdown and the way he ushered her in, as if he were selling her insurance, which was what he did when he was not attending to girls like herself, girls who had been a wee bit naughty, and he smiled and winked, said, 'Now, you just make yourself comfortable, dear,' the towel spread on the carpet, 'Pop off those panties.' And she couldn't stop shaking, because nothing had prepared her for this, the clever girl, bright hope of the family. So he said, maybe she needed something to make her relax, crawling over her where she lay upon the towel and his breath smelled of aniseed balls and he grunted in and out, in and out, and she turned her face away, looking under the bed where she could see dustballs and a pile of newspapers and a discarded woollen sock and she wasn't clever, not in the least, she was a naughty girl and at last he quivered and it was over and he said he'd be right back, and there was some metallic banging about from the kitchen and a kettle coming to the boil and he returned with a brown rubber bag like a football and a long tube and she looked away quickly at the sock while he knelt, forcing it into her, filling her with soapy water and then she was standing, she was heavy, weighed down, sticky, dirty beyond belief, hardly able to breathe for the need to get out of this dim room and she was handing over the money, £75 in an envelope, her entire savings and some from the boy, Kevin, the captain of the first eleven, but not ready for this, not ready at all, but he'd found some money, too, and between them they'd tracked down the man in the brown pullover, and two days later it came away, all in a rush of blood and water and a tiny stick thing that floated in the lavatory bowl and it was all over. She was free to go on and change the world.

'You won't breathe a word, will you?' said Irene, her lips trembling. 'I mean, it's legal over there. It's at a clinic with proper medical staff, but I don't want to lose my job. He doesn't know, you see. He has no idea . . .'

No. Liz wouldn't breathe a word. She sits under the kowhai tree while Sally rides but he's gonna put a stop to all that, he's gonna slow her right down. One mornin' soon, she'll be weepin', yeah, she'll be weepin' . . .

Bullshit.

That's what it was. All of it. The rings and weddings, the babies born legitimate or illegitimate. The whole structure was built upon bullshit. Everything. This house, all the houses on Savage Street, all the houses across this city, across this country, were simply boxes, just as Germaine Greer said: boxes in which women laboured without pay in return for lifetime security. Boxes like the one containing the good Catholic family, tended by the good Catholic mother who cooked and cleaned, though sometimes she talked — though not in her husband's hearing — of going back to work, to nursing. And when she did, her face took on a look of such tender longing.

Bullshit. And no wonder the authorities up in Auckland had arrested Germaine for saying so and would have fined her had she not managed to flee the country first.

Sally rides and rides while Liz sits under the tree reading and thinking, how would it be? How would it be if in all the boxes in all the cities everyone could simply choose to live alone or with their lovers, without legal restraint or the force of custom? *Lovers who are free to go always come back, lovers who are free remain interesting . . .*

Out in the old stable they sing among all the mattresses, frayed and stained with living. But how would it be, thinks Liz from her place under the kowhai tree, if all up and down Savage Street, every chick, every bird in those rows of boxes, could simply spread her wings, and . . .

thirty-five

THE VERANDAH POST

SPRING 1974

...**totara. He** scrapes at the paint and he's sure of it. The verandah posts are totara heartwood. He draws his fingernail down the length of the post and there is that unmistakable red-gold glow, the grain straight and fine.

It is raining, a soft warm misty rain that soaks everything. Leaves hang heavy, water drips from spouting that is yet to be replaced and puddles on the path. Here on the verandah, however, the rain cannot penetrate, held back by the wisteria that winds in a thick tangle overhead. They have had long discussions concerning that wisteria. Should it be removed and replaced with a native climber?

'*Tecomanthe*,' he's said, as the expert who works at the Botanic Gardens, planting out a thousand polyanthus every year in the carpet beds around the fountain, clipping back the salvias in the gardens' pride, the long herbaceous border. '*Tecomanthe speciosa*,' he said.

The amazing plant. The sole survivor, discovered clinging to a cliff face in 1945 on a tiny island 50 kilometres out to sea. A cliff face so steep that even the goats had been deterred. But there it was, hanging on, roots set deep in the rock, with its beautiful glossy leaves. A tropical plant, belonging to the warm sweet north, hanging onto this storm-bashed outcrop. Bearing its clusters of creamy trumpet flowers, so narrow that they must surely have evolved to be pollinated by bats, though none were to be found anywhere on the island. Steve could barely find the words to explain it properly: the amazement of that survival, the careful labour of propagation, of cuttings and setting seed, until now it could be bought at any garden centre. *Tecomanthe speciosa*.

But Min demurred. She liked the wisteria, as she liked the camellias, the rampant rhododendrons, the towering canes of yellow banksia. They sat around the table discussing the fate of the wisteria as they spooned up one of her lumpy apple crumbles, standard fare on house nights when they met for discussion. Should they invest in an electric mower? Or continue to mow the grass with the ancient push mower? Or — Min's idea — forget about mowing entirely and have a wildflower meadow. (A 'meadow'? What was that exactly? 'Oh,' she said, gesturing vaguely. 'You just scatter some seeds.') How could they devise a fairer roster for television viewing? Was it right that everyone paid equal shares for the van's service and registration when some people cycled everywhere and used it rarely? And the wisteria: should it be replaced with a native climber? Should all the plants in the garden, other than vegetables of course, be indigenous species?

'*Tecomanthe*,' said Steve, but Min became emotional: she was pregnant and inclined to tears — and since all decisions had to be unanimous, the wisteria clung on, though as a compromise he had been able to plant *Tecomanthe*, too. Its dark leaves gleamed, a small and spindly thing as yet, bound for support to a post at the opposite end of the verandah. But give it time ...

Steve sits on the verandah step, smoking and scraping flaking paint as the rain pricks at the silence. He likes sitting out here, likes the business of rolling a joint, the precision of joining the papers, centring the thin strip of weed he has grown himself behind the silverbeet, from seed he has saved from year to year as he tries for the super plant with the biggest, fattest heads. He likes the rolling and licking, the little twist at the end, the fizz as it ignites and the long slow draw. He sits on the step watching the rain, the beauty of it, though you could never quite trust it now, could you?

Not as he had trusted the rain in childhood when it hammered against the corrugated-iron sleepout behind the house at Tuatapere. 'It's raining,' their mother used to say approvingly, when she came to take away the candle lest he and his brother burn the place down. 'A good night for sleeping!'

But now the rain is suspect, potential bearer of tiny particles, of plutonium and uranium and unguessable invisible plague. Raining down disease and deformity upon the green islands and wide blue reaches of the Pacific. Forty-six tests, until the boats sailed in, the navy frigate with the cabinet minister on board, the flotilla of smaller craft, yachts and fishing boats sailing right in there, into the test zone, daring the French to do their worst. When the call went out he had wanted to join them, to sail over the horizon, carrying the battle to the very heart, but he was hopeless on a boat. Couldn't swim, got seasick on a lilo only metres from shore.

The smoke curls up. He peels another strip of dry paint. It falls away like fuchsia bark, like the strips he and his brother used to make cigarettes, rolling great fat cylinders that made you cough and your eyes water. 'Hey! Look at me!' (Cough. Cough.) 'Look at me smoking!' The paint peels away from an expanse of perfect timber.

Totara. Probably cut from a forest on the peninsula. Cousin to the bleached remnants that litter the bare brown hillsides, ghost forests, white as bone, gaunt and leafless, the timber still bearing the mark of the saw, and left where they fell.

The timber is smooth beneath his hand, like bare flesh, and for some reason he is remembering Kaniere. The brief enthusiasm to leave the city behind entirely, for Lothlorien was just a stepping stone towards true communality, to the ohu, self-sustaining, a kind of kibbutz in the wilderness. They had driven over to the coast in the van, and there was a bit of land and it was beautiful. There was bush. A stream ran through. There were flat sites for building. But on the way back across the Main Divide, Steve had looked out the window as the landscape switched from west to east. The cloud lifted as the van rattled down from the pass, and the plains stretched ahead to the coast in the dry heat of a nor-west day, the temperature in the thirties, and they'd stopped by a river, a swimming hole among trees, and they had all stripped off and leapt in. The shock of icy water over sweating skin, the thrash of Liz's long bare legs as she executed a neat duck dive, Mack whooping and showing off as usual, jumping from the tallest rock, Min squealing on the edge with her arms clasped across her breasts, Pete swimming up and down with a long even stroke, and himself, floating on his back, looking up at a ring of trees and the steep green hills rising all around dense with birdsong and the river flowing clean and clear from the mountains to the eastern plains, beautiful, eternal. His country.

He strokes the timber. There is something within it. A curve. A thigh. A knee, flexed. It is waiting there, behind all that flaking paint. The house is taking no notice. At the other end of the verandah in the big room, Liz is having one of her women's meetings: wimmin, he corrects himself, for she has become insistent about such things. Wimmin, not woman or women. No hint of the patriarchy. Ms, not Mrs or Miss. People, not man or mankind. She is in there with the wimmin in the wimmin's group, reading their wimmin's books, discussing their wimmin's issues. The windows are firmly shut. There is a quiet buzz of conversation, the occasional bark of laughter.

Out the back, somewhere in the workshop, he has the proper tools. It's a cluttered place to the uninitiated eye, filled with all the things he keeps because they might come in handy: bits of copper piping, parts from assorted vehicles, bikes and machines, lengths of timber, ancient tools, a spade, a mattock, rake and pitchfork, stuff that had been lying around when they moved in, the timber grips worn silky smooth by someone else's hand. He had sharpened and oiled and hung them alongside his own tools: the saws and hammers, screwdrivers and wrenches, the old cocoa tins that held his collection of screws, nails, bolts and washers.

Other people are less particular. A couple of paint trays have been left on the floor, covered in dry paint and containing rollers that have set rock hard, beyond reclamation. Ordinarily this would have caused a surge of irritation and a flicker of longing for his own private shed where his own tools would stay where he had left them. But today is not the time for bad temper. Today, he is in search of the gouger. A V-shaped gouger. And a curved gouger and a couple of narrow-headed chisels and a wooden mallet, carving tools he had picked up years ago, wrapped in a piece of oilcloth in a second-hand yard in Kaiapoi, and never used. Who had time for carving when there were walls to demolish, doors to be rehung, window sashes to repair. And yes, there it was: right at the back of the shelf, the little bundle in its swaddling of grimy oilcloth.

The wimmin talk quietly behind doors firmly shut. He likes that. He wants silence and no interruption while the idea sits fresh within him.

The figure waits within the post: a man, legs flexed, standing upon a monstrous mushroom cloud with jaws and teeth, open and snapping as it is forced down by the weight of the man's big square feet. On his shoulders, a woman, hands splayed over her belly, and on her shoulder, a child, a boy, and on his shoulders, a seabird. He can see them all standing one upon the other, awaiting the tap of his chisel for their release.

He has never carved anything before. At school he had done woodwork: made a little bookshelf for his mother for Christmas, though she never read. Not with four kids and full-time at the Four Square and a husband who had never quite recovered from service in the islands, stooped and pale. When she sat down in the evening it was with the phone in one hand for a long inconsequential chat with her sister in Owaka while her feet soaked up to the ankles in a basin of hot water and baking soda.

She had nevertheless received the bookshelf with every appearance of delight. 'Oh, Stevie! That's beautiful!' And put it on the sideboard with a copy of the *Book of Mormon* she had bought one afternoon from a couple of young men who had come to the door. Americans, and so far from home, from their own people. She had felt sorry for them, in their funny suits, biking around a strange land.

The bookshelf had been a success but woodwork bored him. The master was a bully, one of those plump men you might have mistaken for good-humoured, when his jokes were always at the expense of those he calculated he could bully with impunity. Steve, lacking a forceful father, lacking any older brothers to defend him, was fair game. 'Hey, Hori,' he'd say, catching him staring out the window where the beautiful day waited, hours away at the end of a long afternoon. 'Hey, dreamboat! Catch!' Flinging the blackboard duster unless Steve could snap to attention and grab before it landed painfully on his skull.

In his last year, Steve finally objected. 'Don't call me Hori,' he said. 'I'm not Maori, I'm fucking Spanish. All right?' Campbell stood looking at him, little piggy eyes blank behind the thick lenses, fat mouth opening and closing soundlessly. For a split second, Steve had him on the back foot. Then he recovered. 'All right, Diego,' he said. 'You're on report for language. Now off you go.'

And that was the end of woodwork.

He didn't tell his mother this. Of course not. He hadn't told her anything that really mattered since he was ten years old. It wasn't that he didn't trust her, but there was little time for talk. 'How's your day been?' she'd ask, walking in the door as they milled about making Marmite sandwiches, starving. 'Tina, get your bag off the floor. Someone will trip. Oh God, we're out of milk. Who drank all the milk?' Much easier just to grunt, take a sandwich and beat a retreat to the top bunk in the sleepout. He had told his mother about Campbell only a year ago when he was making one of his infrequent trips south at Christmas. For some reason they were talking about school. That was the part of his life of which she had some understanding: the people he knew, names she recognised, some sense of who he was. She knew nothing of who he had become, where he lived now, how he lived now. School was their common ground.

'Campbell was such a bastard,' he said. 'He had names for everyone. I was Hori. Stupid prick. I wasn't even Maori.'

'Well, actually you are,' said his mother, surprisingly. 'Or at least a bit of you is. My mum's family came from up on the East Coast.'

'So why did you tell us we were Spanish?' said Steve, puzzled.

'Because you're Spanish, too,' said his mother, as if none of this mattered. 'And a bit Welsh on your father's side. And a bit Irish. There's even some Chinese in there. You're a bitzer, Stevie. We all are. Ask Auntie Ga. She knows all that stuff. Now give us a hand with the spuds, will you? You've got me running late.'

A bitzer. One bit coming ashore in hob-nailed boots while another bit watched and waited, wrapped in a dogskin cloak. One bit shouldering a gun, carving off his piece of land, while the other bit swapped taiaha for musket, learning fast, fighting to retain it. One bit coming in search of a golden fortune, while another bit fled famine while another bit breathed in a new plague.

The chisel fits neatly in his hand. A bird is singing in the tangled garden. A grey warbler racing up and down the scale. Riroriro.

He is learning birds as he has been learning plants: riroriro in a kowhai. And another bird chiming, a single repeated note, from the lacebark. Korimako in a houhere. He is making a start on learning where he is, who he is.

He begins the work of uncovering the people who stand poised on top of a cloud. The people of these green islands to whom the wide blue sea has never been a barrier but rather a means of connection. The sea which all the various bits of himself have had to cross to come together at last right here. The seeds that have blown in on the wind and taken root here. And now exist within his skin. On this rainy afternoon.

He taps at the chisel and it leaves a clean bite. He has no idea how this will go. But the post feels solid enough, large enough to accommodate all the little people who wait there, holding up the verandah roof and keeping out the rain.

He taps again and the chisel begins to glide, following the ...

thirty-six
THE RIVER
SPRING 1976

Nothing happens.

Rain falls. The sweet spring rain, dimpling the surface.

She sways in her place by the bank, one long silvery muscled thing, flexing against the current.

Within the recesses of her body, one million eggs, as yet unformed.

Tiny specks in the dark, and a whole lifetime before they are ready for release.

thirty-seven
THE BONFIRE
SPRING 1978

...**surveys perfection.** They have built a bonfire on the lawn by the vegetable garden, burning all the timber stripped from the stable when it was converted into living space. *Their* living space, the one she need share only with Mack and Sunny, for the single room, though ample, had not been large enough for two adults and a toddler. Not a noisy toddler who could waken the entire house at 3 a.m., roaring for Bankie, his baby blanket dwindled to a chewed ribbon with an endless capacity for disappearance down the back of a chair or into the clutter at the back of the van. They had stripped out the stable, relined it with gib and plywood offcuts, added a couple of recycled windows. Space for Sunny to roar. Space, when Zoe was born, for all of them. Perfection.

Sunny is running about the garden now with the other kids who have come to the party. Liz's friend Dee's daughter squeals after them, a small witch in a pointed black hat and gumboots because Dee is American and assumes this is Halloween. And Sunny's friend Manu, whose mother organised the roster for the playgroup sessions that took over the backyard three mornings a week. She can hear his thin high wailing. Min privately thinks Manu is a bit of a sook, too readily driven to tears, though she would never hint at such a thing to his mother, who is trying to eliminate gender bias and gave him a doll for his third birthday. Sunny cut off all its hair one afternoon in a frenzied attack with the dressmaking scissors, then hacked his own hair and Manu's for good measure.

Sweet and bald, the doll sprawls face-down on the step while the children rush about in the twilight, waving sparklers in this odd amalgam of Guy Fawkes with a dab of Halloween, though Min had called it, on the invitations, Beltane. The Celtic festival of spring when the cows returned to summer pastures. ('What are you going to do?' said Mack. 'Release the chickens?') Beltane, when the cows were driven between great fires to render them safe from harm and people daubed ashes from the fire upon their own foreheads. Except, of course, the Celts lit their fires on 1 May and here it is upside down as usual so they have lit their Beltane fire on the first day of November. With sparklers. And rockets veering off from a milk bottle stuck in the lawn to burst as stars above the trees, and Egmont and Flower Pot and Vesuvius exploding in fountains of light and startling bangs that make the children squeal and block their ears. But now, the fireworks over, they race about smudged in ash while the adults sit around the sacred fire on upturned beer crates. Mack is playing his guitar and there's the sound of people coming and going through the french doors onto the verandah and the clatter of plates as someone gets on with clearing away the remains of the feast. A shoulder of mutton spit-roasted by Pete's friend Theo, who is Greek and morphed in an eyeblink from lecturer in mathematics to Samian peasant, efficiently setting up a spit over the fire, then patiently turning and basting with branches of rosemary dipped in oil until the meat fell from the bone. A salad of fresh spring herbs from the garden. A panful of kidney bean lasagne from a recipe in *The Moosewood Cookbook* for the vegetarians.

And now she stands looking down on it all from the turret, Zoe sleeping on her shoulder, her face pressed against her mother's neck. Min sways to and fro, soothing her, though she sleeps well. A dream child after Sunny. Calm and placid. Min holds her close and looks down at the festival of rebirth. She always does this: imagines a party, a feast. Spends hours on its preparation, then finds herself overwhelmed by its reality. She suddenly needs desperately to retreat and contemplate it all, like an outsider, an uninvolved stranger. She stands up here in the room she had painted when they first moved in with swags of flowers, poppies and daisies crudely executed — she's no artist — in primary colours: red, yellow, around each arched window and over the dado, which she painted a dark midnight blue. Perfection.

The room is small and largely taken up by her loom, though she has not used that in some time. Nor the spinning wheel. Handwoven curtains were lovely, but they took ages. And Sunny refused to wear his homespun jersey, though it was warm and so permeated with lanolin that it was virtually rainproof. 'Itchy!' he said, clawing at the lumpy neck. Even the tractor she had knitted on the front in contrasting wool dyed with onion skins could not persuade him. '*No*!' he yelled if she so much as suggested it. He preferred to run naked, even on the coldest days, as he was now, whooping in the dark, a small excited savage. If Doctor Spock was correct and every child repeated the stages of human evolution from single cell to womb fish to mammal on all fours to primate, Sunny had reached the Neanderthal phase. Though the good doctor might have got that wrong, as he may also have been mistaken in suggesting that children were naturally friendly and reasonable, not to mention romantically attached to their mothers. Whenever Sunny screamed and kicked, she wondered if Spock and Freud had the slightest idea.

Nevertheless, looking down at it all, this party, this festival of rebirth and new beginnings, she feels satisfaction. This, she thinks, is how we are meant to be, how we are meant to live. Happy people gathered about a fire, while Mack picks lazily at his guitar and Theo dismantles the spit. The mutton had been delicious, despite its dubious provenance.

It had been a gift from Ronnie Smaill, one of her cases. Ronnie was small and wizened and in possession of a file several inches thick, as were his mum and dad over at Pines Beach, as were his sons, two spotty bantam youths with a gathering record of petty thievery, car conversion and repeat appearances before the Children's Court, as were his daughters, big placid girls of fourteen and fifteen, one hugely pregnant, possibly by Ronnie himself. 'Talk to my dad,' said Leanne, when Min asked who the father was, then laughed when she saw Min pick up her pen to make a note: NFF. Note For File. 'Just having you on, Miss. He couldn't get it up if he tried, eh, Krystal?'

'Nah,' said Krystal, who was also, Min noticed suddenly, suspiciously rotund. 'Stupid bugger,' before they both slumped back on the couch for another episode of *The Love Boat*. White uniforms, romance beneath a tropic moon.

Ronnie was out the back and, despite his chronic and debilitating backache, making a reasonable job of butchering a sheep. Blood on the ground, and flies. Blood on his hands and a boning knife. 'Here you go, nursie,' he said. 'Have a bit of meat', handing her a bloody newspaper parcel. It did not seem like the time to raise the question of possible incest. The parcel leaked into the carpet of the departmental Corolla all the long drive back to the city.

It was easy to feel out of your depth with Ronnie and his wayward offspring, with the foster child who, uplifted from one kind of chaos in Bromley and placed in chilly foster care on a North Canterbury farm, simply walked home. Made her way back down the long roads, hiding in ditches and hedges, returning like a stray kitten to what was known, however precarious. So difficult to know if you had perhaps missed something: not noticed the suspicious stillness of the baby in its cot, presuming sleep when the reality could be injury trauma.

'Ah, good!' said the jolly, authoritative woman who had interviewed her for the job, 'BA in English.' Min had briefly considered anthropology, which was new and exciting, until a weekend field trip spent excavating a pa site on an exposed headland on Banks Peninsula put her off. She knelt with the other students in a freezing southerly chipping away with her trowel at compacted earth, uncovering post holes, middens and the rings of charcoal left by cooking fires. At night the wind howled around their tent, threatening to drag them all out into the Southern Ocean. English seemed a more kindly, more comfortable option, which left her, on graduation, with a good knowledge of the Romantic poets and an ability to read Anglo-Saxon. This did not seem to be any impediment to acceptance for the job. Nor was there any training required. She would simply learn as she went along.

'At least you'll be able to write a literate report!' said the cheerful woman.

This was true. She could write about Ronnie and the knife and the murdered, probably stolen, sheep, and the pregnant daughters.

About the chilly foster mother, prepared to take a baby, so long as it was not 'a baby of colour'.

About the desperate couple wanting a little girl, who show her the nursery with its pile of folded nappies and the freshly painted walls with the frieze of little yellow ducks. But the woman has twice been hospitalised for depression so their chances are virtually non-existent.

About the single mothers who must all, no matter how well educated, no matter how comfortably middle class, be visited to check on the baby's welfare in this very unorthodox situation.

About the women who are receiving welfare but there has been the phone call, the careful voice at the end of the line: 'Look, I know this isn't really any of my business, but I thought you should know that ...' The voice of the sneak. The complacent nark. Though of course she has to follow up. She has to drive out early, at 7 a.m., or late, after 8 p.m., she has to knock at the door, enter the house, sight for herself the double bed, take notes concerning the male boarder who has been staying for the past ten months. NFF. Notes For File. The whole imperfect muddle.

But here, in this garden, this house, she has got it right. The children tumble about. Mack is no longer playing his guitar. He has moved back from the fire, which is burning down now, within a ring of blackened earth and charcoal. He is standing in the shadows by the vegetable garden, talking to Helen, who moved into Liz's room when she moved out to live with Dee. He is leaning down to hear what she is saying, he is placing his hand lightly on her hip. She is looking up at him, laughing. Min stands and watches but she refuses to take note.

Not NFF.

She will not let this tiny detail spoil perfection, for this is what humanity aspires to, isn't it? In its domestic phase. We choose a piece of land, we make a home upon it, we gather those we love about us, we raise our children there, we live and die there, we imbue this particular piece of land with spirit and special power. Generation after generation. And when the men in helmets turn up, rank upon rank, pouring from the buses to evict, to tear down, to burn, it is why people fight back. They resist. They sit down upon that piece of land, and refuse to be moved. They battle for its possession in the courts. They hang on, generation after generation, to the beloved land.

And when they go, as everyone must go eventually, they leave behind the marks of their living: post holes, a midden, a ring of blackened earth, the evidence of fire ...

thirty-eight
THE RIVER
SPRING 1980

Nothing happens.

Leaves burst from the bud. The river colours red as fire at sunset.

She occupies her place beneath the bank, fending off all intruders.
Kokopu. Koura.

The old eighty-million-year adversaries. And trout, too.
Those snappy foreigners.

She drives them off.

This part of the river is hers.

Hers alone.

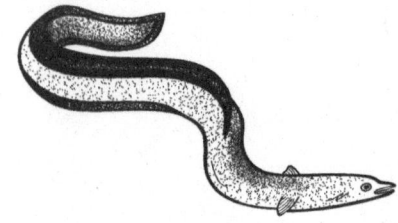

thirty-nine
THE STAIN
SPRING 1982

... **on floorboards** they had spent hours cleaning when they first moved in, lifting metres of ancient carpet and tiny tacks, then sanding and polishing with the mixture of tung oil, spirits and varnish that everyone seemed to think more natural and therefore preferable to polyurethane. And over the boards, unfaded, that wide red stain ...

Mack had been painting a banner.

DAY OF RA he had managed in the red enamel they had used to paint the front door. It was tricky getting the letters even on unframed white cotton. Min had cut the last of the bedsheets in half and stitched it to form a banner long enough to stretch over the whole width of the column. Half a dozen people would march abreast, holding it before them.

He had been planning to add GE. DAY OF RAGE.

And then, if he had left enough room, REMEMBER BIKO, but before he could do that, Sunny had cannoned into him, careless as usual, and knocked over the can. Crimson paint spilled over the banner and pooled on the floor. Little bugger.

Not that anyone in this room was likely to forget Biko. Peter Gabriel was reminding them for at least the twentieth time that morning. They hummed in unison, they called back to him 'Biko! Biko!' from this room where they knelt on the floor making their signs. New signs for a new action because the cops waded in every time, hitting and smashing, so that every time, they had to start again. Get some more cardboard. Rip up another sheet.

It was just as well Min had insisted on sheets. Helen never bothered. She simply laid her sleeping bag on the floor and slept peacefully, wearing nothing but the woolly hat she had bought when she was climbing in Peru. Min, however, preferred sheets. She made them herself, wrestling billowing white cotton like sails through the needle of her machine. It was because of the sparks. When they had first slept together in the flat on Riccarton Road, her body had unleashed an impressive display of sparks.

'Sorry,' she said, as the bedclothes crackled and small shocks flashed between their naked bodies. 'It's the polyester.'

The original electric woman.

So on their shared bed they had white cotton sheets, and in the winter of '81 that proved unexpectedly useful.

Crimson paint all over his jeans. Ruined. He had made a grab for his son who wriggled and kicked, a big boy now and hard to hold. This was the point at which Min would have knelt for a long discussion at child's eye level about the necessity for taking greater care. She would then consider the ruined banner and come up with a solution. She was good at signs, was printing HALT ALL RACIST TOURS on a piece of ply, every letter perfectly formed, perfectly spaced. She would look on the bright side. 'It's not so bad,' she'd say. 'In fact, I quite like it. It looks like blood. Just write round it.'

Like blood from a deep wound. The kind of blood a man might leave who has been beaten, manacled to a window grille, tossed naked and dying into a Land Rover to be taken, when it was already too late, to a hospital. *Di laat my koud*, that Afrikaaner had said. His death leaves me cold.

No. They would not forget Biko. The sun poured through the window, and they painted their signs while every few minutes the whole house shimmied. The street theatre troupe were practising in the front room, chanting and stamping in unison, preparing a performance involving giant masks. Muldoon leered in papier mâché, his stupid lop-sided smirk. He, like the long banner, was a repeat. The first mask had been wrecked as they tried to penetrate the wire round Lancaster Park on the day of the first test, 22 July, the Day of Shame. There was a skinny guy, not an officer but a volunteer, who was standing alongside the cops, holding onto an excitable German Shepherd, and in the scuffle that ensued, the mask had been torn to pieces. But Helen, who taught primary school and was adept at papier mâché, had made another, along with a peace dove with flapping white wings. Another sheet. They had gone through a lot of sheets that winter.

The winter of banners and marches and Red Squad and Blue Squad, all lined up so pleased with themselves in their riot gear. Kiwi plods playing dress-up, fancying themselves as looking at last like real cops, like the ones in movies, if only they could swap that baton for a gun in a bulging holster. ('Is that a baton in your pocket?' Liz had asked, smiling sweetly as the two tribes stood face to face, eyeball to eyeball outside Lancaster Park. 'Or are you just pleased to see me?' Which was gutsy but rash. The cop had come after her when the fighting started and dragged her in a painful headlock to the wagon.)

Mack had always doubted the street theatre.

'It's a distraction,' he said. 'What we need to focus on right now is strategy.'

The big room had been packed, people sitting on the floor, perched on the window seat, gathered for another planning meeting. There were a lot of meetings that winter, in rooms and halls or over at the marae on Springfield Road.

'We need to concentrate all our energy on tactics. How do we mobilise as many people as possible? Then how do we deploy them once they are gathered in the city centre for maximum impact? How can we outflank the enemy, take them by surprise, penetrate their defences?'

'I'd prefer it if we dispensed with the militaristic talk,' said Bradley Bliss, who had taken over Steve's old room and never quite recovered from a first in philosophy. He always preferred talk to action. Endless talk. 'Surely the first requirement is to define our primary objective here? Is it to stop a rugby game, or is rugby just one aspect, a metaphor if you like, for a wider and more complex debate concerning racism? Is our role therefore not to obstruct but to educate, to inform? And if so, is aggression the best way to influence public opinion? Or do we follow Mandela, Gandhi, Te Whiti, and engage in peaceful, non-violent demonstration?'

'Yeah,' said Mack. 'And while you're sitting around singing, kids get shot in Soweto.'

But no one was listening.

Someone up the back was saying, 'Hey, how about we march in single file all the way through the city?'

There was enthusiasm for that. 'In total silence,' said someone. 'They won't expect silence. They'll be expecting "Amand-la" and "one two three four we don't want your racist tour" and all that. Silence would be really effective.'

'And we could march at night,' said Min. 'With candles.' She could see it: the long line winding through the streets like some medieval procession, like pilgrims.

Theatre. They always got hooked on theatre, when it wasn't theatre. It was war.

'But first we need to get the numbers,' said Mack. When they had started all this in February, there had been only a hundred seated in Lancaster Park singing 'We Shall Overcome'. Mack could not stand 'We Shall Overcome', its wavery hope of overcoming something, somewhere, someday, when there on the rugby ground it was all so very clear.

This was not like the protests against Vietnam or nuclear weaponry, where the real targets existed at a distance, in Washington or Paris. In this battle, the enemy had a face. It was that groundsman in Stubbies and sunglasses, giving the fingers, the man outside the RSA as they marched past who flung a beer can, a man who looked exactly like Mack's Uncle Edward. In fact, the enemy was Uncle Edward, all the uncles: mainstays of the district, members of Federated Farmers, men like Mack's own father, who erupted onto the porch when Mack arrived for his mother's birthday and said, 'Get out of my house and don't bloody come back.' While his mother hovered in the hallway saying, 'Oh, for goodness' sake, don't be ridiculous! Why are you all getting so worked up over a stupid game?'

Except it wasn't a stupid game, was it? It was war. On the one side, the privileged son who had been given everything on a plate, never proved himself at Cassino or Alamein — not that Mack's father had either, flat-footed member of the Culverden Home Guard, though he marched anyway on Anzac Day, sporting his red poppy. His father was on the other side, along with the uncles and the cousins who had stayed in the district and could recite names and scores and notable All Black victories all the way back to the Invincibles. That winter of banners and marches was just another episode in the eternal war between two tribes, the war that began in the playground where Mack had learned, as everybody had to learn, which side he belonged to: was he with the side that got what it wanted by force and brutal alliance, or was he on the other side, among the snobs and the loners and the brainy kids who had to figure out other means of survival? This winter of dissent was just another bubbling up of that toxic sludge of resentment and mutual dislike that lurked forever just below this country's gleaming surface. Long hair versus short hair, right versus left, Nat versus Commie, artyfarty versus pig. You had to choose your tribe.

And all of it was tangled with a brilliant winter afternoon and a kid racing down the paddock, slippery ball tucked under his arm, flying away from the pack, the line clearly within his sights, keeping his head down as he has been instructed, while at the edge of hearing there's his dad yelling 'Go, boy, go!' And he's running and no one can catch him, and he's over, he's skidding face-down through the mud. And then there's the ride home in the truck, his knees grazed and stinging a bit, but his dad has bought fish and chips and they're dipping into the newspaper parcel as the truck skids homeward along a white gravel road, held steady between the ruts by his dad's big callused hands, and the mountains are tipped with snow as the sun sets and a plume of golden dust rises behind them like the clouds behind the chariots of gods.

But now it was war and what was needed was determined leadership. Effective alliances must be established with Students Against the Tour, with the unions, with the meatworkers and wharfies. 'That's not as straightforward as it sounds,' said Bradley, who had ditched his PhD for work on the wharves and was therefore expert on all things union-related. 'It's not textbook class theory over there, you know, not when you're actually in amongst it. They might not be exactly Friends of South Africa, but there would be plenty who would come up with some variant of keeping politics out of sport.'

To which the counter-argument was that it was not HART that had introduced politics into sport, but the whole system of apartheid, along with the Rugby Union and its segregated teams and Muldoon himself provoking unrest and anyway, in this country, rugby *was* political and always had been. But this was not the time for the well-rehearsed argument. It was time for *action*.

And eventually, the arguing came to an end and there was action: a winter afternoon, and ten thousand, fifteen thousand, converged upon the Square. Split into four streams, they flowed steadily through the city. Mack marched at the head of one column, wearing his motorcycle helmet for protection from bottles and batons, holding the blood-stained banner. The column wound its way around the grid of streets: families with kids in pushchairs, Maori activists in black leather, the church groups with placards quoting brotherhood, the unionists and all the thousands of others who were not convinced that politics could ever be separated from sport. And the bloody street theatre group with the Muldoon mask. Past his old school where the boys leaned from the windows and catcalled, past the RSA where the uncle-men spat and yelled. On to the wire cordons and the shouting and mayhem and the roar of blood pounding in his ears as he took them all on at last and the law fought back with armlock, arrest, the police van and the formalities of conviction.

A year later, in another spring, the roar is still in his ears. It will never quite disappear. And the stain too, on the polished floorboards, faded but visible. Marking the spot where he had held his son by the arm and smacked him hard for being careless. And left his mark, the outline of his hand, spreading crimson on his son's bare . . .

forty
THE DRAWING PINS
SPRING 1984

'... can't believe he's insisting on sale,' says Min, dumping a copy of *The Whole Earth Catalogue* in a cardboard box that had once held New Zealand apples. 'Is this yours? *The Electric Kool-Aid Acid Test?*'

'Mack's,' says Pete. It was a long time ago and truth to tell he can't remember, but Mack had liked that sort of stuff. *Gravity's Rainbow*, *Slaughterhouse Five*, books about drug-fuelled road trips or war, and none of them real. Pete didn't see the point.

Min tosses it into a rubbish bag with the others destined for the second-hand shop. 'If he wanted it, he should have taken it. I can't believe he's being so selfish.'

'Well, I guess it's pretty much his property,' says Pete, sorting through a pile of papers, newsletters and old copies of *The Savage* that had been stored in the big hall cupboard. He'd forgotten about that: the community newspaper they had produced for a few months in 1972. Somewhere among all this stuff, in this house, there must be the artwork he left behind when he made his bid for freedom back in 1979: posters he had designed for concerts and an outdoor production of *Antigone*, which had been pinned up in the dark hallway alongside the Cubans: Fidel screenprinted among flowers, Che in vivid pink and blue, or spilling rainbows from the star on his beret, Nixon as a blue alien, grinning his shark's teeth smile, the kaleidoscope swirl of arrows designed to draw the people to the central square to celebrate the anniversary of the revolution: Todos a la Plaza! Brilliant posters as vividly self-assured as tropical birds. He had left them all behind that night, packed and fled, knowing if he didn't go that very instant, if he waited only a few hours, until morning, he would be lost. Some of the drawing pins were still embedded on the wall, but of the posters themselves, there was no sign.

'But you had a share,' says Min. 'And I did, too. And Liz and Steve. We all had shares.'

She is looking small and peevish and not in a mood for reason.

'But Mack had more,' says Pete. 'By far. He put in the most back in the day. It's not his fault the place is worth so much more than when we all chipped in together and now you can't afford to buy him out.'

He'd had no idea house prices here had risen so much: $110,000!

'But I found it,' says Min. 'It was my idea. I found it and told the rest of you about it. And everyone worked to make the place habitable. We all put in hours and hours of labour. Steve did all that carpentry and we painted and did the floors. Shouldn't that be worth something? We each put in everything we could afford in time and money.'

'And we've all benefited from that,' says Pete. He has no idea why he is springing to Mack's defence here, not after what happened. Some things said and done you don't forget. Some people you simply can't forgive. But here he is, arguing Mack's corner with Min, who probably deserves his sympathy. He is remembering that she had always irritated him, with her vagueness and romantic optimism. He had always had to repress the urge to pinprick her enthusiasms. Or maybe it's just that he has forgiven Mack? Maybe he really has moved on? Become an incredibly kind and tolerant human being?

'Look, it's nothing personal. It's just maths. Mack put in well over half, so he's entitled to over half. You should have increased your share once you started work.'

'I should have done a lot of things,' says Min. 'I shouldn't have got pregnant or, better yet, avoided Mack in the first place. There was just something about the guitar, the blues, the goatskin coat.

Do you remember the coat? It stank but it looked so cool...'

Pete remembers the coat, the blues.

'You could look at it this way,' he says, becoming even more extreme and why is he doing this? Does he dislike her so very much? 'You could say that Mack has actually been very reasonable. He has left a substantial amount of money in this place for years and you have been able to continue living here rent-free.'

'Raising his children,' says Min. (Why is Pete always so eager to see both sides of a question? Why is he always so bloody reasonable? No wonder he had driven Mack mad.)

'Well, yes,' says Pete. 'But you've been earning.'

'Not as much as Mack,' says Min. 'Not since he started at McClintocks.'

And went over to the other side. Got a job with his uncle. Pete has seen Mack just once since he got back from Melbourne, walking down Colombo Street with a tall blonde. He barely recognised him. Long curls shorn, sleek suit, the woman leggy with big hair and shoulder pads. They looked like the sort they called 'a power couple', the kind who would feature on the social pages raising a glass at a fundraiser or gallery opening in this deadly little village. McClintock. He has seen the name repeatedly on hoardings attached to demolition sites around the central city where some old house or rundown pub was being cleared to make way for development. McClintock Property. Pete watched them walk by with a momentary pang: Mack had filled out, but there was still that easy loping stride, that air of confident entitlement that had always drawn him, made him hang about in the cold room in this ghastly house far longer than he should have done, before Mack turned, the way he could, that icy flick of the knife, the snake-bite flash of revulsion, and Pete had known it was time to quit, to take his broken heart elsewhere. Should have done it years earlier. Seeing Mack, though, was a shock.

'He's loaded,' says Min. 'He doesn't have to toss me and the kids out on the street.' And the image rises unbidden: herself trailing to the supermarket in shabby trackies, alone in a desolate flat with a flagon of cheap sherry, become one of her own clients, NFF.

'Don't be so dramatic,' says Pete. 'He's not tossing you anywhere. He just wants his money out and that's fair enough.'

'Do you know, he wanted to pull it down!' says Min. 'Buy us all out and pull it down! He showed me the plans. He thought I'd be impressed. Hideous townhouses with angled rooflines and a rooftop terrace, so you could stand up there, and see over the trees to the Port Hills. With a courtyard in the middle instead of a garden, for parking. Can you imagine? He kept talking about how it was such "a great location". He actually called the house a "property". A "property" in a "great location". He never used to talk like that.'

'But you put a stop to that,' says Pete. Min's anger is exhausting. He longs suddenly for Thanh, for his quiet unruffled calm. He's been here only a week and already cannot wait to leave. Sign the papers, find his artwork, get back on that plane to Melbourne.

Min drags a carton off to add to the heap in the hall. 'Yes,' she says. 'I did. I wasn't going to let him do the standard McClintock thing: pulling down beautiful old buildings to make way for another tacky concrete monstrosity.'

'Not all new buildings are tacky,' says Pete. 'We've done interiors in some amazing new-builds. And just because something is old doesn't mean it's automatically worth saving.'

'But it's our history!' says Min.

'Well, yes,' says Pete. 'But modern buildings will be history, too, someday. What about the Guggenheim in New York? The Pompidou Centre?'

'Is that the one with the pipes outside?' says Min. 'It looks horrible.'

'It's not,' says Pete. 'It's fantastic. We visited it last year.'

'Lucky you,' says Min. She had never travelled, had stayed anchored to this tiny patch of the planet, to this house in this suffocating little country, while others had come and gone, living here for a time, then moving on.

He tries for local reference. 'The town hall?'

'McClintocks don't build art,' says Min. 'They slap up bog-standard tower blocks and Mack used to love old buildings. He's changed.'

'Well, he's gone,' says Pete. 'And don't fret. Plenty more fish in the sea.'

'I know,' says Min. 'And I'm not fretting. He picks his nose when he thinks no one's looking and there's that revolting outie.'

Pete remembers the outie. Mack's belly button. He remembers the flat on Riccarton Road, the two of them flying on the Triumph on narrow tarmac, heading north to some demonstration. What was it? Agnew? *Truxtun*? He can't remember. What he remembers is the road, the bike, sleeping rough under some pine trees near Kaikoura, the best, the golden time. He remembers the outie. The single flaw on that long lean body, stretched beneath the stars. But now is probably not the time to mention that.

'The thing is, I just don't want to leave this place,' says Min, suddenly dissolving into tears. He'd forgotten how readily she cried. Her nose goes all pink and squashy. 'The kids love it here.'

Sunny is an unappealing little thug who appears to have broken every single window in the conservatory, and Zoe whines.

'They'll survive,' says Pete. 'You'll survive.'

She dabs at her nose with a handkerchief dragged from her sleeve. Disgusting habit. He had forgotten about handkerchiefs: surely everyone uses tissues these days?

'It feels like the end of a dream,' she says. 'All of us living together, sharing resources . . .'

'Arguing over the petrol log for the van,' says Pete. 'And the roster for the TV and hogging the bathroom and not washing the dishes, driving each other mad . . .'

'I know,' says Min, who will not be comforted. 'But it was an attempt to live differently, wasn't it? And it was always interesting. So much better than being parked in the suburbs with fences on all sides, not knowing your neighbours.'

The bitter woman from next door in Brunswick Street who had regarded Thanh with eyes like razors, the quiet man who died in the downstairs flat and wasn't found until the flies swarmed at the windows . . .

'Neighbours can be very overrated,' says Pete. 'Anyway, that was then, this is now. Time to strike out on your own, Minnie. You'll be fine.'

Min sniffs hugely. 'I wonder who will buy it?' she says, looking round at the house with its open windows, its vegetable garden in its higgledy-piggledy selection of reclaimed railway sleepers, car tyres and plastic containers, its compost bins and the old clawfoot bath they had dragged out, rusted beyond repair, and filled with a noisome broth of seaweed and manure. Everything had found a purpose, nothing had been discarded. Under the kowhai the beehive buzzes with its dancing horde, creatures of mystery producing the honey from which she makes a head-splitting mead using a recipe supposedly dating from the Vikings. Even the weeds had their purpose: nettles purify the blood, dandelions, and chickweed and cleavers.

Weeds and clutter, thinks Pete. And nasty little bees that must be given a wide berth. How did he ever stand it?

He shivers. He's felt cold for days now, his head aches and he is so very very tired. He could lie down right now, right here, on the floor.

He stands with a carton in his arms. Sways. Falls heavily against the cupboard.

'Whoops,' he says. 'Sorry, Min. Wrecking the place.'

Min doesn't look up. 'Doesn't matter,' she says, tossing a copy of *Backyard Farming* into a bag. 'Someone else's problem now.' She holds up a copy of *Walden*. 'And this?'

Min sorts books.

Pete makes plans.

His share of $110,000, not a lot, but it will help. The flat in Prahan is inching closer and closer. The place he will buy with Thanh, who has come back to him after all from LA and is at this very moment waiting for him back home.

And the whole lovely future stretches ahead, the future they will enter together ...

forty-one

THE RIVER

SPRING 1986

Something happens.

Death comes as a narrow beam of light, bent to a sharp angle as it hits the surface of the water. The light seeks her out while the cold tip of a wire gaff sneaks down and sidles around her, feeling for a grip.

She is lifted, thrashing in panic, onto the bank, into the raw night air.

She writhes on hard earth, her skin oozing the thick slime of terror.

She slips from their grasp and falls back into the merciful water, surges out into the dark current beyond the light.

And after some time, she returns. Takes up her accustomed place.

But more cautiously.

forty-two

THE INVESTMENT

SPRING 1988

...their salvation.

They had been living at her place, a compact Heartwood crammed onto a subdivided section in St Albans: Stephie and Ben and Paul, and on alternating weekends Paul's son and two tall fair and haughty daughters. The house was resolutely plain, three tiny bedrooms, narrow galley kitchen, living/dining, single bathroom containing the only toilet.

When Stephie bought it, it had fitted her exactly. Then, she had wanted nothing but to curl up in the smallest of spaces, and stop. Stop thinking. Stop talking. Stop listening to the commiserations of others, however well-meaning. Stop breathing. Step away from time, from the split second when the snow cracked under his feet. He gave a tiny gasp, his mate said, and that was it. No scream. Nothing. Gone. His body had never been recovered. It lies there still, amid inaccessible ice and jagged rock below a peak in the Darrans. And if Stephie had to hear another person say, 'Well, I suppose that's how Kurt would have wanted it,' she thought she would scream. Scream and never stop.

She spent that first year curled in a corner of the big empty bed with her face pressed hard against a woollen jersey that retained the musky scent of him, fading month by month. The street light aslant over the covers, she could sometimes fall into a fitful sleep while keeping an ear out for the slightest whimper from Ben's cot. His big boy cot, with one side removed because he kept climbing, too, up and over the rails. She surrounded his bed with pillows so that her son might fall, if he fell, onto the softest of goosedown.

One day, years later, when Ben was eleven, he did indeed fall, from a flying fox on a school trip, and she had the phone call. The one that makes everything stop. Your breath. Your heart. She had been photographing a garden west of the city, a dauntingly labour-intensive creation of elms and oaks and woodland paths winding round a lake cut from the dry plains. Her head was down, lining up a shot of a summerhouse clad in rosy Albertine when the owner came running and everything stopped.

Ben was sitting up on an emergency room bed, arm already in plaster cast and sling and white as a hospital pillow. 'Hello, mate,' said a doctor, swishing aside the curtain and consulting his clipboard. 'Fallen off your motorbike, eh?' She registered curly hair, big hands. 'Or did you trip doing ballet?' Ben's wan face cleared. He smiled. The big bear doctor's hands were square, but very clean, with nails neatly trimmed, a gold band on the ring finger.

And two weeks later, there he was again, opening the door to a house on Scarborough. She was photographing a major feature for *NZ Interiors*. The house clung to the cliff face, a miracle of multi-level engineering. The ocean gleamed through vast windows, all the way to the white tips of the Kaikouras, and light streamed into an interior so pristine that it seemed impossible anyone could actually be living here. Light bounced from pale floors, glazed tiles, the only ornament three silver balls on a glass-topped coffee table alongside a metre-high chrome cylinder containing an arrangement of twigs. All purchasable from Objets, Diane's little design store on Victoria Street. It was beautiful, it was stunning, and it was going to be a complete bugger to shoot with the correct light levels. 'Come in!' said the bear, extending a paw, as she wished devoutly for a duller day. Amid all this glamour, he was the one anomaly: unshaven in saggy jeans and scruffy Springsteen T-shirt, unlike his wife, Diane, who was whippet-thin in snowy white to match the settee, a fine golden chain about her burnished neck.

'Welcome!' she was saying, 'to our little seaside bach!', white teeth smiling, though later, from the kitchen as they fetched coffee, there was a barely audible, 'For God's sake, Paul, go and get changed. I've put some things out on the bed. The least you could do is try to make an effort!' He reappeared as Diane was describing the lap pool she hoped one day to see constructed on the level below the deck, an infinity pool, carved from the cliff — it would be amazing! He was combed and shaven in pressed chinos and a pale linen shirt, like a dog that has been groomed professionally and feels its inner wolf to be deeply compromised. Stephie photographed them seated side by side on the impossibly stylish, impossibly uncomfortable low-backed settee. Paul's arm was placed awkwardly about his wife's narrow shoulders. Her ankles were elegantly crossed.

'I wanted to say thanks,' said Stephie, as she was packing to leave. 'For being so nice to my son.' His face took on that faintly haunted look of people who deal with a lot of strangers whom they will not necessarily recognise again. 'Broken arm, two weeks ago? Sorry — this must happen to you all the time, but I just wanted to say thank you. You were great.' Diane moved a little aside. Clearly this was something that happened often enough to be irritating.

'Good,' said the bear. 'Danny, was it?'

'Ben,' she said.

Diane was still on Scarborough, still selling her objets, still playing tennis twice a week, still largely financed by Paul, who remained, at heart, the altar boy who had abandoned wife and three children, committed the sin of adultery and was therefore required to make restitution for the rest of his life, and possibly later, should purgatory turn out to be true after all.

The house on Savage Street was a solution when those weekends in the Heartwood became intolerable: four kids slamming about the tiny kitchen making cheese toast, banging on the single bathroom door. 'Hey! Bendy! I'm busting! Hurry *up*!' Four kids arguing over Nintendo, over who got to control the console, over who would direct little pixilated Mario as he hopped through the Mushroom Kingdom, bouncing from enemy to enemy and tossing fireballs. Four kids arguing over whose turn it was to choose the video. Four kids alert to any hint of affection between their respective parents.

Stephie dreaded those weekends when she slipped into bed beside Paul, both of them whispering lest they draw the ironic thump on the flimsy wall that separated their room from the one next door, occupied by one of the two fair daughters.

'Ugggh, gross,' they said, should Paul so much as kiss her chastely on the cheek.

She loved Paul, but his children were a nightmare. The son was withdrawn. Asperger's, perhaps. Or, as Ben said, just plain weird. While the daughters had simply loathed her on sight. They barely acknowledged her presence, insisted on endless reminiscence with their father about events from which she was excluded, people she didn't know. That holiday in Fiji, the time Nick fell in the harbour off the Zimmermans' (who?) yacht, the good times when they had been a proper family, before she had entered the scene and ruined the idyll.

Paul seemed blissfully unaware. The only difficulty he could see was lack of space. The house on Savage Street would make everything possible.

He came across it one afternoon when he was out running along the riverbank. Stephie had no affection for old houses, having been raised in a villa on the Taieri where a chilly draught flowed constantly from front door to back and damp seeped through thin walls. But Paul was a romantic. He liked the turret: some lingering memory of childhood and a picture in a book of a knight riding forth through a green forest on a noble quest. He liked the inglenook in the living room, and the high ceilings, he liked the trees and the garden and the riverbank for his morning run, he liked the closeness to the hospital for those times when he was on call. In this house, there would be room for all of them to spread out.

And they could afford it. He, with whatever was left over from maintaining the illusion of domestic continuity on Scarborough Hill, she with the money she had withdrawn from the share club, just in time, before the crash.

It was not prudence or foresight that had saved her. She had joined the club on the recommendation of her sister, Alice, who worked for a bank and knew what she was doing when it came to money.

'Go on!' she'd said. 'Make some decent money for once! If not for yourself, for Ben: for his education, for his future.'

Alice had borrowed against her house to join a group in Mount Eden that included some very savvy individuals: an accountant, a lawyer, a builder, and some people like herself with a sense of adventure and a bit of money to invest. Their first purchase had been shares in Neptune, which went from $20 to $150 in a matter of months.

'You see?' she said. 'It's easy! You're always so cautious.'

'No, I'm not,' said Stephie. Though it was true. She was. (She knew, of course, that you could take a risk, and that you could fall. Without so much as a sound...)

She joined Alice's club. Each month she sent off her contribution, each month she received the financial statement and the report of the club's meetings, each month she read the confident advice of the professional manager they had appointed to direct their affairs.

And then there was Paul. Then there was the house...

That spring, the US sent a missile into an Iranian oil tanker and a great storm bore down on southern England, tearing trees out by the stumps and closing the London exchange and one damp day, Wall Street crashed. Black Monday or, if you lived in New Zealand, on the other side of the timeline, Black Tuesday. The biggest one-day dive in history, taking all the tiny investors down into chaos.

But not Stephie. She had got out only a few weeks before. She had got out just in time. When the crash came, her savings lay invested in weatherboard and corrugated iron, in high ceilings and french doors and an inglenook fireplace. In a turret and a bay window.

And a year later, here she was, living with Paul and safe as...

forty-three

THE WALL

SPRING 1990

... the place reverberated to the sound of saws and hammers. The whole back wall was being torn away to make way for a deck. And a barbecue, and maybe a pool. Seriously. They were thinking of putting in a pool. As if they were all about to play Happy Families, Dad in one of those barbecue aprons with the tongs, flipping hamburgers, Sniffy dispensing drinks from the bifold kitchen windows and all of them, the kids, splashing in a pool in their waterwings. They seriously thought that was going to happen. Sniffy had shown them the drawings. Tiny people lay on deck chairs round a blue rectangle where other tiny aliens threw a beach ball.

'We're going to open the whole place up, so there's a flow from the family room to the deck. It'll be so cool.' She actually used the words 'so cool'. She actually used the words 'family room'.

'What do you think?'

Lydia had glanced at the aliens at play.

'Oh yes indeed,' she'd said. 'I'd say it would be "cool". Or perhaps even "fab"?'

She had no opinion whatever to offer concerning anything about this house. At nights when she had to sleep there, she lay in the dark cave they'd allocated her. The last bedroom because she refused to choose, simply shrugged while the others argued over what was fair. She lay in the empty cave, listening to things crawling in the walls behind her head. Little skittery things and things that sounded swollen and soft and furry, amorphous, boneless things, squeezing their way up into the attic above her room. She could hear sharp nails scratching and the heavy lumpen run across the ceiling. Sometimes, half-dozing, she was woken by them and for a few seconds lay wondering what it was and where she was.

She was in the cave, not in her real room: the one with its big bright window overlooking the bay. You could look down from that room to the surfers, seal heads bobbing about waiting for a wave. You could see the beach where people strolled or sunbathed on the expanse of gleaming sand. You could see the mountains in the distance. You could hear the little kids squealing down in the playground and the waves breathing, that soft insistent accompaniment to her whole life. That was her real room, not this horrible dark cave with its purple walls. Sniffy had said she could have it repainted. Lydia could choose any colour, anything at all, whatever she liked.

'Don't care,' she'd said.

Sniffy surveyed the paint chart.

'What about this?' she said. 'Sandcastle. That's nice.' Pale yellow.

'It looks like spew,' she'd said.

Touché. That little nerve jumped in Sniffy's neck, the one that signalled she'd made a hit. But swiftly suppressed. Sniffy was still trying to suck up to Dad, still trying to make them all join in some stupid version of that TV series they used to watch when they were kids, *The Brady Bunch*. All of them seamlessly melding. The others might have given the appearance of compliance: Nick wouldn't notice anyway. He didn't relate to humans, only to his computer, while Emma was preoccupied with a new boyfriend and indifferent to whatever was happening at home. Which left Lydia. And she had no intention of complying. She was not Marcia Brady. Hell no. She was Lydia and she was not going to read the lines as expected.

'White,' she said.

'Really?' said Sniffy. She looked almost pathetically grateful.

'Yes,' said Lydia. 'Definitely. It's what my mother would advise.'

'OK,' said Sniffy, folding up the chart. 'White it is. Now, who's for pizza and a video?'

They'd given her a poster for her room: quite a nice poster actually that they'd brought back from New York when Dad went over for a conference: *Mäda Primavesi* by Klimt, who was her favourite artist of all time, *The Woman in Gold* the most beautiful painting ever. Mäda looked like a determined girl in a white dress standing among flowers. Lydia had cut it, with some regret, into a hundred squares and dumped them in the rubbish, leaving just one piece on the carpet for Sniffy to discover. No mention was made of it, and the square remained exactly where she had left it, a tiny pink flower, but Sniffy definitely came into the room, snooping. She must have seen it.

The walls of the cave remained bare. Her room at home was covered in posters, and swimming certificates and photos of her friends on a ski trip or at school and photos of Smooch as a puppy, lifted up to smile for the camera with the Christmas tree just visible in the background. Such things belonged in her real room where she lived her real life, not in this weird dark place she stayed in only because her dad had gone all serious one Saturday afternoon as he drove her to netball at the park.

'Lyddie,' he said, hands on the wheel at ten to two, his eyes on the road ahead, 'I know this is hard. I know you don't like Steph. But it's hard for all of us.'

'Well, that's not quite true,' said Lydia. 'It's not quite so hard for you. You're the one that left Mum. You're the one who had the affair.'

Her father concentrated on negotiating the busy turn onto Fitzgerald Avenue. 'That's true,' he said, in his reasonable voice, 'but there are things you don't know, Lyddie, that are none of your business really. Your mother . . .'

'Don't!' said Lydia. 'Don't you dare go blaming Mum for this! Now let me out of the car. I'll walk.'

He kept driving, along the avenue among the Saturday morning traffic. She fiddled with the doorhandle. 'I mean it,' she said. 'Let me out!' The door swung wide, nearly clipping another car.

'Lyddie!' he yelled, all pretence of calm broken. He swerved to the curb.

'Look,' he said, as she scrambled out, 'I just want you to try. What's done is done, and I'm sorry, but we've got to do the best we can.' His voice cracked. He sounded weird. He wasn't, was he? Yes, he was. He was crying. His lips were all trembly.

It was horrible. Like watching a building collapse. Like watching a wall come down. Who knew what could happen now, if her father cried, laid his head on the wheel between his hands, oblivious of people passing on the street? She had been going to slam the door to make her point, but she closed it quietly instead, then walked away along the avenue, her sports bag slung nonchalantly over one shoulder, because that was what she had said she would do and she always did what she said, unlike other people. But everything had changed. A defence she hadn't even known was there, keeping her safe, had been breached. And who knew what could pour from that weakness? She had felt herself, with every step, walking out into new territory.

But ever since, she had tried a little harder. She had slept in the cavern on alternate weekends without enthusiasm, but at least without comment. She had continued to refuse Sniffy's food, because she was vegan, or perhaps in the first stages of anorexia, which would serve them all right.

This spring morning, she sits drinking her breakfast smoothie in the garden as the house shudders under the assault, weatherboards cracking, roofing iron tearing from joists, the wall coming down as walls everywhere, great and small, are coming down, leaving the way open for the happily blended family.

And one of the workmen is waving something he has found, up there in the roof. 'Hey!' he's calling to everyone. 'Hey! Come and look at . . .

forty-four
THE RIVER
SPRING 1992

Something happens.

Snow falls, heavily, to sea level and late in the season. It piles deep in drifts along the riverbanks, all the way to the coast, weighting the branches of trees so that branches snap.

The water rises and spreads over the roads, lapping at fences. It surges. Small creatures are swept to the sea.

But then, that is how it happens, here and everywhere. Small creatures are washed away in their thousands, their millions. Their small bodies are found, piled in ditches.

She swims strongly against the current and is safe.

Then the sun comes out. The snow turns to slush and melts away. The river draws back to its accustomed channel.

A leaf falls.

forty-five

THE HOLE IN THE SKIRTING

SPRING 1994

... **back in** 1991, drilling a hole in the skirting. Large enough to thread a length of two-wire cabling from the phone in the hall to a BT wall socket under his desk. Wire, socket and phonejack purchased that very afternoon. Nick knelt on the floorboards, feeling a deep satisfaction in knowing precisely what he was about: four screws to hold the socket in place, thread the cable through, stick in a phonejack, done. In his bedroom on the other side of the wall, his computer, an AMD 386DX-25, product of birthday and Christmas presents and months of washing dishes at the Dux — waited for connection, glowing in the dark.

The drill whirred in his hand. He peered intently at the bit as it drove into the skirting, lit by the narrow beam of his head torch. The wood was surprisingly tough and he was forced to apply some pressure to force it through when he became aware of a pair of bare feet.

'What the hell are you up to?' said his father, voice muted. 'Do you know what time this is? I've got a big day tomorrow and Stephie has a job in Nelson. She's got to be on a plane at 8.30.'

'Just putting in some cable,' he said. 'Won't be a sec.'

A couple of minutes to link it all up. Already he was planning what he'd post on their BBS to Dev and the others who were at this very instant seated in front of screens all over the world, his widespread tribe gathered around the glow of the campfire. Some like himself who had to work late at night, when there was no necessity to compete with everyone else in the household for a phone connection.

His father had no idea what he was up to. He used the computer as a kind of glorified typewriter, seemingly unaware of its limitless potential.

Nick did have an idea. He had understood its magic from the very start, back when he and a bunch of other kids had persisted in sneaking into the new computer lab over lunchtime, though the duty staff were always trying to throw them out, back into the jungle that was the quadrangle and grounds of the school. When forced out into the open air, they huddled unhappily by the door, merely waiting for the moment when the duty teachers retreated to the staffroom and they were free to return to the reverent hush of the lab, the row of PCs whirring, emanating their seductive, enticing power.

Mr Shaw understood. But then he was an outsider, too, the only teacher who turned up unkempt, in baggy shorts, socks and sandals when the male staff's standard attire was trousers, shirt and, often, a tie. Hagley was unconventional in some ways, and that was why Nick had chosen to go there. No uniform. He was able to grow his hair, apply a whole bottle of Directions Acid Green, then comb and gel the result into a spiky mohawk. He looked like some ancient hybrid creature, part human, part lizard. But Hagley was still a school, with classes and desks and a syllabus he largely ignored. The only reason he attended at all was Mr Shaw and the computer lab.

Mr Shaw's idol was some dude called Richard Stallman, who'd been at Harvard and MIT, which, according to Mr Shaw, was the centre of the universe.

'That's where I'd go if I had the chance,' he said, looking round at the stupid daily notices pinned to the wall, the pile of dumb assignments waiting for assessment on his desk. 'Too late for me.'

Mr Shaw was kind of gloomy. A lot of kids didn't like him, laughed when he passed, or played stupid tricks, delivering a hail of spit balls the moment his back was turned or parading in and out to the toilets during class, but he didn't give a fuck. That's what

Nick liked about him. He truly didn't give a fuck. He also knew a lot about computers, and if he was on duty, he let them into the lab. Nick and a couple of silent boys from form 3 and a Chinese kid and a skinny Goth girl in dead-white pancake make-up and boots so huge it seemed impossible her sticklike legs could lift them.

This guy Stallman was a hacker at MIT (Nick savoured the word: 'hacker'. You could be a 'hacker', a smart pirate, working on the fringes of the system.) He'd been a hacker who had modified the software on a Xerox laser printer in this building at MIT, so that it alerted everyone who was logged-in when it was jammed. Which was kind of useful, as it was on a different floor from most of the users.

But Xerox wouldn't allow them to introduce this modification and blocked their access to the printer's source code. So Stallman said, 'To hell with that!'

'These computers,' Mr Shaw waved at the row of screens 'are tools, whose power is infinite. And that power will soon be freely available, as it should be, to anyone who wishes to adapt this tool to their own use. Thanks to Stallman and people like him, your generation will have access to immense power.'

And as he said it, standing in Room 43, the computer lab, he looked, in his baggy shorts and wild hair, like a wizard, like Gandalf or Saruman, passing his wizardry into the hands of the initiates, to the mutes from form 3 and the Goth girl and the Chinese kid and Nick.

Nick repeated the words as he walked home from school, his green mohawk tremulous in a nor-wester. GNU, UNIX, source code, copyleft, rehearsing the language of the new world. He had tried to speak it with his father, to convey to him the power that lay at his fingertips, but his dad wasn't really interested, though he was vaguely approving of his son's prowess.

'Good for you, mate,' he said, patting him on the shoulder, then went off to carry on with his exhausting, demanding, deadening job.

One thing Nick had always been absolutely certain of was that he would never become a doctor. Not for a single second would he want to spend his life looking up someone's bum, poking and prodding sick people in some dreary shabby stinking hospital. His father's life seemed exhausting. He always had the air of being slightly harassed, even on holidays, never completely free, always checking back on someone or other. When Nick was small, someone had asked him if he was going to be a doctor like his daddy and Nick had said, though he has no memory of this, 'No!' And when they went on and asked him what he wanted to be instead, evidently he had replied, without missing a beat, 'Rich!' Everyone always laughed at this, as if it was a joke, like the way Emma always mispronounced 'hostiple'. But Nick had been deadly serious. He still, deep down, wanted to be rich. Why not? It was as good an ambition as any.

So when his father stood over him that night as he drilled a hole for the cable, it was without comprehension. He had no idea how necessary it was to put in the cable, so Nick kept drilling, nearly there, and his father stood by fighting for calm, saying, 'Nick, there are other people in this household, and you must have greater consideration for them. If you don't want to do so, then you're free to leave. You're old enough. You're perfectly entitled to choose for yourself. But right now, you must stop disturbing everybody. Now, give me the drill. You can finish this in the morning.'

And crouched by the skirting, Nick experienced a revelation. It was true. He could leave. He could walk away from this fucking flatlining city, he could go to Wellington. In Wellington, maybe he could do some course, teach himself Linux, become part of the future.

Which is how he came to be living in a flat off Cuba Street where a mobile of ancient pizzas dangled from the light shade and the walls were ornamented with the interlocking As and Es of Anarchy. And the curtains remained drawn at all times and the dark rooms resonated to Crass and Conflict and the Dead Kennedys and bands whose names began with 'Dis': Discharge, Disorder, Disfear, Disaffect, who were Scottish, fast and thrashy, and there was endless talk about the system, which was totally fucked, and endless beers, and he had an A and E tattooed on one shoulder, and a stud in his nostril and another in his lip where it clinked on the glass.

He got a job washing dishes in a kebab place on Willis Street where there was a girl called Kaz who had yellow hair tied in rows of tiny tight plaits who told the owner to get fucked when he tried to grope her behind the chiller and they both walked out and went straight back to his flat and his grimy bed and then she sort of moved in.

She gave him a jacket, black and heavily studded, that she'd got from a friend who lived in a flat where someone had OD'ed and they were recycling his clothes in his memory. The jacket lay upon his shoulders like armour. And he got another job, with computers this time, at GTech on The Terrace where he worked on a help desk, sorting out problems with UNIX users in the Ministry of Fisheries.

And one afternoon in 1994 he is helping Lorraine, who is unbelievably thick, and he's beginning to wonder if he should just run down to her office and sort it out himself rather than laboriously try to explain, yes, that arrow. The black one, by the toolbar, that's the bar at the top with all the little pictures, can you see it? And the rain falls horizontally, driven by a ferocious southerly, and the flat is growing mould and someone has nicked the dead man's jacket, maybe Kaz who has kind of moved out, and Wellington has lost its glow.

And as he sits there, rain splattering the windows, he experiences another revelation: he hasn't avoided his father's life after all. He's repeating it. He has become a doctor, not ministering to people but to sick computers, and it's every bit as tedious, every bit as exhausting.

And he'll never be rich.

And he'll never realise his potential. He has taught himself C, submitted to the Linux kernel, rewritten a sound card driver.

But here he is, helping Lorraine locate the black arrow.

'Fuck it,' he thinks. And it is a repeat of the revelation by the skirting board. 'I'm free. I can leave.'

And he hangs up the . . .

forty-six
THE GLASS PANEL
SPRING 1996

... **steps out** into the early morning. Mist covers the river as he begins to run, turning east toward the sea. Along one bank for thirty minutes, across at a road bridge, back on the other side. Pounding along in his new trainers. He feels that flicker of satisfaction that always accompanies something new and well designed. The shoes mould to the shape of his foot, with just the right curve beneath the arch. The soles are firm yet spring readily on impact. Each time he buys a new pair of running shoes, the technology gets better.

He checks his watch. (Timex, digital, accurate, lightweight, snug on the wrist: another improvement.) 6:03 and another day lining up. You're never quite sure until you get in, of course. That's what drew him to emergency in the first place: the absolute certainty of uncertainty. On the alert at the frontline, handling whatever comes through the door. And now there is another uncertainty. Bloody Barry. And the deadening panoply of idiocy that has been dropped upon them from above.

Management. It's as if all those zombies you thought you'd left behind in the fourth form have been given new life and walk the earth. The dullards of 4C, destined to spend their lives as salesmen or clerks, or, if they were lucky, a vague attempt at a commerce degree, part-time, arriving on campus after a day spent in some dire office, still wearing collar, tie and pressed trousers, when every other student wore jeans and a T-shirt. But now it's their turn, the office drones. Somehow they have morphed into management. Awarding one another bigger and bigger salaries. Men like Barry.

Barry knows a lot about selling apples, but not a lot about medicine. Yet Barry talks blithely about 'efficiencies'. In the plural. Barry inhabits a refitted office overlooking the river with smart leather chairs and a desk clear of clutter, while he, Paul, a mere functionary on the factory floor, labours in a broom cupboard near the emergency room, its shelves piled high with papers and files. Tidiness had never been particularly valued in 4A. What mattered then was getting good marks in chemistry and maths, what mattered was As in physics and biology, and dux or proxime accessit and a scholarship, then surviving the first year scrambling for admission to med school, and the years that followed of long hours, high on exhaustion and adrenaline as you walked home to some defiantly grotty flat on Cumberland Street. What mattered was doing a fine job, making a calm and considered assessment under pressure: 'Don't *do* something,' as one of the supervising consultants had said to him when he was starting out, 'just *stand* there!' Make the assessment, determine a course of action, set in train a decisive and orderly procedure. Confront day by day the multiplicity of disasters to which frail human flesh is hostage. Do his best for his patients according to his ability and judgement. Do no harm. Heal.

A tidy desk and efficiencies are the priorities of another school of thought entirely.

Mist furls and swans and scaup leave long arrows on the serene surface of the river. He pads along beside it, liking the sound of the tarmac beneath his excellent shoes, liking the in and out of the cool green air, the steady ti-tup ti-tup of his heart. He likes having a house here, close to the river. It had been an economic choice to begin with, beautiful but in need of renovation and on the unfashionable eastern side of the city rather than the more expensive west. It was the best he could afford at the time, given the inordinate cost of sending his children to schools where they received the same education others received free. The kinds of schools that had chapels.

He had protested: What was wrong with the local high school where they would learn to mix with everyone, the way he had in Hokitika? As Diane must have learned, presumably, in its Taihape equivalent? But Diane had insisted, and off their children went to the kinds of schools where it was proposed that the senior students might benefit from a field trip to Pompeii.

'Pompeii?' he'd said. 'What's wrong with a trip to the cheese factory?' Or to Wellington to see the leaders of democracy yawning on the parliamentary benches? Or the trip to the car factory, observing people standing by a conveyor belt, making the same adjustment, over and over, to a Holden chassis? The trip that had persuaded him to stop mucking about, pass exams and work his way up and out.

'Pompeii? And Greece? Who the hell needs to go there at sixteen? It's the bus trip everyone remembers: the kid who throws up, the chance to sit next to the girl you've been eyeing up for months. That's what field trips are for.'

They went, of course. Everyone else was going, it would be a once-in-a-lifetime opportunity, and Diane had hissed that he was being ridiculous, as if he were depriving his offspring of essential nourishment. They went and returned clutching Benetton bags from Milan. So much for the Acropolis. So much for the Doric order.

Now he's glad he lives near the river where, each morning, he can run beneath the trees down to the road bridge and back. He pads along, to that simple, easy, duple beat. Ahead lies a day of argument with Barry and the other graduates of 4C. It's a disaster. An emergency department without enough beds while they witter on about competition between the city's hospitals, as if they were rival companies scrapping for business. Forget Hippocrates. Forget 'do no harm'. This was medicine as profit-making enterprise, sick bodies as marketable assets: roll 'em in, fix 'em up, get 'em out, like some cut-rate garage attending to a succession of broken-down Toyotas.

It took so much time and energy to voice dissent. One of his colleagues had done the maths: quite simply, the department needed more nurses, more staff. In Australia, they reckoned on one full-time equivalent per 1000 patients per annum.

Paul categorically refuses to use Barry-speak: consumers, clients, units. They're patients, damn it. It's a good word, an old word, for people who are waiting as they mostly do, with the touching submission of the ill and damaged, for him or someone like him to do his best to make them well. It is their trust that most appals him yet makes him come in, day after day, to do his job. These are not consumers, fecklessly occupying their free beds, gobbling up some finite resource. They are patients. He makes a point of using the word when talking to Barry and his mates as they chatter in their alien management tongue.

In this hospital, the figure is more like one FTE per 1529 patients-not-clients per annum.

In Australia, they reckon on 27.75 doctors to safely operate an emergency department equivalent to the one where he works in this city.

This department operates with eighteen doctors, often house surgeons, eager and bright but inexperienced, with a registrar, exhausted after long hours on the job, without proper supervision, at risk of making wrong calls.

People could die, unnoticed by distracted, overworked individuals doing their best to cope, not reading crucial notes, missing some detail in the rush of handover, in the muddle consequent on Barry's 'efficiencies', which require the closure of certain wards overnight, the way you shut down a factory line. Patients with head injuries end up in urology, or the medical day unit, or parked for hours in the traffic jam in the hallways, with, always lurking, the constant risk of infection.

And still the Barrys in management and ministry talk in their big cool offices about financial performance. And all of them, the staff, have been locked into their vision, signing absurd job descriptions, while the patients wait on the trolleys with their bleeding heads, their worried relatives.

But ah yes! Savings must be made, $12 million, a figure arrived at by management without consultation with Paul or his colleagues, for they have been relegated to the fourth tier of management in this efficient structure, beneath three tiers of Barrys to whom they must report: the service manager, the general manager, layer upon layer, as in a car factory.

Paul breathes, the green air entering his lungs, cool and clear. On the river the scaup dive and pop up at unexpected angles. He runs beneath the elms along the far bank, crosses the little footbridge and heads for home. Back along the river and onto Savage Street, into the cool shadow of the driveway and up the steps to his own front door. Half an hour to shower, dress, get to work.

And he doesn't mean to, but as he goes inside, he slams the door. It swings to, heavily: so heavily that one of the little pink glass panels set in the doorframe cracks across from side to ...

forty-seven

THE ROSE

SPRING 1998

...**tears at** her skin. Stephie pulls back, secateurs tangled in a whippy snarl of Souvenir de la Malmaison as blood bubbles the length of her forearm. 'Damn,' she says, then sets to licking herself better. She tastes salty and raw beef. Roses are such savages under all the pastel simper. She has never trusted them, not since Alice's friend who had been stabbed in the nose by a rose and developed cancer on the site of the wound.

'Dead within a year,' said Alice. 'Just eaten away.'

Her sister was full of such stories of alarm and sudden death, all instructive of the necessity to seize the day, throw caution to the winds, live as if there were no tomorrow. (And look where that had got her: a unit in Mount Roskill next door to a panelbeater, with another in her collection of hopeless men: too dependent or too independent, violent or addictive or feckless or embarrassing or just plain married already.)

Stephie tries to resist the message, but somehow she is always impressed by her sister's little homilies. This morning, for instance, she carries on, snipping and tying, but inevitably, eventually, gives in. She lays the secateurs aside, goes indoors to the bathroom cabinet, slathers the wound in Savlon. It stings. She likes that. She learned long ago, in childhood, as the iodine was dabbed from the little brown bottle, that that is how things are made all better. You could trust pain.

Then she returns to the roses. There was no time to muck about, not if everything were to be ready by 14 February.

Valentine's Day.

Could anything be more banal? She ties a whippy sapling so that it will drape as planned around the archway through which Melissa will walk in her white dress.

No. Not a dress. A *gown*. A Lara Milligan creation in lace, boned corset and full tulle skirt. $3500. Her son is about to marry someone who has spent $3500 on a frock. She had even flown to Sydney for the purchase, along with the gaggle of young women, her 'girlfriends', who were to be her bridesmaids: a couple of former flatmates, her sister, and one, Kim, her best friend from school, who has unfortunately somewhat run to fat.

Stephie had overheard Melissa discussing this with Ben one evening when they were visiting and out in the kitchen stacking the dishwasher.

'I have to ask Kim,' Melissa was saying. 'She'd be devastated if I didn't, but she's going to have to lose a few kilos. A lot of kilos. I'm going to get her a personal trainer. And I'm going to order her dress in a size twelve so she's got something to aim for. Either she steps up to the challenge or she doesn't get to be part of it.'

At her present girth, Kim would ruin the photos. The click of plates. And Ben — her Ben, kind easy-going Ben whose best mate at high school had weighed in at around 100 kilos — grunting in agreement, going along, it seems with this kittenish torment.

Kim made the cut for Sydney, off for the girls' weekend, teetering with the platoon between shops in ridiculous heels, bubbles on the hotel balcony, voddies in the bar, hunting down The Gown. Back to work on Monday, mission accomplished. Or so Stephie gathered.

Melissa had mentioned the dress when she and Ben came down for Paul's fiftieth birthday.

'It's soooo gorgeous,' she said. 'There was so much choice, more than you'd ever get in Auckland, but the minute I saw it, I knew this was The One.'

'At that price, I'd hope so,' said Stephie, spearing a Brussels sprout.

'Oh, Mum,' said Melissa, laughter tinkling over the table, the good German glasses filled with a sauvignon produced by one of Paul's colleagues, a former anaesthesiologist who had taken early retirement and now applied his scientific rigour to the production of wine on a river flat in Marlborough. There were flowers and the best china. Enormous white dinner plates where each serving occupied a small redoubt at the centre.

Not that Paul would notice. He sat at the head of the dining table, colleagues, friends, family on either hand: Nick had flown back from Dubai for his father's birthday, Emma from Auckland, Lyddie from Singapore. Stephie watched him from the opposite end of the table, stolidly chewing beef Wellington, supposedly his favourite, just as lasagne was supposedly Ben's and Thai salad was hers.

To tell the truth, she was no longer sure if any of those choices was true. Her real favourite, if she were asked to nominate her final meal, if she were on death row in some appalling American prison, togged up in the orange jumpsuit and facing imminent execution, would be buttered toast. And Paul, she suspected, would revert to his origins and nominate baked beans.

And Ben? Who knew? She hadn't known since he left for uni in Auckland and an existence sustained by beer and two-minute noodles. He and Melissa were certainly very specific about drinks, spending an inordinate amount of time stirring and shaking pre-dinner cocktails composed of spirits and liqueurs bought especially for the occasion. Blue stuff and green stuff and clear stuff so potent that a single glass has left Stephie stone cold sober but with doubts about her ability to stand or move her arms.

But there it was: beef Wellington for Paul. You could be defined forever by some random choice made long ago. Right now, Melissa was smiling in her indulgent fashion at another of her future mother-in-law's funny little ways: her caution, her stinginess.

'Ah well,' she said. 'It's once in a lifetime, I suppose.'

'More likely twice,' said Stephie, 'possibly three times, if you check the statistics. Remember Diana? The wedding of the century? The dress? She still ended up in the tunnel. Remember the sea of flowers? I'd hang onto that dress if I were you. You'll probably get a lot of wear out of it.'

'And,' she'd like to add, 'don't call me "Mum". I am not your bloody mother.' But Ben was looking at her disapprovingly. He placed his hand over Melissa's on the tabletop, and when Stephie went out to the kitchen to collect the chocolate cake, he followed.

'Why are you being so rude?' he hissed. 'Melissa's on her own. She doesn't have family here. They're all in Taiwan. She deserves our support.'

'To do what?' said Stephie. 'Spend a ridiculous amount of money on a dress?'

'Her money,' said Ben. 'She's earned it. She works bloody hard.' Melissa worked in marketing. For Lion Nathan.

'She sells beer to New Zealanders,' said Stephie. 'How hard can that be?'

Once Ben would have thought that was funny, but a new seriousness had swept over her son, along with the stubbled jaw, the shaven head. He didn't laugh and Stephie stood holding the cake, knowing she was risking it all: future visits, wedding, grandchildren when they came along, as Melissa had promised they would.

'We both wants heaps of kids,' she'd said, as she stood chopping tomatoes at the kitchen bench, diamond engagement ring twinkling above the knife. Giving Mum a hand. 'So don't worry. You'll soon be a grandma!'

'My life's ambition,' said Stephie, who was washing a lettuce at the time. The water was icy. Her fingers stung.

She carried in the cake — chocolate, Paul's favourite. Or so they all supposed. They sang the song. They cut the cake. Speech speech. He rose. He thanked them all: his family, his friends and colleagues, his wife. They drank a toast in the German glasses. To Paul. Happy Birthday!

Then Melissa tapped her fork upon the glass with tiny fingers tipped blood red. She jumped to her feet. 'I'd just like to take the opportunity to say thank you,' she said. 'To you all. I mean, you have all just so welcomed me into this family, made me feel so totally welcome. I always wanted to be part of a big happy family. It was one of the things that drew me to Ben in the first place, wasn't it?' She looked down lovingly at Ben's shaven head. 'That we were both only children and you just miss out on so much, being raised an only child . . .'

Stephie surveyed the remains of her slice of birthday cake.

Her son.

Her only child.

The child who burst through the blur that fell over her on the day the police officers arrived, standing on the doorstep, saying something to her, something about Kurt, about an accident, their faces wrinkled with concern, their quiet, considered voices. There had been the blur, and darkness and through the darkness, a sudden vicelike grip that seized her body, and began to squeeze, hard, harder and there were sheets, white sheets, flowering scarlet, and voices and people running and a siren howling or perhaps the howling was her and she was tearing in two, she was being ripped apart as she was carried, swaying, through the dream of a dark city and flashing lights and then, oblivion.

And when she woke, there he was: a tiny wrinkled creature covered in raspberry ripples of blood and creamy unguent, skinny legs pedalling at the unimpeded air, arms waving, hold me, hold me, while the doctors and nurses did something urgent to a part of her body that had become distant, irrelevant, devoid of sensation.

And when she woke again he reappeared in a plastic incubator wearing an absurd little knitted cap like an egg cosy. And she sat close, as close as she could without climbing in beside him, unaware of anything, not eating unless someone said she should: here, you must have something. She felt if she looked away for a single second this tiny creature could give a little fluttering sigh and simply disappear. It could happen. It took all her energy to keep him visible, to make him breathe.

And after a long time, days, nights, she can't remember, he was released. They opened the plastic box and handed him over to her, dressed in a baggy babygro, newborn size but still too large, like the lambs they used to find in the rain-soaked paddocks of the Taieri when she was a girl, bony bodies inside baggy jerseys of crimped wool stained yellow with afterbirth, and saved, bearing them home to the warmth of a cardboard box lined with a bit of sacking next to the kitchen stove.

She was a hollow shell. Everything within her had been ripped and torn and taken away. No chance whatever of another. But there he was, her son, who now sat there smiling adoringly at this silly girl he planned to marry.

She looked down the long table at Paul, who was looking straight back at her.

He knew her. He knew her life, as she knew him and his life. About Diane and her affairs — four that he knew of, others he suspected but never asked about to be sure. About the difficulties of work, the problems with management, the times he made the wrong call, lost someone. She knew his fears — of putting on weight, of losing his hair, of sudden cardiac arrest at fifty-two, like his father who had collapsed in front of him, with brutal suddenness, in the garden at Hokitika and how he, twelve years old, had tried to hold him up, stop him falling.

She knew him. The way he hummed when preoccupied, a tuneless repetition of 'Delilah' for some reason, though he didn't even like Tom Jones. The feel of his heart against her head, beating. The solid beauty of him as he walked across the bedroom naked, or as he made his way toward her dressed for work in that public place he inhabited with the same ease she felt when she was out in the darkroom in the old laundry at the back of the house, developing film. She had tried to capture it, this beauty, though he didn't like being photographed. He held his hands up against her camera, pulled a silly face. She had sometimes managed to catch him unawares, just woken from sleep, or walking ahead of her along a beach and he was beautiful then, turning to look straight back at her, through the camera lens.

As now he looked at her, while Melissa talked of meeting Ben.

Paul. The man with whom she was sharing her life. They had not bothered with a wedding. There was no need to stand in front of a whole lot of people, repeating vows that hard experience taught were no more than vague intention. You could have the wedding of the year, kiss upon the balcony before millions, and it still ended in a tunnel, a sea of flowers.

Their agreement had been made on the night when, in the private world of a shared bed, she had told him about Ben's birth. And he had told her about Diane's affairs and that was the moment they had said, you. No one else. You.

Melissa had sat down, and Ben laid his hand over her hand, over the diamond solitaire. But Paul was standing up. He was walking around the table. And he was putting his arms about Stephie, he was holding her, kissing her, in front of everyone. His children, his friends and colleagues.

'Hey,' he murmured so that only she could hear. 'All right?'

'Yes,' she said. 'All right.'

And now it is spring and she is clipping and tying the roses, preparing for her son's wedding. One of the weddings, for there are to be two: one here, one in Taiwan, both requiring months of organisation. She ties Souvenir de la Malmaison to the archway, but one little sapling cane she leaves loose.

It will grow over the next few months. And by Valentine's Day, it might, just possibly, be long enough and prickly enough to snag on the Lara Milligan . . .

forty-eight
THE RIVER
SPRING 2000

Nothing happens.

Above water, things click. Tiny creatures skid about the meniscus. Time shifts from one second, one minute, one day or month or year, to another.

Below water, there is light.

There is dark.

There is light.

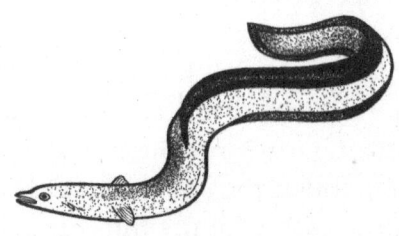

forty-nine

THE DUST

SPRING 2002

... **sometimes people** simply disappear. One morning they go to the airport out among the paddocks at the edge of the city and fly away. Over the ocean, hour upon hour of watery blue, light to dark to light, before touchdown and transfer and more hours, blurry with jetlag across the whole span of the continent until seatbelts are fastened and they sway down at last to solid ground.

This part Emma can imagine. Her father seated by a window, glancing out at America, eager to get there, to check into the hotel, shower, stretch out at last on the long bed and sleep. He hated flying, even in the privileged seats, his big body crammed into the spaces deemed ergonomically feasible for the transportation of the human anatomy.

In theory, he was fascinated by flight, its engineering, its history, bringing back for his children, when they were small, models of early flying machines purchased at some science museum. His gifts tended toward the instructional. He thought it important that they should be scientifically informed. She remembers a microscope, a kit for growing crystals, balsawood dinosaurs. 'Look at this!' he'd say, calling them to examine a monarch breaking free from its green chrysalis, or running a magnet underneath a sheet of white paper onto which he had spilled dust and leaf mould scooped from the spouting. Tiny flecks of black skittered over the page, shreds of molten iron, molten nickel. The air wasn't empty at all, but filled with all sorts of stuff: dust from meteorites and distant deserts and jungle fires and the smoke of cities far away. You didn't notice unless you paid proper attention.

She remembers sitting at the table, glueing a model of a little gondola slung from a giant bird while her brother frowned over some wings attached to a kind of bicycle. People had climbed aboard, putting their faith in paper, feathers and wire, they had leapt from high towers, beating their arms up and down, paddling frantically with their legs strapped to rudders and ancillary wings.

'What happened?' she said, carefully fitting slot B into slot A.

'They crashed,' her father said. But the crash wasn't the point. The point was their spirit of enquiry, their determined optimism. John Damian on wings of chicken feathers flapping into the future.

She has thought of her father as she followed him across that ocean, and as she checked into the hotel: not his, which was by Central Park, near Mount Sinai, but a cheaper place off Times Square selected by the tour company as comfortable and convenient to the city's attractions. She thinks of him as she crawls, buzzing still, into the enormous bed and is finally, mercifully, able to stretch out to full length, for, like her father, she is tall and not designed for hours in economy.

She lies looking up into the dark as her body races to adjust to a new time zone. She thinks of him when she wakes abruptly, ready to go, only to find the city in darkness. Cars pause soundlessly at the lights below her window. She is hungry and would like to go out, but she has never been here before and doesn't know her way around. Best to wait until morning when she can find a diner. It will have bare tables and a tough waitress who will slam down her bagel. She has seen it all on screen and knows how it will be. She eats peanuts from the minibar instead and chocolate, incredibly sweet, which won't help with the pre-race build up.

She feels the prickling at her skin that sometimes washes over her in hotel rooms: that feeling of desolation at the universal black faux leather chair, the pile-up of cushions, colour-coded on the bed. (Why do they do that? Surely everyone just tosses them straight onto the floor?) The universal bathroom with the tiles, bone white, and the bevy of tiny bottles. In their presence she can be overwhelmed by the certainty of her own anonymity. She has to force herself to lie still, close her eyes, breathe slowly, in, and out, in, and out.

She thinks of him then, and the feel of his hand holding her steady as she walked along the top of the seawall at the esplanade, the big waves gnawing at the rocks below, trying to get through. She thinks of him reaching up to hang her bird machine from a thread in the window of her room at Sumner and how it spun in the sunlight. She thinks of him in the photo, seated on the back step of the house by the river, taking off his shoes after a run, his hair damp with sweat and looking up, laughing straight into the camera. She knows it is not her but Stephie he is seeing through the lens, but it doesn't matter. You can see the boy in that photo who existed inside their father, the same boy she heard sometimes through the wall that separated her bedroom from theirs, laughing quietly at some shared private joke. When Stephie said did she want anything, anything at all, she had said, yes, that photo. It is there, in her wallet, in her bag on the black leather chair.

She breathes in, and out, in, and out, switches on the television, watches people sitting on the sofa that is always the same sofa, set dead centre in the same room with the same staircase behind. She watches their mouths opening and closing. She breathes in, and out, in, and out, as the city fades into a pallid autumnal grey and she can go out, find that diner with the grumpy waitress, have her bagel. She walks along streets that feel, after a lifetime of movies and television, weirdly familiar, visits an art gallery, a museum. The trees in Bryant Park are already tipped with gold, and all the time there is that black hole, that absence which she cannot approach, now that she is here. She cannot even come close.

She thinks of him as she lines up for her race pack. She thinks of him as she stands in the early morning in her orange race bib, identity pinned to her chest. 'EMMA' above a row of numbers. The crowds, corralled by the officials, are twitchy with nerves. She is wearing old warm clothes as advised by the tour company, for they have to wait for several hours and it is cold here, in autumn, when she has left behind a country bursting into her leaf. Wear old warm clothes you can toss aside, they said, as you set out, leave them behind for the volunteers to collect for charity. She shifts from foot to foot, talks inconsequential talk with other runners as restless as herself: a woman from Berlin, a team from Minneapolis, a man running his eighth marathon. Nothing like it, he says, and he has run plenty others. In California, in Paris, in London, two a year, but this is the best. The five boroughs, the bridges, the bands, the crowds. You wait, he says, just you wait till you get to Brooklyn! Your first? Wow. You've come a long way for this!

She waits, trying to keep warm, trying for the perfect balance between hydration and the necessity to pee. The men, someone told her, just pee off the bridge, but it's trickier if you're a woman and there are long lines for the portaloos.

And the minutes tick by, the hours, and finally, they're off! Wave after wave, the wheelchair competitors first, and the disabled, the blind with their companions. Then the élite women who lope away, graceful as cheetahs or antelopes or some creature designed by its very nature to do this, to run. And then the élite men, the ones who will chalk up spectacular times, and finally, after hours of waiting, they are released. The ones who have spent the past year running their 10 kilometres, 20 kilometres around the streets of towns and cities or along country roads or through leafy parks, in America and well beyond. Along the waterfront at St Heliers, for example, Rangitoto an elegant curve on the harbour's glisten. She had run thinking of him then and his steady heavy tread, and his big running shoes that smelled of sweat so that they had held their noses when they were little, said, 'Ugggh yuck! Stinky!'

She thinks of him as, one among thousands, she runs steadily upward to the crest of the bridge, legs up, arms swinging, body tilted a little, still fresh but careful to pace herself for the long road ahead.

And at the top she permits herself at last to look. There it is, on her left, the gap in the skyline. The place where flame had billowed forth and tiny people stumbled or fell or jumped from that immense height. They were consumed.

No bone. No body. Just dust blowing through the canyons between buildings. Dust that settled inches thick half a mile, a mile away. Dust that held all that was left, those tiny twisted threads of DNA to be identified in the mud that washed into sewer grates, or brushed from balconies and rooftops. Dust that blew with all the dust we leave behind, dust to dust, ashes to ashes, across continent and ocean to settle with the dust of desert, jungle and distant cities, the particles of meteors and stars, on a roof perhaps on a house on a leafy street. In the spouting. With a handful of leaf mould, perhaps, in a spouting.

People can disappear. She has no idea if this is where her father died. He left no credit card trail, no security camera footage anyone can readily identify. He had taken his passport with him from his hotel room, and his wallet and briefcase, but left behind an open suitcase of clothes and a child's insect-collecting kit with magnifying glass, gift-wrapped, probably for Ben's daughter.

Perhaps he ran toward disaster, driven by instinct and professional training.

Or perhaps he was there already, a tourist in the city, taking in the view from the top-floor restaurant when the world exploded under his feet. Perhaps he, too, blundered about in the smoke, or jumped or fell, diving, or lying on his back for the long seconds it took to meet the ground.

Perhaps he was one of those who grasped a tablecloth, held its corners in both hands, hoping, against all reason, for flight.

Or perhaps he was not there at all, but miles away running another ...

fifty
THE RIVER
SPRING 2004

She is massive now, and old.

One heavy undulating muscle, flat browed, the steel studs of her eyes missing nothing.

She snaps up whatever drops through the water. Holds her place. Waits.

Something must be about to happen.

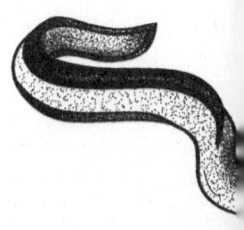

fifty-one

THE UNDERCOAT

3 SEPTEMBER 2010

... **late when** she laid the paintbrush down. They liked doing this, she and Rob, after they'd come home from work, the evening bustle over and the kids quiet behind closed doors in their rooms, asleep or sneakily on their phones or transfixed by the computer's pallid glow.

That was when she and Rob picked up the brushes, put on some music — hits of the eighties had the right swagger for a bit of DIY — and set to work. The ceilings were high so they needed ladders and trestles, or stood on the kitchen table, which was sturdy rimu, a junk shop discovery, something she had always wanted: a giant table, large enough for a family's clutter, the big bowl of fruit, the bills and discarded brochures for Great Holiday Deals, the car keys, the shopping. The walls were wide and bare.

'It's so white,' she'd said to Rob when, heavily pregnant with Poppy, she had walked about in stockinged feet at the open home in 2003. 'It's a lovely house, but God, it's bland. That's going to have to change.' She had already made up her mind: within a minute of arrival, as soon as she walked up the path and saw that absurd little turret with its hexagonal room. She'd paint it yellow. She'd reclad all the rooms in strong colours: vivid blue, acid green, wallpaper with a bold retro print to go with the retro lounge suite she had found in a junk shop in Westport: wooden arms, nubbly orange upholstery, immaculate condition, a triumph. It didn't look as if a single soul had sat on it.

No white. No off-white. No muted beige. Steadily, room by room, over seven years, they had driven the pallor back. Months of work, months of evenings spent humming along to the Boomtown Rats and Dexys Midnight Runners as they coloured in their home. The kitchen bloomed with walls of burnt orange, on which the children's paintings hung in glorious disarray: the bright confident circles of two-year-olds that morphed, in the predictable Lowenfeld sequence, into disembodied faces to which spindly legs and arms were somewhat randomly attached. Then the pink house with the purple tree firmly fixed to a green baseline beneath a blue strip of sky. Then Tom's careful depictions of planes, flying side-on, both wings in full view. And Poppy's ballerinas poised on tiptoe with elaborate hair. The children were older now, well past such naïveté, but she left their drawings pinned beside the refrigerator. She liked them.

Poppy's room they had painted pink, as requested: she had a protracted pink phase. But it was a strong pink, a cyclamen pink, not a pallid tutu pink. And Tom's was charcoal. He hadn't seen the point of all the mucking about, changing things, but if his room must be painted, he wanted it black. Black walls, fitfully lit by the tank that gurgled in one corner with its shoal of tiny luminous fish. The big front room with the bay window and the fireplace had its seventies swirls and curtains in a vigorous Marimekko print, the real thing, from a place in town that specialised in hard-to-find. Two whole bolts of Unikko pattern! It was an extravagance that used up a fair portion of the money put aside for dental bills or when their car, an aged Subaru, finally expired, and there was no real need to replace the existing curtains, which were an inoffensive cream linen of excellent quality. But the Marimekko print would look amazing, and would, she told Rob, last forever!

'Nothing lasts forever,' he said. But he let it go. Janey liked bright things, whereas he did not really care, one way or the other.

The curtains looked great, and on the chimney breast she hung their house-warming gift to themselves: a Sybil Sinclair of a plum tree in full bloom, still recognisable as their plum tree though its trunk had split in some winter gale since the painting was completed. A dark shadow hovered above an expanse of vivid green beneath branches of luminous blossom. It was beautiful, as if it had belonged there always.

And now, at last, their bedroom. The final room to be rescued from terminal pallor. A Friday night in early spring and they were slapping on the undercoat, working themselves to a pleasant state of exhaustion, putting the whole bloody week behind them. Talking while painting was one of their best times together. Rob moaned about the regional council, she moaned about school, but after a while as their brushes moved steadily across the walls and the area of undercoat expanded, all that fell away. They found themselves humming instead. *Come on Eileen, come on.* They could have gone out. It was Friday night after all, and once that would have meant heading into town, a bar, a club with music, a crush of bodies dancing. They could have gone out and had a meal somewhere, pad Thai, then a movie. But the week had been long and filled with minor irritations, so they stayed in and painted instead. Made a start on the undercoat, worked until late, then left the walls half done and opened a bottle of pinot. Sat by the fire.

The new gas fire.

Janey would have preferred to keep the open fire — immense logs blazing within the inglenook — but Rob had said no. There was a good reason why the regional council had banned open fires in the city, and before he could get started on particulates and the air pollution index and rates of asthma, she cut him off. 'Fine,' she said. 'Fine. We'll install gas.' Just so long as it was a proper gas fire with imitation logs, half charred to imitation ash and those imitation flames flaring at predictable intervals. 'If it has to be fake, then it has to be a real honest-to-goodness, in-your-face fake.' Just so long as they retained that absurdly over-the-top inglenook.

The gas fire was fantastic, and the heat output, she had to admit, miles more efficient than any open fire could hope to emulate. They sat on their orange chairs either side of the fake grate where the fake logs burned yet could never be consumed and the efficient fan whirred as the house settled. It was one of the things Janey liked best: the way this wooden structure emitted small satisfied creakings late at night as the timber cooled, like some shore bird settling in the dark upon its nest. She had become accustomed to its utterances: the rattling of the bay window in a southerly, the creak of the loose board in the hallway as Tom padded, half asleep, from his bedroom to the bathroom and back, the tapping of the piece of corrugated iron on the turret that would have to be attended to sometime, but was awkward to reach, would require scaffolding and no doubt prove expensive, so best left till the whole exterior needed repainting.

The house creaked and settled. She had always felt safe and happy here. Some houses had that quality, while others simply didn't. It was an observation based on long experience dating back to a childhood spent trailing after her mother from that dark little cottage in Karamea, to a cabin on a hillside among gorse in Golden Bay, to a flat above a grocery shop in Aro Valley, to a crib overlooking the lagoon at Okarito, to a housebus tinkly with crystals and flappy prayer flags near Alex. Sue was a free spirit, and when she found her wandering man, Zeb, scraggly ponytail and guitar, they wandered freely off to Queensland. But by then Janey was old enough to choose and she did not choose Zeb and those country roads and her mountain momma. She chose instead her aunt, her mother's sister Fern and Uncle Greg who lived in a ranch-style in Palmerston North.

No harm came to her there. Fern and Greg were kind. The house was warm. Yet every time she biked home, head down against the wind along College Street, her heart sank, just a little, at the sight of it.

It was just so featureless. So bland. Whereas this house, with its ridiculous turret, its inglenook and aging roof and night-time creakings, delighted her. It had many layers. When they stripped away the wallpaper in a back bedroom it was to find four different kinds of paper, a pale blue floral over ochre stripes over a pattern of green acanthus, and at the bottom, against the sarking, a layer of newspaper dating from 1910 with pictures of women wearing long skirts and enormous hats. It reminded her of a book she'd read as a child, about a little house that was built upon a hill where it could see the sun and the moon and stars. And steadily, season by season, the world about it changes, from horses and buggies to cars and the city edges nearer until the little house is engulfed by tall buildings blocking out the sun and the moon and stars. It becomes sad and derelict. And then a woman comes by and buys the little house and moves it on a truck far out into the country where it can see the sky once more and is happy. She'd loved that book, with its illustrations of trees in all seasons and the house whose windows were eyes and whose front door was its nose. She'd loved the idea of the building living through change.

And now here she was, living in just such a house, a place that had seen many people come and go, perched on a rise above the river. She loved it for itself. She did not want to restore it to some notion of authenticity, with flowery Edwardian friezes and lumbering antiques. She did not want to retain the off-white good taste of its previous owners. She wanted to play, fill its ample shell with colour, dress it up, a garish old lady with wonky lipstick. There was room for that here. For silliness. For happiness.

So they drink their pinot as the house settles into the dark. It is late, after midnight, when Rob reaches out and touches her hand, the way he does. It's the familiar question to which she feels the familiar response, the bubbling excitement, and they are kissing, they are fumbling on the retro sofa and she is a little drunk, her head somehow not quite attached to the rest of her body, which is tumbling somehow or other onto the mat in front of the fake fire and they are both laughing, but quietly. Tom is staying with his friend VJ somewhere in town, but Poppy could blunder in on them at any time, in flight from some dream, so half-undressed they stumble across the hallway to their bedroom and shut the door. The curtains have been taken down and the windows left wide open to let out the smell of undercoat. The carpet is covered in drop sheets and there are ladders and trestles. It does not look like their bedroom at all. It is strange.

Strangeness has always done it for them. Hotel rooms, for example, where in hushed anonymity, several floors above a city street filled with cars driven by people they do not know, to places they do not know, it is as if they, too, become strangers. Rob becomes the man in the fantasies they sometimes murmur to each another, the man she has just met at a party, or on a beach: the one who picks her out among the crowd, the one whose shadow falls across her as she lies sunbathing naked among the sandhills.

That's the man she meets in the hotel room, not Rob, who wonders if he should get back into surfing, get another job, lose a few kilos, slams in from work, rumpled and fed-up, dragging off his shoes without undoing the laces, kicking them into the corner, saying, 'God, I'm buggered. Bloody commissioners. I need a drink.' Rooting in the cupboard above the fridge where they kept the whisky.

Not that man. On the hotel bed's 500-thread white linen, he is a stranger, someone she picked up ten minutes earlier in the lobby downstairs.

And now, in their bedroom, their bed waits, and it, too, is strange, though they have made love on it, on average three times a week for fifteen years, allowing for interruptions following the birth of each child when she had sat in the dark, feeding, Rob passed out from exhaustion, managing somehow to sleep through the crying. She had leaned against the headboard as first Tom and then Poppy had sucked mightily, while her own body clenched the way it had previously done only at the point of orgasm. And with that clenching came such a surge of love: not the ordinary soppy Valentine's card love, but an all-pervading, fierce attachment to this little creature whose steady slurping relieved the pressure that had built within her breasts. Then there was the time of the wakeful toddler clambering between them at odd hours, squirming into the nest and resisting all attempts at eviction until one of them, usually Rob, gave up and left the child in full possession, chattering away at 2 a.m., while the adult squeezed into a vacated bed among the stuffed toys.

But that time passed. Now the children sleep alone behind doors firmly closed with signs warning off intruders, and two or three times a week, through the tangle of jobs and deadlines and assignments and meetings, she and Rob find their way back to each other. Sometimes a brief coupling before sleep, sometimes a more elaborate business of strangers on a beach or the fiddle of the black lacy outfit Rob had brought back from a trip to Sydney, with suspenders, for God's sake. It slid over stretch marks and cellulite and the scar where Poppy had been cut from her in haste, the ring of masked faces looking down at her as she lay, high as a kite on pethidine. The lacy outfit slid over it all and Rob's hand moved up and under and they were off again.

Tonight they navigate their way over the drop sheets between ladder and trestle to the bed that has been dragged from its customary place by the wall that had once housed a fireplace, long since gibbed over, out into the centre. No time nor need for fiddle, just kissing, unzipping, undoing and falling together onto this strange new bed, and fondling and sucking and she with him between her legs and he with her between his and the rhythm builds, harder, faster, oh oh oh, and his face strange and inward above her and then the groan, the explosion of little lights behind her eyes, the release.

And later, parted now, each sinking onto their own side of the bed to sleep, he murmurs, 'Thank you.' As if she has given him a present. It amuses her, these good manners after they've been writhing round one another, under and over, and here they are, all drying sweat and semen and general stickiness, yet from somewhere, deep in some past training of 'Say "Please"!' 'Say "Excuse me"!' 'Say "May I get down from the table?"' rises this muttered 'Thank you'.

'Thank you,' he says, from a long way off, on his way down the steep slope into sleep. Snuffling at the pillow the way he does in the seconds before oblivion, its soft bulk clearly some primal substitute for the ample breast of his faintly terrifying mother, Ruth, who must once have sat and fed and fiercely loved, though now she exists as dotty doyenne of the Ambleside retirement complex on Edgeware Road. 'Thank you,' as he passes out.

What is he thanking her for? The writhing? When you have been doing something, anything, three times a week for fifteen years, you know how to rate the experience. There is Unsatisfactory. Not Achieved, for those times when they have been too tired, too distracted, too irritable from some earlier argument. There is Satisfactory. Achieved. A little predictable, but pleasant enough. And there is Excellence, for those occasions when everything feels exactly, intuitively right and it has felt like flying, like lifting off.

And tonight? Achieved. Verging on Excellence.

Or is he thanking her for something more general? For their shared life, for the pregnancies, and the children and putting up with his mother, and listening to him moan about the council, for being his friend, his mate? Is he thanking her for being happy to spend Friday night painting a bedroom? Or is the source of gratitude a bit of all that?

'You're welcome,' she says, as she rolls over, drifts out into oblivion. 'And thank you to you, too.'
For all that. The solid structure of their . . .

fifty-two
THE RIVER

Something has happened.

She has stopped eating. She no longer snaps at smaller fish and errant ducklings, their tiny legs furiously paddling overhead.

Her guts have shrunk. Her body is an empty cavity.

Something is about to happen.

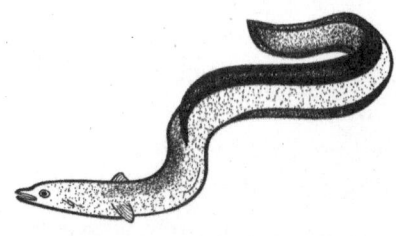

fifty-three

THE FOUNTAIN

4 SEPTEMBER 2010

...is standing at the window, naked, looking out at the dark. Though it is not really dark. Not the darkness he recalls from childhood when he used to let himself out into the night-time world while his parents slept, snoring mightily, in their bedroom in the house overlooking the bay, and his sisters lay in twin beds either side of the rug that was their tightly policed frontier.

Now Rob is a man with a job and family of his own and he is standing at the window in his own home, but every cell of his body remembers wet grass underfoot and the sharp tips of gravel by the sheep yards and the cool watery lick of the wind on his skin, lit by the faint glitter of the river of stars that flows across the universe. And the air was rich with the smell of sheep dung and dry grass and the sea, and it echoed with the strange cries of night birds and the furtive rustling of creatures who belonged, like himself, to the dark, where he, too, was an animal, bare-skinned, pyjamas cast aside, left folded under his pillow. Pyjamas had no place in the world of the animal, the hunter who finds his way about by smell and hearing and the faint light of galaxies.

He is remembering this as he stands by the open window, cool night air brushing his skin, while Janey sleeps on, curled on one side under their duvet. He is fully awake, alert, and not quite sure why. Disturbed perhaps by the blackbird that often sings at night from the walnut tree, deluded by the street lights into thinking it is dawn. The wind shimmies among leaves. His skin prickles.

And then the window gives a little preliminary rattle and something roars up, a rumbling rises beneath his feet, felt in every bone as much as heard, a deep visceral explosion that flings him up into the air, so that he loses balance and falls hard against the sill. Which is in motion, as is the whole house. It sways and jolts as if gathered up by immense hands and brutally shaken, and with the shaking the windows crack and there's the crash of things falling, dwang and soffit splitting asunder as the momentum gathers, stronger, harder and from long training he knows he must get under the doorway. That is the safest place. Beneath a lintel. So somehow as the floor bucks and jumps, he stumbles over trestles and ladders to its protective frame.

Janey has got there before him, flung abruptly from sleep face-down on the floor, scrambling towards the door because above all the din there is a single, high-pitched cry that pulls her like a wire to Poppy's room, to her daughter who is screaming in the jolting dark in her room along the hallway. And she would go to her, but it is like one of those dreams of fever where you cannot move, your legs are trapped though your children are howling as some dark force seizes them, threatens to carry them away. She tries to move, but there are things in the way: a mass of stuff that was not there before, that she must clamber over as it shifts beneath her feet and it is all she can do to stay upright.

She hangs onto the doorframe, to Rob, as the roaring builds, then fades. It seems to pass on towards the east, leaving the house in its wake settling to an uneven rocking, and at last she is able to move out into the darkness that used to be the hallway but, in less than a minute, has become a strange landscape of dust and stone and sharp slivers of glass and unexpected barriers over which, her feet cut and bleeding, she must clamber to her daughter, who is sitting up on her bed, somewhere beyond the mountain range that is her wardrobe fallen aslant a bookshelf and a chest of drawers. And Rob is beside her, grunting as he tries to heave things aside and at last she can reach out, feel about for her daughter, for Poppy, her hair, her frantic little arms, the scream that is like an animal, like a rabbit when it has been hit and cries in the dark.

'The monster!' she cries. 'The monster!' Reverting in an instant to the pre-schooler who had feared monsters beneath her bed, insisting they check before switching off the light, nighty-night. Janey holds her tight as Rob wraps his arms about them and they form a huddle on the bed. Shh ... shhh ... it's all right. It's an earthquake. Janey's shoulders quivering. The wet patch soaking Poppy's nightie.

Rob is all ears. Outside, the sirens are going off: car and house, and every dog in the city has burst into furious barking. The house creaks and groans and under all these noises, there's a strange whispering static he cannot identify. And Tom? Where is Tom? What's the name of his friend? VJ? VJ what?

'Phone,' he says. 'It's on the bench.'

The house sways. They are in the belly of the beast, deep inside some living unpredictable thing. It heaves and moves and there's that breathing, that soft insistent sibilance. He feels his way through the creature's unfamiliar interior to the kitchen. No light to guide him: no comforting glow from the streets outside, no light within from all their various appliances waiting on standby, their computers and heaters and TV and stove. Beneath his feet, the kitchen floor is wet, a sodden morass that smells like vinegar, soy sauce. He feels around and there's his phone dangling from the bench on its charger, and the relief of the message on the tiny screen: 'I OK. U OK?' His fingers are huge and clumsy on the pad but he manages 'We OK. Where U?' The message wings off into the dark as he looks about by the phone's torch light. Every cupboard gapes open, contents spilled at random, the rangehood is detached from the ceiling, the walls split along jagged cracks, a layer of glass glitters on the floor like an unseasonable frost, and there's creamy stuff oozing up between the tiles.

Janey is standing beside him, Poppy glued against her neck. 'Tom?' she says. 'He's okay,' says Rob. The house jolts and there's a cracking overhead. 'Outside!' she says, fumbling at the door. 'Quick!' The door is jammed. But Rob is strong, stronger at this moment than he has ever been. He has the strength of several men. He could lift great weights, run great distances, leap metres into the air. He drags at the door with all this strength and the family steps outside into the safety of the open air.

Except it's not. The torch beam plays over the lawn and it is moving. It shimmers. It gleams and ripples and out here the whispering is louder and he is able at last to identify it. It is the sound of water. It bubbles up between paving stones, it oozes as white silt from tiny cones that have popped up like miniature volcanoes across the lawn, the lawn he mowed only last Sunday. Beside the clothesline a fountain erupts. It rises metres into the air, glittering, before pattering back to earth. It is weirdly beautiful, this fountain rising in their back garden into the night air.

His mind is racing, trying to catch up with his quick attentive body. Liquefied silt, he thinks. Quicksand. Of course. There could be nothing solid beneath us. They could sink into a bottomless morass.

Or drown. A flood. A wave. A massive tsunami like the one recalled from earliest childhood, a card from the Weetbix series of Great Catastrophes. A wave rearing up above tiny straw houses, tiny bending palms and tiny people running hopelessly at its foot. Ant people, like the ant people on the ship that was sliding down into the icy waters, ablaze with light. Like the ant people lying face-down as the volcano's ash fell and buried them and the tiny dog straining hopelessly at its leash.

The wave. He looks out into the dark, listening for the tremor that will announce its arrival, looming above the plum tree, rolling through the dark from Pegasus Bay. The glittering wall surging up Savage Street, gathering to itself all the houses, the cars, the tiny ant people. The torch beam plays feebly over the garage and his bike leaning against the wall and the row of wheelie bins, one fallen, the inorganic one, plastic wrapping floating on the grey ripples, a styrofoam tray that had held last night's steak. Beneath their feet the ground quivers and in slow motion another bin topples. The lid falls open.

And all the time his mind is darting about, fixing on this detail, checking, correcting. If it is this bad here, what must it be like in Wellington, for surely this must be the offshoot of that other distant long-anticipated calamity? The Wairarapa Fault or the Ohariu or the Wellington Fault, take your pick, it could be any one of them, returning at their predictable intervals in this jumpy fractured country, Lambton Quay metres deep in fallen glass, tower blocks slumped, the sea rolling in as it rolled in back in that big quake in 1855, 30-foot-high waves, the harbour emptying, then filling, over and over. Only now it would scoop up Lyall Bay, Kilbirnie, Eastbourne, Petone. Motorway and railway and airport disappearing as the land sinks back below the sea, leaving the ant people to scramble as best they can along the hilltops to safety.

Or maybe it's the Alpine Fault that has shifted. The most active faultline in the world and overdue for its next appearance. Vast avalanches of schist and granite may have fallen, chasms may have opened across the Main Divide, waves may have submerged Greymouth and Westport and the muddy green farms. The whole spine of the island may have been reshaped in a few seconds, and here they are, in steady reliable old Christchurch, experiencing the ricochet.

He has reeled off the figures to meetings and conferences, he has modelled the events: vertical movement on the Kekerengu Bank Fault, the Hikurangi Trench, the Wairau, Hope or Awatere Fault, near-field tsunami, waves of 5 metres, 7.5 metres, 14 metres, frequencies of 150 years, 300 years, 2000 years, 6000 years, shelf resonance on the Canterbury coastline, beach slope, permeability and viscosity, Synolakis' law and the mathematics of wave run-up, and click another graphic for the screen. But now the graph is jumping beneath his feet. The deck is rocking. The lawn is inundated, and the wave, the wave ...

And he is the ant person. His wife. His daughter. His son, wherever he might be at this precise moment. All ant people.

'Holy crap,' says Janey, holding Poppy tight. Her voice is high and bright and strange.

Or maybe this is the symptom of some other event. Not seismic but volcanic. A break somewhere in this country's fragile crust. A cone rising out in the bay like that island off the coast of Iceland. Surtsey. The plume that rose, with no warning, no scientific prediction. A fishing boat found it, went to check expecting fire, a ship in trouble, men clinging to burning wreckage, and found instead churning water about the tip of new land. Taking shape as new land has always taken shape at these opposite ends of the globe. Maybe somewhere out in Pegasus Bay at this very moment, steam is rising and a cloud of ash and this was the tremor that accompanied its arrival.

The water gurgles and licks at the step and he is thinking quickly. The car? Drive to safety? But what if the roads are impassable? And what if Tom returns and finds them gone? What then? He steps from the deck into the dark water, feeling cautiously for something solid under his feet as Janey says, 'What the hell are you doing? Rob! There could be holes!' But the path is intact under that weird sucking mud, so he wades to the shed where the kayaks are stored. He drags one then the other to the deck where he ties them to the railing. Should the water rise on a surge, above the steps, above the house, above the whole city, he will save his family. They will surf the great wave, they will paddle for the safety of the Port Hills while the rest of the city takes its chances.

Poppy whimpers. 'Right,' says Janey in the strange brisk voice. 'We're getting chilled. We need a hot drink. We'll light up the barbecue. How about that, Popps? A late-night barbecue. We'll make Milo. With sprinkles!'

There was, of course, no gas in the barbecue bottle, so no Milo. They should have made sure the bottle was full. They should have had a proper torch, with viable batteries, rather than the selection of dead torches among the rubber bands and birthday candles and general detritus in the kitchen drawer. They should have had a radio, one of those wind-up dynamo types. But they didn't. Instead, while Rob tells Poppy a story about being a kid on the peninsula and how he used to go out at night all on his own while everyone was asleep and pretend to be an animal because he liked the dark, it was exciting, it was an adventure just like the one they were having tonight, Janey fossicks in the wreckage of the kitchen and finds bananas and apple juice. She ventures further in, torch beam picking up the shadowy profiles of strange things: a table, a bookshelf, Rob's maps dangling askew on the hallway walls or fallen, smashed along with Ruth's ornate Victorian mirror. She clambers over the moraine that has materialised on the floor of the bedroom to snatch up warm clothes, shoes, another duvet. She makes her way cautiously to the bathroom at the end of the hall, obeying some long distant injunction, perhaps dating from her brief spell as a Girl Guide back in 1983, to fill the bath with drinking water. And all the time the house shudders, speaking its new language of creak and sigh, its foreign, unfamiliar tongue.

Then they sit together on the swing-seat on the deck wrapped in the duvets, adrift upon the waters, their yellow kayaks moored to the railing. They sit in the dark to conserve the torch batteries, waiting for . . .

fifty-four
THE RIVER

Something is happening.

In the cavity that is her body, the eggs that have hung there all along, tiny seeds in the dark, have begun to swell.

They are globules, twenty million glistening, strung like pearls.

Something is about to happen.

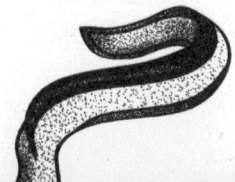

fifty-five
THE BRICKS
OCTOBER 2010

...adds another to the orderly pile by the shed. There isn't much else he can do until the assessors arrive to examine the extent of the damage. Everything must be left exactly as it is except where temporary repairs are necessary for waterproofing or to remove danger. The brick inglenook had collapsed along with two entire chimneystacks, which had crashed through the walls in living room and bedroom. They'd cleared the mess, laboriously moving the bricks outside, and now he is stacking them against the wall of the shed, and with every brick he thinks, feeling the solid weight of it in his hand, thank God.

Thank God they'd moved the bed away from the wall. Thank God they hadn't been buried under a pile of bricks.

He picks up another, knocks away rotten mortar, adds it to the stack. Something to do while they wait for their house to be repaired. The whole process has been laid out for them, clear as day: their house, like houses throughout the country, is insured by the government itself via the Earthquake Commission.

Tsunami, landslip, volcanic explosion, flood and earthquake, a whole line-up of natural disaster could wreak havoc, tear and roar. But here on Savage Street, they are secure. They will be reimbursed for damage up to a maximum of $100,000. Should the damage prove worse, the cost to repair or rebuild estimated at more than $100,000, they can turn to their private insurers. A major international company has agreed to come to their aid. It's all there on the contract he had retrieved from the house when he stumbled back through the mess that had felt like the end and the beginning of the world.

The file box was on the shelf in the room they grandly called the office, though neither of them had ever worked there. If he had to work at home he preferred sitting on the sofa in the living room, laptop on his knee, jazz greats on shuffle, while Janey preferred the big table, computer at one end among piles of mail, flyers, magazines, newspapers, birthday cards and downloaded recipes that would make use of the random contents of the fridge: strawberries, broccoli, a piece of gurnard, some leftover rice. The office was a repository of stuff they mean to organise sometime, a cluttered desk with the PC they no longer use now that they have gone over to the other side, to Apple, a cabinet containing ancient tax returns, Janey's outmoded lesson plans, folders of material they must have once thought it necessary to retain. The file box was on a high shelf, safely above the creamy silt that had seeped from the skirting board into the carpet. It held their important documents: passports, wills, insurance policies, home, contents, car, life, proof that they were covered. A warm quilt of recompense and bureaucratic concern for their welfare lay over them. They had kept the filebox beside them as the sun came up on that bright unreal morning and the birds began to sing as if nothing whatever had happened overnight.

They were covered. Their house had sustained some damage: that was clear. But all would be well. Earthquakes were a predictable part of living in a country balanced upon two opposing tectonic plates. This was not the first time he and Janey had experienced the jolting, nor would it be the last. But for the time being, they were safe, Poppy was safe, Tom was safe. They were not, after all, paddling towards the Port Hills, eating bananas, their documents stored in a dry bag in the hull.

On that strange bright day, Rob had cycled round to Ambleside, grey silt dragging at his wheels, to find Ruth seated in the dining room with some other old women, having an early breakfast. The power in this part of the city still seemed to operate, or perhaps they had a generator. A TV flickered unattended in one corner: an image of a city street littered with masonry, a car buried under rubble. 'Well,' said Ruth, bright-eyed and smiling, 'Jerry put on quite a show last night, didn't he? But we're still smiling! Chins up and carry on, eh girls? Now, would you like a cup of tea, young man?'

On that strange bright day, they had compared notes with their neighbours: with the Tuitamas next door on one side and, on the other side, Bronwyn and Rick, the new tenants. With Sharon, who lived across the road, and the old couple they'd glimpsed sometimes in their garden but had never really known before. The Novaks. Stan and Kitty. Tom had got back around 8 a.m., hero on a skateboard from the wars returning, breathless with the excitement of it all, these huge cracks everywhere, crazy! The power had stayed out, but they had sat in the car, chassis-deep in silt in the driveway, and listened to the radio, where the shaking was calmly measured, a fault, previously undetected, 40 kilometres to the west, 7.1, extensive damage, a single fatality, a man who died of shock.

On that strange bright day they had made a start on the clean-up. They had tossed broken stuff into bags and cartons, wiped a sticky mingled soup from the floors, begun lifting sodden carpet, carrying it out into the sun to dry, shovelling some of the strange grey silt from path and drive. It lay, inert, a dead weight on the shovel, far heavier than ordinary earth, weird stuff that had come from deep below ground where no air could penetrate or lighten. They had a cup of coffee with the old couple. They insisted. Stan was not the kind to let his gas bottles run empty. 'We're all set up,' he had said, skinny and balding, legs like dry kindling in baggy shorts. Plaid shirt. Old army beret. His garden had been an orderly place where the pansies formed ranks and the lawn was firmly under control. He had a selection of shears and clippers that hung on his garage walls with other tools, each over its own black shadow.

On that strange bright day, silt had covered lawn and pansies, and the tools had been ripped from their silhouettes. The old couple's house had slumped toward the river and plaster had fallen from the ceilings, but they had set up the barbecue and lit the thermette. Stan said you couldn't beat a thermette, they'd used them in the desert, and Kitty handed round biscuits, little chewy almond biscuits with an Italian name no one afterward could remember. Kitty was small and neat and had on her lipstick, cherry red, despite the disturbances of the previous few hours. They all sat in the sun and drank their coffee and the strange bright day felt oddly festive.

Now, Rob kneels on grey powdery earth and stacks the bricks. Without its chimney pots, the house looks odd. 'It's lost its ears!' Janey had said. And he can see what she meant. The house does indeed look as if some vital part has been amputated: like a white cat on the farm when he was a child that had lost its ears to sun-induced cancer. Two ragged holes have been left in the corrugate.

On the strange bright day, he had climbed onto the roof clutching a heavy length of blue tarpaulin and some rope. He did not like heights and it was a long way down and the ground shook from time to time. Janey had gone ahead of him and was already straddling the roof ridge, unfurling the other tarp. Between them, as a pesky wind snatched at the heavy plastic, threatening to drag them both off and out, sailing above the garden, they managed to tie the tarps in place, anchoring them as best they could to make a couple of rough patches. They wouldn't last, but this was only a temporary solution, sufficient to keep out the rain for the short time before proper tradesmen would effect proper repairs.

They had used more tarpaulin to patch the gaps within the house where the chimney breasts had avalanched onto the carpet, the last tarpaulins in stock on the strange bright day when they were finally able to drive across town to Placemakers. Everyone was needing tarpaulins. Everyone had fallen chimneys and gaps to patch. They had carried home the tarps as if they were rare treasure, and made their temporary repairs and now, a month later, a new sound had joined the night-time creakings of their house: a soft insistent drip drip drip in the fire cavity whenever it rained and the protection offered by tarpaulin had been breached.

They no longer sleep in their half-painted bedroom, not trusting the cracks that snake over the plaster ceiling from the heavy central rose. It seemed wiser to drag their mattress to a room down the hall, a bare little room with a ceiling mercifully free of decoration. It is a bit cramped. Poppy has refused to sleep in her own bed after the arrival of the monsters, and every night squeezes between them. Tom is less perturbed, though for the first time in years, he sleeps with his door ajar and his window wide open. At VJ's, doors and windows had jammed and he'd been unable to escape.

Rob would never tell him so, but he likes hearing his son across the hall, likes his daughter snug between them, the whole family safe as darkness falls. No background computer hum, no whirring from the fridge, no blue glow from Tom's fishtank, which had smashed, leaving its shoal of tiny fish open-mouthed on the bedroom carpet. No street light glow from behind the curtains. They are like some primate family, reverted to a stage before houses or cities, huddled for warmth in a cave.

They are safe. They have shelter. They have water. If the town supplies were contaminated, there was the tap in the back garden which pre-dated the town system and drew directly from an underground source. They have the barbecue for cooking, and always, now, a spare gas bottle. They have the file box.

They have done as requested: disturbed as little as possible, while they wait for the process of assessment to begin. They have placed all smaller broken things in cartons as advised. *Do not throw away any damaged items unless they are perishable or dangerous. If you do throw away any items, please take photos of them.* They have gathered up the broken cups, the antique ginger jar and the blue and white dinner set Ruth gave to them for safekeeping when she moved to Ambleside for her little holiday, just a loan, mind, I'll be back! They have kept what remained of her Victorian mirror after it crashed from the hallway wall. The cartons wait for inspection on the big table. As back-up, they have photographed everything and added the images to a new file on the computer: EQ Claim.

Steadily, in an orderly fashion, they are putting everything back together, stacking the pieces, brick by . . .

fifty-six
THE RIVER

Something is happening.

Her head is changing its profile. It has become flatter, narrower.

It is pointed like an arrow, lean and full of purpose. Her lips are thinner.

Something is about to happen.

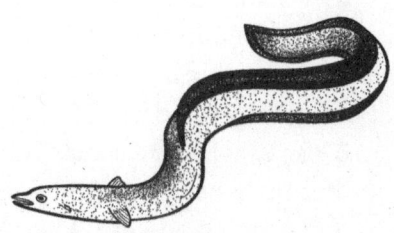

fifty-seven

THE PILES

NOVEMBER 2010

...dry and powdery. Like a bunker in Afghanistan or one of those barren desert places where they're fighting the Taliban and those Muslim dudes with the massive beards. Secure. No one can get at him there. It's dark, too, once he tugs the door closed. It takes a while for his eyes to adjust. The piles of the house form ranks on either side, set at even spaces apart like that buried army. The one they dug out in China with all those soldiers lined up to kill in a battle that was going to last forever. They even had horses and chariots and a carriage for the emperor. Their hands were clenched to hold spears and stuff but the weapons had rotted under the mound so now they were going to fight forever empty-handed. Thousands of them, stood to attention under the ground. Lifesize. The art teacher said they had been painted bright colours, red and blue. Then they'd buried them.

The columns down here form ranks, square and sturdy, fading away into the dark. There's a flicker of light in the furthest corner. A cat maybe. Or a rat. They nest down here for the same reason he comes here: because it's safe, because it's warm. Cats, rats, mice, sometimes a possum. There are bones everywhere: tiny fragile skulls, the pointed teeth bared in a grimace. A complete mummified cat, the skin shrunken around backbone and rib cage, the legs arched as if the animal had died in the act of jumping. As if it was leaping towards something and then froze in mid-air and fell to the ground, dead. Like it had been hit by one of those shells they use in Iraq that were designed to kill people but not smash the real estate, so those guys died looking like they were completely intact, no blood or anything. Except their insides had been completely liquefied, blown to bits.

The cat had lain beside one of the piles, leaping into nothing, its sharp teeth smiling. He had taken it up to his room but his mother said it was gross. She had this thing about skulls and bones. Not in this house, she said. It was like the mummy would bring bad luck. He had hung onto it for a while because he didn't want to do what she said, not right away, but once out of the dry air under the house it began to smell so finally he took it back underground. Tossed it into the dark corner where the cat or rat or whatever it is crouches, eyes burning. People used to think animals had fires inside them and that's why their eyes flared in the dark. That was kind of amazing. Little fires inside the skull. It made sense.

He leans against one of the piles. Above his head he can hear the thud of feet on floorboards. The rapid one two one two of his mother, always at the half run, crossing the dining room to the side verandah. Poppy landing thump thump thump doing her practice in the hall where she uses the dado as a barre. She'll never be a ballet dancer. He's told her so. She's too fat. But she persists. Thump thump, landing with her feet turned out in first position. And that steady tread is his dad moving about in the kitchen. Their voices are muted and far away. Pipes gurgle, emerging from the floorboards, tracking along the bearers before disappearing into dry earth.

He likes it here. He has always liked it, ever since he first discovered the little door behind the hydrangeas. He likes its smell of dry timber and concealment, the way he can slip in, undetected, close the little door behind him. No one knows he's there. He has told no one, not even VJ. When the silt bubbled up his first thought had been for the bunker. It smelled different now, with an added tang of shingle and riverweed, but he has spread some plastic and it is fine. Sometimes the stumps quiver. The whole square-cut army springs to attention as the house sways overhead. To begin with it unnerved him but now it also feels familiar, like a dog twitching as it sleeps, dreaming rabbit dreams. The house twitches and he waits and it settles back on its stumps.

He leans back, and flicks open his laptop. That's another reason he likes it here. The reception. He is right underneath the modem in the living room. He opens a packet of chippies, sets it beside him for a snack and takes down his headphones from their usual place between the bearers as the laptop opens onto the limitless vistas of the Paracosm. Beyond the Iron Plains lie the distant peaks of the Mountains of Lontaz. In caverns below those snow-clad peaks lies the only known source of Parraxium, a substance so hard, so sharp when forged, that nothing can resist it. With a weapon created from Parraxium, you could counter the hordes of Dark Striders who infest the land. You could create tools of immense strength with which to build a fortress on the islands that are rumoured to exist beneath the choking metallic fog that cloaks the Iron Plains, maybe several forts, maybe an entire city.

For years, when he opened his laptop, he has entered the Paracosm. He has set out upon the journey, a young apprentice boy with his companion, the Grimling, Xan. 'You must step forward boldly,' the Grimling had instructed as it lay dying by the road, its belly ripped wide by the talons of a Dark Strider. 'Only for the bold will the Iron Plains offer solid ground. For the timid, they will be nothing but fog through which you will fall into the bottomless Deep that lies beneath the Paracosm . . .'

'A kid's game,' says VJ. 'And the graphics are crap.' When Tom goes to his place, they play Death Zone 2, and it is better, that world of abandonment where Jed Rowstein, the Vietnam vet, and Max the IT genius and Lola the beautiful co-ed fight their way across a city infested with Pathos. Once the Pathos had been ordinary citizens until mutant mosquitoes had spread a virus that transformed them into voracious killers who roam the streets, sucking blood from their hapless victims, passing on a plague that evolves rapidly with every transference in its levels of complexity and evil.

The graphics are undeniably superior. The city a maze of empty buildings in perpetual gloom, filled with dark alleys and shadowy corners where any danger might lurk, the Pathos devising ever more ingenious methods of killing and ever more ingenious methods of disguise. With every weapon at their disposal, Jed, Max and Lola make their way to the town hall where, a dying human has told them, before the virus took hold, a rooftop helicopter exists that might lift them to safety.

Tom usually chooses Max, but sometimes he takes Jed, shooting to kill with speed and accuracy, as they pass through the city, find the town hall in flames, struggle south over forested hills infested with Pathos to a harbour where perhaps they might find a ship that will carry them offshore, though there is no telling if the infection has spread worldwide and nowhere, on this whole infected planet, is safe and no one, on this whole infected planet, can be trusted.

The deaths are more explicit, the narrative less predictable, but still, when he is on his own, Tom returns to the Paracosm. He doesn't see the point of change for its own sake. He likes the Iron Plains under their rolling, though not, it has to be admitted, very lifelike, metallic fog. He likes the limitless world that hangs suspended above the Deep, even if everything in the Paracosm has been reduced to a Lego-block cube. He has played it for so long. The apprentice boy is called Hawk. He stands before the dangerous seething of the Iron Plains. He takes a deep breath, fixes his eyes on the distant mountains, steps into the fog.

The pile at Tom's back quivers. The noise rises, a kind of roaring that approaches fast and the house jolts. Then it passes. There's a pause and the footsteps begin again overhead. Tom helps himself to a handful of chippies. Salt and vinegar. The grains stick to his fingers.

Behind him roam the Dark Striders. There is nothing for it but to advance. Hawk steps into the unknown. For an instant, his foot waves about in empty air. Perhaps he is not brave enough. The fog billows round his legs, chilling him to the bone, then mercifully, with a deafening clang, a cube slides into place beneath him. He stands on a tiny iron platform above the Deep. He finds his balance, takes another breath, steps forward once more and clang! Another plate, as solid as the first. Then another.

The Iron Plains take shape beneath ...

fifty-eight
THE RIVER

Something is happening.

Her eye sockets are enlarging.

Her eyes stare. A blue rim forms about them.

She is all eyes, seeing everything.

Something is about to happen.

fifty-nine

THE OUTSIDE TAP

DECEMBER 2010

... **Poppy and** Talia from next door are bouncing on the trampoline. It's hot. Poppy has on her new togs. They are red with a little frilly skirt round her middle. Talia's are new, too. They are blue with white spots. They have turned on the hose. It snakes across the lawn from the outside tap with the purest water in the world. It never has to be boiled. It comes from a river that flows right under their house. You can't see it but it is there, a long way down, on its way from the mountains to the sea. The water from their kitchen taps sometimes has to be boiled and tastes a bit like swimming pools. The water from the outside tap tastes like ice.

She directs a jet of the purest water in the world above the trampoline. It's her turn to squirt while Talia jumps. When the water hits Talia's bare skin, she squeals. She leaps higher. They have lain side by side for ages on the tramp, warming up on black plastic. Through the fence there's the sound of Talia's dad talking to the big giggly uncles who are visiting for Christmas, and across the back lawn there's the sound of her own mum banging and clattering about the kitchen.

The air smells richly of summer and roasting meat. Talia's dad and the uncles are cooking a pig on a spit. Usually they would cook it on rocks on the ground, but the ground is funny this year: it's dead and heavy so they are cooking it on the spit instead. The pig turns over and over with an iron stick poked through its bottom and out its mouth. From Poppy's house comes the smell of turkey, stuffed and basted. There's a ham, too, a fleshy pink lump that, despite being coated in rings of pineapple and scarlet cherries, is unmistakably the leg of another unfortunate pig, its little black tiptoe foot removed. Poppy has been wondering lately about becoming vegetarian. Lots of people are. And that leg sitting impassively in the fridge since yesterday morning has finally persuaded her. Maybe after lunch …

Poppy's mum is flushed and in a bad mood. Her mum is here. Sue, who lives in Australia. Except she isn't Sue any more, or Nana, or Grandma: she's Sahana, which makes her mum mad, though Poppy finds that puzzling. Sahana is a much nicer name than Sue, and shouldn't everyone be able to choose their own name if they want to?

'No,' said her mother. 'It just confuses everybody.'

'I'd like to change my name,' said Poppy. 'I'd like to be called Beyoncé.'

'No, you wouldn't,' said her mum. 'Now go outside and play. I've got heaps to do. I have no idea why I agreed to this whole stupid family thing.'

Poppy could have said, 'But you do have an idea. It's because it's Sahana's birthday,' but her mother was furiously whipping cream so it did not seem like a very good idea. Ten people for lunch because Sahana had the same birthday as Jesus, and this year she was going to be sixty, which was very old indeed. Sahana and some American she has picked up at a yoga retreat in Bali. 'God knows what he'll be like,' her mother said. 'She has appalling taste in men.' ('Taste?' said Poppy. 'You mean she eats them?' And all the grown-ups laughed as if she had made a joke. 'More or less,' said her mum.)

There was Auntie Fern and Uncle Greg and Uncle Lou, who was Sue/Sahana's brother, and his boyfriend Miguel, who had driven up from Queenstown in Lou's car ('a classic MG,' her dad called it, which was evidently a good thing) with a cake in a big box on the back seat and a couple of manic Jack Russells. Lou was a chef and made amazing cakes.

The dogs race about the lawn, ears flattened, leaping the rows of vegetables in the garden and barking frantically as Poppy lifts the hose's heavy head and the purest water in the world forms a rainbow through which Talia does a kneesie, then bounces back onto her feet, squealing.

Around the trampoline their toys lie in little heaps where they have fallen. Poppy's dolls and teddy and the stuffed koala Sahana brought from Australia, Talia's dolls and Little Pony with its flowing blue mane. It's their favourite game: Earthquakes. You arrange all the toys you can find on the trampoline, then you take turns to see how hard you can jump and how high and far the toys can fly. They bounce off in all directions, faces frozen in fixed expressions of happy acceptance as they spin with stiff splayed legs through the blue summer air.

When Isobel lived across the road their flight was truly spectacular. Isobel had a totally enviable collection of toys sent by her granny in Scotland. A single jump released a blizzard of Barbies and teddies that rained down upon the garden. But Isobel doesn't live there any more. Her mum Sharon didn't like the aftershocks. You could hear her yell after every one.

'Fuck!' she'd scream, which was a very bad word, and she made Isobel and her brother sleep on a mattress under the table because she was frightened stuff might fall on their heads, like in that story about the chicken who thought the sky was falling when it was only an acorn.

It was quite nice, actually, under the table. Isobel's mum put a sheet over so it was like a tent, and she slept there beside the children, with a torch by her pillow and Isobel's dad's hard hat that he used to wear when he was cutting down trees, which was a fairytale kind of job: being a woodcutter. Except one of the trees fell on him. So Isobel's mum kept his hat beside her, yelled 'Fuck!' so loudly they could hear her all the way over the road, and one afternoon Poppy had come home from school to find Isobel standing on the footpath with a big suitcase on wheels and her best teddy. 'We're going on a plane,' she said. 'We're going to live in Scotland. Mum says they don't have earthquakes in Scotland. I'm going to get a puppy.'

She Skyped once or twice. Said it rained a lot in Scotland and it was hard to tell what people were saying. She had had her hair cut. She held up a squirmy brown puppy who was very cute. His name was Bruno. Her voice sounded different. She had a friend called Layla. She stopped Skyping.

Poppy and Talia used to go sometimes to Isobel's house. The gate had a padlock but you could squeeze through a hole in the fence into the garden. It was kind of messy with lots of long grass and when you looked through the windows you could see Isobel's bed, still with her mattress and some toys lined up as usual on the chest of drawers, as if she had just stepped out and was about to come back into the room. Her scooter still leaned against the wardrobe. There were cups on the kitchen shelves and a dead pot plant on the window sill. It was like the Sleeping Beauty's castle, the roses growing up and up till they covered the whole house.

They would not be going again. Last time, they had squeezed through the fence and were standing on tiptoe looking into Isobel's window when a scrawny hand gripped their shoulders and a high witchy voice said, 'And what are you girls doing?'

It was only old Mrs Novak but not quite Mrs Novak, with her glittery eyes and blood-red lips. She made them come to her house, though they had both been told over and over that they must never go into strange houses.

She had seated them on high stools at her kitchen bench and served them biscuits that were probably poison, and orange juice, and while they ate and drank, choking on every morsel, every drop, she had sat stroking her big ginger cat whose name was Zitto and told them about Christmas when she was a little girl, and how everyone went to church in the snow at midnight on Christmas Eve and then they all came home to a feast, a big feast with soup made of thistles, which didn't sound very nice, but she said it was. It was delicious. And fish, seven different kinds, there had to be seven, and a whole stuffed eel as big as your leg, which didn't sound very nice either but exactly the sort of thing a witch might eat.

And next day, said Mrs Novak, on Christmas Day, there was another feast. This time, it was roast lamb and little cakes made of chickpeas and chocolate, and they didn't have Father Christmas but a kind old woman, a good witch who had given the presents meant for her own little baby, who had died, to the baby Jesus instead. So every year she came, flying through the air on her magic broom, and for good children she brought toys and lollies like bits of coal.

'Coal?' asked Poppy.

She knew about coal. It was a black stone that burned. Their teacher had told them about a place where people went to dig coal and there had been a fire and they were trapped under the ground, waiting in the dark, crying and sad, for someone to come and rescue them. She had shown them a picture, smoke pouring from the hole, and she had brought a piece of coal to show them because none of the children knew what coal looked like.

It didn't look like something you could eat. But Mrs Novak was looking sad remembering the coal lollies and the thistles and the eel, and then, appallingly, while Poppy and Talia choked down their poison orange juice, their poison biscuits, which tasted very nice, though that was part of their danger, the old woman sat down at her piano and began to sing, 'Tu scendi dalle stelle,' in a high witchy wavery voice. They sat either side of the bench, heads down, not daring to catch her eye, until finally, every crumb consumed, she released them, with more biscuits in shiny scarlet boxes tied with ribbon for their mums and dads. Poppy and Talia ran as fast as they could, back across the road to the safety of the garden where they dumped the poison biscuits in the hedge.

And they didn't die, and now Talia executes a perfect somersault and Poppy aims the hose so she lands in a shower of diamonds. The sight of the water, gleaming in sunlight, falling and falling, makes her dreamy. She's a bit sleepy anyway, having gone to bed late. Sahana had suggested the midnight service, though none of them, said her mother, had been inside a church in years apart from weddings and the occasional funeral, but hey! Why not? Everyone except Poppy's dad, who said religion was bullshit. Even Tom came, who asked if there'd be monks.

There were no monks, and no snow, just the big cathedral doors open to a warm wind blowing dust round the Square. They sang carols, some of which she knew from school, and then the people stood up and sat down and murmured words. And Tom took out his phone until Janey reached over and shook her head, no. And Poppy must have gone to sleep and been carried to the car because she woke some time later in her own bed. In the darkness she could hear voices. Next door, Talia's dad and mum and all the cousins and uncles and aunties were singing. It sounded nice. She went back to sleep.

And in the morning there had been presents, the new togs, the Jack Russells, Sahana in pink silk, the table set with flowers on the deck, the turkey, the pig's leg. And the trampoline. Which is always bouncy. So bouncy you can't feel the rest of the world bouncing. You can't feel it shake. Because the world does shake. It can do all sorts of things you don't expect. It can roar and crack things and it can go on fire. It can explode and you can be trapped in the dark, so she holds the hose high. She points it straight to the sky and Talia from next door bounces up, hair flying, into a dazzling arc made of the purest ...

sixty

THE RIVER

Something is happening.

She has changed colour.

No longer an anonymous shadow in the water.

Her back is darker, but her belly has become silver.

She gleams.

She is different to others of her kind.

Something is about to happen.

sixty-one
THE BOTTOM SHELF
JANUARY 2011

… **is looking** for the tent pegs. They used to be kept with the tent in a box Rob had labelled in black felt-tip 'Camping Gear' and stored on the bottom shelf at the back of the garage. But that box had been buried when the earth bubbled up, then set like concrete. They'd had to dig it out, along with all the other stuff that had lain submerged in silt. It had been like an excavation, hacking away to uncover the evidence of past lives: the bundle of carabiners from the Pre-Child Era, when hanging from a rope over a sheer drop seemed like fun. Preserving jars from her Maternal Era of ferocious gardening, pickling and preserving that came to an end when she returned to full-time teaching. Crates of bottles from Rob's Home Brew Era. Paint pots, trays and rock-hard rollers smeared with earlier colour schemes. A bundle of plastic that was the deflated paddling pool into which Poppy had slid at birth, in the hushed warm dark of the living room that would be, forever after, her daughter's room. The exact place where she was born. The feeling of newborn skin against Janey's shoulder, Rob beside her, the two of them looking for the first time into their daughter's wrinkled, wonderful little face. The pool had lain half buried in the garage, along with nuts and bolts and discarded tools, furls of electrical lead, assorted metal parts

belonging to forgotten appliances that might yet find a purpose.

They had dug it all out and tossed most of it onto the pile destined for the dump, for future purpose now seemed uncertain. Off to the dump, along with the cartons of broken stuff — the remains of cups and glasses and Ruth's blue and white dinner set — that they had been keeping as instructed for the assessors.

Des and Craig. Big and bluff, they turned up a few weeks after the quake, filling the hallway with a kind of flat-footed assurance that could only mean police. And they were. Ex-cops from Queensland, come over to give you Kiwis a bit of a hand. They did not seem especially interested in the cartons and the remains of Ruth's dinner set. Instead, they walked heavily about, glancing at the cracks, the tarpaulins, the patches, the broken roof, the little door that led to the crawlspace under the house, for surely they would want to examine the piles? Janey had been dubious about that door: could it accommodate the generous bulk of Des or Craig? She need not have worried. The assessors were no more interested in the piles than the remains of a blue and white gravyboat. They walked about, filled in paper forms attached to a clipboard, tick tick tick, and they were done. 'Yeah, well ...' said Des, '... you look like honest folk. You'll be hearing back in a couple of weeks.' And off they went, filled with kindly Anzac hands-across-the-Tasman goodwill to the next place. 'That was weird,' said Janey to Rob, watching them walk down the path. 'It didn't feel like they were assessing the house at all. It felt like they were assessing *us*.'

The tent hangs to air over the clothesline. But the pegs. Where the hell are the pegs? The ground shimmies under her knees. Three point four, she thinks with that tiny part of her brain that pays automatic attention to such things. Hundreds of aftershocks have rattled through, sometimes several a day, a swarm overnight. At first they ran, found their shoes set ready by the bedroom door, but now they scarcely waken. 'Four point two,' she'll mutter to Rob before falling back to sleep. 'Three point eight,' he'll mutter in reply and in the morning they'll check on Geonet. Each shock registers as a tiny bubble, popping over the map of the city like a raindrop falling on a pond.

The shelves rattle overhead as the ripple passes eastward to dissipate in the waters of Pegasus Bay. They had it right, she thinks: the old people, when they saw the earth as a woman lying on her back and this little baby, this Ruaumoko, in her belly, kicking, quivering, rolling over. Not setting out to hurt or harm, but simply moving the way her babies had moved within her. There was the quiver under the navel that announced their presence, like a butterfly flapping its bright wings within cupped hands. And as the sack grew tighter round the growing body, there was the squirming, the tiny mounds that were elbows or knees nudging against her skin. The upheaval of rolling over, alive within her in that miraculous private fashion that could not be shared completely with anyone, not even Rob.

Janey kneels on the dry grey earth in the garage thinking they had it right and everything was alive, everything was breathing. She hadn't known it properly before, not with her whole body the way she knows it now, and the knowing comforts her. When the earth quivers, stuff could fall on her head: jars of nails, a roll of chicken wire. Concentrating on the baby and the aliveness of things helps to calm her.

She does not panic as Sharon used to panic, yelling 'Fuck!' across the road before her precipitate escape, but in city shops, at the movies, in her house, she no longer feels quite safe.

The shocks jolt and rattle. The experts say this is to be expected; in fact a steady release of tension is desirable. There is a predictable pattern to these natural events. While that pattern unfolds, she and Rob have taken some sensible precautions. They sleep in the back bedroom, keeping the window always open, they have stored away anything that might fall and smash, they have tied the kitchen cupboard handles so they cannot swing open, spilling their contents, they have criss-crossed all the glass in the windows with strips of black electrical tape for reinforcement.

She still startles at sudden noises — a truck clanging over a loose manhole cover, a gate slamming — but this will pass. The aftershocks will dwindle in size and frequency. They will all recover. House and city will be repaired. This is the way things are.

Just the same, she longs for the tent. She wants to find the pegs, pack the car, head out onto the main road south, the plains stretching wide in summer sunlight edged by mountains dabbed with summer snow. She longs for shelterbelts of eucalypt and wattle and macrocarpa, the resinous scent borne on a dry wind through the open window. She longs to take the bridges one by one, car wheels clipping across the joints and the swirl of water below, though Rob says, as he always says as they cross the bridges, Look at that, no water, they're buggering the whole place up, and when he was a kid they used always to stop around here and have a swim, there used to be a beautiful swimming hole just there, by those willows, but now look at it. What a bloody mess.

And she should care, she does care, for she also remembers how it was to swim in river water, smooth grey pebbles underfoot and willows overhead, resonant with the sawing of cicadas.

But all she can think about is the tent. The tent pitched in the corner of the O'Malley's paddock by a river that gushed, small and clear close to the source, and the road has dwindled to a track barely visible in dry brown grass and magpies quardle ardle in the trees. Christmas a receding memory. Baking, roasting, vacuuming, the tree, the lights, food and drink served in the random selection of bowls and glasses that had survived the quake.

'What a pity,' Fern said, surveying the cartons of broken stuff. 'All that lovely china.'

'It's just stuff,' said Janey.

'Ah yes,' said Sahana, bracelets tinkling. 'We all learn the emptiness of earthly possessions.'

She was ensconced in the sleepout over the garage with the American, an astonishingly flexible yoga instructor whom you came across at odd moments, upside down in an immaculate handstand or twisted into Astavakrasana beneath the plum tree. The others had checked into a motel, Fern and Greg because they didn't want to be a nuisance and Lou and Miguel after Sahana objected to the dogs.

'Not inside,' she said. 'They give me asthma.'

This house gave her asthma, the city, the entire country. It was a major reason she chose to live in Australia.

'Dogs didn't bother you when we were kids,' said Lou. 'Remember Monty? You were fine around Monty.'

'I've become sensitised,' said Sahana.

'And our dogs are our family,' said Lou.

'But they're not really, are they?' said Sahana. 'They're not your actual children. Yours and Miggle's.' (She never pronounced it properly.) 'They're animals.'

Her breath was becoming rattly. She left the room to do some intercostal breathing while the dogs whined at the french doors, scratching at the glass.

They all left at last, Fern after making a trip to town on Boxing Day from which she returned ashen-faced, clutching a box.

'I thought you needed something pretty,' she said. Six delicate little German coffee cups. There'd been a shock, a most awful bang, while she was in the china department, glass and crystal shaking all over the place.

'This is a dark place,' said Sahana. 'It has a most dreadful vibration.'

But now they have gone, back to their stable, sunny lives, and all Janey can think of is that lightweight temporary shelter, the deck chair in the sun, miles from timetables and classes and bells dividing the day into 50-minute segments, staff meetings with everyone lined up at 8.10 on their favoured chairs clutching their favoured cups filled with tasteless instant coffee, miles away from Year 9, Year 10, the press of adolescent bodies coming through and coming through her door in their shapeless brown gingham, their smooth hair drawn back in regulation ponytails, their ebullient energy, their confident strident laughter. (Does anyone laugh again the way they laugh at fifteen?) Increasingly they make her feel small, these girls. Each year they seem bigger, louder. The senior girls wear straight skirts and jackets laden with badges: the DP insists upon the jackets. She argues that it gives the students of Richmond Girls' High School 'a more corporate look', as if the highest aspiration of education ought to be to turn out young women who look like the employees of some company marketing financial services.

Miles away, no mobile coverage, no iPad, no laptop. Tom grumbled mightily.

'You can take a break for a few days,' she said. 'You could read a book. We could play cards.'

'Or we could make our own butter,' said Tom. 'Or weave our own shoes.'

With nothing more over her head than the tent, their frail temporary home, so light, so flyaway. And when they were ready to leave, they could pack it all up, everything they really needed, and carry it away. And she would look behind as she always did and there would be no sign that they had ever been there. Just a patch of crushed grass beneath the big blue bowl of the summer sky, receding in the rear view …

sixty-two
THE RIVER

Her body has swollen about its cargo of eggs.

She is heavily freighted.

Twenty million.

Something is about to happen.

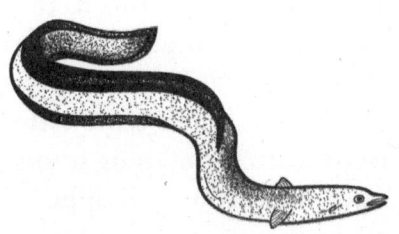

sixty-three
THE ANIMAL FRIEZE
FEBRUARY 2011

… crouches before the screen in his tiny room, every shelf, every surface crammed with report and analysis, like a rat in its nest of shredded newsprint. So much for the paperless office and no evidence whatever that five months ago he had taken advantage of disruption to tidy up. Shelves had been torn from the walls, his computer lay face-down on the desk, ceiling tiles drooped at odd angles and everything was coated in plaster dust. There was no option but to impose order.

Fifteen years of work sorted. On the day they were eventually let back into the building, the engineers having checked every shaken centimetre and given it their blessing, he had cleared a space and got down to it. This to the bin, this to keep, this to the carton destined for a purgatorial half-life in the spare room at home to await a switch in the political weather.

For some time, surely, there must be change? A different government, a different minister. Bloody Smith and even more bloody Hide must disappear some day, Smith exploding in a bloodshot frenzy, Hide tippy-toeing off to dance among the stars. Voted out and off to the blissful nirvana that awaits right-wing politicians in this bloody country: multiple directorships of this or that, comfortable consultancies, an embassy on some tree-lined boulevard. Surely, sooner or later, they'd go and the current regime would be dismantled? The overpaid, out-of-town commissioners appointed to rubber-stamp the region's irrigation projects would fly north again. The government had overturned the regional council elections to enable their arrival, but another government could as easily reverse that.

They could reinstate elections, re-establish a proper regional council and he and his colleagues would be free at last to stop planning an environment fit only for vast herds of dairy cows. Those poor bloody creatures you saw everywhere now, moping on big bare paddocks, wagging the stumps of their amputated tails, exposed to the full force of summer sun and howling gale, winter snow and driving rain because shelterbelts and shade trees got in the way of the irrigator arms and must be rooted out. Poor bloody cows. Reluctant mainstay of the country's economy. Just big pink sacs really, on their skinny legs, squeezing out milk powder for Chinese baby formula, Chinese ice cream, Chinese dietary supplements. And hadn't he read somewhere that the Chinese were allergic to lactose?

Some day he would be able to stop thinking about all that, and the water being drawn up from the dark aquifers to turn dry plain to green pasture. He could stop thinking about plans for reservoirs and canals to hold all that water. He could stop thinking about cows and turn to planning environments fit for other creatures: fish, for example.

The marine reserve.

His project, his fifteen-year preoccupation. It gleams in the mind: pristine waters bordering the tawny bulk of the peninsula, edging into all the little bays between ancient outpourings of lava, lapping at the foot of basalt cliffs and tiny islets. Surging with forests of kelp and all the multitudes that live within their shadows. Silver moki and freckled blue cod fanning their fins, pouting trumpeters, orange roughy a hundred and fifty years in the growing, red cod feeling their way across the seafloor with that single spiky barbell, canny ancient hapuku in their crevices of rock, battalions of crayfish marching up submarine hill and down submarine dale on their long route around the coast, little blue penguins rafting up of an evening for a chat before the laborious commute on stumpy feet uphill to their burrows.

He had dedicated himself to their welfare. Those mysterious millions. He had worked to counter the ravages of the trawlers and the squid boats, the rows of humming factories moored at the 12-nautical-mile limit, dragging their kilometres of lines or hoovering the seafloor. He had stood and argued the case for a reserve with recreational fishermen who bellowed at the slightest hint of intrusion into their preserve even though he had the data, he had the figures to prove that their catch beyond the borders would improve. And then there were the bad boys who didn't bother with argument, didn't give a fuck, reserve or no reserve, they'd carry on regardless, filling the catchbags with undersize paua and crays to trade with crims and down at the pub.

Fifteen years of meeting and consultation and bellowing and reports in the attempt to hold it back: the empty seas, the dead forests, the whole sad depleted calamity that has haunted him since childhood.

He sits at night reading his daughter a bedtime story. She is tucked up under her duvet, sucking her thumb the way she has done ever since the quake, though now she sleeps in her own bed unless an aftershock sends her stumbling to the bulwark of their big parental bodies.

It's a baby story really, but one she has always liked, about two polar bear cubs who run off on an adventure, tumbling through the snow. Her room is dimly lit by her bedside light. The shade has a pattern of little elephants running nose to tail. It rotates slowly, casting soft shadows on the bedroom wall. Poppy is warm against his arm, her hair still damp from her bath, her skin smelling of soap. Above her head is the frieze of animals Janey stencilled on the walls when Poppy was little: dancing zebras and smiling giraffes, a plump hippopotamus half-submerged in a blue pond. Beside her, arranged across her pillow, are her stuffed toys: a couple of teddies, Sahana's stuffed koala, Monkey, grubby and well loved, and Choochoo, who is a panda and lacks one ear.

Rob reads the story of the polar bear cubs and Poppy sucks her thumb dreamily, believing it all. This fantasy of carefree cubs frolicking in the snow while Rob can think only of the cubs' mother, her big white legs pawing at the water in that endless blue looking ahead for the ice shelf that has receded since last year, is shrinking still, faster, faster.

He sits reading to his daughter as the elephants (down to 600,000 because of the fucking poachers, the fucking ivory carvers) slowly circle the walls. She cuddles her panda (1864 at last count, and there is something so infinitely depressing about that '4', the exactness of it). Monkey sprawls beside her head, the goofy long-limbed orangutan without whom she cannot go to sleep (400,000, declining by around 1000 a year to make way for fucking oil palms). And she has tucked the koala (100,000, dying by the dozen from disease and dog bite and suburban encroachment) under her duvet.

His daughter sleeps each night surrounded by dying species and he can hardly bear it, this terrible fairytale he must keep telling her of cute polar bears and happy elephants and cuddly monkeys when the reality is cubs starving to withered corpses, their bodies empty leather on windswept rock, their teeth like pearls, the sea levels rising and warming, the dead birds, dead fish, the silent empty world.

He's done his best, day after day, biking into the office, a quick sprint on the rowing machine in the basement gym, a shower and at his desk by 7.30, ready to do his best for the moki and the cod, red and blue. And then overnight it was all shelved, cast aside in the rush to approve plans to turn plains of skimpy grassland over river shingle into lush green dairy pasture.

There had been rumours in 2008 as soon as the Nats got in. Veiled hints at meetings or in public statements. Comments passed on by a mate of Rob's who had moved to the ministry in Wellington and knew how things were moving. Central government was 'not happy' with the Canterbury council's performance, it was 'dysfunctional', it was obstructing progress, in its niggling nanny-state fashion, getting in the way of the canal and dams that would ensure prosperity for the region and, by extension, the economy of the entire country. Straws in the wind, followed as inevitably as night follows day by the ministerial directive, the performance review, the official report — written, of course, by another Nat, former cabinet minister and deputy PM, one of those reports where, Rob's mate said, the conclusion had been written first and was going to be attached to whatever the review uncovered.

And after that came the sacking of the elected council, and the arrival of the government's own appointed commissioners, like some SWAT team dropping from the sky to deliver dazzling efficiency. No report to be more than a single side of an A4 sheet. No meeting to last longer than one hour. All non-essential work to be cast aside for that monocular focus on irrigation, on dairy cows. All hands to the pump. All eyes on the irrigator.

Rob crouches before the screen, preparing for the afternoon while things are relatively quiet. Colin from next door, who has never quite adjusted to office existence, still operates like man alone, voice booming from a bare mountainside, is off at the Carlton for his lunchtime pint. Sarah will be back at one, and then they'll head out to Prebbleton, rattling along companionably in one of the council utes to check water quality in a well that has been repeatedly condemned, unfit for human consumption, especially dangerous for babies, laden with nitrates and phosphorus, seething with faecal coliforms.

Brian, the farmer, doesn't give a stuff. His feedlot is a shitty mess, the drain-off inadequate. His fences are broken and crudely mended, unable to restrain his stock who break through to stand, as they yearn to stand, in the river's cooling waters, soothing udders strained to bursting to produce more milk than any cow was ever designed to produce to feed its calf in her unmodified lifetime. Brian will stand by, arms folded in barely repressed resentment, while he and Sarah dip and test the toxic residue of a once-pristine aquifer. Ahead lie argument, rage, injured innocence, delays, mitigation, summons, lawyers, a fine for an amount that may or may not act as a deterrent, depending on this month's milk solids payout. A mere slap on the wrist.

But first there'll be the trip, window down, out of the office with Sarah, who is good company, her long brown legs in summer shorts, her long hair flying, making the drive tolerable: along the road by the dead lake with its flaccid eels, its toxic algal bloom, over the dry streams where bikes scream about among the broken bottles and plumes of dust rise, a rim of willow the only evidence that once there was water, glittery with dragonflies and iridescent millions and herons motionless at the rim and bitterns among the reeds and all the beautiful shadows of species long dead, long gone.

He reaches for his coffee. And in that split second, a new fault ruptures and the building leaps into . . .

sixty-four
THE RIVER

Something will happen.

The river is high with spring melt. Creamy with silt.

She hangs in the water as the moon passes overhead, waiting.

Not yet.

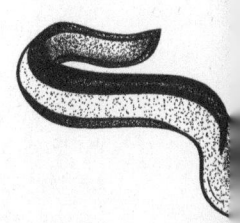

sixty-five
THE BOOKSHELF
MARCH 2011

...arranges what she has been able to grab on the shelf in the spare room. It's a fairly random selection, made in the half-dark that afternoon in the clutter that had once been her classroom. Tau stood in the doorway keeping an eye on the time. 'Fifteen minutes,' he'd said, as he handed them their hard hats. 'Fifteen minutes to get in and out. Okay?' They didn't need warning: massive cracks had opened over the brick Edwardian façade of the main block and the roof was broken-backed. She followed Sandra down the darkened corridor, each of them wearing an absurd little hard hat which would be no use whatever should the earth choose that moment to adjust itself and the whole buckled structure fall.

Amazing it stood at all, a month after the second quake that had sent them scurrying from the concrete modernism of the town hall and the orderly agenda of the PPTA meeting out into mayhem. That day on which she had trudged among all the others, cloaked in dust, with single-minded intent towards whatever place they called home. Across the city, over the Port Hills, out to the suburbs, or further still to the surrounding townships. Looking down, watching her feet negotiate cracks and broken glass and expanses of silty water, while her head repeated 'Poppy. Tom. Rob. Poppy. Tom. Rob.' For her phone was dead. The air jammed with all those thousands reciting other names, over and over. U OK? U OK?

And those who weren't OK, who would never be OK. Who were broken, buried, dying. They haunt her dreams, will haunt her always, those messages flying in their many tongues from beneath the slabs of fallen concrete in the central city.

She has scooped up what she could in the darkness that had been her room. Her laptop, a stack of books: Patricia Grace, *King Lear*, Mansfield, *Looking for Alibrandi*, Janet Frame, *English Basics*, *English in Aotearoa*, Carol-Ann Duffy, Tusiata Avia, poems and short stories found scattered, face-down, butterflied among fallen plaster and shoved in a cardboard box before Tau said, 'Right. Time to go. Let's get outta here.'

She took her carton and left, the main block creaking round them. It was to be demolished. The site would be cleared and then, who knew? Meanwhile, they must improvise. The girls will be bussed to a school on the opposite side of the city, the western, less damaged side. She will share a classroom. In the mornings, it will be occupied by one school, in the afternoons, by the other.

So she sits in the spare room, dusting off the books in readiness. All these words with the ideas and little pictures they contain in each tiny framework of line and circle. All the words she spends her professional life handing to the girls in the brown gingham and pony-tails. The dolls' house with its little lamp, glowing against war and death and disease. The children walking to the reservoir at the end of the world. The old man on the train, going to see those people about his land.

Out early today old man. Business, young fulla.

I give you an onion. It will blind you with tears like a lover.

Come, let's away to prison: We two alone will sing like birds i' th' cage.

Ahead of the girls lies love, despair, ecstasy, birth, unfairness, injustice, resistance, acceptance, bereavement, a whole tumult for which they may need words if they are not to become lost.

Rob has taken over the room that they have always called the office. He has cleared a space on desk and shelves for computer, file boxes, printouts, whatever he could grab in the fifteen minutes he had been allotted to run up four flights in the tilting tower, scramble over fallen shelves and retrieve what was essential. Whatever he thinks might be necessary to work from home over the next weeks or months, however long it might take to reassemble.

In adjoining rooms at the back of the house they improvise. Elsewhere, ceilings and walls have cracked wide, floorboards are hillocky over uneven piles, joists have collapsed. When she first saw the damage after her long trudge home, her heart lurched. But no one had been underneath. Everyone was safe.

There was Rob, cycling home along a road that had reverted in an eyeblink to primeval swamp, holes and crevices opening into which cars had toppled nose-first. The manhole covers that hinted at the web of pipes and wiring below ground that held everything together, had each risen like little conning towers clear of the surface. They required careful negotiation. There was Poppy, lined up with the other children on the playground at her school waiting for someone to come and find her. 'The wheels on the bus,' she sang with her good, kind teacher, whose own children waited over the hill at Lyttelton for her to be free to come and find them. 'Round and round, round and round . . .' And there was Tom, who had not been at school that afternoon, but sitting on the back step at home, fixing his skateboard. And when it struck he thought of Poppy, poor old Popps, and went to find her. Tears were rolling down her plump cheeks. 'The wipers on the bus go swish swish . . .' when suddenly there was her brother in his beanie hat and she had run to him and hugged him so tight he could hardly breathe. And there they were walking together along Savage Street, hand in sticky hand. And Ruth was already in Dunedin, evacuated immediately with all the residents of Ambleside and flown south to another complex, another armchair, another cup of tea.

Everyone was safe.

Across the road, the Novaks were moving out of their house into their garage. The house was knock-kneed and had shed all its concrete block cladding. It had fallen away in heavy sheets over lawn and pansies, leaving the inner frame of wood and tarpaper exposed. The windows were empty sockets.

'Is stuffed,' said Kitty, her arms full of bedding. 'We sleep out here.'

'Come and stay with us,' said Janey. 'You can have our sleepout. There's a bed and everything.' Four-square and corrugated iron, the sleepout had flexed mightily but remained intact.

Kitty shrugged.

'Stan want to stay here,' she said. 'On his own land. Keep an eye on things. We be okay.' She looked tired, smaller than before, though the lipstick bloomed poppy-bright.

'Well, if you change your mind,' said Janey, 'the sleepout's always there.'

They had helped the Novaks shift their bed from the house to the garage, along with a couple of armchairs and Kitty's piano. They stood looking slightly incongruous against the silhouettes of saws and hammer. Stan set up a gas ring on his workbench, dug a bucket latrine in the liquefaction in the back garden and placed the thermette on some bricks, handy to the garage door. On that first night, the Tilley lamp flared blue from the little window. Up and down Savage Street tiny pools of light punctuated the darkness. Candles in windows, a brazier around which shadowy people gathered. The wind rattled dry leaves and the river was audible, running high and creamy white between broken banks. It was as if time had abruptly changed gear and gone into reverse, to encampments and fire.

Now many of the houses stand empty, and at night Savage Street is quiet, too quiet, and dark, too dark. The Tuitamas have gone to stay with family in Auckland while they wait to hear the fate of the state houses. Bronwyn and Rick, who rented the place next door, have moved to Napier. The massive glass window that fronted their house had cracked from side to side and could not be repaired. The entire framework of the house had twisted.

Sometimes Janey met the Novaks at the portaloo. It arrived one morning to stand a little wonkily on the verge outside the house, and Poppy hated it: refused point blank to go out after nightfall, and never on her own, though she would never say quite what frightened her. Maybe it was the way it shook in the aftershocks and what if it fell over with her inside, amid all that poo? Or was it spiders? Or was it that she feared someone she didn't know knocking on the door? Or did she not like the smell? She wouldn't say, but there was a lot of hanging about, waiting on the verge.

'How are you getting on?' Janey asked Kitty, and always she said, 'Okay, we fine, no worries.'

And sometimes Janey feels as if it is the end of the world. The darkness on Savage Street washes over her and she thinks it will never end. Everything will fall away: walls and roofs and roads and cathedrals and schools and concerts and art galleries and sewerage systems and electrical systems. It can all just stop.

But she cannot think like that. She pushes the thought away. She dusts off *King Lear*, switches on her laptop. She'll get some work done: plan for the year ahead. NCEA Level 3.

1. Establish context. Introduction to Elizabethan Period.
2. Summarise concept of Great Chain of Being:
   i. *Every being has its place within a rational hierarchical universe designed by God.*
   ii. *The King's God-given role is to rule his subjects with wisdom and justice. Lear refuses to accept the truth of Cordelia's love, and unwisely transfers his power to Goneril and Reagan whose deceitfulness and ambition make them unfit to fill this role. He violates his responsibility to his subjects and upsets the natural order.*

The loose catch on the windowsill rattles. The familiar signal for another aftershock. There have been thousands now, the earth constantly twitching. She pauses, hands lifted over the keyboard. The window rattles, the house jolts, the shock passes. Four point two. She carries on.

3. Stoic philosophy and Lear: *Seneca. De Beneficiis/On Benefits*:

'I will show you what the highest in the land stand in need of, what the man who possesses everything lacks: someone who will tell him the truth. A man believing himself to be as great as he hears he is brings on wars that are useless and will imperil the world, and breaks up a useful and necessary peace. Led on by a madness that no one checks and believing that what has already reached its highest development and is even now tottering will last forever, such men cause vast kingdoms to come crashing down on themselves and their followers.'

Another rattle. They often come in pairs. She pauses. It passes. Three point six, maybe three point seven.

Ah, Lear. Howling naked in the storm. Learning that 'unaccommodated man is no more but such a poor, bare, forked animal'. Learning that it's all just stuff.

She opens the text, scribbled with marginal notes dating back years, to the time she had read the play in first-year English at uni. She props it up against the carton containing all the other texts and then she settles, in half a house, to the business of improvising an education, a . . .

sixty-six
THE RIVER

The riverbed has risen.

Water laps at creviced banks.

Waste oozes from broken pipes.

She hangs, silver and swollen with promise.

Amid shoals of shit, flotillas of filth.

She waits.

Soon.

Soon.

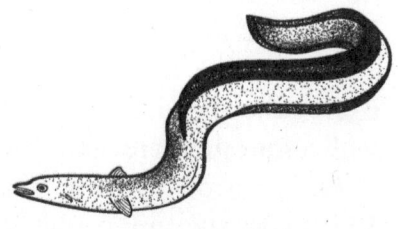

sixty-seven

THE BEDROOM DOOR

APRIL 2011

...to begin with, a tank, drawn up by the bridge into the central city, and soldiers with that casual but watchful look he'd seen before only in movies. The tank has gone, but the checkpoint remains and wire cordons line the riverbank, the houses corralled behind for their own safety. Ordinary everyday houses, some already taking on a look of abandonment, their curtains drawn.

He stands by the lights that blink red green red green at an empty avenue, wondering if he should chance the checkpoint. One of the soldiers has noticed him. He's not a lot older than Tom. Maybe eighteen, but short and muscly with that don't-fuck-with-me look, that I've-got-my-eye-on-you look. Tom stands feeling weird, exposed, in his hoodie and jeans holding a skateboard like a little kid, instead of a gun. That guy won't let him through. No way.

The soldiers lounge about, talking loudly. A white ute drives up, pauses, they bend down, talk through the window, the ute reverses with a squeal of tyres and drives off down the avenue.

On a narrow street beyond the soldiers and the cordon stands VJ's house, the tiny cottage he shares with his dad and his dad's brother who has that thing, kind of chunky with big bulbous eyes. Downs. VJ has a caravan in the backyard. No one bothers to come and tidy VJ's caravan. He's fixed hand-grips so he can get into his bed by climbing over walls and ceiling, spider-like, from grip to grip, without once touching the floor. He can stay up all night if he likes, and no one notices or cares. When Tom visits, they play Death Zone 2 till dawn, then fall asleep in the caravan's happy doggy stink.

He can see VJ's house behind the wire. He's probably still asleep, sprawled under a couple of sleeping bags. Pale and skinny, already with a faint moustache on his upper lip, his long limbs coated in fine gingery hair. Sometimes, curled on a heap of VJ's doggy clothes on the caravan floor, Tom has wanted to reach out and stroke that arm, flung wide, the smooth skin at the wrist, the fine hair, the fingers lightly flexed, VJ breathing evenly with a little runnel of spit seeping onto a faded Batman pillow dating from when they were kids and into that kind of stuff. Jumping off the shed roof at Savage Street, aiming to fly to the top of the walnut tree, sticking nails into an electric socket with the general intention of developing superpowers. Wrestling each another, trying to trip or get a hold, training to be heroes. He lay on the floor, looking at VJ's arm. A shaft of bright sunlight fell through a hole in the window blind. It caught in the fine hairs so that he seemed coated in a red-gold pelt, like a dog or some wild animal. He moved his hand slightly, so slightly, closer; he could touch them, brush against them.

'What?' said VJ, one bleary eye open, watching. Tom's hand shot back. He had been careful, ever since the fight.

They had been fighting in Tom's room, the old room with the fish swimming in their tank and everything as it always had been, a whole house still in existence beyond his closed door. He'd usually won when they fought, wrestling for supremacy. He'd always been stronger, but recently VJ had grown, was now the tallest kid in the class and the weight imbalance was swinging in his favour.

But finally, Tom had him pinned. Both arms down, while VJ thrashed and bucked beneath him. And he'd found himself leaning down, breathing heavily with the effort to hold him, until their faces were almost touching. VJ's eyes slid into a single Cyclops eye in the centre of his forehead. His breath smelled sour of salt and vinegar chips. And suddenly everything went very still, like you could hear air spinning, like lots of tiny molecules were spinning and the whole world was made up of these tiny spinning particles and then VJ gave one mighty shove and he fell off and hit his head on a chair leg.

'Faggot,' said VJ, rubbing his wrists hard to get back circulation. His eyes were bright and mean and Tom had sat on the carpet sick with sweat and embarrassment and a kind of giddy excitement unlike anything he had ever felt before. And then Poppy was in the doorway. They hadn't noticed her before. She had totally ignored the notice to knock. 'What are you doing?' she said. 'It's dinner time.' On the way down the hallway, VJ had tried to deadleg him. He'd been forgiven. But he had to be careful.

And now, behind the cordon, VJ is walking with the new slouchy walk he has been perfecting to go with his new long body. Kind of loose and whatever. Tom has tried to imitate it, looking at himself in the mirror in the strict privacy of his bedroom, but he looks stupid. He'll have to work out his own walk. VJ walks toward the checkpoint carrying his skateboard because the streets on that side of the river are too wrecked for boarding. He says something offhand to the soldiers who nod, then skates across the road. 'Hey,' he says.

They rattle down the avenue. It's a reconnaissance mission, seeking out the best locations. The deepest crevices, places where slabs of concrete have uptilted leaving a clean kerb or a ramp, rails on an empty stretch of street outside abandoned shops, a place someone has told them about where there are cars partly buried by rubble in a garage where the walls are wide open and that could look really good. And some café tables and office stuff left lying around in abandoned buildings that they could drag out onto the street. Desks and that. VJ's got a camera. Not a GoPro. He'd really like a GoPro, but his dad had said he wasn't about to send him off with $400 on his head, and especially not right now when they didn't know where they'd be living next year or what expenses they were likely to have. VJ had managed to find a cheap action camera instead on Trade Me. It would have to do.

The main thing was to catch the moment, this never-to-be-repeated time when the city had turned itself inside out, into a vast untended park, a place that looked at last like the places in the background on the video clips. Places with big empty factories and shadows and a vast tagged emptiness where they used to make cars and fridges and stuff. At last they live in a city that looks as a city is supposed to look. One that looks like it belongs with the soundtrack. A city that is finally, unmistakably *real*.

The boards rattle over uneven ground as Tom follows VJ into the YouTube clip, the one where he will ollie effortlessly over crevices, grind the rails outside some video store, attempt to jump off some half-buried Toyota, where they'll find the angles, he on his board leaping into the flare of . . .

sixty-eight
THE RIVER

Her eyes are ringed with blue.

Her belly glistens.

She gleams.

sixty-nine
THE SPIRIT LEVEL
MAY 2011

... **levels off** the concrete. He is going to make a brick oven, one of those outdoor pizza ovens with a domed profile. He has plenty of material after all. A whole stack of bricks by the shed. It made sense to use them for something.

'Why?' said Janey.

'Well, you've always said you wanted one,' said Rob. 'Jamie Oliver and all that: cooking pizza in the garden.'

'That was before,' said Janey. 'Why are you doing it now? We don't even know what's going to happen to the garden. We don't know what's going to happen to the house.'

They have had the visit. The one that will determine the extent of the new damage to their home, whether it is to be repaired or rebuilt, over or under that $100,000 cap, whether they will have to engage their insurers, whether they will stay or leave, whether their lives will take this path or that. Another couple of inspectors from the Earthquake Commission have shown up, another couple of Aussies. Trevor, who was trim and brisk and balding, and Faye, who was steely-eyed beneath plucked eyebrows raised in permanent surprise.

'This must have been such a lovely home,' said Faye, as she flipped open a laptop. 'It's a beautiful area. I bet you loved living here.'

'We still do,' said Rob. Why was she talking as if they had already gone? 'We still like living here.'

Faye looked round at the kitchen, crowded now with all their living.

'Yeah,' she said. 'Course you do. These old veelas. They've got so much atmosphere.'

They set to work. 'No need to come around with us, sir,' said Trevor, in a voice that precluded objection. 'We don't want to disturb you. Just carry on.' And Rob felt himself dispatched to sit on the deck, waiting, hearing the mutter of their voices as they moved about inside his house. The narrow red beam of the surface laser sketching the profile of the hallway with its sloping floor, the hillocks above uneven piles in the front bedroom, the sunken tongue and groove in living room and dining room.

The rooms were dark. He had boarded the broken windows with ply, closed off the hall midway along its length. It sloped perceptibly now from right to left and a wide crack had opened around the frame of the front door through which a steady autumn breeze blew.

'Just nail one of the living room curtains over it,' Janey said. 'Don't bother buying ply. It's a waste of money. We can just shut the doors on the rooms with broken glass.'

It was weird. She'd been the one who fell in love when they first visited and insisted on the huge mortgage they were still servicing and would be servicing for years. She was the one who was forever repainting, hanging different curtains, who talked of the house having a 'personality'. Now she didn't seem to care.

'I don't see the point of fussing,' she said. 'Not when it's probably coming down anyway.'

He sat on the deck looking out at the back garden while Trevor and Faye murmured and took their measurements. It was like waiting for a diagnosis on a sick relative: like waiting to hear how Ruth might recover after she fell that last time, trying to find the toilet (she'd have said 'lavatory'. 'Never "toilet", darling. It's vulgar.') in the dark confusion of her new room in Dunedin.

The minutes ticked by. Out here in the garden the leaves were turning gold. The walnut, the plum, the elms along the back fence. He should go in, get some work done at the desk in the spare room, just carry on as Trevor had suggested. But the inspectors' presence made him restless, their casual appropriation of those darkened rooms, that careless past tense in speaking of his home. As if they presumed it was already dead. As if from the depths of their professional expertise they had already assessed its fate.

Those bricks, he thought. Just going to waste. When they would make a first-rate pizza oven.

There was some movement behind him. Trevor and Faye emerged blinking into the sunlight, computer and laser level in hand, just a few details to fill in before they leave. They'd taken less than an hour.

He was unable to restrain himself. 'So, what do you think?' The anxious son.

Trevor was concentrating on his laptop. 'I've seen worse,' he said.

'What about the floors?' said Rob. 'In the hall, in the living room?'

'Well, some of that damage will be pre-existing,' said Trevor.

'Pre-existing?' said Rob. 'What do you mean?'

'It's an old place,' said Trevor, tapping away at his keyboard. 'And old places are pretty robust but they always have some cracking and earth movement. That's part of their charm, eh?'

'Charm?' said Rob. 'It's slumped by 300 mill at least, by the bay window.'

'Yes, sir. We know. We have the data,' said Trevor. He snapped the laptop shut. 'Right. We'll get out of your hair. Our people will process this over the next few weeks and get in touch.'

'So it's a repair job?' said Rob.

'Bit early to tell, sir,' said Trevor. 'You'll just have to wait till we've been able to attend to it. It's a big job, as you'll realise.'

'But off the record, in your opinion,' said Rob, 'as a surveyor? Or are you an engineer?'

'Matter of fact, I'm neither,' said Trevor.

An airline pilot. Retired. And Faye was 'in real estate back home'.

'So do you think they had any idea what they were doing?' said Janey when she got home that evening and they sat having a glass of wine in the kitchen.

'Hope so,' said Rob. It all depended on that little gleaming red eye, like something feral, burning like a tiny flame in the dark.

It's simpler really to concentrate on the oven. He has dug a foundation not too deep. The website advised 200 millimetres and it wasn't easy in the strange dense soil that now covered the garden.

It lay heavy on the spade, but he'd worked away at it when he felt like a break from work. One of the problems with working at home was that there were fewer interruptions. No one came and stood in his office doorway, in the way that had always annoyed him when he had an office and a doorway. Colin didn't hover, talking about the difficulties of fencing his lifestyle block at Tai Tapu, Sarah didn't pop by to tell him about the cycle race at the weekend, bloody amazing, central city to Akaroa along the summit roads, but God, it was tough, 28 degrees. None of that happened. Sometimes, he wondered about ringing Sarah, just to see how she was getting on. Maybe even Colin. But instead, when he wanted to stop, he went outside and worked on the oven.

Odd things emerged from the soil. He found an Edwardian penny, lead-topped roofing nails, a rusty compass. He placed them on the kitchen windowsill.

He has dug a hole 1200 millimetres square and cut a piece of tarpaulin to fit. He bought concrete, ready-mix, and poured a base.

Everything was a mess: the house, the road, the whole city, but right now, he is here in the garden as it turns golden, and maybe it's for the last time? Who knows? He has the garden to himself. The broken house to himself. Janey is at work on the other side of the city, the kids are at school. His colleagues are scattered, working from bedrooms and living rooms about the city. The whole orderly grid that had hung on the hallway wall, the map devised by a couple of Englishmen seated in a tent on the riverbank, simply presuming to lay down a city on land bought for a song from the inhabitants. The casual appropriation of empire. All that's a mess right now.

He kneels in his old jeans, no need to dress for work, rough clothes will do. He takes up the spirit level and lays it on the concrete base he has poured. If he gets that right, the whole structure — and it could weigh a tonne once all the bricks and mortar are in place — the whole thing will be stable. (The earth tips a little, rolls back: 4.1.) The tiny bubble rolls from side to side in the tube then settles dead centre. He's got it . . .

seventy
THE RIVER

Something happens.

A dark night. Moonless. A dim sprinkling of stars.

There is a shift within her. A kind of urgency. Some force, some new taste to the water, some vibration, some need.

She turns, for the first time going with the current, rather than facing it head-on.

She turns and begins to swim downstream between creviced banks and trees tilting on damaged roots.

This is not memory that guides her, or knowing, but something deeper, older.

She swims, one long silvery muscle, past the embankments with their settlements of broken houses, out into the estuary. Her big eyes look about. She is full of purpose.

She can taste it now, the salt water that lies beyond the bar. She finds the gap and swims through into the wide acres of the bay.

And once there, this force, this need, draws her north, into the deepest, darkest ocean.

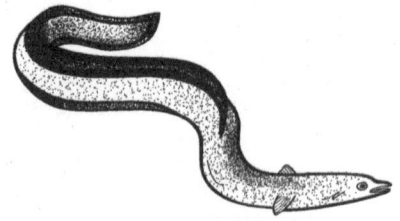

seventy-one

THE DADO

JUNE 2011

... a rellevay, fingers on the dado rail, just the tips, not hanging on, head up so she is tall, tall as a giraffe, with a long long neck. Eyes looking straight ahead, feet turned out in second position, bottom tucked in, tummy tucked in. And up one two with all her toes on the floor. And down three four. She'd like to be able to see herself in the mirror that used to hang here, her face rising up one two, down three four in a thick frame of carved wooden fruit and flowers with the fat baby at the top. Poppy had not much liked the fat baby. Her mother had said it was Cupid, the god of love, but he didn't look much like a god of love to Poppy. How could he be a god of anything with his fat bare bottom and dimpled legs.

Her mother had hung it among Dad's maps in the hallway when Grandma Ruth went into the hospital. She thought it might brighten it up. She was always trying to brighten things up.

'What do you think, Popps?' she'd say, head on one side contemplating a streak of green on the living room wall. 'Will that brighten things up?'

'It's already bright,' said Poppy.

'It's white. Everything's white,' said her mother. 'I hate white as a colour.'

'White isn't a colour,' said Poppy. 'Mrs Ngatai said. It's achromatic.'
But her mother wasn't listening.

The fat god has gone, along with the maps, smashed to bits when the thing beneath her bed exploded.

She had always suspected it existed, the Thing that had made her insist upon the light being left on in the hall. The Thing that had made her take a deep breath when she finally had to leave the warmth of the sitting room where everyone was slumped on the sofas watching TV, for her distant bed. She'd paused in the doorway, then leapt in three giant strides across the room to the safety of duvet and pillow. When she was little she had imagined something big and hairy like the Wild Things in the picture book who danced with Max. She'd imagined a long skinny arm reaching out to grasp her leg and drag her down down into the dark. She'd never confessed this fear, but Tom must have guessed, because once after she'd broken one of his Transformers, he had hidden under her bed and grabbed her leg and she had screamed. She had peed in her pyjamas and screamed so hard she couldn't stop, even when her mother came running and held her close and said there were no such thing as monsters under the bed, there was just Tom who was being very silly.

'Why are so mean to your sister?' she'd said, Poppy a damp bundle in her arms. And her father had told him to grow up.

That was a long time ago when monsters could inhabit cupboards and dark corners and the dolls in her dolls' house could walk about leading small intricate lives and her bike could become a pony and fly. Such times pass.

But on that night the Thing had risen up, and it was real after all. It lay under her bed. Under the house. Under the entire city. It was strong enough to break the mirror and tumble the chimneys. It could collapse the front porch so the posts stood at awkward angles, and wreck the turret. It cut a big crack across the front path and when Mum poked a broom handle down to see how deep it was, the handle waggled in empty space. The Thing had opened a great hole beneath the house, maybe a hole under the whole city into which they could all tumble.

It was more powerful than she had ever imagined. It had pushed over the cathedral in the Square. Talia had been in the city with her mum getting her eyes tested because she needed glasses, when the steeple fell down and heaps of shops and a big tower where people were killed. The dust gave Talia asthma. If she laughed too much she began wheezing and had to fumble for her inhaler and squirt the asthma stuff into her mouth and that was one reason she had gone away. In Auckland maybe she wouldn't need the asthma stuff.

The Thing was all-powerful. At night she lay in bed looking up into the dark awaiting its arrival. It tapped at the window, trying to get in. Over and over. It was better when they slept in the tent. For a while, after the terrible day when she had sat in the playground with the other kids waiting for someone to come and find her, they had dragged mattresses outside and gone camping in their own garden. She had liked that, snug in her sleeping bag, her hat over her ears because Isobel had once told her about this girl in Scotland who had lain down on the grass and an earwig had crawled into her ear and eaten all the way through her brain and come out one of her eyes. She tugged the hat securely, then lay between the reassuring bulk of her parents, Tom sleeping on the outer edge, all of them in a row, playing Guess as the aftershocks rattled through. 'Four point two,' she'd say, 'Four,' said Tom or Dad or Mum, and in the morning they'd check on Geonet and whoever came closest got a chocolate. She was really good at guessing. In the garden the shocks were less alarming. They felt like a kind of ripple under your sleeping bag, like riding over a wave when you were in one of the kayaks. Outside, the Thing lost some of its power.

But after a couple of weeks, Mum had said they might as well move back into the house. A builder had examined it and said the back rooms were safe enough. They slept once more in their own rooms.

Her mother sighed with relief. 'Ah,' she said. 'That feels a bit more like normality.'

Except it wasn't normal, was it? The Thing still lay there, under her bed, breathing slowly, quietly in the dark. She had dared once to look into the darkness. Something glistened there, right at the back. A big brown mushroom. There was a whole row of them growing from the bottom of the wall. She had reached out and touched one tentatively and it was sticky, like honey, and stank of toadstools. Just the kind of thing a Thing might eat. She didn't dare tell anyone. If they saw it, they'd take it away and then what would the Thing eat instead? She lay in the dark, listening to the mushrooms growing, spreading.

Nothing was normal. People were going away. Their houses had holes in them or were nailed shut with bits of plywood. Yesterday on the way to school she had passed a house where a boy called Luca used to live. A tall red crane stood outside, its skinny head swaying above the trees.

From its clamped jaw a window dangled. A whole window, slowly turning in the air, while another machine tore at a wall, ripping a huge hole. The front of the house was already gnawed away, left bare like a dolls' house so you could see inside, where everything was black. Someone had got in over the weekend and set a fire, a man said.

There were things inside the blackened house: a cupboard on the top floor, still with all the coats and clothes lined up in a row. 'Bloody vandals,' said the man. 'Some people.'

The machines roared, and when she scootered home that afternoon, Luca's house had all gone. Just a big bare open space with a black mark where it had been.

Houses left, and people, and her school, too, might go away. Mrs Ngatai said because lots of kids had left and the school was damaged with fences blocking off the playground, they might all be going to another school and wouldn't that be cool? They'd meet heaps of new friends.

Poppy didn't want to go to another school. How would she find her way? She wasn't very good at finding her way. When she was little she got lost at the A&P Show. She stood alone in a forest of legs, her hot dog leaking tomato sauce over her hand. Around her the legs shifted, a wall of shorts and bare knees and skirts and jeans. Dense, impenetrable and she very small on a patch of crushed summer grass. And then suddenly the forest parted and her dad was there, reaching down and saying, 'Ah, there you are, Popps! Why did you wander off? We were wondering where you'd got to.'

She often got lost finding her way back to the car at the supermarket. She got lost the first time she tried to go to this school on her own. She was supposed to walk with Talia but Talia had flu so she decided to go alone and ended up on her scooter miles away near the mall, crying, until a nice lady stopped and said, 'Now, what's the matter with you, sweetheart?' And the school was in a fuss, and her mother came running when she and the nice lady turned the corner at last onto Savage Street, her hair all mussed-up and hugging her far too tight, saying, 'Poppy! What on earth were you thinking?'

After she'd calmed down she drew a map of the way to school with the things that Poppy recognised: Talia's house next door, then a little further along, the house with the black cat who often sat on the stone wall to be patted, his eyes two lemon slits. And beyond that, the house with the fuchsia bush where she usually stopped to pop some buds. And further along, there was the house with the barky dog, and the place with the red letterbox decorated with daisies where Luca lived, then she walked along the street by the river towards the silver footbridge, and just past that was the school. The map helped, though now all the details had changed: Talia had gone and Isobel, and the black cat no longer sat on the fence. Instead there was a sign pinned to the gate with a blurry photo. BILBO. Our much-loved cat, lost February 22, $100 for safe return. The barky dog had gone, too, which was a good thing, but Luca's house was that big black patch and the little silver bridge had been twisted and hung over the river like a length of silver rope with a sign saying DANGER.

The map would be no use for a new school. She would need to make a new one if she was to find her way.

And their house, too. Would it stay? Dad said it was Orange. All the houses were either Red or Green or Orange. Red meant they would be pulled down. Green meant they were okay. And Orange meant no one knew for sure. It was already uncertain, especially since the witchy lady had moved into their sleepout. Mum said Mr and Mrs Novak were too old to be living in a garage over the winter. It was the least they could do, until everyone was sorted. Poppy saw her sometimes at the sleepout window, and looked away quickly before she could see the wave, the dangerous smile.

And all the time the Thing bangs and jumps and Poppy stands in the twilit hallway, hanging onto the dado with her head up, looking straight ahead at the crack in the wall, dips down into a pleeay, one two and up three four. Shoulders down, head up. And again. One two and up . . .

seventy-two
THE RIVER

The river flows between bare branches, stripped by hail and a chill wind.

She is swimming northward along the coast. Past forests of kelp, and the strange creatures that flicker in their shadows.

She knows the way.

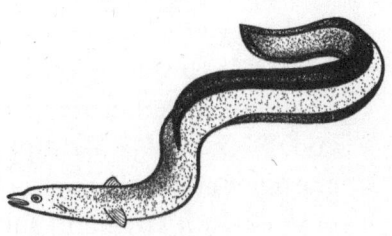

seventy-three
THE SLEEPOUT
JULY 2011

... **standing by** the window in his baggy striped pyjamas, his hair tousled, keeping watch. She often woke to find him there, peering out at Savage Street, or moving about restlessly among the clutter in the cramped quarters above the Morrisons' garage. The sleepout was dry, it was warm, it would be better for her cough. But it was crammed with their suitcases and plastic bags and cardboard boxes. She'd wake to the rustling of paper or plastic to find him lifting out some treasure: his indoor bowls trophies, the crystal water jug, the whisky glasses. In the morning they would be scattered over the carpet.

But equally often he simply stood at the sleepout window watching the street, their house. He wanted to keep an eye on things.

She rolls over. 'Stan?' Speaking quietly for sometimes he isn't quite awake. Even when he was in the grip of the nightmare, thrashing from side to side, tearing at the quilt, crying out, 'No! No!', it did not do to waken him too abruptly. If she reached out, touched him, said, 'Wake up! Wake up!', he could spring up, half unconscious, grasp her about the neck, thumbs pressing at the vein until her eyes popped with stars, and she had to be calm, say 'Stan! Stan! It's me, caro! It's Kitty!', before she passed out completely.

And then he woke and lay beside her babbling about poor bloody Thommo and those blokes in the hold when the Poms hit the *Jason* and it doesn't make much difference, German torpedo, Pommie torpedo, not to the poor bastard who's in the way when it comes through the wall and Jesus the sound of them, Get us outta here! Get us outta here! But those Itie bastards weren't hanging around to let us out, over the side into the boats as soon as it hit, just left us bloody drifting, didn't give a monkeys, two thousand of us locked down and drifting dunno how long onto the coast and you never heard blokes so happy in all your life to go aground and then they got us over to Italy, a camp, Tuturano, yeah Italy and a year later, they're off again, the Ities, out of it, out of the war, just buggered off and left us to it, and then the Jerries took over, different bunch altogether and they had us marching over to Aquila, yeah Camp 102 Aquila, you know Aquila, what a bloody mess, what bloody mess that was . . .

And Kitty, lying beside him as he went over it and over it, poor bloody Thommo, didn't give a monkey's, left us to it, thought, L'Aquila, yes, I know L'Aquila.

The little city with its ornament of towers along the skyline, the wide green valley at its foot, the snowy peaks of the Sasso at its back, the rush of streams and rivers. Yes. I know L'Aquila. She lies waiting as the recitation comes to its conclusion, the part where the men are being loaded onto a train, off to some other bloody camp in Germany and all packed in like sardines, locked down and you could hear planes coming up along the valley, you could tell they were Yanks, B-25s, and there's this guard, little pansy kid, couldn't have been more than nineteen and he just stands there, won't unlock, just stands there while the Yanks get cracking, and you've no idea, the whole bloody shooting match goes up, poor buggers torn to pieces, you know, what a bloody mess . . .

She lies while the words stream out, tracers into the dark, and eventually, they come to an end. She keeps still as he quietens. Slowly he returns to now, to this room, this bed. To himself. To her. 'Ah well,' he says. 'Maleesh. A long time ago. Maleesh.' And when he says that, she knows it is safe to reach over, switch on the Capodimonte lamp with the little couple dancing, he in velvet jacket and knee breeches, she in frilly crinoline. To say, 'Okay, you want a cup of tea?' Offering that strange Kiwi panacea: a cup of tea and a wine biscuit.

Ah yes. She knows L'Aquila, and the young man who fell from the wall into her aunt's garden. Tumbled down at her feet in the long grass by the pigshed.

She is standing holding an armload of washing, on her way back from the fountain where ninety-nine spouts spill into long troughs and the women go to work, sleeves rolled up, arms crimson to the elbows in the icy water for it is December, almost Christmas. In her arms the linen lies cold and heavy, good shirts and dresses and the cloth for the Christmas table. She has carried them in the woven basket from the fountain, walking quickly along the road at the foot of the city wall. Something is going on at the corner by the railway station, a lot of soldiers, grey German uniforms, marshalling columns of men. She keeps her eyes down. The Germans are unpredictable and, right now, Italy no longer aiding them, filled with rage. The rumour, her aunt tells her, is that a few days ago they murdered an entire village, children, old men, women, even babies, in the mountains near Rivisondoli. Only one child survived, concealed beneath her grandmother's skirts.

'Be careful,' she says.

Kitty needs no encouragement. She passes the soldiers as you pass a dangerous dog, eyes averted, trying for calm, but relieved nevertheless when she reaches the safety of her aunt's garden. And then beyond the stone walls, there's the steady thrum of engines from the south, planes flying up the valley, towards the city and then the detonation, the explosive thump, the rattle of machine guns strafing the railway yards, and she is on the ground by the pigshed, head down among the damp washing, arms over her head though that's pointless, as the planes drone away to the north and gunfire is replaced by the sound of voices that must be men, though they could be mistaken for pigs, pigs at the instant when the knife strikes home and the blood arcs into the basin. She stands and gathers up the washing, covered now in dirt, as a column of oily black smoke rises into the blue winter sky.

She straightens up, a little giddy and seeing stars, when there's some scrambling overhead and the young man falls at her feet. He lies looking up at her: dark curling hair, face streaked with blood and ash, saying nothing but smiling up at her, a sudden confidential smile she does not need words to understand. When the Germans come looking, slashing open the sacks of chickpeas and grain stored for the winter, tumbling their survival into the dust, he is safely stowed in the pit under the pigshed. Concealed for days, fed by her aunt until he is ready to rejoin his army, but by then it's done, isn't it: curly black hair, wide smile, they have talked, in the few words they need, and she loves him, he loves her, she will follow him to the ends of the earth.

Yes: she remembers L'Aquila.

And tonight here at the end of the earth he stands in his baggy pyjamas looking out the window, keeping guard, fully awake.

'Come and look at this,' he says.

In the dim light of a fitful moon she can make out a white ute parked outside the empty house several doors down. As she watches, a couple of figures emerge from the shadows of the drive carrying something between them. They lift it with practised ease onto the tray and a split second later she hears the clang of metal hitting metal.

'They're taking those gates,' says Stan. 'Bastards.' And he is stumbling through the dark between the clutter of cartons to the door.

'What you doing?' she says. 'Stan! What you doing?'

She switches on the Capodimonte lamp with its velveteen couple. Stan is fumbling for his shoes.

'I'm going to go down and sort them out,' he says.

'No!' she says. 'No, Stan! Is not worth it for a gate! Call the police.'

'They'll be gone before the police have left the station,' says Stan, stiff fingers tugging at Velcro fastening.

The light must have alerted them. There's another clang, then the ute roars into life, executes a skidding u-turn and is off down Savage Street and around the corner.

Stan sits on the bed, one shoe on, puffing and reaching for his tablets while she puts on the kettle, makes the tea the way he likes it: caramel brown, a dash of milk, two sugars though he isn't supposed to have sugar because of his heart. All these parts of self that are failing within their bodies, giving up, falling out of tempo, clagging with fat, swelling dangerously or producing strange growths and little lumps or blocking breath, so that you cough, cough, cannot stop. All the tiny failings that will eventually, and probably quite soon, carry them both away.

She makes the tea and they climb back into bed to drink it companionably, just her and Stan, no child to remember them or grieve when they're gone because that is how it turned out to be: some gap, some failing within her or within him. Just the two of them, the girl with the armful of white linen, the young man in the long grass, drinking their tea now, sitting up side by side in their borrowed bed. It's too narrow really, a queen when they had always slept on a king, but their bed would not fit up the narrow stairs to the sleepout. She sleeps as far to the right as possible, careful not to nudge Stan when they turn to sleep at last and he sets off once more to that dark hold, locked into sleep. She lies still and tries not to cough and waken him.

This is how it happens, she thinks, when things fall apart. As they do. As they have done, over and over again.

Anything can happen anywhere to anyone at any time at all. In the blink of an eye, in a few seconds, everything can fall away. She has known this all her life: towns and cities fall. That little city on the hilltop has fallen many times. Sometimes a partial collapse: a church tower or two, a few buildings in a street. Other times the destruction has been total, and each time the people rebuilt. Stone by stone, they put it back: the square, the theatre, the palazzo, the cathedral. And no sooner have they finished, stood back and regarded their new city, than it has been shaken into ruin again. And when everything collapses, some people behave with dignity and kindness, while others steal the gates.

And that, she thinks, poised on the very edge of sleep in the Morrisons' sleepout, is just the way things . . .

seventy-four

THE RIVER

The river flows, dimpled by rain.

She swims northward, drawn by the force of the earth, the spinning of spheres.

She is a silver thread in the water.

On her way.

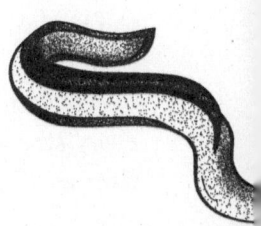

seventy-five

THE GLASS DOOR

AUGUST 2011

… in the dark, the girls board the bus. They shove one another, school bags bumping and jamming the narrow aisle. They find seats next to one another, young female voices a single undifferentiated racket like starlings settling.

'Got everyone?' says the driver and she says yes, all checked. Chantelle, Holly, Madison and the rest present and accounted for in their short short winter skirts and tights, and their long long hair tied back in ponytails. No one has short hair any more. The staff are all short-haired, but the girls are uniformly long-haired. In imitation of Kate. The princess in the white gown. Or Pippa with the buttoned bottom.

The girls cram the bus, school scarves tucked tightly against the cold for winter has come at last after fooling everyone into thinking it was spring. Pink blossom on the cherry trees along the avenue, a magnolia in full bloom last week as she rode across the park. But today cloud has clamped down, heavy over the city. Curtains of rain have swept over the sports field outside her window all afternoon.

The rain has stopped but the carpark is shiny with puddles and every street light has its aureole of fog. Janey stamps her feet in her thin work boots: beautiful boots, but not terribly waterproof. She'd have to get some sheepskin liners for nights like this when it's her turn on duty. At last the bus revs into gear and begins its heavy trundle back to the eastern side of the city. The sound of voices fades as it lumbers from the carpark, nudges its way out into the crush of cars along the avenue, and finally she is free to go back inside.

The corridors are empty with that weird sigh of relief that floods through them after hours, and that dense smell, that universal school smell that has been the same wherever she has taught: the bouquet of massed youth with all their glands and sweat and shampoos and deodorants mingled somehow with wet wool and bananas — always bananas — and chemicals from the science labs and cleaning compounds as the cleaners move in for the evening: the whirr of a floor polisher, thump of wastebins being emptied into bigger bins.

The workroom is dazzling after the darkness of the carpark. It takes her a moment to make out Sandra working at her cluttered desk amid the tangle of cords hanging like jungle vines from the ceiling to accommodate all the additional computers. (A flicker: 3.5.) Their own computers and the ones belonging to the morning shift, the home team, with whom they now share, have shared since the day the cracks burst across the main block.

Sandra looks over as Janey gathers up her bag.

'Hey!' she says. 'How's it going?'

'Good,' says Janey. 'Bloody freezing out there.'

Sandra leans back, stretches, rubs her eyes. 'Are you done with *Alibrandi*? Thought I might try it on my Year 10s. They're definitely not into *Romeo and Juliet*, that's for sure, even with Leonardo. They just keep asking, "But what's it *for*?"'

'And saying "It's a sublime work of literature" doesn't really cut it,' says Janey, slipping off the wet boots, the skirt, dragging on tights, fluoro jacket, sneakers.

'Not with Tina Foley, it doesn't,' says Sandra. 'She's set on a career doing eyelash extensions. It's good money evidently, and there's a course you can do with someone called Natalya. She's a Russian lash master.'

'Sounds excellent,' says Janey. 'Yeah, I'm done with *Alibrandi*. I should have picked up more than one copy.' A class set, one for each girl, but it had been such a muddle, such a rush. And it wasn't so bad: she had read aloud instead from the solitary copy, and the girls had liked it, reverting in an instant to four-year-olds, with that dreamy attentive calm. She'd forgotten that: how easy it could be to read aloud, how pleasant it could be to simply listen to a story. She likes reading aloud, likes having the mornings free, likes cycling across the city to work, likes the novelty of a new school, new staffroom, new shared room. David, her host teacher, is nice. Young, energetic, relaxed about her arrival. 'I've cleared some shelves for you. And if there's anything you need, anything useful, just help yourself.'

Sandra hates it.

'I'm a morning person,' she says. 'I don't function well after midday.'

She hates sharing a room, a desk, a wall. 'There's these posters: Barry Bloody Crump. The one with the cigarette. I hate Barry Crump, all that matey crap, survival in the bush, killing pigs, when they were probably living on Crunchie bars or nipping out for fish and chips. And even bloodier Baxter, that photo where he's pretending to be Jesus when he was writing poetry about incest. *I handled you like bone china.* I have to look at those pricks every single day.'

In the evenings Sandra drives home to a motel on Clyde Road. A blank corporate one-bedroom unit with not a single item belonging to her past. Her apartment is in an Art Deco building in the central city placed off-limits from the minute the quake hit. No chance of retrieving books, her first editions of New Zealand novels. Or paintings, the Gretchen Albrecht, the Doris Lusk she had inherited from her aunt, the beautiful little Sybil Sinclair of a dog sleeping. Or her collection of New Zealand pots, the big Zeke Wolf bowl ornamented with leaves and oranges, the jars and jugs. Or her photos of friends smiling on some Provençal terrace, glasses raised, the careful portraits of great-grandparents side by side on their wedding day seriously contemplating the future, the photos of nieces and nephews from babyhood to the family wedding. Or her clothing, her dark angular New Zealand tunics, Karen Walker, World. Or her shoes, acquired over years and cared for immaculately. They were up there still in her apartment, beyond the cordon, books flung every which way, paintings slewed or fallen, pots smashed or whole, clothes and shoes probably mouldy in the wardrobe on the third floor, food rotted to slime in the fridge.

She hates their loss. Hates the loss of the Art Deco building creviced by cracks, hates the loss of cinemas and the town hall and galleries and shops and restaurants and libraries and plays and the ballet and the opera and concerts. 'You know: civilisation,' she says. 'I miss that.'

Janey leaves Sandra marking in the workroom, delaying as long as possible the return to the barbarous frontier of Unit 12 in the Arizona Motor Lodge, and goes to find her bike. Rain dimples the puddles in the carpark as she straps on her helmet, flicks on every light she can muster. Blinking and twinkling like Christmas, anything to avoid being clipped by a truck. There are a lot of accidents at present: broken roads, diversions, shrunken lanes lined with orange striped cones, distracted drivers, not to mention the psychopaths in the 4WDs who clearly believe cyclists are a nuisance, best eliminated.

Blinking and twinkling, she heads out into the traffic. It's still commuter slow, bumper to bumper, but at least they'll have a chance to spot her and her illuminations pleading Don't hit me! Don't hit me! along the avenue and around the park. In the past the traffic would have built as she neared the centre, but now in this strange season, it dwindles. The streets empty. She cuts down the main street, which ends now at a wire cordon where the road slams into darkness, not a soul in sight.

Beyond the cordon the city's towers are shadows against a stormy sky. Towers and shops, the town hall, the art gallery, cinemas and cafés and theatres: does she miss them? Does she miss civilisation? Yes, she thinks as she pedals through the puddles. Of course. But there's a kind of pleasure, too, in tiny unexpected details: that light, for instance, that single neon light at the end of the street right up against the cordon, reading OPEN. All by itself among the blank boarded windows. The smell of olive oil, fish, the Mediterranean, the brief blare of voices and music, and then it's gone and she is turning the corner, riding eastward.

Her headlight picks out potholes and cracked tarmac. On her right behind the cordon, the towers of the CBD lean at dodgy angles, the cathedral is a beached whale in the Square, a great hole gouged in its side, the cafés with cups and plates and food cabinets left just as they were, rats moving in and plagues of cats and gulls.

The galleries and shops filled with stock on racks and rails, empty theatres, abandoned cinemas, parks reverting to weed around the statues and emblems of empire. Civilisation. Does she miss it?

Ahead at the corner, a girl stands all by herself under a street light, high heels, skimpy dress despite the cold. They used to work further south on Manchester Street among the bars and massage parlours, but now the girls work here, in the rain on the blank streets outside the cordon.

'Hey, Ms Morrison,' says the girl as Janey approaches a traffic light, red on an empty street.

'Hi, Rakelle,' says Janey. 'How are you doing?'

'Not bad,' says Rakelle.

Rakelle Vincent. Year 9, 2008. She draws deep on a cigarette, goosebumps pimpling plump white breasts. A car comes around the corner, throbs toward them along the kerb. She flicks her cigarette away. 'Gotta go,' she says. 'You take care now, Ms Morrison.'

'You too,' says Janey.

The light changes.

She pedals on across the bridge and along the river. Here the darkness is more absolute. Some houses lit, fewer, it seems, each week, while others are already blank-eyed in overgrown gardens.

And there at last is Savage Street, their house, still partly liveable, still perhaps repairable, no one seems to know for sure. The front of the house is boarded over, but around the back the lights are on in the kitchen. She stands, taking off her helmet, switching off the twinkling, looking in through the kitchen doors. Rob is by the stove stirring something in the wok. Tom is slouched at the table staring fixedly at his phone. Poppy is talking to Rob, standing on one leg with the other stretched into an arabesque. Her family. They seem lit up at that instant with an innocent, unbearable vulnerability.

Above and around them stands the house, the place she had loved, and chosen. But now it seems a heavy looming thing, not entirely to be trusted. The kitchen is brightly lit through sliding glass doors criss-crossed with lines of black electrical tape. Her family look as if they are caught behind a web. And the kitchen lies wide open. Like a jaw. It could snap shut at any . . .

seventy-six
THE RIVER

Snow covers the banks, smooths out the cracks, calm and cold.

She is away from the coast now, heading up into the open ocean.

Currents surge from west and east.

Her narrow head points north.

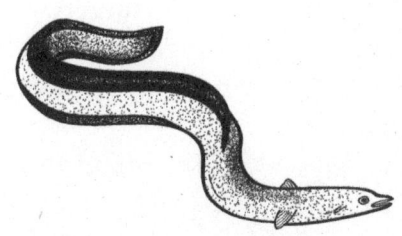

seventy-seven

THE FRAMEWORK

SEPTEMBER 2011

...on the phone to Vida. 0800DAMAGE. Vida is a cheerful woman.

'Not sure what's going on here,' she says. 'I can't see your file.'

'It's there,' he says. 'CLM/2011/029286.'

The phone cord is twisted. They bought a plug-in analogue last year after mobiles and cordless phones died of shock on that day, airwaves clogged, cell sites knocked out, power down, back-up batteries and generators collapsed from overload. The cord tangles round his fingers.

'No,' says Vida. 'Not here. You're sure? 029286?'

'Yes,' he says. 'Yes. 029286.'

'Look, I'll just pop you on hold for a minute,' says Vida. And leaves to have open-heart surgery. Or a short break in Fiji. Rob stays behind, fingers tangled in the phone cord, being entertained by Richard Clayderman. 'Moon River'. Followed by 'Candle in the Wind' and—

'Right,' says Vida. 'I'm going to pass you over to Queensland. They'll be able to help you.'

...'Somewhere over the Rainbow', 'Autumn Leaves'... The tip of his little finger tangled in the cord has lost all feeling, all colour.

'So, my dear,' says Carla in faraway Brisbane, 'what seems to be the problem?' And he wants to yell, 'Not seems: *is*. There *is* a problem, which is that you have managed, yet again, to lose my file. And incidentally, don't call me "dear".' But it would not do to irritate Carla at her office desk, three hours behind, on the upper floor of the glass tower overlooking the museum grounds and the river beyond. Not if he wants to debate the estimate.

$80,000 for repairs? You've got to be kidding. Have you seen the fallen turret, the buckled floors, the broken walls? What exactly are you proposing to repair? He can't check. The scope of works is confidential. Since July no homeowner has been able to access their scope of works. They have been placed off-limits, behind a tight bureaucratic cordon.

'02928sex?' says Carla.

'Yes,' he says. '02928sex.'

'Right, my dear,' says Carla. 'I'll just pop you on hold . . .'

Monks chanting over a disco beat . . .

Sometimes he feels himself to be at the bottom of an immense structure, a tiny ant in its basement. Above him are layer upon layer of inspectors, claim handlers, project managers, supervisors, and executives and CEOs, and the government minister in Wellington, the Big Buffoon, and the Earthquake Commission and the company they have nominated to handle earthquake claims with its Australian office and its bevy of handlers and supervisors and managers and CEOs and Carla, of course, placid Carla, and beyond them Head Office in a plaza in Iowa. He has looked it up, moved the little Google man to stand at ground level before the shiny tower which is, it seems, filled with people guaranteeing to go beyond the expected, to deliver the best possible outcomes to those who have suffered loss. Their mission: To Serve and Assist. There's a photo on the site of a child in a burnt-out building clutching a teddy bear, the company's 'Emissary of Empathy', ready for distribution to the traumatised in any one of the seventy-five countries around the world in which it manages claims.

His claim, for instance, which seems at this moment to be lost.

The disco beat goes on, a weird mix of Ibiza rave and Spanish cloister.

And should his claim be reassessed, which it must be — one of Colin's mates has visited, an engineer who said, at a rough estimate,

$380,000 to fix the fallen turret, buckled floors, broken walls — more layers will be added to the framework: the assessors and claim managers and project officers, the handlers and executives of their personal insurers in this country, and on across the Tasman to the managers and officers and executives at the Australian office and beyond them there are other layers all the way back to the company that insures their insurers.

He has looked them up, too. He has moved the little digital man to stand before their headquarters among the bicycles on Köninginstrasse. Yellow walls, steep-pitched tiled roofs and Doric columns, and a park with a charming summer house. Solid, dependable, emitting that nineteenth-century Bavarian rectitude, the sober company that, uniquely, survived the massive payouts consequent on the San Francisco earthquake of 1906.

The weight of process and distance and time lie over him. He is such a tiny figure in all this, though it is his minuscule premiums that hold the whole structure up. His and millions upon millions of other tiny premiums. The ants that fill the basement.

And despite the rhetoric of serve and assist, behind the battalions of teddies, there's hard-headed business based on retaining as much as possible of those multitudes of tiny premiums, giving out as little as possible in claims, and ensuring a healthy dividend for their shareholders.

He is a very small ant indeed.

Around him the framework flexes, and on the walls of his temporary office in the spare room his maps rattle. (Three point five, he thinks, barely noticing.) He has removed the broken glass with tweezers and reframed them all. Marine charts of bays and inlets with their shoals of fathoms. There's a map of a tough little South Westland settlement of baches on a shingle spit where the waves rear up and fall with a boom like thunder and driftwood surges ashore, yet here it is as it was planned back in London with streets and a university and a seaside promenade. There's a hand-tinted copperplate engraving by Bellin of the *Mer du Sud*, the islands of Nouvelle Zélande no more than a wriggly sliver of coast. There's Andersen's map of the peninsula, a ragged wheel of land coated in an overgrowth of names, Maori and European. There's a *Map of New Holland with adjacent countries and New Discover'd Islands* from a copy of the *Universal Magazine of Knowledge and Pleasure*, 1787, where New Zeeland has taken shape and has Cook's orderly ranks of pointed alps lined up across Toai Poonamoo. A map of the world from his old school atlas, with all the empire's possessions tinted pink.

He has always liked looking at the maps, seeing his country rise on paper, like a fish, taking on its present form. He likes the angle of view, the godlike vision, looking down. He likes the way maps transform the chaos at ground level to something orderly, manageable, packed within a grid.

The phone plays on, some soothing crap, the sort of stuff his father used to play for the cows at milking on the peninsula, the same stuff they use to keep trapped humans calm in lifts or as several thousand tonnes of steel prepare to come to earth on a narrow runway.

He sits there, waiting to be told what is going to happen to his house. They cannot leave, though Janey says she'd like to leave. Just get out, take the kids, go to America, or Europe or somewhere, buy a van, have an adventure. 'But what will we live on?' he says. And she waves her hand, says, 'Oh, we could work on farms, I could do some English-as-a-second-language teaching, we could pick fruit. Whatever.'

It was what he had liked about her when they met. There had been a party. Over in Lyttelton. He hadn't wanted to go.

'Come on,' said his flatmate. 'Get your fat arse off that sofa.'

'Nah,' he'd said. He had wanted to leave his fat arse precisely where it was. But Ryan wouldn't let go, got his mate Shane to help and they'd half-dragged, half-heaved him into the back of Shane's Nissan.

'Here. Have one of these,' Ryan had said, handing a pill over the seat. 'Relax. You never know. That chick — what's her name — Becca? Donna's sister — she'll be there. You might get lucky.'

And what do you know? He did. Not with Becca, who was weepy drunk by the time they got there, but with this girl who was sitting outside by the brazier, not taking any notice. Just sitting. He'd gone outside himself because the pill had left him buzzy without the lift he'd hoped for. It had done nothing to deaden the deep conviction that nothing whatever in his life had changed, nothing would ever change, and he was doomed to spend the rest of his existence in endless, circular repetition.

He had been away five years, working in Sydney, and he knew he shouldn't have come back. He'd liked it over there, had driven with this girl, Amy, up the east coast, the Pacific bluer than it ever was at home, lizards like small dragons rearing up on red inland roads to face down their spinning wheels, the great arc of the night sky overhead, and a feeling of limitless possibility. He'd never quite lost a certain timidity at the multitude of creatures this place could come up with that could sting or bite or rip off your leg while you were swimming in that blue ocean, but he'd begun to think it could go on forever.

Except there had been the 'It's not you, it's me' conversation, Amy nibbling at a nail the way she did when she was nervous, and it had all come to a grinding halt. He'd been flung sideways by it, cracked apart. He hadn't expected to feel like that.

So he'd come home, and had known it was a mistake the minute he stepped from the plane. There was the airport looking like a tin shed and the flat streets where everyone had left or died of boredom and his mum in the same kitchen cooking the same lump of meat and his dad out in the garage at his lathe, turning out yet another twisty lampstand, and it was as if the past five years hadn't happened.

He'd got a job and a flat, but it was only until he'd saved enough for a ticket out.

But there she was by the brazier, looking up at him, arms wrapped tightly round her body. A slim body from what he could make out, firelight shadowing one side of her face, glinting in her eyes.

'Hi,' she'd said. 'Do you want to walk me home?' He'd taken a second to realise she was talking to him. 'Okay,' he'd said and, as they began climbing one of the port's little steep winding streets, 'Just where is it you live?'

And she'd said, 'Opawa.'

'That's the other side of the hill!' he said.

'Yep,' she said. 'We'll go over the top, on the track. There's a full moon.'

And there was. As they climbed higher the street lights became fewer, then came to an end and the moonlight lay, clear and blue, over the harbour, over the port clanging with cranes and containers. Maybe it was the sudden blast of cold air, but suddenly the pill seemed to kick in. Everything was gilded. The leaves on bushes as they brushed past, the stones ahead on the path, this girl's hair when she turned her face to speak, the outline of her body walking easily ahead up the steep hill. He'd never done this before: climbed some vertical bloody cliff with some girl, everything turned to silver and shadows of deep velvety black, the crunch of their shoes on a path of glittering stone, and at the top, the city spread across the plain, no longer the place of boring forever and ever, but a web of brilliant light, lines of light, where anything might happen.

But here she is, talking about picking fruit and a van when nothing's settled. They have a house, they have a mortgage. They can't sell, they can't leave, they can't simply walk away, they have to get the place repaired without having any idea what those repairs might include, they have to hang on listening to a piano while somewhere in the framework above and around, Carla in Brizzy is looking for their ...

seventy-eight
THE RIVER

The trees that remain after snowfall, hail, wind, the shaking earth, break into new leaf.

Far to the north, she is swimming into warmer waters.

She dives down to the cooler depths.

The cooler, darker waters.

seventy-nine
THE TAG
SEPTEMBER 2011

...mark the first anniversary of the quake together, as a family.

'We could have a picnic,' she said.

But everyone had other plans. Poppy wanted to go to the group hug in the gardens with her new friend, Gina, and her mother.

'What's a group hug?' she said.

'A lot of people hugging each other,' said her mother. 'Cheering themselves up.'

'People I know?' said Poppy.

'Not necessarily,' said Janey.

Poppy looked dubious.

'You don't have to go if you don't want to,' said Janey. But after the hug Gina's mum was going to take them for a Happy Meal. Poppy would get a Smurf. Gina had almost a complete collection. Little blue figures with pointed hats, including Smurfette who wore tiny white high-heeled shoes. Poppy privately didn't like Smurfs much, but to admit it would have been like saying you didn't like Katy Perry. Everybody liked Katy Perry: Gina, especially. She could do the dance from 'Hot n Cold'. She and Poppy practised it, over and over, using the sofa as a substitute for Katy's car, the one she stands on while the brides dance around. She said Poppy was really good at it, and maybe they could do it for assembly? Poppy could be one of the brides.

Poppy set off happily for the park, the hug and the Smurf, along with Gina and her mum, a cluster of red and black balloons bouncing from the windows of their Mitsubishi.

Tom had stayed over at VJs. 'A picnic?' he said, as if she'd suggested something completely bizarre. 'Why?' He didn't see the point in picnics: carrying food to eat it somewhere boring, with extra sandflies. 'I thought we should do something for the anniversary,' his mum said. Nah, said Tom. He'd just hang out at VJ's.

The cordon had receded, the wire fences now forming a narrower defensive circle around the CBD. At night they ringed the tilting towers and shadowed streets where demolition cranes reared up into the dark sky and security patrolled with slavering German Shepherds.

Tom didn't like German Shepherds, the way they strained at the leash, tails clamped between their haunches, ready to spring. On the eve of the anniversary he had watched one crossing a demolition site from a vertiginous viewpoint four floors up on a building off High Street. On the ground floor of this building stood VJ's dad's pretzel shop, now a dusty, empty shell. VJ's dad had been pissed off. All these celebrities were being escorted round the central city, that guy from *Gladiator* and Prince William and some model, Rachel whatever, getting their photos taken in front of the cathedral, while he couldn't get in to clear out his property. And when he had finally been permitted through the cordon, it was to find everything had gone: the whole place had been stripped bare, tables, chairs, equipment. And, of course, the till. 'Now there's a surprise,' said VJ's dad. 'Who'll protect us from the protectors?'

From the fourth floor where Tom was crouched with VJ behind the fire escape, the German Shepherd's panting was clearly audible, an eager, drooling whoosh whoosh whoosh as torchlight slid over the walls. They lay unmoving, scarcely breathing, and then, amazingly, the crackle of a two-way radio and the guard walked on, his voice echoing in the silence as his footsteps receded and the dark came down again.

'Shit,' said VJ. His voice buzzy against Tom's ear. 'That was close.'

The fine was $5000. Or three months in prison. Not to mention endless trouble with their parents, no matter how much they might have been pissed off about the guy from *Gladiator* and Rachel whatever.

'But,' said VJ, as he showed Tom the way through the cordon, 'fuck it! It's our city, not theirs.'

Their city lay around them, streets slamming into darkness as Tom fumbled in his backpack and handed up a can to VJ. He was way more confident up there. Tom preferred the security of the railing. It was a long way down. He kept his eyes averted, watched as VJ threw them up, the letters of his name, each tip a spear point, wild style, taking possession.

He worked quickly, but then he'd perfected it over several weeks, working out style and design among the cracks on the living room wall at Tom's place. It didn't matter: no one went in there, in the dark and damp behind the plywood patches, and the walls would be coming down eventually. Just the same, they went there only when everyone was out and they had the house to themselves. Parents could be unpredictable about things like that.

This building, too, would come down and take its tags with it. The demolition cranes stood by. But four floors up on the parapet, for a few seconds, Tom and VJ owned the Death Zone.

Rob didn't want a picnic either. He simply wanted to get on with his pizza oven. It now stood on the lawn like a little domed cathedral. Its base was a three-sided structure of concrete blocks scavenged from the Novaks' house across the road. ('You go ahead and use them, young fella,' said Stan. 'No point in it all going to waste at the tip, is there?')

The base had a space where wood for the oven could be stored to dry properly. On top of the blocks he had laid a concrete slab, carefully levelled, and then the bricks, arranged in an igloo around a central layer of firebricks. The dome was beautiful. Rob had cleaned each brick of old mortar and laid it precisely, abutting its neighbour at a perfect angle. He had supported the dome of bricks with a couple of old beer crates while he was building, then filled the whole cavity with some of the silty soil that had bubbled from the ground and now lay in a pile by the back fence. Nothing was going to waste. Everything had its purpose.

And now the mortar holding the bricks in place was dry enough for its outer layer of insulating concrete and this afternoon was the perfect time to start. He'd work on the oven and then maybe he'd go out for a paddle. Sometimes he just wanted to slip through the water, the kayak responsive to every shift in balance, his passing leaving scarcely a ripple.

The river was filthy, he knew that. But he wasn't alone in deciding to ignore the fact. Stan had always put out a whitebait net on the riverbank at the end of Savage Street and saw no reason to stop now. 'Anything that was going to kill me would have done it long ago,' he said, sprawled happily on the grass by the 'Fishing Prohibited' sign very early that morning, smoking a cigarette while keeping a wary eye out for the authorities.

'Always some miserable bastard these days running around trying to tell you what's good for you,' he said when Rob stopped for a chat. 'And the bait are running this year. Never seen so many. It's like they know. They've just been sitting out there, waiting for everyone to bugger off.' There was a blue plastic bucket on the grass beside him, half-filled with tiny silvery squirming fish. 'Well,' he said, getting to his feet. 'Lucky for some. Here: take a few.' He scooped a generous serving into an ice cream container, emptied and neatly washed. 'There you go: enough for a feed!'

Rob received his gift with every appearance of delight. He was certainly not about to join the ranks of miserable bastards preaching caution, but as soon as he got the container home, he tipped it into the compost. He had read the data. Knew the pollution levels. He wouldn't be eating whitebait from the river again any time soon.

But the kayak, the paddle, the herons lifting on slow lazy wings from the banks, a single white spoonbill standing motionless on the muddy bank of Naughty Boys Island. There seemed to be more birds around now, maybe taking advantage of human abandonment, of the shoals of bait making a dash for it. There were fewer dogs now the houses were empty, and fewer cats. And from the kayak, low in the water, even though the river had risen in its bed, the sad suburbs were barely visible beyond the stopbanks.

First, though, the insulation: six parts Perlite to one part cement, and water to mix. He sat on the back step stirring it in a bucket ...

Janey watches him through the kitchen window. It's impossible to say how much this slow purposeful stirring, this nonsense with the pizza oven, infuriates her. It is supposed to be for her birthday, but it is so terribly pointless. Their house has avoided the red zone and automatic demolition by the narrowest of margins. It may yet be red-stickered, demolished, the site cleared for rebuilding, taking everything, house, pizza oven, garden and all with it. It could perhaps be repaired, but, either way, Janey doesn't want to be here any longer. She has fallen out of love and can't go back to that earlier infatuation.

She is making herself a sandwich. If no one else wants to come on a picnic to mark the day, she'll go alone. Bike up the Port Hills to the point where the roads are closed because of the risk of rock fall. Sit in the sun to eat her sandwich. Think about Before. Think about After.

Above the bench on the kitchen wall hangs the photo board, crammed with the imagery of Before: Tom as a toddler, digging in the sand on the beach at Sumner, Poppy seated in the front of the double kayak on the river, or in their togs, or on Santa's lap, in their sleeping bags in the tent, blowing out the candles on a birthday cake with chocolate icing, Rob and Tom playing chess, Poppy holding a fish on the pier at Brighton, an old photo of herself and Rob with dreadlocks at a dance party on top of Takaka Hill, long before the arrival of the children, who now regard that photo with derisive disbelief, laughing hilariously at their parents' youthful absurdity.

And if she looks further back, at some picture of Rob's parents snapped by the photographer in their best going-to-town clothes walking along Colombo Street, the spire of the cathedral visible in the background, the 'before' seems even more remote. A time of careless indifference to masonry and stone. Buildings would always stand, cities were forever.

But they weren't, were they? New Orleans had been swept aside in a single night, villages at Fukushima have disappeared while the cameras circled soundlessly overhead, filming the little white car that races along the road just ahead of the relentless wave rolling over farmhouse and settlement and you watched it as it played over and over on the news, saying, 'Go, little car! Go! Run away! Escape!'

As she wants to go. To run. She's said as much to David. They've taken to having a quick coffee while he clears up after his teaching and she comes into the room to prepare for hers. The brief interval before the room fills once more with jostling adolescence.

'Yeah,' said David, 'It's a weird time, eh.' He'd been back only a few months, returned to teaching after a couple of years crewing on a yacht sailing from Stockholm to Tahiti. It had been fantastic, even the moment when he'd glanced back over one shoulder somewhere close to Rapanui and seen this great bloody wave rolling down on them and nothing he could do about it but hang on, keep hold of the tiller ... He was restless, didn't know what to do next, where to go. When he talked about the boat, about *Lista Light* — she's this old wooden gaff ketch, a fishing boat to begin with, built for the storms in the North Sea, sturdy as — his legs jiggled as if he was about to run. He had her image as his screensaver, fully rigged before a tropic sunrise, ready to go. He was here only because his father hadn't been well, thought he should come home for a spell.

'Yeah,' he said when Janey confessed to wanting to just pick up and leave. 'I know exactly what you mean.'

It was such a relief that someone knew exactly what she ...

eighty
THE RIVER

The trees burst into spring leaf.

Two thousand kilometres to the north she swims through the dark, 700 metres down.

Without doubt or distraction.

The dark waters part before her.

eighty-one
THE IDEAL CITY
OCTOBER 2011

... is drawing a city. Everyone has been asked to draw a city. Just the middle part, not the suburbs with houses, but the middle part of offices and shops where there was a lot of damage. Many of those buildings would have to be demolished, which was a bit sad, but the good part was that now, Mrs Ngatai said, they could build an even better city. The city council wanted everyone to tell them what they thought would make it the best city in the world.

Cities needed all kinds of things. She wrote a list on the board as everyone called out what cities needed: shops, parks, roads, 'Toilets,' said Poppy, which made everyone laugh, but Mrs Ngatai said it was true. That was very important. Cities needed proper toilets and a sewerage system, instead of horrible spider-webby smelly portaloos.

'And now,' she said, 'you can add whatever you like. Imagine your ideal city! Imagine something new and exciting!' It was very important that the city council heard from children because the ideal city would be their future.

Poppy sits in the sun at the kitchen table with her felt tips and a piece of paper to design the future.

It's quite hard to think about an ideal city when you can still remember bits of the old one. Mrs Ngatai had said they could change the streets if they liked. It was a blank canvas. So Poppy draws a circle. A round city would be cool, maybe with water all around it, like an island. Everyone would go into the city across bridges or on boats. The water could be a giant swimming pool, with beaches where people could have picnics and there would be kayaks and pedal boats. She draws blue waves around the city.

She likes drawing. It is quiet when she draws. She puts on her headphones and listens to an audiobook as the line emerges from the tip of the pen. No one and nothing can reach her, here inside the voices of the book, the line on the page. Beside her on the table is the yellow plastic basket containing the Novaks' laundry, dried and neatly folded by her mother because they are old and don't have a washing machine any more and it's no trouble, not in the least.

The Novaks' washing is disgusting. Big grey knickers and funny old underpants and saggy singlets and faded nighties, all smelling, despite the detergent, of age: that horrible fishy smell of old dry skin and thin hair and yellow teeth and some sweet cloying soapy perfume...

She no longer believes that Mrs Novak is a witch. Her mother told her to grow up when she admitted that that was why she avoided going to the portaloo. She hated that dark figure seated by the window overlooking the street, or walking with infinite slowness across the road to put out milk for Zitto. Zitto had run away on the day of the quake, but still she put out milk and meat at their old house, just in case he came back. Mr Novak said they had the best-fed rats and hedgehogs for miles around, but still he went with her every day, holding her arm to steady her across the potholes.

The thought of seeing Mrs Novak at the window, or encountering her unexpectedly as she walked to find her cat, unnerved Poppy. It was a worse thought than the spiders, worse than the thought that someone might come along and tip over the portaloo while she was still inside.

'Don't be such a baby,' her mother said. 'There's no such thing as witches. Mrs Novak is just an old lady who isn't well and wants to stay near her home as long as possible and we must be kind to her and to Mr Novak.' But still that smell lingers, that dank ancient buried smell...

Poppy is supposed to deliver the washing to the sleepout and she is putting it off as long as possible. She is hiding inside the book where Stacey, the girl detective, is figuring out what happened to the diamond ring, while she tries to think about what to draw next. What should go at the centre of the ideal city? A row of shops? But when she tries to draw that, all she can see is the row of shops that were always there with the sushi place they went to on Friday nights, or the store where they had the Christmas windows every year, with the wolf who sat up in Grandmama's nightcap, his stiff grey mouth opening and shutting while a voice told the story. She is not supposed to draw these things. She is supposed to be imagining something new and exciting. Maybe she could draw shops with gardens on their roofs because why shouldn't people walk along the roofs, rather than on the street all the time? There could be a path all the way along for skateboards and scooters...

'Poppy!' The headphones are lifted away. 'How many times do I have to...'

She picks up the basket. Usually when she delivers something to the sleepout she runs up the steps, knocks at the door then runs away again, before the Novaks can answer. But today the door is wide open and Mrs Novak calls out as she climbs the stairs and she has no option — we must be kind — but to go inside.

The old-person smell is thick and rank. The room is crammed with bags and suitcases and cardboard boxes and Mrs Novak sits on an armchair among the clutter, in her hand a tin can, the lid bent back with a jagged edge.

'Ah, Poppy,' she says. 'Che fortuna! Stan is at supermarket and I am not feeling flash. You put the dinner for Zitto, please?' Not waiting for her to say yes or no, simply handing over the can and a milk carton, so there is no option but to take it — the catfood is stinky fish — to cross Savage Street, let herself through the gate into the garden where the Novaks' house sits knock-kneed and naked without its bricks, though Stan still mows the lawn, trims the edges.

And there, sitting on the front step as if he had been there all along, is Zitto, skinnier than before, his fur matted but calmly licking his white paws. He bows as she comes toward him, and wraps his skinny body round her bare legs. He allows himself to be picked up and carried, purring, across the road and up the stairs into the sleepout.

'Zitto! Zitto!' says Mrs Novak. 'Oh, Poppy! You bring him back! I knew you are good luck!"

And she reaches out and takes the cat in her arms and sits stroking him, smiling and not looking in the least like a witch, as Poppy sets out milk in a saucer, and catfood. Then they sit watching Zitto as he gulps down his dinner, and Mrs Novak asks her what she is doing so Poppy tells her about drawing the ideal city. 'Ah,' says Mrs Novak. 'The ideal city . . . So, it must always have a square at its heart, always — a big square where anyone might go, with beautiful buildings all around, not high, like here used to be, but low so there is light and sunshine, and a fountain and a place serving the most delicious ice cream and . . .'

Zitto's neat pink tongue laps at the milk, and Poppy and Mrs Novak imagine the ideal . . .

eighty-two
THE RIVER

The moon rides over the city, lays down a path on the river.

She is far away, coming closer, closer.

She feels some change, some taste, some sound, some vibration that reaches her in the deep water and draws her up.

Up towards the dazzling surface.

eighty-three
THE PIZZA OVEN
NOVEMBER 2011

'...fantastic!' says Janey and everyone laughs, clinks glasses. A random selection of tumblers and wineglasses. They've never replaced the ones that broke. 'Happy Birthday!'

Rob slides the first pizza from the oven and onto the table. 'It's a bit burnt,' he says. 'There's a knack to the fire. You have to move it round, heat one side then the other, then scrape all the embers away. I haven't quite got it yet.'

'Doesn't matter,' says Sarah, wielding the pizza cutter. 'It looks good.'

Mozzarella trails away in a long strand as she lifts a slice from the board. She wraps it round her finger. 'Tastes good. That's all that matters!'

She's right, of course. What matters isn't how things appear, but whether they serve their essential function: does food taste good? Is a lake sustaining life? Is a house deeply damaged or are the cracks merely on the surface?

The oven stands at the end of the lawn some distance from the deck, on account of the smoke. From where Rob stands, sliding in the next pizza, the deck looks like a theatre stage, framed with bunting and fairy lights.

Poppy had insisted. 'It won't be a party if you don't have decorations.' Decorations and candles and bunting. Happy Birthday!

Decorations and the rituals of the cake, the candles, the song. She becomes frantic these days about such things: what should happen, how things should be done. 'You've got to do it properly,' she said. So they did.

Heat pours from the oven door. Three minutes only. Sarah approaches, bearing the empty platter. 'Here, chef,' she says. 'You cook. I'll be your wait-person for this evening.' She has bare arms, a loose blue dress and sandals.

Over on the deck, their friends move about, voices already becoming louder and more dishevelled, the shout of laughter, music playing, Salmonella Dub, that loose summery slide. Janey's birthday has always felt like the beginning of summer, the first night when it is usually warm enough to eat outside. The doors onto the deck are wide open. There are salads in big bowls on the picnic table, and paper plates and the clink of bottles, the pop of that bubbly stuff Janey insists on drinking on such occasions. From down here at the end of the garden, it really does look like a party. You would never guess at the half-house, the broken windows, the empty street. It's pasteboard, like a film set, like the saloon in some old Hollywood western. He slides another pizza — also slightly charred on one side, he'd have to sort that — onto the platter. His arm brushes Sarah's as she turns to go.

'Do you want another pinot?' she says.

Of course.

Janey is up there centre stage, receiving a gift: Oh, you shouldn't have. I said strictly no presents, but she is smiling at the donor just the same. Some tall guy he doesn't recognise. One of her colleagues maybe, or someone from her yoga class, someone she's just met or someone she's known for years. Whatever. She reaches up and kisses him lightly, that silly kissy kissy affectation everyone has taken on, as if we're all actors in some French movie, entering a smart Parisian apartment or arriving for a lengthy luncheon in the campagne. He never knows what to do now: to kiss or not, both cheeks or not. Or his usual solution, knocking noses in the middle. To hug or not. To shake hands or not or to opt for his preferred stance: to stand back, nod and grunt in a way that he hopes will be construed as reasonably affable.

The gift-bringer seems unfazed anyway. He bends down to receive his kiss, then, Rob cannot help but notice, keeps one hand lightly against Janey's back as she leads him through to the table, come on I'll get you a drink, what are you having ... The crowd parts to let them pass.

Another pizza. He hopes the oven will hold the heat. It seems to be okay, though he's only fired it a couple of times when, on-line, they recommend five pre-firings to dry the mortar thoroughly. If there's any moisture in the walls it can turn to steam with intense heat. And it has to be intense to build up the high temperatures required for perfect pizza. The walls can crack.

Sarah's back with the platter and his drink.

'Going down well, chef,' she says. 'Best pizza ever. What wood did you use?'

She seems genuinely interested, and he is able to say, 'It's plum wood. Amazing, eh? You have to use a really dense hardwood that will burn slowly: most people use manuka. But our plum tree went over in the snow and the wood's perfect, once it's dry. It's supposed to give a good flavour.'

He's talking too much, getting caught up in the detail, but Sarah is nodding. 'It does,' she says. 'It's a great oven. And it's good to build something when everything is such a mess.' She reaches out a hand and strokes the dome. 'I love this curve.' Her fingers are long and slender, she's wearing a heavy silver bracelet. He's never seen her in a dress before, always sensible work clothes. Her hair is tied up somehow so that it falls around her neck. And when she brushes her hand over the curve on the oven, he finds himself suddenly suffused with some rush of feeling that is not desire but something more complicated altogether.

Attraction is part of it, yes. Of course. She's gorgeous. But right at this moment, standing there at the end of the garden, what he feels primarily is a kind of gratitude. She sees the point.

He has known it was ridiculous, all this careful labour to build something more complicated than he has ever attempted in his life before. He's been at best a couple of bookshelves man, a coathook man, no DIY master with a shed like Stan's across the road, everything to hand and an easy familiarity with the hardware aisles.

He knows he's been driving Janey mad with his steady

application to assembling bricks and mortar on uncertain ground, nine thousand aftershocks and counting. A risk, a waste of time. But then everything is driving her mad at present. Last week she slammed a letter on the bench as he came in from work. Insurer's letterhead. 'Here for YOU!'

They were now officially over the cap, the original estimate for repairs revisited. '$190,000!' she said. 'Didn't that engineer mate of Colin's say $380,000?' As if it was Rob's fault, this discrepancy, as if the file fattening on the desk of printouts, emails, estimates, reports, was his responsibility, not their shared future. He feels buried by documentation, claim and counter-claim, estimate and revised estimate, by figures that slip from his fingers at the slightest touch, going up, going down, argument over apportionment, when precisely this crack appeared in their foundations . . .

'What are they going to repair?' she said, and he said, as he always says, 'I don't know. No one knows. You know that.' *We cannot release information that may be prejudicial to the ongoing investigation of this claim.*

'We should demand to know,' she said. 'We should stand up to them.'

'There's no point,' he said.

And she said, 'Why are you being so bloody feeble?'

And he said, 'I'm not being feeble. We could get a lawyer. We could get a full engineer's report.'

And she said, 'But that'll cost a fortune,'

'Exactly,' he said. 'But if you think we should stand up to them . . .'

'We can't afford it,' said Janey. She picked up the insurer's letter, stuffed it roughly back in its torn envelope. 'So, I guess we send another email? Say we think the repair estimate is too low?'

'If you think it'll make any difference,' he said, the shiny towers of handlers and adjustors and managers and CEOs stretching away across oceans and continents, the ranks of empathetic teddies heavy overhead.

'Or we do nothing?' said Janey.

And on and on, till she slammed out to sit on the sofa, the laptop cover raised like a wall. He went to bed before her, face turned away in the spare room when she came in, late, slipped under the duvet, then tugged it tightly around her. A cold gap opened at his back.

But here they are, having a party that looks, at first glance, like all the other parties they have ever had in this place. The fairy lights, the music and Sarah is handing him a drink, saying, 'Here you go, chef,' as he slides the pizza (Hawaiian cheese and pineapple) from the oven. And there's a little pop, and a crack opens right across the cement shell of the . . .

eighty-four
THE RIVER

It happens.

In sunlight, streams of ova pour from her body.

She floats on the surface in dazzling light, around her the bodies of others like herself. Great heavy females releasing themselves into the warm tropic sea, the little whiplash males exuding millions of wriggling sperm.

The whole churning mess of fertilisation, sperm drawn into the body of the egg.

And it's done.

She drifts.

An empty sack.

Gulls gather.

eighty-five
THE CEILING
DECEMBER 2011

... **looking up** at the ceiling. Some trees have been removed from the riverbank, judged too unstable to remain, and sunlight on this summer afternoon reflects from the water, sending circles of light dancing across the sleepout ceiling. Kitty misses the trees, but the lights, she thinks as she settles to her nap, are very beautiful.

It's quiet. Just a bird racing up and down a scale, the wind rustling in the leaves of the walnut tree by the fence. The Morrisons have gone camping, a 'no-fuss Christmas'. So it's just her and Stan. Alone in the sleepout. Keeping an eye on things.

It's necessary. Now that so many houses stand empty, the utes and vans have become casual, almost entitled. They turn up at all hours, sometimes in the middle of the afternoon, a couple of men wearing hi-vis vests for the illusion of legality, calmly helping themselves to water cylinders and piping for the copper, to windows, french doors, fittings. Yesterday afternoon, while Kitty and Stan were at the doctor's — the pills were no longer working, she needed something stronger — they had returned to find the Morrisons' rockery gone. Just holes in the ground where those big smooth rocks had lain. There was a good market for rocks at present, the policewoman told them when she came to record the theft. Rocks, stone walls, seats, plants, shrubs, cacti. Anything that could fetch a dollar as people shifted about the city, making new homes, new gardens elsewhere.

Stan keeps guard nightly. He has moved as much as possible from the garage across the road to the sleepout, back and forth, back and forth until only the largest most immovable things are left behind. The fridge. The washing machine. No one wants them, not even the men in the utes. 'Too old,' said the policewoman. 'They won't bother with those.' Or her piano.

It stands at the back of the garage under an old bedspread with the stool containing all her music. Sometimes when they first moved from the house she had played. Rolled up the garage door so the sun came in and sat at the keyboard, stiff fingers fumbling after a carol, a Chopin prelude, a little Bach minuet. But since they had come up here, to the sleepout, she had stopped. She had not played for months.

But this morning she had thought, why not? The sun was out, the air was sweet and warm. Perhaps it was the new pills, but she felt a surge of energy. Her fingers when she flexed them moved smoothly. She would go over to the garage, Stan would roll up the door and she would sit and play.

It took a while to get down the steps, Stan holding her steady. Zitto ran ahead as they crossed the road, his tail straight up in the air with that little curl at the tip. The garage was dusty, but when the door rolled back there was her piano, cloaked in faded pink chenille before a wall bearing the shadows of all Stan's tools.

Stan pulled out the stool, then sat himself down on an old deck chair in the sun to roll a cigarette while Kitty began to play. Schubert. 'Von Fremden Ländern und Menschen'. Nice and slow to start. Her fingers touched the keys.

A muffled twak twak twak and the key stuck fast. Something was in the way, blocking the music and she simply could not bear it. It all rolled over her. She lifted her hands, hit the keys, hard, so hard it hurt, hit the wooden frame, because this was how it ended, how it always ended. Trees fell and houses and ideal cities and little villages with children playing. They all came down. Young men, young women and the music of distant lands, it all ended in discord and jangling and a muffled twak twak twak and she could not bear it. She howled. She could not bear it.

But Stan lifted the piano lid. He looked inside. He reached in and lifted something from the interior.

'Well, what do you know,' he said. A little nest, a perfect little nest lay cupped in his hand. It was lined completely with tufts of pink chenille. 'Little buggers,' he said. 'Get in everywhere.' The nest was a soft pink cup. It would have been so warm over the winter, tucked inside her piano, with its cluster of tiny naked bodies.

Without the nest the piano was a little jangly and untuned but possible and her fingers, once she warmed up, moved more freely than they had in ages. Stan sat peaceably smoking in the sunshine while Kitty played. 'Don't need a flash concert hall,' he said. 'Got my own concert hall right here.'

And after she had finished, they shut the piano, replaced the bedspread with its nibbled holes, and crossed back over Savage Street. She was tired now, very tired. The sleepout steps were steep. But Stan said, 'Here you go, girl. Upsy-daisy.' And he lifted her, as if she were young again, and he, too, a young man taking her up to their shared room.

He set her down, both of them laughing at the silliness of it.

'I make coffee,' she said. And she was just reaching down their cups from the shelf above the bench when she heard a little Oh! behind her back. As if Stan had been surprised by something. As if something completely unexpected had suddenly burst through the wall of the sleepout and startled him. And she turned and he was falling, straight back, onto their bed . . .

And now she is lying on the bed, too, looking up at the lights of the river dancing in shining circles on the sleepout ceiling. Stan lies beside her, on his back with his head on the pillow, eyelids closed on that startled stare. She has combed his hair and put on his good tie, his best leather shoes. She has put on her best dress, too, and a warm angora cardigan and high heels she hasn't worn in years. It has taken her all afternoon to get ready, moving slowly about the room, putting out food for Zitto and a thank you note for the Morrisons. She leaves the door unlocked for the nurse's visit in the morning.

She lies on the bed. She has had her coffee. Washed down all her pills. The bird races up and down the scale, the wind blows through the walnut tree leaves, the river lights dance on the ceiling. She takes Stan's hand, already cold, but still recognisably his hand, with its familiar calluses, she twists her rosary beads around them both. God will understand. Not that old man god with his rules and retribution, but the baby god who perched, weightless, on his mother's arm, one hand raised in blessing, the other holding the golden apple of the world. The first god, whom she met long ago standing with dusty boots beside her aunt in the sanctuary at Roio Poggio. He will understand. She's sure of it.

He has sent a sign: lights dancing across the white ...

eighty-six
THE RIVER

Summer on the river.

Cicadas sawing away on the willow trees.

Seven years under ground. A few hours above ground to fit it all in: flight and breeding and death. A life.

Their legs saw. Pick me! Pick me!

Far to the north, a tiny silvery leaf wriggles in a warm ocean.

Charged with life. With nerves and gut and eyes and mouth.

Floating.

eighty-seven

THE DRAFT PLAN

JANUARY 2012

...**looks down** as the plane circles low over the central city in a fierce nor-wester. It sways and bucks and she grips the armrest. The man next to her seems unconcerned, deep in some grim Nordic thriller. How weird that countries that consistently score top in those international happiness polls come up with such innovative ways of killing, maiming and torture. The plane dips suddenly and there's a sharp intake of breath, an involuntary aahh from the interior of Flight NZ517. Her, too. The man looks up, smiles at her, turns a page.

Maybe he's a helicopter pilot, search and rescue, accustomed to sudden downdraughts. Or just a show-off. She concentrates on the scene below, the streets in early evening stretching across the plain from the foot of the Port Hills, the cluster of buildings at its heart, the gaps where buildings once stood. Big gaps now, hundreds of demolitions, five or more a week. 'Getting the old dungers down,' as the Big Buffoon puts it. 'Levelling the city's heritage,' as the letters to the editor more often put it. From above, the city seems covered in bald patches, like some ailing creature. Beside her, the man folds down a corner of a page and closes the book: the abused heroine has drugged the serial rapist, handcuffed him to the radiator, is switching on the drill . . .

She feels strange. Floating. Detached. The undercarriage is down and the wind tips them from side to side as they sway in, lower now over the western suburbs: long straight roads lined with the corrugated-iron roofs of light industry, warehouses, malls. From up here, they seem barely damaged. Nothing has changed.

That's the strangest thing about their lives now. She lives in half a house with water running down the hall in a southerly, with argument with insurers and dispute over surreal detail, while only a few kilometres away lives go on pretty much unchanged. The sense of unreality becomes even greater once you leave the city entirely.

As she has just done.

She has been in Auckland. For a conference. Three days in a lecture theatre at AUT, little plastic label pinned to her jacket, the schedule of talks and seminars folded in her bag. She has sat at the opening session listening to an academic who hasn't been near a high-school classroom in twenty years delivering a careful analysis of conceptualisations of knowledge and learning in the something curriculum something meta-ethnography. Something.

And all the time, her feet are jiggling under the desk and there's a quivering in her stomach that has nothing to do with meta-ethnography.

He had left at Christmas. Was living aboard a yacht up in Auckland helping a mate get a 35-foot sloop ready to sail up to Fiji over the winter. David thought he might go with him.

'If you're in Auckland, get in touch,' he'd said. 'I'll be there till May, early June.' It depended on the wind.

So she did. Of course she did. And he had texted back, Marina gate, 1pm? And she had texted back Great! CU.

The sloop was out of the water. It looked long and sleek, but solid, he said, with a deep displacement, long bluewater keel, she'd handle the conditions out there, and he waved vaguely towards the little islands that ringed the harbour, the gulf and the open ocean beyond.

Janey hadn't gone back to the conference. She hadn't slept in the enormous bed at the Best Western, but in the cramped cabin of a yacht, moored in a little bay at the bottom end of Waiheke. The boat rocked under them, then settled to a gentle swaying as he fell asleep, one arm flung back behind his head, while she lay beside him in the narrow berth thinking: So, this is it. Cheating. Being unfaithful. Committing adultery. If I lived in Saudi Arabia, I'd be dragged to a pit and stoned. Beside her, David stirred. 'Hey,' he said. He reached out a lazy hand and touched her face, and off she went again. Piling up more stones.

And in the morning she could have gone back. There was a lecture on the exploration of identity and integrity in teaching. She'd put a ring around it on the schedule, but the birdsong in the bay was loud that morning so she did some yoga stretches under a pohutukawa tree in full blossom, red stamens raining down, and swam back to the boat where David had made coffee: strong black coffee, and the wind was right it seemed to sail up to Kawau . . .

For three days she floated. They dawdled round little bush-clad islands that rose like mirages from the lustre of the sea. She phoned home a couple of times, said 'Everything okay?' as if she were looking out at the Sky Tower from her hotel. 'Fine . . . fine . . .' The voices, hers and theirs, sounded strange, as if they were actors speaking lines of dialogue.

She was no longer Janey who folded the washing and picked up Poppy from ballet, not Janey who slept beside her husband in the spare room, not Janey standing in the rain doing bus duty. The boat quivered, but it was not like the quivering of earth, that abrupt jolt that came from the east, from the fault that snapped somewhere off the coast near Brighton. Nor the slower, lurching gait of the shocks that rolled through from the west, from the fault that had split across a paddock near Darfield. The boat moved constantly but it was to be expected. The sea moved beneath the hull, making the halyards rattle, sending pots and jars rolling about the lockers in the galley. It was supposed to move, and that movement calmed instead of startling.

Out here, on this shifting surface she was someone else. Someone from a movie, with salt in her hair. Someone who dived over the side naked into the blue waters of the gulf, someone who sat on deck drinking margaritas in a sarong (and why had she packed a sarong? Had she planned this all along?) as the sun went down in a sudden flare of glory, unlike the slow dwindling summer twilight further south. Janey who lay in the narrow berth against a smooth brown body while stars rocked overhead, Janey who could in an eyeblink simply keep right on sailing, from island to island across the wide blue Pacific.

'Why not?' he said.

The plane sweeps over the city's edge, where the bulldozers are already assembled in paddocks being swiftly transformed into subdivisions of open plan and en suite and grey cladding to accommodate those whose homes have been destroyed elsewhere. Everything is being reconfigured. She has seen the plan. Rob had brought home a copy. Computer-generated citizens walked along tree-lined boulevards and cycled along a riverside path, light-rail systems traversed the city, the centre was a pedestrianised zone where people would 'live, work and play'. It was just a draft, just a suggestion, yet to be approved by the minister in charge of the city's recovery, the Big Buffoon, but 'It looks all right, doesn't it?' said Rob. She'd glanced at the plan. The computerised citizens had a kind of airless unreality, elongated shadows on the boulevards, living, working, playing. But yeah. It looked all right.

The plane lands with a bump. And now she must wake up. No longer floating, but back to the quivery earth. Back home where ...

eighty-eight
THE RIVER

Nothing happens.

Light dances on the water.

Thousands of kilometres to the north, the silver leaf is caught by the current.

She is carried southward.

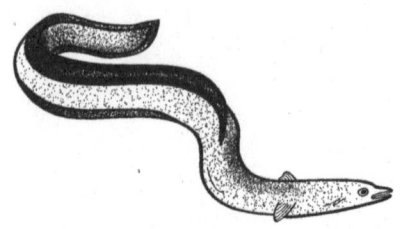

eighty-nine

THE CUBES

FEBRUARY 2012

... to move out. Just for four months while the house is repaired. A month to clear the place and find somewhere else. Janey is lying on the sofa (1.3 cubic metres) scrolling through the listings on Trade Me looking for a rental. Three bedrooms, not too far away from here and the children's schools.

He is measuring up their belongings for storage in a secure unit, a grey steel container on an industrial site near the estuary.

'You're lucky to get this,' the owner said. All those red-zoned houses, not to mention the thousands not red-zoned but red-stickered whose homes had to be rebuilt, or the thousands like themselves who had to leave while their homes were repaired.

'That's a whole lotta storage,' said the owner. 'We're chokka.' And he handed them a leaflet promising electric gates with swipe-card entry, monitored security for total peace of mind, regular pest control and a courtesy trailer.

Thirty-five cubic metres should do it easily, he had said. But just to be sure, Rob is filling in the company's calculator. It reduces all their belongings to cubic meters: freezer – 1 square metre. Armchair – 0.48 square metres. Desk – 0.80 square metres. He walks about the house ticking them off. Some items are a puzzle.

'What's a whatnot?' he says. 'Do we have one?'

'No idea,' says Janey. 'Hey, how about this? Ah, no ... not short-term ...'

She has been distracted, but then she always is at this time of year: getting back to work after the summer break. And this year she has been caught up in the move back to their old site, now cleared of debris, to a prefab behind the netball courts that will serve as her classroom until the Education Department decides the final fate of the school. She's restless: spends hours at the gym, or at yoga, or closed away in that private space that exists behind the raised lid of her laptop.

And he is busy, too, working from a temporary office next to a mall in Papanui. His colleagues are scattered about the city in other temporary offices: in a conference centre out at Lincoln, sharing space with one government department or another among the offices and warehouses in the commercial zone off the southern motorway. But at least he's out of the spare room.

That room was already empty. A stack of orderly cubes contained the books and maps and things they planned to keep. Outside on the verge stands a skip already half-filled with the things they no longer need. Janey is in a mood of frantic discarding.

'I'll never read these books again,' she'd said as she dumped a carton of ancient university texts in the skip. '*The Faerie Queene*? *Sons and Lovers*? I don't think so.' Out went bundles of clothes no longer worn, broken toys, complicated board games they'd got for Christmas and never had the patience to learn. The items grew larger as she became more reckless: a chair everyone avoided because it was slippery and dumped you on the floor, a painting they had inherited from his mother: a landscape vaguely reminiscent of the peninsula hills with a stylised kereru in flight. 'I've always hated it,' she said with such vehemence that he was taken aback. He hadn't known she had disliked it so much.

And the stuff they had inherited from the Novaks. He had not expected that either: the little note on a floral card, Kitty's uneven wavery hand thanking them for their hospitality as if she were leaving a party. The proceeds of the house were to go to the son of a cousin in distant Abruzzo, but the contents were all theirs.

What was useful has gone to the charity shops, though these are full to bursting as others like themselves discard. Poppy wants the piano (2 square metres) and the lamp with the dancing lady in her flowery dress, the man in his red velvet jacket, their fingers lightly entwined.

'Are you sure, Popps?' said Janey.

'Yes,' said Poppy. 'It's pretty.'

They had also inherited Zitto, which made finding a rental a little more difficult.

'How about this?' says Janey from the sofa. 'Ah, no. No pets.'

The pressure's on. The red-zoned, the red-stickered, the temporarily displaced for repairs, those who owned their homes, those who rented houses that are coming down, all are scrambling for accommodation. Rents are rocketing. $650 per week, $700, $1000. But that, the Buffoon says, should not be construed as evidence of any housing crisis. It is simply the market at its divinely appointed task, a predictable outcome, business as usual. There are the stories in the paper, stories Rob hears at work of people camped out in garages, or with relatives, sleeping on sofas, or like a friend of Sarah's sister who is living in a caravan in a park trailing back and forth with her two kids to the communal toilets, lost her job in town, couldn't get a rental, long waiting lists for a state house and the government's selling them all off anyway, divesting to the private sector. The private sector which will, of course, deliver greater efficiencies and better management. Rob stands ticking off items, thinking that sometimes he feels as if he has landed in some strange island cult, surrounded by believers waving their hands in the air and chanting 'Opportunity! Choice! No taxation!' with a mad-eyed fervour.

Sometimes it feels as if everything is being reduced to cubes.

His home is just the start. Around the house, the entire city is being chopped up, rezoned, remapped, reconfigured. The Buffoon has turned down the council's draft plan, with its light rail and modest renewal. He is set, it seems, on something more glitzy, more whizzbang altogether. His department has taken over a tower in the central city, one of the few to remain undamaged. It's right next to the city council's building, but it's higher. The Buffoon's appointees sit up there overlooking the centre, where the demolition gangs have been at work, tearing down the dungers, clearing a space, exposing a blank slate of grey gravel and endless opportunity. Sometimes when Rob comes into the city on the way to some meeting or other, he finds himself at an intersection wondering where he is exactly. What street is this? What stood at that corner? He has to get his bearings, his inner map in disarray.

And now, up in the tallest tower, the appointees, the Blueprint 100 Team have one hundred days to come up with the new map, making way for a new wave of opportunity. Surveying plots of land again, carving up the wilderness into squares and rectangles. Cubes.

The government has taken direct control of the centre because you can't, after all, it seems, really trust the market and free choice. The Buffoon has taken over the CBD in a manner which is distinctly unliberal, as keen as any tinpot communist dictator to keep control. In one hundred days, he says, there'll be a new plan, a revised plan. (Rob ticks off the kitchen table – 1 square metre, the kitchen chairs 0.35 square metres.) At the centre it's all under direct government control, but out here, in the suburbs, they're on their own. Out here on Savage Street, it is, as the Buffoon has said, 'All over to the insurers.' Rob fills in the storage form in a suburban kitchen, the ant below the functionaries and multiple layers that have complete, unregulated control over how and when and where he will live his life. He's a figure on a balance sheet. A profitable item. An asset.

Not an independent citizen in a sovereign state.

And not just him. His family. His house. All the houses on Savage Street. All their neighbours. And all the houses and people in this city, in this entire country. All, all of them, assets, items, figures on a balance sheet, stock. And all the land on which they live their lives and all the institutions that keep them healthy and fed and educated, all cubed and reckoned, all assets. Readied for sale.

And this country becomes, as the Buffoon's boss, that smirky little currency trader of a prime minister, puts it, 'A place where it is good to do business.' How has it happened, thinks Rob (fridge – 1 square metre), that this country, which he loves with a kind of pang, its hills and rivers and ridiculous enthusiasms, his country that, a hundred years ago, led the world as the Workers' Paradise, would dwindle into a place whose highest hope is to enable some fucking multinational to make a buck?

'Or this . . .' says Janey. 'Three bedrooms. "Some EQ damage." But it must be okay or they wouldn't be renting it. It must be habitable.'

Small and bare and bald but not too far away and no mention of a prohibition on pets. 'That'll do.' Bare and bald will be fine. $750 is just manageable and, besides, it's for only four months.

He can hear her talking to the agent as he goes outside with the calculator: trampoline (dismantled) – 1 square metre. Picnic table and benches – 2.5 square metres.

There have been more visits, claims handler, loss adjustor, quantity surveyor, muttered talk from other rooms to which he has not been party. They have been assigned a builder, officially approved by the company the government has contracted to oversee the city's post-quake residential construction. The government says this will prevent cowboy builders profiteering from disaster.

All will be well. Their house will be repaired. The centre will rise again. The rivers will run clear. The dairy cows will graze on lush green pasture. The milk will flow. The honey, too. The economy will boom. It will be rock star, a phenomenon.

And, temporarily, all their worldly goods will fit easily into 35 cubic . . .

ninety
THE RIVER

The river bears its tainted cargo to the sea.

She is a silver thread in a vast ocean.

She seems to be swimming.

She seems to know where she is going.

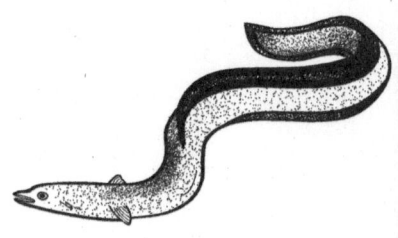

ninety-one
THE CRACK
MARCH 2012

...**are times** when she catches sight of herself in a window: a shop window for instance, when she is crossing a road. Or now, as she closes the windows on the prefab that is her classroom. It stands, one of an encampment of prefabs lined up in tight ranks on the cleared ground that had once housed two storeys of imposing Edwardian red brick, those dim and hallowed halls. The prefabs are poised well clear of the ground on steel foundations. Their floors bounce under the impact of dozens of adolescent feet in solid school sandals. Devoid of acoustic insulation, they resound to the racket of adolescent voices. They feel light and flyaway, ready to move at a moment's notice. Flexible. Adaptable.

The perfect metaphor really. Sandra knows someone in the ministry who has told her the city's schools are to be rebuilt to a new paradigm. No longer will there be classrooms in which individual teachers work with small groups, but instead, huge open spaces, 'innovative learning environments', where hundreds of students will mingle and teachers will move among them, working together in easy collaboration. The classroom with its desks belongs to the old industrial model. The future will require students educated to become the citizens of a global world, endlessly flexible, instantly adaptable, in spaces as open as a call-centre. No walls. No desks. No chairs. They will sit on flexible beanbags.

'I don't think I'm quite up to an innovative learning environment,' said Sandra.

Janey moves about her outmoded room, clearing up, switching off screens, picking up cardigans and a phone someone has left behind, dumping a half-eaten apple in the bin. Another day over. Not perfect, beginning with the realisation that the electronic system was on a go-slow, so that even taking the roll had been tedious. Sometimes she longed for a roll book and a pencil. Or a quill and parchment. Or a rock and a sharp stick.

She is closing a window when a face floats towards her in the glass. Her mother is outside, hovering in the narrow gap between the prefabs, looking in at her. Her mouth has that characteristic whimsical twist, her brow is slightly furrowed. It takes Janey a second to recognise her. Not a ghost, some version of Hamlet's father floating in to goad the hero into action. Not Sahana, having mastered the ability to manifest as ectoplasm, drifted in across the Tasman to startle her daughter.

The elderly face is not her mother's, but her own. Forty-two years old, and dead on target with the mid-life crisis. Behind her lies her youth. Ahead lies the furrowed brow, the wrinkles, menopause, increasing decrepitude, old age, The End. Janey feels herself poised above the crack.

She had come across it one morning after a swarm of aftershocks. It had opened the whole length of the path from the gate to the red front door of the house on Savage Street. She had fetched a broom and poked the handle into the gap. It went all the way down, waggling about in nothing. A hollow lay under the front path. They were standing on the flimsiest of surfaces, a thin layer of tarmac only, and who knew how far this hollow reached. Maybe no deeper than the holes that had opened on roads near the river into which cars had fallen head-first, tails in the air. Maybe all the way down.

Cracks had opened everywhere, and not just on footpaths and living room walls and across the façades of buildings. Everything was cracked.

Her marriage, for example.

She had always known there was a crack. The differences between herself and Rob had delighted them, a source of endless amusement. His caution, her impulsiveness. When she had suggested at the end of that first day they spent together, the day after they walked home in the moonlight over the hills, that they should chuck in their jobs and go to Vietnam — 'I've always wanted to go to Vietnam. The people are supposed to be really nice and the food's fantastic' — he had laughed. He thought she was joking.

She had found his caution equally unlikely. His seriousness, the way he planned, examined the map before departing, examined every purchase, compared from shop to shop, did the research.

'It's a toaster,' she said. 'It heats bread. I don't know exactly how a hydro lake heats bread, but it does. And all the toasters in the world probably come out of the same factory in Chengdu. So don't worry about it.'

And usually it worked out. He loved Vietnam. And their toaster lasted. It did not explode on the day after the warranty expired.

He enjoyed her impulsiveness. She liked his caution. Maybe it was because of a childhood spent trailing after her mother from place to place, from school to school, from one classroom of strange faces to another. 'This is going to be such an adventure!' her mother would say as they headed off yet again down the highway, as they stood in the doorway of the broken-down caravan at Arthur's Pass that was going to be their home for ever and ever. Rain dripped from the faded awning and moss grew lush and green along the window frames.

When Rob said let's think about it, no rush, her first impulse might have been a rush of impatience, but deep down there was also a kind of calm. He held her in place. She could flap about, but she was anchored on solid ground.

And then the ground exploded beneath her and the crack opened. His caution now maddened her. The way he sat poring over the file labelled 'Quake/Insurance 2010–2011–2012', the way he carried on, maintained routines — after-work drinks on Friday evening, kids' sports on Saturday, cycle around the hills on Sunday. And building that bloody pizza oven.

She had lain beside him in that hideous house that could so easily fall and harm, barely able to touch him for sheer impatience.

Sometimes there really were times when it made sense to head down the highway. And calmly, in the dark, she'd hear him sigh and say, 'But we can't just get up and go! All our capital's tied up in this place. We've got to wait until the repairs are done. We can't sell till we've signed them off, and we can't rent it out in the meantime, not in this state. We've just got to hang on, keep paying the mortgage and the rates. We've got kids, we've got jobs, we can't walk away.'

And she'd known all that was true. True and unbearable. And this was their life. And life ended.

She had been the one who found them. The Christmas camp had been rained out, the tent sagging, the creek rising. It had made sense just to pack up and head back early to the city.

Zitto was waiting at the sleepout door. It was open so she'd tapped lightly and called and then she'd seen them, in their best clothes, their best shoes. She had never seen death before. The stillness of it. The quiet composure of their leavetaking, hand in hand. She had stood looking down at the Novaks while Zitto wrapped himself around her legs the way he did when he wanted to be fed.

'So sad,' said the nurse when she arrived for her morning visit, 'but I'm sure this was how they would have wanted to go.'

Was it? Was this the way the Novaks would have wanted to go? Was it the way she would want to go, hand in hand with the man with whom she had spent her life? Was this how she would want it to end?

Because it would end. Everyone ended. She would end. A bare forked animal.

The cracks have opened, around her and within her, and when you look down into the crack, the broom handle waggles in ...

ninety-two
THE RIVER

Nothing happens.

Late summer, the leaves beginning to turn.

She is in the wide ocean, her body undulating.

She is being drawn toward the south.

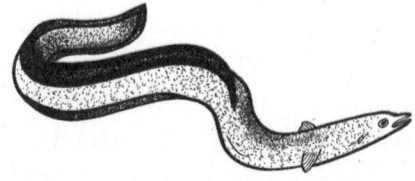

ninety-three
THE WALNUT TREE
APRIL 2012

...there, in the long grass, beneath the golden sweep of the walnut tree. Tom sits on the side verandah next to the post with the little figures carved one on top of the other, with their three-fingered hands splayed over their bellies. He likes that post. It's warm here, out of the wind. Sheltered by the big glossy leaves of the vine that has taken over one end of the verandah. Behind him the house is shuttered with plywood over all the doors and windows. Some scaffolding pipes are stacked in the garden, but other than that there is no sign of the builders. They were supposed to be here last month to start repairs but there was some problem, something that made his father slam the table, making them all jump. He never slammed. And his mother shrugged, said, 'Well, what did you expect?'

Someone has been in. They've tagged the plywood. Not well. VJ would have scoffed. 'Toy shit,' he'd have said. 'No style.' But VJ isn't here. He's gone. His house in the Loop was red-zoned. It was going to be torn down. The pretzel shop had relocated, but the rent was astronomical and no one wanted to drive all the way to Woolston to buy pretzels and really, his dad said, he couldn't be bothered with all the hassle. He was going back to Switzerland, where there were lots of rules and regulations but no worse than here. New Zealand had turned into something different from the free and easy place he'd expected when he emigrated.

'Fuck Switzerland!' said VJ. 'Soon as I can, I'm back here.'

That wouldn't be for years.

Sometimes Tom looks at their video. It's not much good. Others have done it better, with music and proper editing and those clips have gone viral. But there is one bit, just a few seconds when he'd had the camera and filmed VJ ollying a crack that had opened across the road by the river, leaving a sharp ledge. There are some orange cones strung with plastic KEEP CLEAR tape and he skates in from the left, approaches the ledge and Tom keeps him in tight focus and the screen flares as VJ jumps up and the sun explodes around him, then he lands and skates off down the street and out of shot. That bit's good.

The sun sifts through golden leaf. It's a long detour on the way home from school to their new place, but he wants to come back here. It feels sad and full of absence and that's how he wants to feel right now. Sad and full of absence.

Houses have come down all along Savage Street. They have left gaps of rough gravel between hedges or a driveway going nowhere, or a hollow concrete square where a house once stood, or a single tree, some tied with strips of yellow plastic that his mum said was to tell the demo people to leave that tree standing because it was special: a dog was buried there, or someone's ashes. Dead things among the absence. On their side of Savage Street some houses still had cars in the driveway, but others are like theirs, boarded up and empty.

The sun flares in the walnut tree among leaves of brilliant gold. Then, the movement . . .

'Hey!' he says. 'What are you doing?'

There's a girl by the walnut tree. Hair in a plait under an orange bobble hat, blue puffer jacket over baggy pants. Beside her on the ground there's a shopping bag and it is full, he notices, of walnuts. More crunch under his feet as he walks towards her, a crackling carpet fallen in the gales under the golden-leaved tree. The girl straightens and turns to look at him.

'It's okay,' he says. 'I'm not a rapist or anything.'

But she doesn't seem startled or worried. He recognises her. She's one of the older kids at school: Dana? Mila?

'Hey, Tom,' she says. She has a freckled face and small mucky hands in those fingerless gloves. They look like the paws of some forest creature with dirty nails. 'Do you live here? Is this your house?'

'Not right now,' says Tom. 'It's being repaired.'

'So it's not being pulled down?' says Molly. Yes. Molly. That was her name. Molly. 'That's good. I like that tower thing. It's cool. If I lived here, I'd sleep up there when it's fixed. You'd be able to see for miles.'

Tom turns to look. The tower thing is wrecked, all the little arched windows covered in ply, twisted iron peeling from the roof with its curly metal finial. But yes. It is cool. And when it's fixed, that's exactly what he'll do. Sleep up there, above the trees.

'Hope you don't mind about the walnuts,' says Molly. 'I thought this place was empty, like all the others. It's crazy: people buying fruit when there's all these apples and stuff just lying around rotting.'

'Help yourself,' says Tom. 'Take as much as you like.' Now he looks around he sees that there are other bags under the tree: apples. Pears. Grapefruit.

'See?" says Molly. 'That's all from your garden.'

'What do you do with it?' he says.

'Eat it,' she says. 'Or give it away. People always like free fruit. And it's not sprayed with toxic chemicals.'

And because she has already turned away and is picking up walnuts, he picks some up, too. Their small hard wrinkled shells sit comfortably within his hand. He presses two together and one splits open, revealing the nutmeat inside.

'It looks like a brain,' he says, and instantly regrets it. It's the kind of comment that makes some people look doubtful, think he's weird. But Molly says, 'Yeah, that's because they're good for your brain. That's nature telling you to eat walnuts if you want to think clearly.' Plants had all sorts of shapes that told people what they were good for: like some plants had leaves that looked like lungs with spots and they really did help people who had TB, and tomatoes were shaped like hearts and they were good for heart disease, like plants are really amazing, there's all this old lore about them that people have forgotten because they've come to depend on supermarkets and packaging and food has been industrialised, but look: everything we need to be healthy is just growing here, all around and free for the taking ...

She pauses. Looks up at him. 'Do you think that's weird?' she says. 'No,' he says. She smiles. 'Good,' she says. She picks up one of the bags.

He helps her carry the bags to her bike, which is parked by the fence with a wooden trailer on old pram wheels attached to the back. They load it up, along with some apples from a tree in what used to be the Novaks' back garden. And some cactuses that were growing in the rough grass next door. Molly says she'll take them into the city and plant them. They're planting stuff on the rubble because no one cares about it, but plants are amazing and heaps of people are coming into the city and making little gardens where the buildings had been, just cactuses and things that are tough and can survive and all these butterflies and insects are coming back now the buildings are gone, things that haven't been in the city for years ...

And then they set off down Savage Street, Molly riding slowly on her bike with its laden trailer, he on his skateboard and looking round, not at absence but at apple trees and pear trees and grapefruit trees, laden with ripe fruit and free for the ...

ninety-four
THE RIVER

Nothing happens.

The nights are lengthening. Mist lies over the river.

She is swimming into cooler waters, rising closer to the surface and the remembered warmth of the sun.

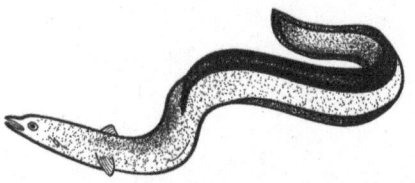

ninety-five
THE OPEN DOOR
MAY 2012

'...Zitto!' she calls. He'll be here somewhere, sitting washing his face and waiting for someone to put out his food.

She has left a note on the table back at the new house, propped up against the fruit bowl. 'I am going to find Zitto. xx Poppy' with the 'o' turned into a smiley face.

They were arguing in the sitting room, a quiet argument that they think no one can hear, but she can. She can hear all the arguments in that house. The walls are very thin and the rooms are very small. Last night she heard them arguing in their bedroom next door. Not the words exactly, though usually it starts with some stuff about the house and money before moving onto other things. Last night had been the worst. Her mum had said something that made her dad really and truly mad, yelling, slamming doors. 'Is this what you want? Is this what you really want?' And her mum had started crying, her face gone all red and rubbery and her mouth stretched down at the corners, not looking like her mum at all, though they had stopped when they saw her at the door and put on these stupid fake smiles.

Her dad said, 'I'm going out', and he roared off in the car and didn't come home for ages but when he did, they started all over again. And later, when she got up to have a pee, she found him sitting in his sleeping bag on the sofa watching soccer. All by himself in the dark watching tiny Englishmen running about kicking a ball while thousands of people sang. She didn't know which was worse: the arguments or the long sulky pauses in between.

Gina said that's what her mum and dad did before they split up. They argued all the time and her mum slept in the spare room and then they sat her and her brothers down and had The Conversation. The one they have in movies where they sit the kids around the table and say, 'Now, look, kids, your mom and I have something to tell you.' The one where they say that there's nothing to worry about, it will all be fine, but your father and I have been having some difficulties lately and we think it might be best for us, for all of us, if we lived apart. The one where they said that nothing would change, they'd still get together for birthdays and Christmas just as usual and then the clincher: And remember, kids, we both love you very, very much.

Gina said it was all lies. Your dad moved in with his boyfriend and your mother started wearing stupid short skirts and going out on dates with people she met online and you had to spend weekends at your dad's house in Akaroa which was miles away and you always got sick driving over the hill to get there and you didn't know anyone when you did get there. And you had to live with your mum during the week in this horrible unit because neither of them can afford to buy a proper house now they've split their money, but the good thing was you could get them to buy you stuff out of guilt: like, she had sushi all the time, whenever she wanted it, and inline skates and her dad said she could have riding lessons and she thought there was a chance she might be able to get them to buy her a pony.

Poppy had no intention of spending weekends in Akaroa. She had her scooter. She knew exactly what she was going to do. She had a plan. If no one was thinking properly, then she would.

She had worked out how to get there. All you had to do was to keep the Port Hills in front of you. Go straight towards them. Their big brown bulk rose reassuringly at the end of every street, until at last she reached roads she recognised and she was turning the corner onto Savage Street. It looked different. One side of the road was totally empty, except for a few trees. All the houses had gone. Isobel's house, and the Novaks' and Talia's house too. Their house stood dishevelled behind its hedges and garage. She opened the gate, fumbling a bit because her fingers were freezing. She had forgotten her gloves in the rush to leave before anyone saw and stopped her.

It feels strange. The gate latch clicks under her hand the way it always has done and the gate swings shut behind her as she pushes her scooter up the path, bumping it over the big crack. Pale sunlight filters through bare branches strung with spider webs and the morning's rain. Snails and worms, driven up to the surface by the soaking, have left wavering threads of shiny silver across the path. The windows along the front are still boarded up awaiting the builders, but the front door stands ajar, shiny red with those little blisters of paint she has always liked to pop and around it are the panels of coloured glass where you could stand and look out and see the garden change from ordinary green to pink or bright acidic yellow.

The hall is dark so she pushes the door wide to see properly. Light falls on dusty floorboards, picks out the hooks and nails on the walls where the maps used to hang, casts a dim shadow around the hall cupboard where they used to hide when they played Sardines at birthday parties, all squeezed in trying not to giggle as someone trailed about, looking. Coming ready or not! The door to the sitting room opens onto a twilit mess, gaps in all the walls, big holes where the fireplace used to be, the tiles of roses set into the surround, some cracked but still pretty.

A water bottle lies on the carpet and someone has tagged all the walls. It's a bit spooky thinking that people might have been in their sitting room, so she goes out into the sunshine. Around the back of the house there is still the mark where the trampoline used to be, and through the kitchen windows she can see the cupboards still in place and the space for the fridge and the corkboard that used to have all their photos, now cleared, ready for the builders when they come to fix the walls and the foundations and stop arguing among themselves.

'Zitto?' she calls. 'Zitto?'

They will come and find her. They will know where she has

gone. They will be here any minute, both looking anxious. They will run up the path, hand in hand, united in their concern for their daughter who could have been abducted, dragged into a car, taken off to live the rest of her life in a cellar like that girl Gina told her about who had babies and everything but it was in Germany or somewhere. Things like that were always happening overseas: girls living in cellars, and wars and assassinations and massacres and refugees in leaky boats and famines with sad babies and huge cities, four times bigger, six times bigger than the whole of New Zealand, all the people squashed into enormous high buildings, hundreds of times bigger than anything in this city. They have all sorts of things overseas, weddings with carriages and white horses and school kids taking guns and shooting their teachers and planes flying into buildings. And girls living their whole lives in cellars.

But not her. Not here. Here, her parents will come running around the corner and find her sitting on the deck, calmly patting Zitto. They will say, 'Oh, my God, Poppy! What did you think you were doing? Why did you leave without saying anything? Oh, my darling, we were so worried!' And they will both put their arms around her. They will stand together on the deck hugging each another tightly, knowing that they can never never part. They will stay together forever like William and Kate. They will love each other, they will come back to this house, which will be repaired, and just the way it always was, and the houses will be rebuilt and everyone — Isobel and Talia and Luca and Zitto — will come back and they will all live on Savage Street and be happy.

The house stands before her. A bird warbles up and down, the wind rattles in a pile of dry dead leaves. And listen . . .

ninety-six
THE RIVER

Rain falls. The cold hard rain of winter that peppers the surface of the river as the year slides to the shortest day.

The stars that mark the turn of the year have sunk below the horizon. They have disappeared entirely.

She is swimming now close to a booming coast.

Heading south.

And the first star lifts its tiny head.

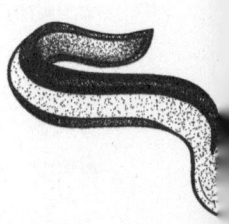

ninety-seven
THE SIREN
JUNE 2012

...midwinter, 2012. The dark heart of the year. The sun slides to its northernmost point. It appears to snag on the horizon. Stops.

Drops freeze on the leaf. Puddles lie unruffled under a brittle meniscus. Worms curl motionless in their winter dark burrows of sleek clay.

The city lies bareheaded beneath the wide arc of the sky. Its houses, some whole, some brokenbacked, line the grid of streets laid down across the plain, or stare, blank-eyed from the hillsides. At the centre, the muddy rectangles of demolition await their opportunity. The figures are good, says the man surveying the city from the highest tower: record freight movements are being reported through the port and airport, unemployment is down 5 per cent, demolition companies are flooding into the city, 150 of them at last count, scrambling for business and the 43.1 million dollars' worth of contracts being let by the government. It's a boom, he says to the reporter. It's a bonanza, a gold rush! The city is going gangbusters, it's flat out. The investors will soon be here, the big overseas investors with the very deep pockets who will drop like gods from the machine.

The city is being reconfigured. A new map is taking shape, a blueprint for the future. At present it exists as little cardboard cutouts of anchor projects which the Minister, who is a tactile man, can move about at will. Sports Precinct *here*. Rugby stadium *here*. Convention Centre *there*. The city is going to be rebranded. It is on its way to becoming The City of Sport.

The sun snags and a chill winter wind blows in from the sea. It crosses the city, rattles the windows of a room that smells of orange peel and the damp wool of winter tartan. Youth taps the abbreviations of hope and love and C U while the old man scrapes at the glass with his wild, mad claws saying poor, bare, forked animal. *Poor, bare, forked animal, as thou art.* Youth takes no notice. That's for later. Right now, they are certain they will never join him, unaccommodated in the storm. Nor will they ever set off to war to die for some grand delusion. Nor will they suffer too greatly in its opposition. They will never give way to despair, they will never risk too much. They will hate sometimes, and lie and deceive. That's inevitable. Everybody does. But not for long, and not too disastrously, and not in a fashion that will cause lasting harm to others or themselves. They will not love unwisely, nor die at the hands of fanatics. They will be wise and avert disaster. They will save the planet. They will spread a net and capture the sun.

The wind stirs the long grass by the river where Zitto pauses, paw raised, listening, eyes alert, every muscle tensed to spring. The wind eddies about an office block in a new business park by the motorway where an adjustor pauses, too, hands raised over the keyboard, waiting for the spreadsheet to shift a point. That tiny shift that means profit again after the unfortunate events of last year, the little hiccup, but all is well once more. The company is charging higher premiums. And away from the city, in other offices in other cities, in other countries, the points are shifting, too, up and up, and the great invisible flood of capital is flowing as it should, like an ocean current, in its customary direction.

The sun snags, the wind blows, and beneath the city streets, beneath the silt and layers of shingle, beneath clay and rock in the deep, dark belly of the earth, the god baby waits, forever curled in the dark, forever in a state of being about to be. He breathes within the skin of his big dark mother who reclines holding everybody on the surface of her body: tiny inconsequential creatures, like naked kits.

When the baby kicks, mountains shimmy and hills leap and all the structures the tiny creatures have built for their shelter creak and snap. The framework of their lives stretches, adjusts, weakens. Their houses with all their evidence of living: their scratches and cracks and scuffs, their layers and patches and fallen brick. They creak whenever the god baby kicks out. Things break.

The sun snags. Pauses. The wind blows, a bird sings, a siren wails along a city street. And then at 11.09 a.m. precisely, the sun and earth make some adjustment. At least, that's how it seems from here. There's a turning, a revolution, and the sun begins its long rolling progress back along the shining line toward . . .

ninety-eight
THE RIVER

Something happens.

Out in the bay, the shoal of silvery fish swims to shore. They find the gap at the tip of the sandspit where salt and fresh water meet.

They swim through, one shimmery silvery throng, and find their way across the estuary to the river. They swim upstream, between banks of mud and flax, beneath the waving plumes of toetoe laden with silvery frost. No nets, this early before the season, get in the way.

She swims in her new element, with its dense scent of raw earth and waste and green waterweed.

She comes to a place where the bank curves over the water, leaving a dark and secret shadow.

She swims into it.

She'll stay there.

ninety-nine

THE NAIL

JULY 2012

... **rained overnight** and the ground was clagged and heavy. In the shade under the trees, puddles are filmed with a thin coating of ice and he shivers despite T-shirt, jeans and the jacket supplied by the company. Jacket, hi-vis vest, boots, to be paid off in deductions each week. The jacket was a size larger than he'd have preferred. They'd run out of his size by the time it was his turn to be kitted out, but it was warm. Way better than nothing. He'd been warned.

'It's cold down there,' Uncle Joe said before they left. But he had had no idea. Not until he walked off the plane, backpack over one shoulder, hours of flying behind him, watching all the movies, good Chinese action movies, drinking all the wine, eating all the food and the little packs of peanuts. Asking for extra. He had paid for it, after all, out of his own pocket. Might as well make the most of it.

Beside him, Uncle Joe had slumped into heavy sleep from the moment of take-off, his head lolling. Around him the others slept or sat in tiny pools of light playing games or watching some superhero leap and kick, the body count rising. Some he recognised from the time doing their assessment task, proving their skills doing renovations to the agency office.

There'd been four hundred waiting for interview. A great milling crowd of men like himself from all over, all gathered outside the Aspiration International Placement Agency off Don Quijote Street. Lining the stairs, clutching their CVs, ready to answer the questions: Where have you worked? (Dubai, he answered. And Iraq. US bases, big companies, lots of experience.) Proving he knew his job, was a good worker, a skilled worker, not some new boy fresh from the provinces trying to break in. Proving he could do the calculations, knew how to measure, knew how to estimate, doing his best in a few minutes to stand out from the crowd.

'Are you excited to work in New Zealand?' the employer had asked, a big unsmiling Kiwi with white hands. 'Helping with the rebuilding of the city after the earthquake?' And he had replied, 'One hundred per cent, sir! Oh yes! One hundred per cent excited!' Only twenty places.

And then the two-month assessment for those who had been shortlisted, doing renovations at the agency offices, all of them putting in the hours, sleeping on the floor so they could get an early start. Then another assessment, another month at some resort on the coast, some fancy tourist place where they worked fast, they worked hard, proving their CV was no lie, the slow, the lazy ones dismissed on the spot. Off you go. Not wanted.

But he had made it. Borrowed his costs — airfare, visa processing, agency fee, accommodation, clothing, tools — from a lender Uncle Joe had recommended: not cheap but reasonable, not someone who'd send round the heavies to threaten the family should there be a problem. Would not demand his collateral. Would not seize the house. At least, not right away. A hundred and fifty thousand pesos at 18 per cent.

But soon he'd be earning. A three-year contract. He'd pay it all off, debt and interest. He'd prove himself, obtain good references, apply for an extension to his visa, set about getting residency, for himself and for his family. He had it all planned as he took his place among the chosen ones, waved goodbye to Maria, the press of her body still with him, to his daughter, who had clung though she had known him only six months, who was not accustomed yet to this father who arrived, then left again. She had been suspicious at first, watching warily, thumb in mouth, considering this stranger in her house. Then abruptly fell in love, climbed onto his lap, hung onto his hand, stayed as close to him as she was able. The imprint of her arms was still tight about his neck. And the boys, who watched from behind the barrier, wide-eyed, as their father joined the line of men filing through the gate, learning how it was done, this leaving. And his mother, who had pressed a little crucifix into his hand as she kissed him goodbye, weighing him down with her usual protection, the candles already lit in San Agustin, the prayer cards already purchased. He would fly once more with angels. Or Uncle Joe. A plump angel.

The cabin door had opened onto the icy air. It smelled empty. And the airport, when they walked through, was silent as if everyone had been vaporised, disappeared. The streets, too. He had sat in the van the company had sent to collect them that morning, looking out at the low wide ranks of houses rising from fog like alien craft, unanchored. Adrift. And he felt that familiar clutch of longing for home.

He'd get over it. It never lasted long. He'd work, start sending money to Maria and the point of what he was doing would take care of the longing. The hostel was company-owned, $150 a week for a bed in a shared room in one of those houses. His roommates were Filipinos, a couple of Brazilians had the room next door, and the front of the house was occupied by some men who might be Irish, he couldn't tell. Just workers, like himself, caught up in the global tide, swept this way and that as they were required to build this, demolish that. A great flood of men in knock-off Nikes, jeans and sweatshirts bearing the logos of Harvard, or Oxford, or some other noble institution. Some of that shoal, washed into this bywater, playing cards around a kitchen table, waiting until the time is right to Skype over the time divide, to talk to the child's face peering into the screen to find him, holding up the picture she has drawn at school of the plane flying through a blue strip of sky and that's you, that's you sitting in the window looking out. In red felt-tip, one of the floating world, the drifting world of men who fly about the planet from one site to another. The world is full of such people, such sites.

This one is demolition. A big house in a garden near the river. They've already got the trees out, sawed them down to stumps in order to let the machinery in. It's going to be a messy job. The place has been partially burned, leaving joists and rafters turned to charcoal. The ground is littered with shattered glass, buckled iron and smoke-blackened bricks. They're loading the rubbish into a dump truck for disposal at some waste site, buried under the earth or dumped into a harbour for reclamation.

'Here you go, Tarzan,' said one of the Irishmen, handing him his tool kit. 'Straighten out that lot. Might get something for that.'

It's a kind of turret propped up with scaffolding to one side of the house. Little arched windows, wooden panelling, more or less intact and untouched by the fire. Something here might be salvaged. He sets his hard hat straight and starts work. The sun is up. Light catches the drops of water strung on every length of old timber. It gleams on broken glass, melts the ice puddle under the broken trees. The earth steams where the light falls. He takes the hammer he has been given, not the best quality, not the best fit to his hand, but it will do, and he sets the tines about a nail. He tugs. He pulls up and away.

The nail doesn't loosen. It has been well hit, driven firmly into the wood, but he works at it and suddenly it comes away. A piece of framing splits apart. It falls to the ground.

And up on the roof, where they are wrenching off the iron, and already stand in the full light of the winter sun, someone begins to whistle ...

One hundred
THE RIVER

A leaf falls.

She is a silver thread in the shadows by the riverbank.

Living her life.

Waiting for something to happen.

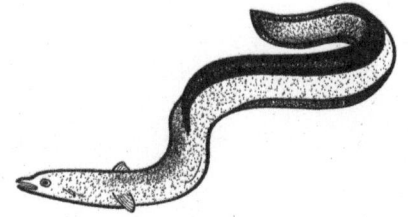

Author's Note

This novel is a companion volume to a non-fiction book, *The Villa at the Edge of the Empire*, both prompted by the earthquakes that struck my home town, Christchurch, in 2010–11, and their aftermath. Fiction and non-fiction offer complementary perspectives, one factual, one imaginative. I am normally a writer of fiction, but in 2010–11 fiction felt irrelevant. What mattered was reality. What mattered were the factual narratives, thousands of which have been recorded and deposited in archives across the city. Faced with such accounts, fiction fell back, abruptly exposed as an expression of ego, a mere display of technique with its roots in Enlightenment notions of individualism.

I think this may be a common response to disaster. When I began thinking about it, I could come up with no novels, for example, written during the Blitz by any of the writers who were living in London at the time. The first I could recall was Elizabeth Bowen's *The Heat of the Day*, written not during that appalling era, but long after the war was over, in 1948, and from a great distance, in southern Ireland.

Writing, however, is something I need to do to understand what is going on around me. I was puzzled by the city in its post-quake phase and by the decisions those in power were making concerning its reconstruction. I began collecting newspaper reports, articles, hearsay. I began taking notes, talking with people, thinking in a focused way about the current state of my city and my country and how we might have got here. Eventually, those folders of data became a work of non-fiction, *The Villa at the Edge of the Empire*, which was published in 2015.

But fiction has its role, and it's one I love and value. It can go straight to the heart of things, into private and secret places. It allows multiple points of view, sometimes almost simultaneously. It plays with metaphor, connecting this with that. It gives shape to the random narrative of existence.

It also operates within a different version of time. I became acutely aware, in writing *The Villa at the Edge of the Empire*, of the impossibility of achieving that over-worked word, closure. In non-fiction, there's no such thing as an ending, just a pause in the continuous flood of reality. Time is at work, changing meaning, adding further details, even before your fingers have left the keys.

Fiction, on the other hand, is a structure that exists outside time. Events can conceivably have a beginning, a middle and end. Fiction is classical, designed to arrive at that final, orchestral ta-dum! While non-fiction is improvisatory, a perpetual jazz riffing around facts.

Both these books use the same data base, and I hope that between them they will tell a single story: about my city and my country and what was laid bare when the walls fell down one spring morning in 2010.

Fiona Farrell
Christchurch
2017

First and foremost, to Creative New Zealand and the 2013 Michael King Fellowship.

This novel could not have been written without the help of the expert librarians at Christchurch City Libraries, who have advised and retrieved material from storage in a city that is yet to rebuild a fully functional central library.

Thank you, too, to the journalists present and past of *The Press*. And for detailed information, thanks to Trish Allen, Dr Mike Beard, Rev. Jim Consedine, John Dodgshun, David Gregory, Al MacDuff, Lisa Mackay, Phil May, Leonida Miller, Rod Naish, James Norcliffe, Steve Parker, Susannah Poole, Ursula Poole, Victor Rolton (HRNZ), Morrin Rout, Dr Dame Margaret Sparrow, Hugh Wilson and Dr John Wilson.

Thanks, also, to my publisher, Harriet Allan, and the staff at Penguin Random House New Zealand, and to Anna Rogers, for her skilful editing.

And, as always, to Doug Hood.

Non-fiction finalist,
Ockham New Zealand Book Awards, 2016.

A provocative and insightful exploration of rebuilding our homes, communities and cities after their devastation. Where are we? How did we get here? Where do we go now?

From nineteenth-century attempts to create Utopias to America's rustbelt, from Darwin's study of worms to China's phantom cities, this work ranges widely through history and around the world. It examines the evolution of cities and of Christchurch in particular, looking at its swampy origins and its present reconstruction following the recent destructive earthquakes. And it takes us to L'Aquila in Italy to observe another shaken city.

Farrell writes as a citizen caught up in a devastated city in an era when political ideology has transformed the citizen to 'an asset, the raw material on which . . . empire makes its profit'. In a hundred tiny pieces, she comments on contentious issues, such as the fate of a cathedral, the closure of schools, the role of insurers, the plans for civic venues. Through personal observation, conversations with friends, a close reading of everything from the daily newspaper to records of other upheavals in Pompeii and Berlin, this dazzling book explores community, the love of place and, ultimately, regeneration and renewal.

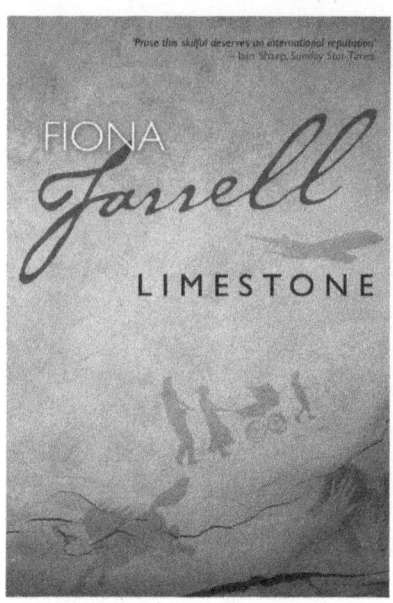

Finalist for the Montana New Zealand Book Awards, 2010 and longlisted for the International IMPAC Dublin Literary Award.

A fabulous multi-levelled novel.

Clare Lacey is on a quest. In Ireland to attend an art history conference, she sets out to find her father who walked out one day to buy a packet of cigarettes when she was a child, and disappeared. She is urged on her way by chance encounters: with a woman in a high tower, a blind man at a crossroads, a singer whose song she does not understand . . . Clues lie all around on a labyrinth of walls – but the final clue lies deep within.

With Irish roots and a nod to the Irish classic, *The Year of the Hiker* by John B. Keane, this is a contemporary novel about inheritance, belief, art, love . . . and limestone.

Longlisted for the International IMPAC
Dublin Literary Award, 2009.

*An historical, pastoral, satirical,
scientific romance, with mustelids!*

A young man out poaching. A beautiful maiden in a mysterious house. A perilous voyage to distant islands. All the ingredients of a highly coloured Victorian romance are played out in the context of the great colonial experiment. Exotic species travelled back to stock the collections of Europe, while useful species were dispatched to found new colonies in the antipodes. Walter Allbones really existed. So did his ferrets. From these facts, Fiona Farrell has spun a delicate, satirical fantasy about human folly and the perils attendant on disturbing the subtle balance of nature.

Finalist, Deutz Medal for Fiction, New Zealand Book Awards, 2005.
Longlisted for the International IMPAC Dublin Literary Award, 2006.

An evocative and moving mix of memoir and fiction from an award-winning novelist.

As war is waged in the Middle East, a woman in New Zealand has her nose in a book. Kate is immersed in other battles, engrossed in eyewitness accounts of an earlier war in ancient Persia. She has grown up, left her Otago home and returned, and in all these years books have shaped her life and made sense of the world – offering mystery and solace, entertainment and enlightenment.

From *The Little Red Hen* to *Owls Do Cry*, from T.S. Eliot to Aphra Behn, this frequently funny, always original novel is another extraordinary offering from the author of *The Hopeful Traveller*.

***On 22 September 1960, six girls gather
behind the school toilets to read* Peyton Place:**

Caroline the leader, Heather the caregiver, Kathy the actress, Raeleen the explorer, Greer the mystic and Margie the rebel. Like the historical heroines whose stories are repeatedly held up to them as models, these girls confront in their various ways the uncertainty and fears of adolescence.

On 22 September 1995, we meet them again, confronting the issues of middle age. Caroline's on the way up, Raeleen's now Ra, Margie climbs higher and higher. They're all re-learning in the process the joy of making that vital, terrifying, thrilling leap 'out into the sun' . . .

Finalist, Deutz Medal for Fiction, New Zealand Book Awards, 2003.
Longlisted for the International IMPAC Dublin Literary Award, 2003.

A fascinating novel of hope, love, idealism and human progress, made up of two separate stories, which can be read in isolation and yet reverberate against each other.

Sometime in the 1860s, in an isolated valley on Banks Peninsula, Harry Head, 'the Hermit of Hickory Bay', experimented unsuccessfully with flight. His story forms part of the exuberant blend of fact and fiction which constitutes this tale. The author takes us back to the beginnings of novel-writing, as philosophical play and serious entertainment. Think Crusoe's island, think Utopia.

Twelve characters, driven by obsession, hope or the vagaries of chance, come ashore in widely different circumstances onto the same island. Once there, the game can begin. Written in two halves, this is a book to be read from either end. Begin with the past and race toward the future, or begin with the present and circle back towards the past. Time may separate the two sections, yet subtle links and twisting events bring them together into a varied, intriguing and compulsive whole.

Winner of the Fiction Section, New Zealand Book Awards, 1993.

Fiona Farrell's first novel – always moving, often hilarious – is a breathtakingly accomplished debut. It presents a head-on confrontation with a New Zealand psyche rarely found in history books.

Skinny Louie, daughter of Shanghai Lil, has a baby in the Begonia House on the day of the royal visit. Maura finds the baby and takes it home. Tia grows up with magical powers into the brave new world of the twenty-first century.